**"You're better than I expected,"
said his lordship,
mollified by this docility.**

"I daresay something can be made of you. Watch
your cousins, and take your tone from them!...
Between 'em, he and Anthea can teach you pretty
well all you need to know. *She* was born and bred
here, knows all the ways of the place, all our history,
every inch of my land! Not married, are you?"

"Married!" ejaculated Hugo, taken-aback. "Lord,
no, sir!"

"No, I didn't think you could be," said his lordship.
"I recommend you to get on terms with your cousin
Anthea. She doesn't want for sense, and she's a spirited, lively girl, and would make you an excellent
wife, if she took a fancy to you....

"I'm going to send for her," said his lordship. "She
can take you up to the picture-gallery for a start."

The Major, showing alarm for the first time, tried
to protest, but was cut short...and awaited in considerable trepidation the arrival of his cousin Anthea.

Also by Georgette Heyer
from Jove

GEORGETTE HEYER
THE UNKNOWN AJAX

THE UNKNOWN AJAX

Copyright © 1959 by Georgette Heyer

All rights reserved

Published by arrangement with G.P. Putnam's Sons

All rights reserved. No part of this publication may be reproduced or transmitted in any form or by any means, electronic or mechanical, including photocopying, recording, or any information storage and retrieval system, without permission in writing from the publisher.

These pages for printing.

First Jove edition published September 1981

J

A JOVE BOOK

THE UNKNOWN AJAX

Three previous printings
First Jove edition published December 1981

First printing

Printed in the United States of America

Jove books are published by Jove Publications, Inc.,
200 Madison Avenue, New York, NY 10016

1

Silence had reigned over the dining-room since his lordship, midway through the first course, had harshly commanded his widowed daughter-in-law to spare him any
more steward's room gossip. As Mrs. Darracott had merely
been recounting to her daughter the tale of her activities
that day the snub might have been thought unjust, but
she accepted it, if not with equanimity, with a resignation
born of custom, merely exchanging a droll look with her
daughter, and directing one of warning at her handsome
young son. The butler glanced menacingly at the younger
of the two footmen, but the precaution was unnecessary:
Charles had not been employed at the Darracott Place
above six months, but he was not such a whopstraw as to
make the least noise in the performance of his duties when
his lordship was out of humour. That was the way Chollacombe described as knaggy an old gager as ever Charles
had had the ill-fortune to serve. Still-rumped, that's what
he was, always nabbing the rust, or riding grub, like he
had been for months past.

Charles had thought himself lucky to have been taken
on at Darracott Place, but he wasn't going to stay above
his twelve-month, not if he knew it! It might suit James,
being Kentish born, to work in a great, rambling house
stuck down miles from anywhere, in a marsh flat and bare
enough to give anyone a fit of the blue devils, and with
never a soul, outside the Family, coming next or nigh it,
but when Charles went after another place he was going
to London. Let alone he was always one for a bit of life,
you could earn extra gelt in London, for there were always
errands to be run, or notes to be delivered, and you got

a shilling every time you were sent off to execute such commissions. If messages had to be carried in the country it stood to reason they were taken by one of the grooms; while as for the throng of open-fisted guests his Dad had told him it would be his duty to wait upon—well, a houseful of guests might have been what his Dad was used to in his day, but it wasn't what they was used to at Darracott Place!

Such visions as Charles had indulged when he had first blessed his good fortune at being hired to fill the post of second footman in a nobleman's establishment! A proper take-in that had been, and so he would tell his Dad! Dad, honourably retired from employment as butler to a Gentleman of Fashion, had assured him that to be hired to serve in a lord's country seat did not mean that he would be immured in rural fastness throughout the year. My lord (said Dad) would certainly retire to Kent during the winter months; but at the beginning of the Season he would remove to his London house; and at the end of the Season (said Dad) the chances were that he would hire a house in Brighton for the summer months. And from time to time, of course, he would be absent, visiting friends in other parts of the country, during which periods his servants would enjoy a great deal of leisure, and might even be granted leave to go on holiday.

But nothing like that had happened at Darracott Place since Charles had first entered its portals. My lord, whose grim mouth and arctic stare could set stronger knees than Charles's knocking together, remained in residence all the year round, neither entertaining nor being entertained. And no use for anyone to tell Charles that this was because the Family was in mourning for Mr. Granville Darracott and his son, Mr. Oliver, both drowned off the coast of Cornwall in an ill-fated boating expedition: Charles might only have been second footman at Darracott Place for a couple of months when that disaster occurred, but no one could gammon him into thinking that my lord cared a spangle for his heir. If you were to ask him, Charles would say that my lord cared for no one but Mr. Richmond: he certainly couldn't abide Mr. Matthew Darracott, who was the last of his sons left alive; while as for Mr. Claud, who was the younger of Mr. Matthew's two sons, it was as much as anyone could do not to burst out laughing to see my lord look at him as if he was a cockroach, or a bed-bug. Nor, though he didn't look at him like that, could you think he cared a groat for Mr. Vincent neither; while as for poor Mrs. Darracott, as kind a lady as you'd find anywhere, even if she was a bit of a prattle-box, it seemed like she had only to open her mouth for my lord to give her one of his nasty set-downs. He didn't, it was true, do that to Miss Anthea, but that was probably because Miss Anthea wasn't scared of him, like her Ma, and would maybe give as good as she got: it wasn't because he was fond of her, as you'd think her granddad would be. It wouldn't be Miss Anthea as would coax him out of his sullens; it would be Mr. Richmond.

But Richmond, his grandfather's darling, after one thoughtful glance cast under his lashes at that uncompromising countenance appeared to lose himself in his own reflections. Some pickled crab, which he had not touched, had been removed with a damson pie; and his sister saw, peeping round the massive silver epergne that almost obscured him from her view, that he had eaten no more than a spoonful of this either. Since he had partaken quite liberally of two of the dishes that had made up the first course, she was undismayed by anything other than her grandfather's failure to notice his present abstention. In general, Lord Darracott would have bullied Richmond into eating the pie, imperfectly concealing his anxious affection for the youth, whose earlier years had been attended by every sort of ailment, under a hectoring manner, to which Richmond, docile yet unafraid, would submit.

As little as Charles the footman did Anthea, or Mrs. Darracott, or even Richmond understand the cause of his lordship's brooding ill-humour; rather less than Charles did any one of these three believe that it sprang from grief at the death of his eldest son. His lordship had both disliked and despised Granville; yet when the news of that fatal accident had reached Darracott Place he had been for many minutes like a man struck to stone; and when he had recovered from the first shock he had horrified his son Matthew, and Lissett, his man of business, by saying several times over, and in a voice of icy rage: "Damn him! Damn him! Damn him!" They had almost feared for his reason, and had stood staring at him with dropped jaws

3

until he had violently ordered them out of his sight. Matthew had never dared to enquire what extraordinary circumstances had provoked his outburst, and this lordship neither offered an explanation nor again referred to the matter. Only a black cloud seemed to descend on him, rendering him more unapproachable than ever, and so brittle-tempered that Mrs. Darracott quite dreaded having to address him, and even Richmond several times had his head bitten off.

Dinner was always a protracted meal; tonight it seemed interminable; but at last it came to an end. As the servants began to remove the covers, Mrs. Darracott picked up her reticule, and rose.

His lordship's hard, frowning eyes lifted; he said curtly: "Wait!"

"Wait, sir?" faltered Mrs. Darracott.

"Yes, wait!" he repeated impatiently. "Sit down! I have something to say to you!"

She sank back on to her chair, looking at once bewildered and apprehensive. Anthea, who had risen with her, remained standing, her head turned towards her grandfather, her brows a little raised. He paid no heed to her; his eyes were on the two footmen, and it was not until they had left the room that he spoke again. So forbidding was his expression that Mrs. Darracott, in growing trepidation, began to search wildly in her mind for some forgotten error of omission or commission. Chollacombe softly shut the door on the heels of his subordinates, and picked up the port decanter from the sideboard; he perceived that his master's hands were clenching and unclenching on the arms of his chair, and his heart sank: there had been a storm brewing all day, and it was going to burst now over their heads.

But when my lord again spoke it was as though it cost him an effort. He said: "You will be good enough, Elvira, to inform Flitwick that I expect my son and his family here tomorrow. Make what arrangements you choose!"

She was so much surprised that she was betrayed into uttering an unwise exclamation. "Good gracious! Is *that* all? But what in the world—I mean, I hadn't the least notion——"

"What brings them here, sir?" asked Anthea, intervening to draw her grandfather's fire.

4

He looked for a moment as though he were about to utter one of his rough snubs, but after a slight pause he answered her. "They are coming because I've sent for them, miss!" He paused again, and then said: "You may as well know now as later! I've sent for my heir as well."

At these bitterly uttered words Chollacombe nearly dropped the decanter

"Sent for your heir *as well?*" repeated Richmond. "But my uncle Matthew is your heir, Grandfather—isn't he?"

"No."

"Then who is, sir?" demanded Anthea.

"A weaver's brat!" he replied, his voice vibrant with loathing.

"Oh, *dear!*" said Mrs. Darracott, breaking the stunned silence that succeeded his lordship's announcement.

The hopeless inadequacy of this exclamation dragged a choke of laughter out of Anthea, but it caused his lordship's smouldering fury to flare up. "Is that all you have to say? Is that all, woman? You are a wet-goose—a widgeon—a—take yourself off, and your daughter with you! Go and chatter, and marvel, and bless yourselves, but keep out of my sight and hearing! By God, I don't know how I bear with you!"

"No, indeed!" said Anthea instantly. "It is a great deal too bad, sir! Mama, how could you speak so to one so full of compliance and good nature as my grandfather? So truly the gentleman! Come away at once!"

"That's what you think of me, is it, girl?" said his lordship, a glint in his eyes.

"Oh, no!" she responded, dropping him a curtsy. "It's what I *say*, sir! You must know that my feather-headed Mama has taught me to behave with all the propriety in the world! To tell you what I *think* of you would be to sink myself quite below reproach! Come, Mama!"

He gave a bark of laughter. "Tongue-valiant, eh?"

She had reached the door, which Chollacombe was holding open, but she looked back at that. "Try me!"

"I will!" he promised.

"Oh, Anthea, *pray——!*" whispered Mrs. Darracott, almost dragging her from the room. She added, as Chollacombe closed the door behind them: "My love, you *should* not! You know you should not! What, I ask you, would become of us if he were to cast us off?"

5

"Oh, he won't do that!" replied Anthea confidently. "Even he must feel that once in a lifetime is enough for the performance of *that* idiocy! I collect that the *weaver's son* is the offspring of the uncle we are never permitted to mention? Who is he, and what is he, and—oh, come and tell me all about it, Mama! You know we have leave to marvel and chatter as much as we choose!"

"Yes, but I don't know anything," objected Mrs. Darracott, allowing herself to be drawn into one of the saloons that opened on to the central hall of the house. "Indeed, I never knew of his existence until your grandfather threw him at my head in that scrambling way! And I consider," she added indignantly, "that I behaved with perfect propriety, for I took it with composure, and I'm sure it was enough to have cast me into strong hysterics! He would have been well-served if I had fallen senseless at his feet. I was never more shocked!"

A smile danced in her daughter's eyes, but she said with becoming gravity: "Exactly so! But a well-bred ease of manner, you know, is quite wasted on my grandfather. Mama, when you ruffle up your feathers you look like a very pretty partridge!"

"But I am not wearing feathers!" objected the widow. "Feathers for a mere family evening, and in the country, too! It would be quite ineligible, my love! Besides, you should not say such things!"

"No, very true! It was the stupidest comparison, for whoever saw a partridge in purple plumage? You look like a turtle-dove, Mama!"

Mrs. Darracott allowed this to pass. Her mind, never tenacious, was diverted to the delicate sheen of her gown. She had fashioned it herself, from a roll of silk unearthed from the bottom of a trunk stored in one of the attics, and she was pardonably pleased with the result of her skill. The design had been copied from a plate in the previous month's issue of *The Mirror of Fashion*, but she had improved upon it, substituting some very fine Brussels lace (relic of her trousseau) for the chenille trimming of the illustration. Her father-in-law might apostrophize her as a wet-goose, but even he could scarcely have denied (had he had the least understanding of such matters) that she was a notable needlewoman. She was also a very pretty woman, with a plump, trim figure, large blue eyes, and a quantity of fair hair which was partially concealed under a succession of becoming caps. From the moment when she had detected a suspicion of sagging under her jaw she had made her caps to tie beneath her chin or (more daringly) her ear; and the result was admirable. She was neither learned nor intelligent, but she contrived to dress both herself and her daughter out of a meagre jointure, supplying with her clever fingers what her purse could not buy; and she had never, during the twelve years of her widowhood, allowed either her father-in-law's snubs or the frequent discomforts of her situation to impair the amiability of her disposition. Her temper being cheerful, and the trend of her mind optimistic, she seldom fretted over the major trials which were beyond her power to mend. Her daughter, of whom she was extremely fond, was twenty-two years of age and still unwed; her spirited young son, whom she adored, was kept kicking his heels in idleness to serve his grandfather's caprice; but although she recognized that such a state of affairs was deplorable, she could not help feeling that *something* would happen to make all right, and was able, without much difficulty, to put such dismal thoughts aside, and to expend her anxiety on lesser and more remedial problems.

Anthea's quizzing remark brought one of these to her mind. Smoothing a crease from the purple-bloom satin, she said very seriously: "You know, dearest, it will be excessively awkward!"

"What will be awkward? The weaver's son?"

"Oh, him——! No, poor boy—though of course it *will* be! I was thinking of your Aunt Aurelia. I am persuaded she will expect to see us in mourning. You know what a high stickler she is for *every* observance! She will think it very odd of us to be wearing colours—even improper!"

"Not at all!" replied Anthea coolly. "By the time my grandfather has demanded to be told what cause *she* has to wear mourning for my uncle and my cousin, and has made her the recipient of his views on females rigging themselves out to look like so many crows, she will readily understand why you and I have abstained from that particular observance."

Mrs. Darracott considered this rather dubiously. "Well, yes, but there is no *depending* on your grandfather. I think we should at least wear black ribbons."

7

"Very well, Mama, we will wear whatever you choose—at least, *I* will do so if *you* will stop teasing yourself about such fripperies and tell me about the weaver's son, and the uncle who must not be mentioned."

"But I don't know anything!" protested Mrs. Darracott. "Only that he was the next brother to poor Granville, and quite your grandfather's favourite son. Your papa was used to say that that was what enraged Grandpapa so particularly, though for my part I can't believe that he held him in the slightest affection! Never, never could I bring myself to disown *my* son! Not though he married a *dozen* weaver's daughters!"

"Oh, I think we should be obliged to disown him if he married a dozen of them, Mama!" Anthea said, laughing. "It would be quite excessive, and so embarrassing! Oh, no, don't frown at me! It don't become you, and I won't fun any more, I promise you! Is that what my uncle did? Married a weaver's daughter?"

"Well, that's what I was told," replied Mrs. Darracott cautiously. "It all happened before I was married to your papa, so I am not perfectly sure. Papa wouldn't have spoken of it only that there was a notice of Hugh's death published in the *Gazette*, and he was afraid I might see it, and make some remark."

"When did he die, Mama?"

"Now that I *can* tell you, for it was the very year I was married, and had just come back from my honeymoon to live here. It was in 1793. He was killed, poor man. I can't remember the name of the place, but I do know it was in Holland. I daresay we were engaged in a war there, for he was a military man. And I shouldn't be at all astonished, Anthea, if *that* is what makes your grandfather so determined Richmond shan't enter the army. I don't mean Hugh's being killed, but if he had not been a military man he would never have been stationed in Yorkshire, and, of course, if he had not been stationed there he would never have met that female, let alone have become so disastrously entangled. I believe she was a very low, vulgar creature, and lived in Huddersfield. I must own that it is not at all what one would wish for one's son."

"No, indeed!" Anthea agreed. "What in the world can have possessed him to do such a thing? And he a Darracott!"

8

"Exactly so, my love! The most imprudent thing, for he cannot have supposed that your grandfather would forgive such a shocking misalliance! When one thinks how he holds up his nose at quite respectable persons, and never visits the Metropolis because he says it has grown to be full of mushrooms, and once-a-week beaux——! I must say, I never knew anyone who set himself on such a high form. And then to have his son marrying a weaver's daughter! *Well!*"

"And to be obliged in the end to receive her son as his heir!" said Anthea. "No wonder he has been like a bear at a stake all these months! Did he know, when my uncle and Oliver were drowned, how it was? Was that what made him so out of reason cross? Why has he waited so long before breaking it to us? Why——Oh, how provoking it is to think he won't tell us, and we dare not ask him!"

"Perhaps he will tell Richmond," suggested Mrs. Darracott hopefully.

"No," Anthea said, with a decided shake of her head. "Richmond won't ask him. Richmond never asks him questions he doesn't wish to answer, any more than he argues with him, or runs counter to him."

"Dear Richmond!" sighed Mrs. Darracott fondly. "I am sure he must be the best-natured boy in the world!"

"Certainly the best-natured grandson," said Anthea, a trifle dryly.

"Indeed he is!" agreed her mother. "Sometimes I quite marvel at him, you know, for young men are not in general so tractable and goodhumoured. And it is *not* that he lacks spirit!"

"No," said Anthea. "He doesn't lack spirit."

"The thing is," pursued Mrs. Darracott, "that he has the sweetest disposition imaginable! Only think how good he is to your grandfather, sitting with him every evening, and playing chess, which must be the dullest thing in the world! I wonder, too, how many boys who had set their hearts on a pair of colours would have behaved as beautifully as he did, when your grandfather forbade him to think of such a thing? I don't scruple to own to you, my love, that I was in a quake for days, dreading, you know, that he might do something foolish and hot-headed. After all, he *is* a Darracott, and even your uncle Matthew was excessively wild when he was a young man." She sighed.

"Poor boy! It was a sad blow to him, wasn't it? It quite wrung my heart to see him so restless, and out of spirits, but thank heaven *that* is all over now, for I couldn't have borne it if your grandfather had agreed to let him join! I daresay it was just a boyish fancy—but Richmond has such good sense!"

Anthea looked up, as though she would have spoken; but she apparently thought better of the impulse, and closed her lips again.

"Depend upon it," said Mrs. Darracott comfortably, "he will never think of it again, once he has gone to Oxford. Oh dear, how we shall miss him! I don't know what I shall do!"

The crease which had appeared between Anthea's brows deepened. She said, after a moment's hesitation: "Richmond has no turn for sholarship, Mama. He has failed *once*, and for my part I think he will fail again, because he doesn't wish to succeed. And here we are in September, so that he will be more than nineteen by the time he *does* go to Oxford—*if* he goes—and he will have spent another year here, with nothing to do but to——"

"Nothing of the sort!" interrupted Mrs. Darracott, bristling in defence of her idol. "He will be *studying!*"

"Oh!" said Anthea, in a colourless voice. She glanced uncertainly at her mother, again hesitated, and then said: "Shall I ring for some working-candles, Mama?"

Mrs. Darracott, who was engaged in darning, with exquisite stitches, the torn needlepoint lace flounce to a petticoat, agreed to this; and in a very short space of time both ladies were deedily employed: the elder with her needle, the younger with some cardboard, out of which she was making a reticule, in the shape of an Etruscan vase. This was in accordance with the latest mode; and, if *The Mirror of Fashion* were to be believed, any ingenious lady could achieve the desired result without the smallest difficulty. "Which confirms me in the melancholy suspicion that I am quite lacking in ingenuity, besides having ten thumbs," remarked Anthea, laying it aside as Chollacombe brought the tea-tray into the room.

"I think it will look very elegant when you have painted it, my love," said Mrs. Darracott consolingly. She looked up, and saw that Richmond had followed the butler into the room, and her face instantly became wreathed in

10

smiles. "Oh, Richmond! You have come to take tea with us! How charming this is!" A thought occurred to her; her expression underwent a ludicrous change; she said apprehensively: "Does your grandfather mean to join us, dearest?"

He shook his head, but there was a gleam of mischief in his eyes, which did not escape his sister. His mother, less observant, said in a relieved tone: "To be sure, he rarely does so, does he? Thank you, Chollacombe: nothing more! Now, sit down, Richmond, and *tell us!*"

"What, about the weaver's son? Oh, I can't! Grandpapa snapped my nose off, so we played backgammon, and I won, and then he said I might take myself off, because he wants to talk to *you*, Mama!"

"You *are* a detestable boy!" remarked Anthea. "Mama take care! you will spill that! Depend upon it, he only means to throw a great many orders at your head about the manner in which we are to entertain the heir."

"Yes," agreed Mrs. Darracott, recovering her complexion. "Of course! I wonder if I should go to him immediately, or whether——"

"No, you will first drink your tea, Mama," said Anthea firmly. "Did he tell you *nothing* about our unknown cousin, Richmond?"

"Well, only that he's a military man, and was in France, with the Army of Occupation, when my uncle Granville was drowned, and that he has written that he will visit us the day after tomorrow."

"That must have been the letter James brought from the receiving office, then!" exclaimed Mrs. Darracott. "Well, at least he can *write!* Poor young man! I can't but pity him, though I perfectly appreciate how provoking it is for us all that he should have been born. Still, even your grandfather can't blame him for that!"

"For shame, Mama! You are under-rating my grandfather in the most disrespectful way! Of course he can!"

Mrs. Darracott could not help laughing at this, but she shook her head at her too-lively daughter as well, saying that she ought not to speak so saucily of her grandfather. After that she finished drinking her tea, begged Richmond not to go bed before she returned from the ordeal before her, and went away to the library.

Anthea got up to fill her cup again. She glanced down

11

at Richmond, sunk into a deep chair and smothering a yawn. "You look to be three parts asleep. Are you?"

"No—yes—I don't know! I had one of my bad nights, that's all. Don't cosset me—and, for God's sake, don't say anything to Mama!"

"What a fortunate thing that you've warned me!" said Anthea, sitting down in her mother's vacated chair. "I was just about to run after Mama, before procuring a composer for you."

He grinned at her. "Pitching it *too* rum!" he murmured. "I wonder what Grandpapa *does* want to say to Mama?"

"I don't know, but I hope he may say it with civility! How *could* you stand there, and let him speak to her as he did at dinner, Richmond?"

"Well, *I* can't stop him! What's more, I've more sense than to rip up at him as *you* did! It only puts Mama in a quake, when she thinks he may fly into a passion with you or me: you should know that!"

"He doesn't like one the less for squaring up to him," she said. "I will allow him *that* virtue: I don't know that he has any other."

"He may not like *you* less, but you're a female: the cases are different."

"I don't think so. He liked Papa far more than he liked Uncle Granville or Uncle Matthew, but I can't tell you how often they were at outs. I daresay you might not remember, but——"

"Oh, don't I just!" he interrupted. "Grandpapa abusing Papa like a pickpocket, Papa as mad as Bedlam, the pair of them brangling and brawling to be heard all over the house——! *Not remember?* I don't remember anything half as well! Too well to court the same Turkish treatment that Papa got: you may be sure of *that!*"

She looked curiously at him. "But you're not afraid of him, are you?"

"No, I'm not afraid of him, but I detest the sort of riot and rumpus he kicks up when he's in a rage. Besides, it doesn't answer: you'll get nothing out of Grandpapa if you come to cuffs with him. I'll swear he gives me more than ever he gave Papa!"

She reflected that this was true. Lord Darracott, who grudged every groat he was obliged to spend on anything but his own pleasure, pandered to his favourite grandson's every extravagant whim. If coaxing did not move him, it was seldom that Richmond failed to bring him round his thumb by falling into a fit of despondency. That was how Richmond had come by the beautiful headstrong colt he had himself broken and trained. He had coaxed in vain. "Do you think I'll help you to break your neck, boy?" had demanded his lordship. Richmond had not persisted, and even so clearsighted a critic as his elder sister had been unable to accuse him of sulkiness. He was as docile as ever, as attentive to his grandfather, and quite uncomplaining. But he made it very evident that his spirits were wholly cast down; and within a week his dejection, besides throwing Mrs. Darracott into high fidgets, had won the colt for him. Anything, said Lord Darracott, was better than to have the boy so languid and listless.

It had been to cajole him out of silent despair at being told that under no circumstances would my lord buy him a pair of colours that his yacht had been bestowed on him. Suddenly Anthea wondered if the possession of a sailing vessel had been what he had all the time desired. She turned her eyes towards him, and said abruptly: "Do you still wish for a military career, Richmond?"

He had picked up one of the weekly journals from the table at his elbow, and was glancing through it, but he looked up quickly at that, his expressive eyes kindling. "I don't care for anything else!"

"Then——"

"You needn't go on! Why don't I persist? Why don't I do this—or that—or the other? Because I know when my grandfather can't be persuaded by anything I could do or say! That's why! I'm under age—and if you are thinking that I might run off and take the King's shilling, it's the sort of hubble-bubble notion a female *would* get into her head! That's not how I wish to join! I—oh, stop talking about it! I *won't* talk about it! It's over and done with! I daresay I shouldn't have liked it, after all!"

He turned back to his journal, hunching an impatient shoulder, and Anthea said no more, knowing that it would be useless. She was deeply troubled, however, and not for the first time. He was spoilt, and wilful, but she loved him, and was wise enough to realize that his faults sprang from his upbringing and were to be laid at Lord Darracott's door.

13

He had been a sickly, undersized baby, succumbing to every childish ailment: not at all the sort of grandson that might have been expected to occupy Lord Darracott's heart. His lordship, indeed, had paid scant heed to him until it was forcibly borne in upon him that the frail scrap whom he despised was possessed of a demon of intrepidity. But from the day when a terrified groom had carried into the house a baby who screamed: "Put me down, put me down! I *can* ride him! I *can!*" and had learned from this trembling individual that his tiny grandson had (by means unknown and unsuspected) got upon the back of one of his own hunters and put this great, rawboned creature at the gate that led out of the stableyard, he had adored Richmond. There had been no bones broken, but the child had been stunned by the inevitable fall, and shockingly bruised. "Let me go!" he had commanded imperiously. "I *will* ride him, I will, I will, I *will!*"

Nothing could have made a greater hit with my lord. Himself a man of iron nerve, he was at once surprised and exultant to discover in the weakling of the family a fearlessness that matched his own. There was no more talk of puling brats or miserable squeeze-crabs: thenceforward little Richmond figured in his grandfather's conversation as a right one, game as a pebble; and my lord, who had suffered scarcely a day's illness in his life, very soon became more morbidly anxious about the state of his darling's health than was Richmond's fond mama. Poor Mrs. Darracott, labouring for six years under the stigma of being a doting idiot who cosseted her whelp to death, suddenly, and to her considerable bewilderment, underwent a transformation, changing, almost overnight, into an unnatural parent to whose callous neglect every one of her son's ailments could be attributed. She bore the slur with fortitude, too thankful for my lord's change of heart to resent the injustice to herself. She had dreaded the day when she would be forced to send her delicate son to Eton, but when that day dawned it had been my lord, not she, who had decreed that Richmond must be educated at home. At the time, Anthea, four years older than her brother, had been as glad as she that Richmond was not to be subjected to the rigours of boarding-school; it was not until several years had passed that she realized,

14

looking back, that by the time he was eleven Richmond had largely outgrown his delicacy of constitution. Today, a little more than eighteen years old, he was certainly a thin youth, but he seemed to have no other weakness than a tendency towards insomnia. As a child, the slightest stir in his room had jerked him wide-awake, and this idosyncrasy had remained with him, causing him to choose for his own a bedchamber as far removed from the main body of the house as was possible; to bolt his door; and to forbid his solicitous family to come near him once he had retired for the night. None of them ever did so, but it was only Anthea who suspected that the prohibition sprang from a strong dislike of being teased by offers of hot bricks, drops of laudanum, supporting broths, or saline draughts, rather than from an inability to drop off to sleep again once he had been roused. No one, she thought (but privately), who suffered from disturbed nights could be as energetic as Richmond.

He was certainly looking heavy-eyed this evening, yawning from time to time, as he flicked over the pages of the journal; but as he had begun to bring his hunters into condition, and had spent the morning at trotting exercise, following this up by soundly beating his sister in several games of battledore-and-shuttlecock, before going off to shoot rabbits in a turnip-field, it would have been surprising had he not looked weary at the end of the day.

He glanced up presently from the journal, as a thought occurred to him, and said, with a gleam of decidedly impish amusement: "I wouldn't be in that fellow's shoes for a fortune, would you?"

"Our unknown cousin? No, indeed I wouldn't! If he's not up to the rig, Grandpapa will behave abominably, and we shall all be put to the blush. What do you think he will be like, Richmond? It seems to me that if he's a military man he can't be *very* vulgar. Unless—Good God, he isn't just a common soldier, is he?"

"Rifleman. No, of course he—Lord, I never thought of that!" said Richmond, in an awed tone. He grinned appreciatively. "Well, if that *is* the way of it it *will* mean the devil to pay, won't it? I wonder if my uncle knows what Grandpapa has in store, or whether—Vincent, too! I'll tell you what Anthea, I don't give a fig for Uncle Matthew,

15

but I think it's a curst shame that Vincent should be cut out by this mushroom!"

She did not answer, for at that moment Mrs. Darracott came back into the room.

2

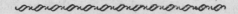

It was instantly apparent to her children that Mrs. Darracott had not been summoned by her father-in-law to discuss such trivialities as the arrangements to be made for the reception of his heir. She was looking slightly dazed; but when Anthea asked her if my lord had been unkind, she replied in a flustered way: "No, no! *Nothing* like that! Well, that is to say—Except for—Not that I regarded it, for it was nothing out of the ordinary, and I hope I know better than to take a pet over a trifle. I must own, too, that I can't be astonished at his being vexed to death over this business. It is excessively awkward! However, he doesn't lay the blame at *my* door: you mustn't think that!"

"I should think not indeed!" exclaimed Anthea between amusement and indignation. "How could he possibly do so?"

"No, very true, my love!" agreed Mrs. Darracott. "I thought that myself, but it did put me on the fidgets when Richmond said he wanted to see me, because, in general, you know, things I never even heard about turn out to be my fault. However, as I say, it wasn't so today. Now, where did I put my thimble? I must finish darning that shocking rent before your aunt arrives tomorrow."

"No, that you shan't!" declared Anthea, removing the work-box out of her mother's reach. "You are big with news, Mama!"

"I am sure I haven't the least guess why you should think so. And you shouldn't say things like that! It is most improper!"

"But not by half as improper as to try to bamboozle

17

your children! Now, Mama, you know you can't do it! *What* has Grandpapa disclosed to you? Instantly tell us!"

"Nothing at all!" asserted the widow, looking ridiculously guilty. "Good gracious, as though he ever told me anything! How can you be so absurd?"

"Now, that is trying it on much too rare and thick!" said Richmond accusingly.

"Foolish boy! You are as bad as your sister, and what your poor papa would think of you both, if he could hear you, I'm sure I don't know! And you ought to be in bed, Richmond! You look worn to a bone!"

At this, her masterful offspring converged upon her, Anthea sinking down on to a stool at her feet, and Richmond perching on the arm of her chair.

"And *we* don't know what poor Papa would think of you for shamming it so, dearest!" said Anthea. "Grandpapa has told you all about the weaver's son. Confess!"

"No, no, I promise you he hasn't! He told me nothing about him—well, nothing to the purpose! Only when I ventured to ask him if it had not been a great shock to him to learn of the young man's existence, he said he had known of it for ever. My dears, would you have believed it? It seems that poor Hugh wrote to tell your grandfather of *this* Hugh's birth, twenty-seven years ago! And not a word has he uttered to a soul until today! Unless, of course, he disclosed the truth to Granville, but I am positive he never did so, for your Aunt Anne and I were the closest of friends, and she must have told me, if she had known anything about it. Oh dear, poor soul, I wonder how she does? I wonder how it will answer, living with her daughter and her son-in-law? To be sure, Sir John Caldbeck seemed a most amiable man, and I daresay *anything* was preferable to Anne than continuing here—though I always used to think that Grandpapa was by far more civil to her than——"

"Yes, Mama," interrupted Anthea. "But all this is fair and far off, you know! So Grandpapa has known from the start how it was, has he? We needn't marvel that he said nothing about it while my Uncle Granville and Oliver were alive, but how can he have allowed my Uncle Matthew to suppose all these months that he was now the heir to the barony? It is a great deal too bad, besides being quite crackbrained! Did he hope the young man might be

18

dead? He can't, surely, have forgotten him!"

"Well, I fancy, from something he said to me just now, that he had the intention of disinheriting him, if it might be done, only from some cause or another—but I don't precisely understand about settlements, so—or do I mean any entail? No, I don't *think* it was that, and naturally I shouldn't dream of asking your grandfather to explain, for nothing provokes him more than to be asked questions, though why it should I can't conjecture!"

"I didn't know one *could* cut out the heir of one's title," objected Richmond.

"It seems to be established that Grandpapa, at all events, cannot," said Anthea.

"Sequestration!" suddenly and triumphantly exclaimed Mrs. Darracott. "That was the word! I thought very likely it would come back to me, for very often things, do, and sometimes, which always seems extraordinary to me, in the middle of the night! Well, that was it, only it can't be done, and so Grandpapa feels that there is nothing for it but to make the best of this young man."

"Did he say that, Mama?" asked Anthea incredulously.

"Yes, he did," nodded Mrs. Darracott. "Well, it was what he *meant!*"

"But what did he *say?*" demanded Richmond.

"Oh, I can't recall exactly what he said! Only he seems to think he might go off at any moment, though why he should I can't imagine, for I never knew anyone so hearty! In fact, it wouldn't surprise me if he—Well, never mind that! Dear me, I have forgotten what I was about to say!"

"It wouldn't surprise you if he outlived us all," supplied Anthea helpfully.

"Certainly not!" stated Mrs. Darracott, blushing. "Such a thought never entered my head!"

"Lord, what a rapper!" remarked Richmond, palliating this undutiful criticism by hugging her briefly. "You're trying to cut a wheedle, but if you think you can turn *us* up sweet, you're a goose, Mama!"

"*Richmond!*"

"How many more times is Mama to tell you not to speak to her so saucily?" interpolated Anthea severely.

"You are two very silly, impertinent children!" said Mrs. Darracott, trying not to laugh. "And what your Aunt Aurelia will think of you, if you talk in that improper style, makes me quite sick with apprehension!"

"We won't," promised Anthea. "We will remember that a want of conduct in us reflects directly upon you, love, and, we will behave with all the propriety in the world."

"*If* she stops trying to gammon us," amended Richmond.

"Oh, that is understood! *How* does Grandpapa mean to make the best of our new cousin, Mama?"

"Well, my dears," responded the widow, capitulating, "he seems to think that it will be necessary to lick the unfortunate young man into shape. At least, that's what he said."

"Unfortunate young man indeed!"

"I own, one can't but feel a great deal of compassion for him, yet it can't be denied that it *is* a severe trial for your grandfather to know that he must be succeeded by quite a *vulgar* person. I should be very much vexed myself, and heaven knows I don't set half the store by my consequence that your grandfather does! Oh dear, how uncomfortable it will be! I did hope, when I learned that he is a military man, that he might be quite gentlemanlike, but your grandfather says that the army has grown so large, on account of the war's having dragged on for such a time, that it is full of what he calls shabby-genteel officers— though how he should know that, when he never stirs from home, is more than I can tell! And to make it worse the poor man is in the wrong sort of regiment."

"What?" ejaculated Richmond, kindling. "He's in the 95th! A Light Division man! I should like to know what is wrong with that!"

"Well, dearest, I don't know anything about such matters myself, but Grandpapa spoke of its being newfangled, which, of course, would account for his not liking it."

"If that's the way my grandfather means to talk he'll make more of a Jack-pudding of himself than ever this cousin could, even if he is a rum 'un!" declared Richmond hotly. "Of all the antiquated, top-lofty——"

"Well, don't put yourself in a passion!" recommended his sister. "You cannot suppose that anything other than a cavalry regiment, or the 1st Foot Guards, would do for a Darracott!"

"Balderdash!" said Richmond. "I don't mean I wouldn't wish for a cavalry regiment myself, but if I can't—

couldn't—join one, I'd as lief be a Light Bob as anything else. And if Grandpapa says something slighting—oh, lord, I shan't know where to look! I wonder if this man marched to Talavera? Do you know that——" He broke off, seeing his mother look quickly up at him, a stricken expression in her face. "Oh, well!" he said, shrugging. "It's of no consequence—only I do hope to God Grandpapa doesn't make a cake of himself! Go on, Mama! How is our cousin to be licked into shape? Does my grandfather mean to undertake the task himself? The wretched victim will seize the first opportunity that offers of escaping from the home of his fathers!"

"Oh, no!" Mrs. Darracott said. "That is—no, I am persuaded your grandfather doesn't mean—He said something about Vincent's being able to *hint* him into the established mode."

"Vincent! He won't do it!" said Richmond positively.

"No, well—well, at least your grandfather seems to feel that we ought, all of us, to use the young man kindly!" Mrs. Darracott perceived that both her children were regarding her with a mixture of surprise and disbelief, and her colour rose. She began to rearrange the Paisley shawl she wore draped round her shoulders, and said, rather too airily: "I am sure it is greatly to his credit, and not at all what one would have expected! Poor young man! Your cousin, I mean, not Grandpapa! I daresay he will feel sadly out of place here, and we must try to make him welcome. I shall certainly do so, and I hope you will, too, dearest Anthea. Grandpapa is—is particularly anxious that you should make yourself agreeable to him. Indeed, I don't know why you should not! Not that I mean..." Aware that two pairs of fine grey eyes were fixed on her face, she found herself unable to finish this sentence, and tried hurriedly to begin another. "Dear me, how late it is! Anthea, my love,——"

"Mama!" uttered Anthea accusingly. "If you don't tell me precisely what it was that my grandfather said to you I'll go to the library and ask him!"

This dreadful threat threw Mrs. Darracott into instant disorder. She scolded a little, wept a little, asseverated that my lord had said nothing at all, and ended by divulging to her children that my lord had conceived the happy notion of bringing about a match between his

21

shabby-genteel heir and his only unmarried granddaughter. "To keep him in the *Family!*" she explained earnestly.

That was all that was needed to send Richmond into shouts of laughter. His sister, in general a girl with a lively sense of the ridiculous, found herself easily able to withstand the infection of his laughter. She waited in ominous silence until his mirth abated, and then, transferring her gaze from him to her mother, asked with careful restraint: "Does it ever occur to you, Mama, that my grandfather is a lunatic?"

"Frequently!" Mrs. Darracott assured her. "That is— oh, dear, what am I saying? Of course not! Perhaps he is a trifle *eccentric!*"

"Eccentric! He's a mediaeval bedlamite!" said Anthea, not mincing matters. "Upon my word, this is beyond everything!"

"I was afraid you would not quite like it," agreed her mother unhappily. "Now, Richmond——! You will be in whoops if you don't take care! Foolish boy! There is nothing to laugh at!"

"Let him go into whoops, Mama! They may *choke* him!"

Mrs. Darracott was shocked by this unfeeling speech, but thought it wisest, after one glance at Anthea's stormy face, to beg Richmond to go away. He did go, but it was a moment or two before Anthea's wrath abated. She had jumped up from the footstool, and now took several turns about the room in a hasty, impetuous way which filled Mrs. Darracott with foreboding. However, she soon recovered her temper, and, although still incensed, was presently able to laugh at herself. "I should know better than to fly up into the boughs for anything that detestable old man could say or do! I beg your pardon, Mama, but it puts me in such a rage when he behaves as though he were the Grand Turk, and we a parcel of slaves——! So I am to marry the weaver's son, am I? I collect that *I* have nothing to say in the matter: has the weaver's son? Has he been informed of the fate that awaits him?"

"Oh, no! That is—I *did* venture to suggest to your grandfather—But he said—you know his way!—that the poor young man would do as he was bid!"

"And he will!" said Anthea. "That's to say, he'll try! Wretched, wretched man! I pity him with all my heart!

22

He will be miserably ill-at-ease, miserably out of place, and will arrive to find himself under fire! Grandpapa will overawe him within five minutes! Mama, it is *infamous!* Did you tell my grandfather that I shouldn't consent to such a scheme?"

"Well—well, I didn't say *that*, precisely!" confessed Mrs. Darracott, in acute discomfort. "To own the truth, my love, I was so much taken-aback that——"

"Then I will, and immediately!" declared Anthea, going towards the door.

She was halted by a small, anguished shriek. "Anthea, I forbid you—I implore you!—He would be so angry! He will say that he told me not to say one word to you about it, and he *did!*"

Anthea could not be impervious to this appeal. She paused; and, pursuing her advantage, Mrs. Darracott said: "My dearest, you have so much good sense! I know you will consider carefully before you—Not that I would urge you to marry him if you felt you couldn't like him! I promise you I would never, never—But what will you *do*, Anthea? Oh, my dearest child, I'm cast into despair whenever I think of it! You are two-and-twenty, and how can you hope to receive a respectable offer, when you never meet anyone but the Family, or go anywhere, or—And here is your grandfather saying that you frittered away your chances when he was so obliging as to frank you to a London Season, and so you must now be content with a husband of his choosing!"

"During my one Season," said Anthea, in a level tone, "I received two offers of marriage. One came from a widower, old enough, I conjecture, to have been my father. The other was from young Oversley, who, besides being next door to a moonling, had the fixed intention of continuing under his parents' roof. Between Grandpapa and Lady Aberford I am persuaded there wasn't the difference of a hair! I haven't watched the trials you've been made to endure only to stumble into the same snare, Mama!"

"No, and heaven knows, dear child, I must be the last person alive to wish to see you in such a situation," sighed Mrs. Darracott.

"I could, I think, have developed a *tendre* for Jack Froyle," said Anthea reflectively. "But he, you know, was obliged to hang out for a rich wife, and thanks to the

23

improvidence for which the Darracotts are so justly famed my portion can't be called anything but paltry. Does Grandpapa consider that circumstance when he talks of the chances I have frittered away?"

"No, he doesn't!" replied Mrs. Darracott, with unaccustomed bitterness. "But *I* do, and it utterly sinks my spirits! That's why I can't help thinking that perhaps you ought not to set your face against this scheme of your grandfather's. Not until you have met your cousin, at all events, my love! Of course, if he should prove to be impossible—only, you know, his *is* a Darracott on *one* side!"

"The side I should like the least!" said Anthea.

"Yes, but—but you would be *established!*" Mrs. Darracott pointed out. "Even if the young man is a coxcomb, which I do pray he is not, *your* position as Lady Daracott would be one of the first respectability. Anthea, I cannot bear to see you dwindle into an old maid!"

Anthea could not help laughing at this impassioned utterance, but Mrs. Darracott was perfectly serious, saying very earnestly: "How can you help but do so when no eligible gentleman ever *sees* you? Dear Anne was used to say that when Elizabeth and Caroline were off her hands she would invite you to stay in London, because she entered into all my sentiments on that head; but now that your uncle Granville is dead, and she has gone away into Gloucestershire, it would be useless to depend on her. Aurelia has still two daughters of her own to bring out, and although I *could* write to my brother——"

"On no account in the world!" exclaimed Anthea. "My uncle is the most amiable soul alive, but I would far rather dwindle into an old maid than stay for as much as two days with my aunt Sarah! Besides, I don't think she could be prevailed upon to invite me."

"No, nor do I: she is the most disagreeable woman! So what, I ask you, is to become of you? When Grandpapa dies we shall be obliged to leave Darracott Place, you know. We shall be reduced to seeking *lodgings*, very likely in some dreadful back-slum, and eat black-pudding, and turn our dresses, and——"

A peal of laughter interrupted this dismal catalogue. "Stop, stop, Mama, before you fall into an incurable fit of the blue-devils! We shall do nothing of the sort! With *your* skill in dressmaking, and *my* turn for making elegant reticules, we shall set up as mantua-makers. In Bath, perhaps, on Milsom Street: not a large establishment, but an excessively modish one. Shall we call it Darracott's, to enrage the Family, or would it be more tonnish to call ourselves Elvira? Yes, I'm persuaded we should make a hit as Elvira! Within a year every woman of fashion will patronize us, because we shall charge the most exorbitant prices, which will convince the world that we *must* be top-of-the-trees!"

Mrs. Darracott, while deprecating such a nonsensical idea, could not help being strongly attracted by it. Anthea encouraged her to enlarge upon the daydream; and soon had the satisfaction of seeing her volatile parent restored to her usual optimism. Not until they retired to bed was the unknown cousin again mentioned. He came into Mrs. Darracott's mind as she picked up her candle, and she ventured to beg Anthea not to speak of the matter to her grandfather. She was much relieved when Anthea, kissing her, and giving her shoulder a reassuring pat, replied: "No, I shan't say anything to Grandpapa. I am sure it would be quite useless!"

Mrs. Darracott, much cheered, was able then to go to bed with a quiet mind. She was to deeply occupied with household cares on the following morning to have a thought to spare for any other problems than which bedchamber it would be proper to allot to the heir; how best to hide from Lady Aurelia that there was not a linen sheet in the house which had not been darned; and whether the undergroom would be able to purchase in Rye enough lobsters to make, when elegantly dressed, a handsome side-dish for the second course at dinner that day. She, and Mrs. Flitwick too, would have been glad to know for how many days my lord had invited five guests to stay at Darracott Place, but neither considered for as much as a minute the eligibility of applying to him for information on this head. Nothing but a rough answer could be expected. My lord would be unable to understand what difference it could make to anyone. He would also be unable to understand why the addition of five persons to his household should make any appreciable difference to the cost of maintaining his establishment. As he would, at the same time, cut up very stiff indeed if fewer than seven or eight dishes were provided for each course, the task of catering to his satisfaction was one of the labours of Hercules. "For, ma'am," (as Mrs. Flitwick sapiently observed) "I dare not for my life tell Godney to use the mutton in a nice haricot, or toss up some oysters in an escallop: his lordship will want everything to be of the best."

It soon transpired that there was one thing which his lordship did not want to be of the best. When Mrs. Darracott asked him if he wished Poor Granville's bedchamber to be prepared for the reception of his successor, his reply was explosive and unequivocal, and carried the rider that the weaver's brat would think himself palatially housed if put to sleep in one of the attics.

The first of the guests to arrive were Mr. Matthew Darracott and Lady Aurelia. They came in their own travelling-carriage, drawn by a single pair of horses; and they reached Darracott Place shortly after noon, having left town the day before, and rested for the night at Tonbridge.

Of my lord's four sons, Matthew, the third, was the one who had caused him the least trouble and expense. His youthful peccadilloes had been of a venial nature, committed either in emulation of his elder brothers, or at their instigation. He had been the first to marry; and from the day that he led Lady Aurelia Holt to the altar his career had been at once blameless and successful. It had been a very good match, for although Lady Aurelia was not beautiful her fortune was respectable, and her connections excellent. She had also a forceful personality, and it was not long before Matthew, weaned from the Whiggish heresies in which he had been reared, found himself (under the aegis of his father-in-law) with his foot firmly set on the first rung of the political ladder. His progress thereafter had been steady; and although it seemed unlikely that he would ever achieve the topmost rungs of the ladder, it was only during the brief reign of "All the Talents" that he was out of office; and although there were those who did not scruple to stigmatize his continued employment as jobbery, no one could deny that he discharged his duties with painstaking honesty.

His political apostasy notwithstanding, it might have been expected that so worthy a son would have occupied the chief place in his father's affection. Unfortunately Lord Darracott was bored by virtue, and contemptuous of those whom he could bully. Matthew had always been the meekest of his sons, and although his marriage had rendered him to some extent independent of his father, he still accorded him a sort of nervous respect, obeying his periodic and imperious summonses with anxious promptitude, and saying yes and amen to his lordship's every utterance. His reward for this filial piety was to be freely apostrophized as a pudding-heart, with no more pluck in him than a dunghill cock. Since his conduct was largely governed by the precepts of his masterful and rigidly correct wife, my lord was able to add, with perfect truth, that he lived under the sign of the cat's foot.

What Lady Aurelia thought of my lord no one knew, for she had been reared in the belief that the head of a family was entitled to every observance of civility. So far as outward appearances went, she was a dutiful daughter-in-law, neither arguing with his lordship, nor encouraging Matthew to rebel against his autocratic commands. Simple-minded persons, such as Mrs. Rupert Darracott, were continually astonished by Matthew's divergence, on all important issues, from his father's known prejudices; but Lord Darracott was not a simple-minded person, and he was well-aware that however politely Lady Aurelia might defer to him, it would be her dictates Matthew would obey in major matters. In consequence, he held her in equal respect and dislike, and never lost an opportunity to plant what he hoped would be a barb in her flesh.

According to Granville, whose own son had found little favour in his grandfather's eyes, it was with this amiable intention that my lord encouraged Vincent in a career which his parents were known to think ruinous. More charitable persons suspected that in Vincent my lord saw a reflection of his own youth; but, as Granville once bitterly remarked, it was strange, if that were so, that my lord's feeling for him fell far short of the doting fondness he lavished on Richmond.

It must have been apparent to the most casual observer that Matthew Darracott was labouring under a strong sense of ill-usage. He was rather a stout man, not quite as tall as his father, or any of his brothers, and with a chubby countenance. When he was pleased he looked what nature had intended him to be: a placid man with a kindly, easy-going disposition; but when harassed his expression changed to one of peevishness, a frown dragging his brows together, and a pronounced pout giving him very much the look of a thwarted baby.

As he climbed down from the carriage, he saw that Chollacombe was waiting by the open door of the house. Leaving James, the footman, to assist Lady Aurelia to alight, he trod up the shallow terrace-steps, exclaiming: "This is a damned thing, Chollacombe! Where's my father?"

"His lordship went out with Mr. Richmond, sir, and is not yet come in," replied the butler.

"Has that fellow—*I* don't know what he calls himself!—Has he arrived here?"

"No, sir. You are the first to arrive. As you no doubt know, Mr. Matthew, we are expecting Mr. Vincent and Mr. Claud also, but——"

"Oh, them!" said Matthew, dismissing his sons with an impatient shrug.

By this time he had been joined by his wife. She never reproved him in public, and she did not now so much as glance at him, but said majestically: "Good-day, Chollacombe. I hope I see you well?"

"Very well, thank you, my lady. Mrs. Darracott is in the Green Saloon, I fancy. Perhaps your ladyship would——"

He broke off, for at that moment Mrs. Darracott came hurrying across the hall. "Oh, Matthew! My dear Aurelia! How glad I am to see you! I did not expect you would be so early—but so delightful!"

"We lay at Tonbridge," said Lady Aurelia, presenting her cheek to her sister-in-law. "I do not care to travel above thirty or forty miles at a stretch: it does not agree with my constitution."

"No, it is very disagreeable!" agreed Mrs. Darracott. "The road from Tonbridge, too, is so horribly rough! I am sure——"

"Elvira!" interrupted Matthew, thrusting his hat into James's hand, "what do you know about this appalling business?"

"Oh, my dear Matthew, *nothing!* That is, only——But won't you come into the Green Saloon? Unless you would wish to take off your bonnet and pelisse, Aurelia? I will take you upstairs—not that there is any *need* to escort you, for you must feel yourself to be quite as much at home as I am."

This, however, her ladyship disclaimed, saying graciously that she considered herself a guest in the house, her sister-in-law being its unquestionable mistress. Mrs. Darracott, though privately thinking that there was a good deal of question about it, accepted this, and the two ladies went upstairs, leaving Matthew to get what information he could from Chollacombe. But as the butler knew very little more than he did, the only tidings he was able to glean were that the heir was not expected to arrive until the following day, and that my lord was (if Chollacombe might venture to say so) a trifle out of humour.

"Ay, I'll be bound he is!" said Matthew. "Well, it is enough to put a saint out of temper! What's more, I shouldn't wonder at it if the fellow's an impostor!"

Chollacombe thought it prudent to return no answer to this; so, after fidgeting about the hall for a few moments, Matthew took himself off, saying that if my lord was out riding with Mr. Richmond he might as well go down to the stables to meet him on his return.

In the event, he reached the main stableyard to find that his father had already returned, and in time to see the two sturdy coach-horses being taken out of the shafts of Matthew's travelling-carriage. He himself was bestriding a neatish bay cover-hack, but Richmond, as his uncle resentfully perceived, had just dismounted from the back of a high-bred hunter which had probably cost my lord anything from three to five hundred guineas.

"So you've arrived, have you?" said my lord, by way of paternal greeting. "I might have known this paltry turnout was yours! What did you give for that pair of commoners?"

"I don't recall—but they are not commoners, sir! Pure-bred Welsh, I assure you!" responded Matthew, nettled.

"Cleveland machiners!" said his lordship, with a bark of sardonic mirth. "You've been burnt, my boy! If ever I knew such a slow-top!" He pointed his whip at Richmond's hunter. "Now, *there's* a horse of the right stamp! Breed in every inch of him, perfect fencer, flying or standing!"

"Hardly the right stamp for carriage-work, sir!" said Matthew. "A goodlooking horse, however, and carries a

29

good head." He held out his hand to Richmond, adding kindly: "Well, my boy? And how are you?"

"Pretty stout, sir, thank you," replied Richmond, shaking hands with him. "I hope you are well? And my aunt, of course. Is my cousin with you?"

The note of eagerness did not escape Matthew; he smiled faintly. "No, neither of them. I collect, though, that you meant Vincent: I expect he will arrive presently."

"You may be sure that he will!" interpolated his lordship, dismounting, and handing over his bridle to the waiting groom. He then looked his son over, remarked that he was becoming as fat as a flawn, and strode off towards the house, imperatively commanding Richmond to follow him.

But Richmond, who disliked being made to stand by in acute embarrassment while my lord insulted his son, had already slipped away into a wing of the stables, and it was Matthew who, swallowing his resentment, caught up with my lord. "Father, I must ask you—indeed, I must insist——"

My lord stopped, and turned, his grasp on his riding-whip tightening. "Oh? So you must insist, must you? Go on!"

"Well, I must say that I think you owe me—well, that an explanation is due to me!" amended Matthew sulkily.

"If you think you'll get an explanation out of me, other than what I choose to tell you, muffin-face, you're a bigger clunch than I knew! What I choose to tell you I have told you, and it's all that concerns you!"

"No, sir!" said Matthew resolutely. "That don't fit! You don't like me; you didn't wish for me to step into your shoes; but when—after what happened in June—I was your heir: no question about it!"

"You were not."

"No! As it now appears, and if this fellow who has sprang out of nowhere is not an impostor! And that, sir, is something even you will own I've a right to ask!"

"He is not an impostor."

"I beg your pardon, but what proof have you of that? For my part I think it damned smoky, Father! If the fellow is my brother's son, I should like to know why he never approached you before! Upon my word, a very neat thing this is! If he had had the impudence to put forward his

30

so-called claim to *me*, I'd have set Lissett to enquire into his credentials, and you may depend upon it we should soon have found that it was nothing more than an attempt to run a rig! Well, I've seen Lissett, and he tells me you didn't desire him to do any such thing, but merely to write a letter informing the rascal you would receive him here. Now, Father——"

"Damn you, when I want your advice I'll ask you for it!" broke in his lordship roughly. "I'm not in my dotage yet! I've known for twenty-seven years that this cocktail existed!"

"Good God!" gasped Matthew. "Known for——And never *told* us?"

"Why should I have told you?" demanded his father. "D'ye think I was proud of a weaver's spawn? D'ye think I ever imagined I should be succeeded by a whelp I thought never to set eyes on? As for approching me— laying claims—you're fair and far off! He never did so! He's coming here because I've sent for him—and he's taken his time about coming!" he added grimly. "If you've seen Lissett, no doubt he told you that the fellow's a soldier. *I've* known that these five years and more."

"Do you mean to say you've followed his career?" asked Matthew incredulously.

"No, I don't! I never gave the whelp a thought. Old Barnwood ran against him when he was out in the Peninsula, and had the curst brass to come up to me in Brook's, and ask me if I knew I'd a grandson in the 95th. I damned his eyes for it, meddling busy-body!"

Matthew said slowly: "So when my brother was drowned you knew! And yet you——For God's sake, sir, why didn't you tell me *then*? Why——"

"Because I hoped he might be dead, chucklehead, or that there might be some way of keeping him out of my shoes!" replied Lord Darracott, his face working. "Well, he's not dead, and there's no way of keeping him out! When I'm booked, he'll be the head of the family, but I'm not booked yet, and, by God, I'll see to it he's been licked into shape before I get notice to quit!"

Vincent was the first of Matthew's two sons to reach Darracott Place, driving himself in a curricle to which were
harnessed three magnificent black geldings, random-tan-
dem; and by the time that Richmond, who had been on
the watch for him, let out a halloo, and exclaimed: "Here's
my cousin at last! Oh, he's driving unicorn! He's the most
complete hand!" even Mrs. Darracott, with whom Vincent
was no favourite, felt a certain measure of relief. In her
view, Vincent was a dangerous blade, with a viperous
tongue, and a deplorable influence over her impressionable young son; but after spending three hours in an at-
mosphere of deepening gloom, she would have been
much inclined to have welcomed the arrival of Beelzebub
himself. My lord having shut himself up in the library, it
had fallen to her lot to entertain his guests: an exercise
which consisted of lending a sympathetic ear to Matthew's
complaints, rhetorical questions, and dire forebodings.
Not a very arduous task, it might have been thought; but
Mrs. Darracott (like her son) was impressionable, and long
before Matthew had talked himself into a more cheerful
frame of mind the depression which hung over him had
communicated itself to her, quite sinking her spirits, and
exhausting her vitality. Every effort to introduce another
topic of conversation than the blighting of Matthew's pros-
pects failed: he returned mechanical answers only, and
at the first opportunity returned to the grievance that possessed his mind.

Anthea too was glad to know that Vincent had arrived.
She had not been subjected to so severe a strain as her
mother, but she had been obliged, after Lady Aurelia had

rested for an hour on her bed to recover from the rigours of her journey, to escort that rather formidable lady on a stately and prolonged tour of the gardens. In her youth, Lady Aurelia had been an enthusiastic gardener; since her marriage she had had no other home than a tall, narrow house in Mayfair, but she had forgotten none of the botanical lore so zealously acquired, and was perfectly ready to place it at the disposal of the various friends and relations whom it was her custom to visit (often for weeks at a time) during the summer months. She never uttered an adverse criticism, but her hostesses had been known to uproot whole borders only because she had said, with flat civility, "Very pretty;" and her way of ignoring the presence of a weed could cover the hardiest with shame. Anthea, no horticulturist, had much to endure, but she was spared the trials her mother was forced to undergo. Beyond stating, in a voice totally devoid either of sympathy or interest, that her husband was sadly put out by the appearance on the scene of the rightful heir, Lady Aurelia made no reference whatsoever to the event which filled the minds of the Darracotts. She did not say it, but no one blessed with a modicum of intelligence could have doubted that to an Earl's daughter the succession to a mere barony was a matter of indifference.

Her peregrinations had brought her within sight of the avenue which led from the crumbling stone entrance-gates to the north front of the house, when Vincent's natty curricle swept into view. The arrival of her eldest-born seemed to be a matter of equal indifference to her, but she raised no objection to Anthea's suggestion that they should go to meet him.

Before they had reached the avenue, Richmond had bounded out of the house, and was standing beside the curricle, smiling a little shyly up at his magnificent cousin. "What a hand you are! I have been watching for you this hour and more!"

The Corinthian in the curricle looked down at him, his brows lifting in exaggerated surprise. "But, my dear boy, you surely cannot have supposed that even *I* could accomplish more than sixty-two miles in less than five hours? Our beloved Regent, I would remind you, took four-and-a-half hours on his memorable dash to Brighton, and *that* road, you know, was vastly superior to this, even in those archaic times. Or did you think that my eagerness to reach the home of my ancestors—*not*, I apprehend, to be one day my own—would set me on the road before I had swallowed my breakfast?"

Richmond laughed. "No! Oh, lord, what a curst thing it is!—*you* to be cut out by this miserable fellow from Yorkshire! But what's this new quirk, Vincent? You were always used to drive that bang-up team of grays in your curricle! Is it now the high kick of fashion to drive—unicorn, do you call it?"

"Yes,—or Sudden Death," replied Vincent, transferring the reins into the hands of his groom. "And *no*, little cousin, you may *not* drive them. We have had enough sudden deaths in the family."

From no one but Vincent would Richmond have tolerated such a form of address, but a cousin, nearly ten years his senior, who, in addition to being carelessly kind to him, was a buck of the first cut, might bestow whatever opprobrious epithet upon him which happened to occur to him. He protested, but with a grin; and before Vincent could roast him into defending hotly his ability to drive any number of horses, Lady Aurelia and Anthea had come up to the group.

"Well, Vincent!" said Lady Aurelia.

He had climbed down from the curricle, and he now swept off his beaver, bowed, and with incomparable grace kissed first her hand, and then her cheek. "My dear Mama! Ah, and my dear cousin Anthea as well! A double pleasure!"

"And so unexpected!" she retorted, shaking hands with him.

His eyes glinted at her. "I never expect to find each time I come here that you are in greater beauty than the last time I saw you. It is really quite remarkable."

She was not in the least disconcerted by this, but only laughed, and said: "Yes, and I so stricken in years! Remarkable indeed! Where is your brother? Did you chance to see him on the road?"

"Now, that puts me in mind of something that causes me to feel the gravest concern!" he exclaimed. "I *did* see him—in fact, I passed him, driving, as I can't conceive, unless it might be that at the fatal moment my attention was diverted by the new lining he has had made for his chaise (maiden's blush I believe that particular shade of pink is called), but I very much fear that I may have ditched him."

Richmond burst into a crow of joy. "Lord, what a famous lark! I wish I might have seen it! Hunting the squirrel!"

"No, no, how can you say such a thing?" protested Vincent, in a pained voice. "How often have I told you that such tricks as that are not at all the thing? I wonder if I can be losing my precision of eye?"

"A stupid and ill-natured prank," pronounced Lady Aurelia, with measured severity. "If I find that Claud has sustained any injury I shall be excessively displeased."

"Then I do most sincerely trust he has escaped injury, Mama. Unfortunately, a sharp bend in the road almost immediately hid the scene from my view, so I can give you no very certain information on that head. But never mind! Crimplesham is following me, with my luggage, you know, and I am sure we may depend upon him to render my brother all the assistance in his power. What is the time? Should I, do you think, present myself to my grandfather at once, or——No, I perceive that it lacks only ten minutes to five. I have brought my evening-dress with me, but it will take me quite an hour to dress without Crimplesham's aid. You *do* still dine at six, I daresay? Such a depressing habit I find it! And my anxiety about Claud to make it worse! Poor fellow! But he shouldn't have urged his postboys to hold the road when I wished to give him the go-by: really, I think he almost deserves to sustain some injury for being so foolish!"

When Mrs. Darracott learned of this episode, which she very soon did, from Richmond, who could not keep such a good story to himself, she was much shocked. It all went to show, she told Anthea, that everything she had ever felt about Vincent had been correct: he showed an unsteadiness of character which she would be very sorry to see in any son of hers; his temper was jealous; he was idle and expensive; and, unless she much mistook the matter (which was not at all likely), he had such libertine propensities as must cause his poor father to suffer the gravest anxiety. Or, she amended, the penance she had undergone that afternoon still fresh in her memory, they would have done so if Matthew had the smallest regard

35

for anything but his own troubles. As for the stoic calm with which Lady Aurelia had received the news of what might well prove to have been a serious accident, *that*, said Mrs. Darracott, was something that quite passed her understanding. Had any son of *hers* been overturned into a ditch she would have had the horses put-to immediately, and dashed to his rescue. She was extremely attached to Lady Aurelia, but it was impossible to forebear the thought that if Claud were to be presently borne into the house with his neck broken it would be a judgment on her.

But no judgment fell on Lady Aurelia. Claud, arriving at Darracott Place half-an-hour later, had sustained no injury, except to his temper. This, however, had been seriously impaired, and he complained so bitterly and at such length of the usage to which he had been subjected that his father lost patience, and said testily: "Oh, that's enough, that's enough! Vincent forced your near wheels into the ditch, and it cost you twenty minutes to haul the chaise back on to the road! Very vexing, but no harm done! If you're at outs with Vincent, go and plant him a facer! Don't come whining to me, like a sickly girl!"

Even Richmond, who wholeheartedly despised Claud, felt that this advice was unkind. His dislike of all forms of violence apart, Claud was both slighter and shorter than his brother: no match for him under any circumstances. He said, with pardonable indignation: "Dash it, he'd throw me out of the window!"

"Well, go away and change your dress!" said Matthew. "It won't be Vincent, but your grandfather, who will throw you out of the window if you keep him waiting for his dinner!"

This dreadful warning had the effect of sending Claud out of the room with much the mien and speed of a coursing hare. His father and Richmond both laughed, but Mrs. Darracott was moved to say that she thought the boy had been very unkindly treated.

"Oh, pooh!" replied Matthew impatiently. "If he had ever had one half the tricks played on him which *I* had to endure when I was a lad it would have been the better for him! Besides, it's his own fault, with his silly daintification, and his finicking ways. *I* don't blame Vincent for making game of him!"

It was on the tip of her tongue to say that making rough game of a younger brother was conduct quite unbecoming in a man of eight-and-twenty, but Matthew had begun to pout, and so she refrained, knowing as well as everyone else that the ill-will Vincent bore Claud was to some extent shared by him, and did not spring in either of them from any particular dislike of Claud's dandyism.

Five years separated the brothers. In appearance they were not unalike, each having the aquiline nose and rather sunken eye which made them unmistakeable Darracotts; but Claud was by far the better-looking, his features being more delicate, his complexion less swarthy, and his countenance unmarred by the deep, almost sneering lines that characterized both Vincent and Lord Darracott. In general, Claud's expression was one of slightly vacuous amiability; Vincent's was sardonic, and frequently unpleasant.

In all but their features they were dissimilar. Vincent had a reckless intrepidity which drove him into all manner of dangerous exploits; Claud, though not (he hoped) henhearted, felt not the smallest impulse to ride straight at the worse oxer in the county, or to take the shine (at the risk of his neck) out of every other top-sawyer on the road; while as for putting on the gloves with Gentleman Jackson, there was almost nothing he less wished to do. But he was not without ambition. It was his ardent desire to become just such a leader of Fashion, such an arbiter of Taste, as Mr. Brummell had been, until so short a time ago. He grudged Vincent none of his fame as a member of the Corinthian set; it would not have gratified him in the least to be hailed as an out-and-outer, a regular dash, or a right cool fish: his heart was set on becoming the chief Pink of the Ton.

This ambition found no favour at all in the eyes of his parents, and would, indeed, have been impossible to realize had not a stroke of amazing good fortune befallen Claud. Hardly had he reached his majority when the maternal uncle after whom he had been named died, and left him the heir to a comfortable independence. Nothing then stood between him and the achievement of his goal but a want of genius. Try as he would he could neither create a new quirk of fashion, nor hit upon some original eccentricity which would make him instantly famous. He was obliged to exaggerate the prevailing mode, and to adopt as his own the tricks and mannerisms of other and more ingenious dandies, and somehow these expedients did not quite answer the purpose.

Vincent, of course, recognized every one of these plagiarisms, but what would have amused him in a young brother no plumper in the pocket than he was himself became a matter for bitter contempt when Claud inherited an easy competence. Vincent, with nothing but his allowance and the erratic generosity of his grandfather to depend on, lived precariously on the edge of Dun Territory. He was a gamester, and his luck had more than once saved him from being run quite off his legs; but he had several times been out-of-town, as the saying was; and he was no stranger to an obliging individual known to every gentleman seeking to raise the wind as Old Tens-in-the-Hundred. Envy and resentment changed his indifference to Claud into rancorous dislike. He was irritated by everything Claud did, whether it was wasting his blunt on the relining of his private chaise, or being such a muckworm as to travel behind job-horses. Nothing short of seeing Claud rolled-up would soften his dislike, and of that there was small likelihood: Claud's fortune was genteel rather than handsome, but he had no taste for gaming or racing, and, like his mother, he knew how to hold household.

It was an added source of exasperation in Vincent to know that his tongue had no power to wound Claud. Nothing short of being tipped into a ditch stirred Claud to resentment; and if he thought about Vincent at all it was with no other emotion than a sort of mild surprise. None of his brother's hazardous exploits awoke in his breast a spark of envy or of emulation: he envied Vincent only his splendid shoulders, and the incomparable blacking which made his boots shine like mirrors. Unfortunately both these desirable possessions were beyond his reach. Nature had seen fit to add drooping shoulders to his willowy form; and the secret of the blacking was locked in Crimplesham's bosom. Buckram and wadding could supply what Nature had withheld, but neither guile nor bribery would ever win from Crimplesham the least clue to his secret.

If it cost Claud a pang to know that Vincent's Hessians outshone his own, this was nothing to the rage and the despair that filled his valet's soul. Nor was the hostility that flourished between the brothers comparable to the feelings of jealousy, hatred, and contempt which filled the hearts of their valets. If Crimplesham excelled in the arts of polishing boots, and keeping buckskins in perfect order, Polyphant's genius lay in his skill with an iron, and his flair for evolving new and intricate modes of tieing a neckcloth, or dashing styles for his master's curled and pomaded locks. He believed himself to be by far the more expert valet, and it galled him beyond endurance to know that, while Crimplesham's one excellence was apparent to all, his own talents must inevitably go to his master's credit. Few people would suspect any aspirant to high fashion of entrusting the arrangement of his hair, or of his neckcloth, to his valet; none would suppose that any gentleman would black his own boots.

By the time Claud hurried into his bedchamber, Polyphant had unpacked his portmanteaux, and had even found time to press the creases from a longtailed coat of superfine, and a pair of black satin knee-breeches. These Claud eyed with disfavour, uttering a protest: "No, I'll be damned if I'll wear that rig here! Dash it, it ain't the thing, Polyphant!"

"No, sir, and well do I know it!" agreed Polyphant, in a feeling voice. "The proper mode, of course, would be pantaloons, since it is hardly feasible to suppose you will be taking a look-in at Almack's." He ventured to point this pleasantry with a titter, but it did not answer; and upon Claud's demanding peevishly how the devil he could take a look-in at Almack's in September, and from Darracott Place, he at once banished the smile from his face, and said: "No, sir. Very true. But it *might* be wise to consider his lordship's prejudice. Not that I would presume to dictate. I *did* venture to enquire of his lordship's man if the custom of wearing knee-breeches every evening still obtains at Darracott Place. He assured me that it *does*, sir."

The sinister nature of this warning was not lost on Claud, and he said no more. It vexed him very much to be obliged to present himself to his family in a costume so out-dated as to amount to a sartorial solecism, but he had his reward in that he incurred no censure from his grandfather other than the comprehensive disapproval contained in that gentleman's greeting. "Twiddle-poop!"

39

said his lordship, as Claud minced up to him to make his bow, and thereafter paid no heed to him.

Dinner, in Mrs. Darracott's view (for her expectations had not been high), passed off very well. No lobsters had been obtainable, but Godney had procured some partridges, which, with some dried salmon, cleverly dressed in a case, quite made up this deficiency, and drew praise from Matthew, who was known to be a *gourmet;* and although the family reunion could hardly have been described as convivial it was not rendered hideous by any explosion of wrath from Lord Darracott.

When the gentlemen rose from the table, my lord, recommending his son, and his younger grandsons, to join the ladies, bore Vincent off to the library, saying, as soon as they had reached this sanctuary: "Your father's as sick as a horse over this business."

"And who shall blame him?" returned Vincent. "I'm not chirping merry about it myself, you know, sir, and I should suppose that *you* are not thrown into transports precisely."

"No, by God!" His lordship poured brandy into two glasses, tossed off the contents of his own, and refilled it. "I did my best to keep the fellow out, but the trap's down. Got to lick him into shape."

"I feel sure you'll manage to do so, sir. How old is he?"

"Much your own age: seven-and-twenty."

"If he is as old as that, he's irreclaimable," said Vincent cynically.

"We'll see that!" snapped his lordship. After a moment he added grudgingly: "He won't eat with his knife, at all events. He's a military man: one of these new regiments, but still——!"

"A military man! Oh, I was expecting a yokel in homespuns! Er—commissioned, sir?"

"Major," replied Lord Darracott shortly.

Vincent's eyes opened wide at that. "The devil he is!" For a moment his expression was inscrutable; then he gave a short laugh, and said: "Well it's to be devoutly hoped that he's up to the rig, for you can scarcely send a Major back to school, sir!"

"Can't I?" said my lord, looking grimmer than ever. "This whipstraw is my grandson, I'll have you remember! He'll dance to my piping, or I'll send him packing!"

"Am I to understand, sir, that you have the intention of *keeping* him here?" demanded Vincent.

"Yes, if he behaves himself. I want him under my eye. The thing turns out not as badly as I feared, but there are plenty of rum 'uns with military titles these days, and this fellow was reared the Lord knows how—in a weaver's hovel, I daresay! If I'd known—if I'd ever dreamt——!" He broke off, his hands clenching and unclenching as they always did when his rage threatened to master him. He glanced under his craggy brows at Vincent. "Well! Between us we should be able to give him a new touch!"

"Between us?" repeated Vincent. "My dear sir, I would do much to oblige you, but bear-leading a cousin I heartily wish at the devil is a feat quite beyond me."

"I didn't say you were to bear-lead him. You're an idle, extravagant dog, but your ton is good: you'll serve as a model for him to copy!"

"If I had had the remotest guess that that was why I was invited I shouldn't have come!" said Vincent.

"Oh, yes, you would!" retorted his lordship. "And, what's more, jackanapes, you'll stay for precisely as long as I choose, unless you have a fancy for paying your own debts in future!" He observed, with satisfaction, that he had at once infuriated and silenced his grandson, and smiled derisively. "Ay, that's where the shoe pinches, isn't it? Scorched again?"

Regaining command over his temper, Vincent replied coolly: "Oh, no! Just a trifle cucumberish! I own it will suit me pretty well to remain here for the next few weeks—until the quarter, you know!"

"The allowance your father gives you won't bring *you* round," remarked his lordship.

"No, sir, but the first October meeting may!" countered Vincent.

"I wish I may see it! Well, I didn't send for you only for that. Since I can't keep the fellow out of the family you'd best meet him at the outset, all of you!"

"*All* of us?" said Vincent. "Are we to have the rare felicity of seeing my aunts here, sir? Not to mention their numerous progeny, and——"

"Don't be impertinent, sir!" barked his lordship.

Vincent, who knew very well that he was perfectly indifferent to his three married daughters, and, indeed, to all his female descendants, bowed meekly. My lord glared at him for a moment, and then said: "I don't care how soon the rest of 'em take themselves off, but I want you here." He paused, frowning. "It's the boy!" he said abruptly. "I'm not going to have that fellow putting ideas into his head: I've had trouble enough over that silly business!"

Vincent raised his brows. "Richmond?"

"Ay, Richmond. It's gone off now, but he was devilish set on joining, six months ago. Fell into flat despair when I told him I wouldn't have it. Well, as I say, the notion seems to have gone off, and I don't want him to start moping and pining again. He's a good boy, but he's got an odd kick in his gallop, you know. For two pins he'd hang on this fellow's lips—make a hero of him, I daresay! Well, he won't do that while you're here."

"Won't he?" said Vincent. "Er—what do I do if I find him talking to our unwanted cousin? Take him by the ear, and haul him off?"

A sardonic smile curled his lordship's mouth. "You won't have to. Think I don't know what he makes of *you*? Whistle him to heel, and you'll have him following like a tantony-pig!"

The prospect of having an eager stripling following him like a tantony-pig was not one which Vincent could bring himself to contemplate with enthusiasm, but he said nothing, reflecting that it would probably be unnecessary to do more than keep Richmond in a string. There would be no difficulty about that, for it was true enough that the boy liked and admired him. He would almost certainly take his ton from his Corinthian cousin, for to win his approval, to emulate his sporting prowess, had always been the top of his desire.

As though he had read Vincent's mind, Darracott said: "He won't sit in your pocket. Won't tease you either. But while you're here, and he thinks there's a chance you may take him off to see a mill, or some cocking, or teach him how to handle the reins in form, he'll pay precious little heed to anyone else."

Vincent nodded. "Very well, sir: I'll engage to charm him away from this——What *is* the fellow's name?"

Darracott's face twitched; he replied shortly: "Same as

his father's. Signs himself Hugo. Don't know why, and don't like it."

"Oh, you've had letters from him, have you, sir?"

"I haven't. He wrote to Lissett—a damnable scrawl!"

A smile flickered in Vincent's eyes for an instant, but he swiftly lowered his lids. My lord's own handwriting would have led no one to suppose that he was a man of birth, far less of education; but it would plainly be unwise even to hint as much. Instead, Vincent asked: "Did he— er—put forward his claims, as my father appears to believe?"

"No, I'll grant him that: he didn't. Never gave a sign of life till I told Lissett to write to him. Seems not to have known he was the heir, unless he was shamming it. Very likely! He wrote that he was sorry to hear of Granville's death. Gammon!"

"Oh, mere civility!"

"Ay! So I might have thought if he hadn't added that he didn't see what was to be done about the business, but would as lief not step into his uncle's shoes! Dry-boots!"

"Oh, that is pitching it very much too rum!" agreed Vincent. "Demonstrably an underbred person: we can do nothing for him!"

"*You* may not; *I* shall! I don't deny I thought myself done-up at the start, but I've never been outjockeyed yet, and I fancy I've hit on a way to button it up tolerably well. The fellow shall marry Anthea."

Vincent had been idly twirling his quizzing-glass on the end of its riband, but he was so much startled by this announcement that he let it drop, and gave an audible gasp. "Marry *Anthea?*"

"Yes, lobcock!" said his lordship testily. "Why not?"

Vincent drew a breath. "I can think of a score of reasons why *not*, but it seems that I must indeed be a lobcock, since I can't think of one why he *should!* How very humiliating! I've always believed myself to be a man of reasonable intelligence."

"You're as muttonheaded as the rest of 'em! It's the best way out of a curst hobble. He ain't likely to form a more eligible connection——"

Up went Vincent's brows again. "A Darracott of Darracott?" he said.

"A half-bred Darracott!" my lord said savagely. "Ten to one he'd choose a commoner like himself, if I gave him his head! Well, I won't do it! No, and I won't have him making a figure of himself in what passes in these days for the ton! I'll have him legshackled as soon as I can, and depend on Anthea for the rest! She'll do the trick: she doesn't want for sense, and she doesn't want for spirit either. She's a girl of rank and character, and he may think himself lucky if she takes him."

"Certainly he may! And what may *she* think *her*self, sir?"

"She may think the same. She's not a pea-goose, like her mother! She had her chance, and a pretty penny that cost me! Either she frittered it away, or she didn't take: *I* don't know. I do know that Oversley offered for her, and she wouldn't have him. If she don't want to end up an ape-leader she'll take her cousin, and make the best of him."

"Which," Vincent told Anthea on the following day, "leads me to hope, for your sake, my poor girl, that this intrusive relation of ours is married already."

"Yes, but what an uproar there would be! Has Grandpapa informed everyone of this splendid match he has made for me? It is too abominable! However, I imagine you can none of you suppose me to be so meek and dutiful as to acquiesce in such a scheme!"

"If *I* thought that, my love, I should feel constrained to marry you myself."

"Is that a declaration?" she demanded.

"Certainly not! I *don't* think it."

"I wish it had been!" she said longingly. "How unhandsome of you! When you know how few pleasures come in my way, you might have granted me the indulgence of refusing you!"

He laughed, but said, a certain gleam in his eyes: "I wonder if you would?"

She met his look without a trace of embarrassment, a good deal of amusement in her face. "Dear Vincent, with enthusiasm! You must never marry. Don't, I do earnestly beg of you, allow yourself to be taken in by any lure thrown out to you! You cannot hope to find a lady who will like you better than you like yourself."

He was nettled, but made a quick recover. "Not *like*, sweetest cousin: *appreciate!*"

She only smiled; and, as a few drops of rain had begun to fall, turned towards the house. As they entered it, they were met by Matthew, who was looking peevish. He exclaimed: "It's to be hoped this fellow don't dawdle on the road! Your grandfather may say he doesn't want to clap eyes on him, but here he is, fretting and fuming already! and it's barely past noon! *I* don't expect him to show a minute before three o'clock!"

By three o'clock, however, there was still no sign of Major Darracott, and my lord was fast working himself into a passion. He strode into one of the saloons, with his watch in his hand, and demanded explosively what the devil could be keeping the fellow. Since no one knew, no one answered, whereupon he asked if they were a set of dumb mutes.

"Mute, but not of malice," murmured Vincent. "Claud, where is your cousin?"

"Which cousin?" enquired Claud.

This instantly brought him under fire. He was apostrophized as an impudent young idiot, and warned not to try his grandfather's patience too far. He looked very much startled, and protested earnestly that nothing was more remote from his intention. "Not such an idiot as that, sir!" he said, with a placating but nervous smile.

My lord, regarding him with loathing, said awfully: "It's my belief you're queer in your attic!" His gaze swept to Lady Aurelia, tatting, by the window, and he added with relish; "He must take after your family, my dear. We Darracotts never bred a mooncalf yet!"

"Very likely," responded Lady Aurelia.

My lord, balked, stood fulminating, and Claud, who had been turning the question put to him over in his mind, suddenly said: "Oh, *that* cousin! Well, I'll tell you!" He discovered that everyone but his mother was staring at him in surprise, and blushed, saying modestly: "I may not be a clever cove, but I can answer *that*. Well, what I mean is, nothing has happened to him. I don't precisely know where he is, mind, though I've a notion about that, too." He looked round the circle with mild pride, and enunciated triumphantly: "Tonbridge! Won't be here for an-

45

other three hours. More, if the postboys lose the way, which I daresay they will. Dashed difficult place to find, this. Lost the way myself once."

After this burst of loquacity he subsided. His grandfather, a most alarming expression on his face, was still struggling for words with which to annihilate him when Lady Aurelia intervened, saying calmly: "No doubt you are right. Indeed, I see no reason to expect the young man before dinnertime."

"Oh, you don't, ma'am?" said his lordship, abandoning Claud for a worthier prey. "Then let me tell you that my orders to Lissett were that the fellow should be sent off post not an instant later than eight o'clock! He will have to learn that when I give an order I expect it to be obeyed to the letter!"

"It seems reasonable to prophesy that he will," remarked Vincent, as the door shut with a decided slam behind his lordship.

"Oh, dear!" sighed Mrs. Darracott. "Since your grandfather seems to *want* him, I do wish he hadn't chosen to be late! I can't help feeling that we shall have a very uncomfortable evening."

By twenty minutes to six, the Major still not having arrived, my lord was in a mood of cold rage, as surly (as Claud confided to Richmond) as a butcher's dog. The ladies of the party had not yet come down from their respective bedchambers, but the gentlemen had prudently changed their dress in good time, and dutifully assembled in the Green Saloon. My lord tugged the bell-rope, his brow black, and upon the butler's coming into the room, told him that dinner was to be served punctually at six o'clock.

"Very good, my lord," Chollacombe said, "but——"

"You heard me!"

It was apparent from Chollacombe's raised head, and straining expression, that he had also heard something else. He said: "Yes, my lord. But I fancy that the Major has arrived."

"Bring him in here immediately!" commanded his lordship.

Chollacombe bowed, and left the room, carefully shutting the door. An indistinguishable murmur of voices pen-

46

etrated to the saloon, as though an argument had sprang up.

"Wants to change his dress first," said Claud, explaining the pause, and nodding wisely. "Very understandable. I would myself."

"Whipper-snapper!" said my lord.

The door was opened again. "Major Darracott!" announced Chollacombe.

4

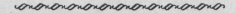

The Major trod resolutely over the threshold, and there stopped, pulled up short by the battery that confronted him. Five pairs of eyes scanned him with varying degrees of astonishment, hostility, and criticism. He looked round, his own, very blue orbs holding a comical expression of dismay, and a deep flush creeping up under his tan. Three of the gentlemen had levelled their quizzing-glasses at him; and one, whom he judged to be his grandfather, was scowling at him from under a beetling brow.

For a nerve-racking minute no one spoke, or moved. Surprise was, in fact, responsible for this frozen immobility, but only Richmond's widening gaze and Claud's dropped jaw betrayed this.

The Darracotts were a tall race, but the man who stood on the threshold dwarfed them all. He stood six foot four in his stockinged feet, and he was built on noble lines, with great shoulders, a deep barrel of a chest, and powerful thighs. He was much fairer than his cousins, with tightly curling brown hair, cut rather shorter than was fashionable, and a ruddy complexion. His nose had no aquiline trend: it was rather indeterminate; and this, with his curly locks and his well-opened and childishly blue eyes, gave him an air of innocence at variance with his firm-lipped mouth and decided chin. He looked to be amiable; he was certainly bashful, but for this there was every excuse. He had been ushered into a room occupied by five gentlemen attired in raiment commonly worn only at Court, or at Almack's Assembly Rooms, and he was himself wearing leathers and top-boots, and a serviceable riding-coat, all of which were splashed with mud.

"Good God!" muttered Matthew, breaking the silence.

"So you've shown at last, have you?" said Lord Darracott. "You're devilish late, sir!"

"I am a trifle late," acknowledged the culprit. "I'm sorry for it, but I missed the way, and that delayed me."

"Thought as much!" said Claud.

"Well, don't stand there like a stock!" said Darracott. "This is your uncle Matthew, and the others are your cousins: Vincent—Claud—Richmond!"

Considerably unnerved by his reception, the Major took an unwary step forward, and very nearly fell over an unnoticed stool in his path. Vincent said, in Richmond's ear, not quite under his breath: *"The lubber Ajax!"*

If the Major heard him, he gave no sign of having done so. Matthew caught the words, and uttered a short laugh, which he changed, not very convincingly, into a cough. The Major, recovering his balance, advanced towards Lord Darracott, who waved him, slightly impatiently, to his uncle. He turned, half putting out his hand, but Matthew, not moving from his stand before the empty fireplace, only nodded to him, and said: "How do you do?"

The Major made no attempt to shake hands with the rest of the company, but when he had exchanged formal bows with Vincent and Claud, Richmond, whose colour was also considerably heightened, stepped forward, with his hand held out, saying with a little stammer: "How—how do you do, Cousin Hugh?"

His hand was lost in the Major's large clasp. "Now, which of my cousins are you?" asked the Major, smiling kindly down at him.

"I'm Richmond, sir."

"Nay!" protested the Major. "Don't call me sir! I'd as lief you didn't call me Cousin Hugh either. I was christened Hugh, but I've never answered to anything but Hugo all my life."

Lord Darracott broke in on this. Having by this time had time to assimilate the fact that Hugo's clothes were freely bespattered with mud, he demanded to know the reason. Hugo released Richmond's hand, and turned his head towards his grandfather. "Well, you've had some rain down here, sir. I should not have come in till I'd got rid of my dirt, but I wasn't given any choice in the matter," he explained.

"Chaise overturn?" exquired Claud, not without sympathy.

Hugo laughed. "No, it wasn't as bad as that. I didn't come by chaise."

"Then how did you come?" asked Matthew. "From the look of you one would say that you had ridden from town!"

"Ay, so I did," nodded Hugo.

"Ridden?" gasped Claud. "Ridden all the way from London?"

"Why not?" said Hugo.

"But——Dash it, you can't do things like that!" Claud said, in a shocked tone. "I mean to say—no, really, coz! Your luggage!"

"Oh, that!" replied Hugo. "John Joseph had all I need, loaded on my spare horse—my groom, I mean—my private groom!"

"How very original!" drawled Vincent. "I rarely travel by chaise myself, but I confess it had never before occurred to me to turn any of my cattle into pack-horses."

"Nay, why should it?" returned the Major good-humouredly. "Maybe you've never been obliged to travel rough. I don't think I've gone in a chaise above two or three times in my life."

Lord Darracott stirred restlessly in his chair, gripping its arms momentarily. "No doubt! You are not obliged to travel rough, as you term it, now! My orders were that a chaise was to be hired for you, and I expect my orders to be obeyed!"

"Ay, I'm that road myself," agreed Hugo cheerfully. "Your man of business was mighty set on arranging the journey for me. He said it was what you'd told him to do, so there's no sense in blaming him. And not much sense in blaming me either," he added, on a reflective note. He smiled down at his seething progenitor. "I'm much obliged to you, sir, but there's no need for you to worry your head over me: I've looked after myself for a good few years now."

"Worry my head——? Richmond! Ring the bell! You, sir! Did you bring your valet, or haven't you one?"

"Well, no," confessed the Major apologetically. "I used to have a bâtman, of course, but, what with one thing and another, I haven't had time to think about hiring a personal servant since I came home."

"No valet?" repeated Claud, gazing at him incredulously. "But how do you manage? I mean to say, packing—
your boots—your neckcloths——!"

"Hold your tongue!" said his father, in an undervoice.

"If you had been listening," interpolated Vincent severely, "you would have heard our cousin say that he has
been in the habit of looking after himself. Except when
he had a bâtman, that is."

"Ay, but I'm a poor hand at packing," said Hugo, shaking his head over this shortcoming.

"How much longer is dinner to be kept waiting?" demanded Lord Darracott. "Ring that damned bell again,
Richmond! What the devil does Chollacombe mean
by——Oh, you're there, are you? Have Major Darracott
taken up to his room, and tell someone to wait on him!
We shall dine in twenty minutes from now!"

Claud was moved to protest, his sympathy roused by
the plight of anyone who was expected to dress for dinner
in twenty minutes. "Make it an hour, sir! Well, *half* an
hour, though I must say it's coming it a bit strong to ask
the poor fellow to scramble into his clothes in that short
time!"

"No, no, twenty minutes will be long enough for me!"
said Hugo hastily, a wary eye on his lordship. "If I'm not
down then, don't wait for me!"

Chollacombe, ushering him out of the saloon, and
softly closing the door behind him, said: "I will take you
up myself, sir. I understand you haven't brought your
valet with you, so his lordship's man has unpacked your
valise!"

"Much obliged to him!" said Hugo, following him to
the broad, uncarpeted oak staircase. "It seems as if Mr.
Lissett ought to have warned me not to show my front
here without a jack-a-dandy London valet at my heels."

"Yes, sir. Being as his lordship is, as they say, rather
a high stickler. Not but what Grooby—that's his lordship's
man, sir—will be very happy to wait on you. We were
very much attached to the Captain, if I may venture to say
so."

"My father? I never knew him: he was killed when I
was just three years old. I'm afraid I don't favour him
much."

"No, sir. Though you do remind me a little of him."

51

The butler paused, and then said with great delicacy, as they reached the upper hall: "I hope you won't think it a liberty, sir, but if there *should* be anything you might wish to know—his lordship being a trifle twitty at times, and not one to make allowances—I beg you won't hesitate to ask me! Quite between ourselves, sir, of course."

"I won't," promised Hugo, a twinkle in his eye.

"It is sometimes hard to know the ways of a house when one is strange to it," said Chollacombe. "*Anybody* might make a mistake! Indeed, I well remember that I was obliged to give my Lord Taplow a hint, when he stayed here on one occasion. He was a friend of Mr. Granville's: quite in the first style of elegance, but he had a habit of unpunctuality which would have put his lordship out sadly. This way, if you please, sir. We have put you in the West Wing."

"It's to be hoped I don't lose myself," remarked Hugo, following him through an archway into a long gallery. "If ever I saw such a place!"

"It *is* rather large, sir, but I assure you there are many that are far larger."

"Nay!" said Hugo astonished.

"Oh, yes, indeed, sir! This is your bedchamber. I should perhaps tell you that Mr. Richmond sleeps at the end of the gallery, and must not on any account be disturbed."

"Why not?" enquired Hugo.

"Mr. Richmond suffers from insomnia, sir. The least sound brings him broad awake."

"What, a lad of his age?" exclaimed Hugo.

"Mr. Richmond's constitution is not strong," explained Chollacombe, opening the door into a large, wainscoted room, hung with faded blue damask, and commanding a distant view of the sea beyond the Marsh. "This is Grooby, sir. His lordship dines in fifteen minutes, Grooby."

The valet, an elderly man of somewhat lugubrious mien, bowed to the Major, and said in a voice of settled gloom: "I have everything ready for you, sir. Allow me to assist you to take off your coat!"

"If you want to assist me, pull off my boots!" said Hugo. "And never mind handling them with gloves! If I'm to be ready in fifteen minutes, I shall have to be pretty wick, as we say in Yorkshire."

Grooby, kneeling before him, as he sat with his legs

stretched out, had already drawn one muddied boot half off, but he paused, and looked up, saying earnestly: "*Don't*, Master Hugh!"

"Don't what?" asked Hugo, ripping off his neckcloth, and tossing it aside.

"Say what they do in Yorkshire, sir. Not if you can avoid it! I'm sure I ask your pardon, but you don't know his lordship like I do, and you want to be careful, sir—*very* careful!"

The blue eyes looked down at him for an inscrutable moment. "Ay," Hugo drawled. "Happen you're reet!"

The valet heaved a despairing sigh, and returned to his task. The boots off, he would have helped Hugo to remove his coat, but Hugo kindly but firmly put him out of the room, saying that he could dress himself more speedily if left alone. He shut the door on Grooby's protest, let his breath go in a long *Phew!* and began, very speedily indeed, to strip off his coat and breeches.

When he presently emerged from his room, he found Grooby hovering in the gallery. Grooby said that he had waited to escort him back to the saloon, in case he should have forgotten his way; but it was evident, from the expert eye he ran over his protégé's attire, that his real purpose was to assure himself that no sartorial solecism had been committed. It was a pity, but not a solecism, that the Major had not provided himself with knee-smalls, but his long-tailed coat was by Scott, and well-enough; his linen was decently starched; and his shoe-strings ironed. He favoured a more modest style than was fashionable, wearing no jewelry, sporting no inordinately high collar, and arranging his neckcloth neatly, but with none of the exquisite folds that distinguished the tie of a dandy or a Corinthian. Grooby regretted the absence of a quizzing-glass and a fob, but on the whole he was inclined to think that so large a man was right to adopt a plain mode.

The Major entered the saloon one minute before the stipulated time, thereby winning a measure of approval from his grandfather. Lord Darracott's brows shot up; he said: "Well, at all events you're not a dawdler! I'll say that for you. Make your bow to your aunts, and your cousin! Lady Aurelia, Mrs. Darracott, you'll allow me to present Hugh to you; Anthea, you'll look after your cousin: show him the way about!"

The Major, receiving a formal bow from a Roman-nosed

matron in a turban, and the smallest of stiff curtsies from a tall girl who looked at him with quelling indifference, turned his eyes apprehensively towards the third lady. Mrs. Darracott, her heart wrung (as she afterwards explained to her daughter), smiled at him, and gave him her hand. "How do you do?" she said. "I am so happy to meet you! So vexed, too, that I wasn't dressed quite in time to welcome you when you arrived. Not but what that might have made it worse for you—I mean, so many strange new relations! I daresay you must be perfectly bewildered."

He did not kiss her hand, but he shook it warmly, and thanked her, smiling down at her so gratefully that she almost wished she had braved my lord's displeasure, and placed Hugo instead of Matthew beside her at the dinner-table.

She and Chollacombe had arranged the table, and an arduous labour it had been, necessitating the use of a slate and much chalk. The result was not ideal, but, as Chollacombe very sensibly pointed out, the ideal was not to be achieved with a party of nine persons, all of them related, and too many of them brothers. In this unexceptionable way Chollacombe was able to convey to Mrs. Darracott the unwisdom of placing Claud within Vincent's orbit. She perfectly understood him; and he perfectly understood that when she said that his lordship would certainly wish to have Vincent on his left hand she meant that she was not going to expose the hapless newcomer to the full force of his lordship's trenchant conversation. In the end, though the table was necessarily uneven, with Lady Aurelia, Richmond, and Claud on one side, and Vincent, Anthea, Hugo, and Matthew on the other, Claud was as far removed as was possible from Vincent, Hugo from Lord Darracott, and Anthea had been placed between Hugo and Vincent, in which position she must willy-nilly shield Hugo from Vincent's tongue.

The arrangement was not entirely happy, however, as Mrs. Darracott soon perceived; for although Vincent was keeping his grandfather amused, and Richmond was nobly trying to entertain his aunt, Matthew divided his attention equally between herself and his plate; and Anthea, determined to cold-shoulder her intended-suitor at the outset, replied to his tentative attempts to engage her interest with icy civility, and in a manner that did not encourage him to persevere. Mrs. Darracott, scandalized by such a display of gaucherie, tried several times to catch her daughter's eye, but never once succeeded.

Hugo, with a hostile uncle on his left and a frozen damsel on his right, meekly ate his dinner, and took stock of as many of his relations as came within view. Of these the most attractive were Mrs. Darracott, and Richmond, who was not quite obscured from Hugo's sight by the epergne in the centre of the table. Hugo thought he seemed a friendly boy: a trifle resty, perhaps; light at hand, like so many high-spirited but spoilt youngsters. He was talking to his aunt: a most alarming female, Hugo thought, eyeing her in awe, and admiring Richmond's address. Then Richmond chanced to turn his head away from Lady Aurelia, and, seeing that his cousin was looking at him, he smiled shyly. Yes, a nice lad: worth a dozen of the Tulip beside him! Not that Hugo had the least objection to the fops of Society. Being blessed with a vast tolerance he was able to regard Claud with amusement, enjoying the extravagances and the affectations which exasperated Lord Darracott and Matthew. Claud was wearing a coat which represented the highest kick of fashion, and had come (he said) straight from the hands of Nugee. His father told him that it made him look ridiculous, which of course it did, with its wasp-waist, and its shoulders built up into absurd peaks, but there was no need to comb the lad's hair in public; and certainly no need for that brother of his to have said that he couldn't help but look ridiculous.

Hugo ventured to steal a glance at the unyielding profile on his right. Not a beauty, his cousin Anthea, but she was pretty enough, and not just in the common style. Her figure was tall and graceful, and she had remarkably fine eyes, with long, curling lashes; but she looked to be a disagreeable girl, every bit as contemptuous as the appalling old windsucker at the head of the table.

He was debating within himself how soon he would be able to escape from the home of his ancestors when he found that he was being addressed by his uncle, who told him, rather sharply, that Mrs. Darracott was speaking to him.

She had, in fact, seized the excuse afforded by Lord Darracott's asking Richmond some question, across Lady

Aurelia, to try to draw into conversation the poor young man who was being, she felt, shamefully neglected. She wanted to know if he had found all he needed in his bedchamber, and to tell him, with a motherly smile, that he had only to ask her, or the housekeeper, if there was anything he wished for. He thanked her, but assured her that there was nothing: he would be very comfortable.

Claud, satisfied that his grandfather's attention was being engaged by Vincent, shook his head. "You won't," he said. "Couldn't be. I don't know where they've put you, but it don't signify: there ain't a comfortable room in the house."

"Nonsense!" said Matthew impatiently.

"Why, you said so yourself, sir!" exclaimed Claud. "What's more, you always say it. The last time you had to come down here you said——"

"Oh, be quiet!" interrupted his father. "It is a very old house, and naturally——"

"Yes, and falling to bits," corroborated Claud.

Matthew, eyeing him almost with dislike, said: "That remark, my good boy, is as false as it is foolish!"

"Well, if it ain't falling to bits you can't deny it's being eaten to bits," said Claud, quite unabashed. "The last time I had to come here, I was kept awake half the night by rats chewing the wainscoting."

"Oh, not *rats*, Claud!" protested Mrs. Darracott. "Only a mouse! Not but what it's perfectly true that the house does need repairing, while as for the linen, and some of the hangings, I declare I feel positively *ashamed!* Well, you know what it is, Matthew! Nothing I can say will induce your father——However, we won't talk of that now! Though I do sometimes feel that if I have to spend another winter here, which, of course, I shall, I shall be *crippled* with rheumatism! None of the windows fits as it should, and the draught *whistles* through the house!"

"More like a hurricane," said Claud. He nodded at Hugo. "*You'll* find it out, coz. Of course, it's summer now, so it ain't so bad, but you wait for the winter! Take my advice, and don't let 'em light a fire in your room: all the bedroom chimneys smoke, so you're worse off than before."

"Not *all* of them!" said Mrs. Darracott. "At least, not

very *much!* Only when the wind is in the wrong quarter. I do hope—for it has begun to get so chilly in the evening now that Mrs. Flitwick is having a fire kindled in *your* room, Hugh! Oh, dear, I wonder if the wind *is* in the wrong quarter?"

"Nay, don't fidget yourself on my account, ma'am!" Hugo said, laughing. "I'm not so nesh as my cousin! I've been used to sleep in a room that had a fire in the middle of the floor, and not so much as a vent to off the smoke, so it will need more than a puff or two blown down the chimney to make me uncomfortable."

His voice, which was a deep one, had a carrying quality. His words were heard by everyone in the room, and were productive of a sudden, shocked silence. He glanced innocently round the table, and added: "A mud floor, of course."

"How—how horrid for you!" said Mrs. Darracott faintly.

Chollacombe, with great presence of mind, refilled the Major's glass at this moment, contriving, as he did so, to give him a warning nudge. The Major, not susceptible to hints, said cheerfully: "Oh, it was noan so bad! I was glad to have a roof over my head in those days!"

Mrs. Darracott looked wildly round for help, and received it from an unexpected quarter.

"Don't look so dismayed, my dear aunt!" said Vincent. "The locality of this dismal dwelling-place was not, as I apprehend, Yorkshire, but Spain."

"Portugal," corrected Hugo, as impervious to insult as to hints.

"Most interesting!" pronounced Lady Aurelia majestically. "No doubt you have seen a great deal of the world during the course of your military service?"

"I have and-all!" agreed Hugo.

"The billeting arrangements in the Peninsula," stated her ladyship, "left much to be desired."

"Ay, sometimes they did, but at others, think on, they were better nor like," said Hugo reflectively. "After Toulouse I shared quarters with the Smiths in a château, and lived like a prince. That was in France, of course. A château," he explained, "is what the Frogs call a castle—though it wasn't a castle, not by any means. You might call it a palace."

"Our ignorance is now enlightened," murmured Vincent.

"We all know what a château is!" snapped Lord Darracott.

"Ay, you would, of course," said Hugo, on a note of apology. "Eh, but I thought myself in clover! I'd never been in such a place before—except when I was in prison, but you can't reetly count that."

James, the first footman, let a fork slide from the plate he had just removed from the table, but Charles, deftly nipping away the plate before Lady Aurelia, maintained his equilibrium. James was shocked, but Charles was storing up these revelations with glee. A rare tale to recount to his Dad, so niffy-naffy as he was about the Quality! Properly served out was old Stiff-Rump, with a jail-bird for his grandson!

"What?" thundered his lordship, glaring at his heir. "Do you tell me that you have been in *prison?"*

"Ay, but it wasn't for long, sir," replied Hugo. "Of course, I was nobbut a lad then, and it seemed a terrible thing to me. I had the fever, too, mortal bad!"

Claud, perceiving that the rest of the company was deprived of speech, made a gallant attempt to respond. "Nasty thing, jail-fever," he said chattily. "Not had it myself, but so they tell me! Very glad you recovered from it, coz!"

"It was being transported set me to reets," said Hugo. "A rare, tedious voyage we had of it, but——"

"Transported?" interjected his lordship, gripping the arms of his chair till his knuckles shone. "You were *transported*, sir?"

"We all were," said Hugo. "The most of us three parts dead with fever, and that ashamed——! Eh, it doesn't bear thinking on! Such a voyage as it was, too! Close on five months it was before we landed, for the transport I was on carried away its rudder in a gale, and we ran four hundred miles out of our course before the *Swallow* towed us into Falmouth, and then we had to sail on to the Downs before they'd let us ashore."

A delightful chuckle broke from Richmond. "I thought that was it! You are the most complete hand, Cousin Hugo!"

"I collect," said Matthew coldly, "that when you speak

58

of having been imprisoned, and—er—transported, you mean that you were a prisoner-of-war?"

"Why, what did you think I meant?" asked Hugo, much astonished.

"You must forgive us!" said Vincent, leaning forward to speak to him across Anthea. "The thought that you had been imprisoned for poaching, perhaps, did, I fancy, occur to some of us."

"Nay! I've always been respectable!" countered Hugo.

At this point, Anthea, who had been surprised into turning her head to stare at him, lowered her eyes rather swiftly to her plate again, and took her underlip between her teeth. Matthew, far more conscious than his parent of the presence of the servants, said, with a tolerable assumption of amusement: "You are, as Richmond says, a complete hand. From the length of time your voyage lasted I am led to suppose that you took part in our ill-fated expedition to South America?"

"That's reet," nodded Hugo. "I joined as soon as I left—as soon as I was seventeen. I was gazetted to the 1st Battalion just in time to set sail with Whitelock. A rare piece of good fortune I thought it, but all I got out of it was a fever that mighty near carried me off, and a horse. I paid three dollars for him, I remember. Eh, but I was a Johnny Raw! I could have had him for two."

"Did you take part in the assault on Buenos Ayres?" asked Richmond.

"I wouldn't, myself, call it an assault," replied Hugo.

"A disgracefully mismanaged affair!" said Matthew.

"Ay, we suffered a bad back-cast. Our people wrote up that General Whitelock was a coward, or a traitor, or maybe both, on all the street-corners in Montevideo, but, myself, I think he was no more than a sackless hodgobbin." He drank off his wine, and grinned. "The men used to drink success to grey-beards but bad luck to white locks," he disclosed.

"And then?" Richmond prompted.

Hugo smiled at him. "Oh, then I was packed off home, on sick furlough, for there was nothing of me left but skin and bone!"

"Poor boy!" said Mrs. Darracott, her motherly instincts stirred. "How shocked your mama must have been! But I am persuaded she soon nursed you back to health."

"Nay, my mother died a year before I joined," he answered.

"Oh, *poor* boy!" she exclaimed, braving her father-in-law's displeasure. "But perhaps you have other relatives?"

"I'd my grandfather," he said. "Mother was all the children he had. Happen it was Yorkshire air and good Yorkshire food that plucked me up."

"Were you at Corunna?" asked Richmond.

Hugo nodded; but before Richmond could beg for further information Lord Darracott intervened, saying harshly that he desired to hear no talk about the war at his dinner table. Hugo, accepting this snub with what appeared to be unshakeable placidity, then retired from the conversation, to discuss with an excellent appetite a large helping of apple pie.

The rest of the meal passed without incident. For perhaps the first time in all the years she had lived at Darracott Place it was with reluctance that Mrs. Darracott gave the signal for the departure of the ladies from the board. Her compassion had been roused, and it went to her heart to leave her enormous but hapless nephew to the mercy of his hostile male relations.

In the event, it was not Hugo but Claud who drew my lord's fire. When the cloth had been removed, it was the custom of the house that not only decanters of port and madeira should be set before his lordship, but that three jars of snuff should be placed on the table. My lord was a connoisseur; he mixed his own sort, but provided for his guests Old Bureau, King's Martinique, and Hardman's '37. He invited no one but Vincent to help himself from his gold box, and was amused rather than offended when that elegant young man, declining the honour, drew out a box of his own, and snapped it open with a flick of his thumb, saying: "Try some of mine, sir! I shall value your opinion."

"Mixed it yourself, did you?" said his lordship. He helped himself to a pinch, and inhaled it critically. "Too much Brazil!" he said. "Why don't you come to me for a recipe? All the same, you young——" He broke off suddenly, his gaze fixed in wrath and stupefaction on Claud, who had produced a small silver shovel and a haresfoot from his pocket, and was preparing, in happy unconsciousness of the baleful stare bent upon him, to scoop some snuff out of the jar in front of him. "What the devil——?" demanded his lordship, in such stridulous accents that Claud, startled, looked up, and promptly dropped his little shovel. "Well?" said his lordship. "Well, popinjay?"

"Put that thing away, you young fool!" said Matthew, in a vexed undervoice. "Making a figure of yourself——!"

"I ain't making a figure of myself!" returned Claud indignantly. "Assure you, sir! Quite the go! You take the snuff in the shovel, to save dabbling your fingers, and if you spill any on your coat you brush it off in a trice with the haresfoot, like——"

"I'll have no such infernal foppery in my house!" declared his lordship. "Good God, that any grandson of mine should find nothing better to do than to spend his time thinking what extravagant folly he can next commit!"

"My dear sir, you are blaming the innocent!" said Vincent. "The guilty person is Thingwall: the Trig-and-Trim dandy, you know. That's one of his tricks. It is the tragedy of Claud's life that he has never yet been able to hit upon a new quirk of fashion, but is always obliged to copy other men."

"Well, *you* needn't sneer!" retorted Claud, flushing. "You only started driving pickaxe in the Park because Brading did so!"

"Not at all, brother. Brading followed *my* lead."

"That's enough, that's enough!" interposed Matthew, removing the snuff-jar from Claud's reach, and pushing it towards Hugo. "Help yourself, if you like this sort!"

"Nay, I don't like it," Hugo said. "I'd rather blow a cloud which is a habit I got into in Spain."

"It is not a habit you will indulge in here!" said Lord Darracott. "Smoking is a filthy and a disgusting misuse of tobacco: intolerable!"

"Well, I was never one to beat squares," said Hugo equably. "I'll smoke my cigars in the garden, and that road we won't fratch."

"Won't do what?" asked Claud, interested.

"Fratch—quarrel! It's what we say in Yorkshire," explained Hugo.

"Possibly not in the first circles, however, so don't copy

it, Claud," said Vincent coldly. "Permit me to point out to you, cousin, that you are chased."

Hugo, finding the port at his elbow, begged pardon, filled his glass, and passed the decanter on, his demeanour one of unruffled amiability.

5

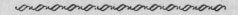

Breakfast at Darracott Place was not served until eleven o'clock, early risers being obliged to sustain nature until that hour on a cup of chocolate and a slice of bread-and-butter, brought to their bedchambers. The custom was not an unusual one; in many country houses of ton, noon was the appointed hour for the first meal of the day; but to a soldier, accustomed to much earlier hours, it was both strange and unacceptable. Major Darracott, awaking betimes from a night of untroubled repose, thrust back the curtains that shrouded the four-poster in which he lay, and pulled his watch from under the pillows. The tidings it conveyed were unwelcome enough to make him utter a despairing groan, and sink back, resolutely closing his eyes in an attempt to recapture sleep. After spending half-an-hour in this barren endeavour, he abandoned it, linked his hands under his head, and lay for a time with his eyes fixed abstractedly on the line of light seeping through the join of the curtains drawn across the windows, and his mind roving over the events of the previous evening. What he thought of them no spy could have guessed, for even in solitude his countenance afforded no clue to whatever thoughts might be revolving behind the blankness in his eyes. There was something rather bovine about its immobility: Vincent had already told his grandfather that he lived in momentary expectation of seeing his ox-like cousin chew the cud.

It had been a daunting evening, judging by any standards. When the gentlemen had risen from the dining-table, Vincent had challenged Richmond to a game of billiards, and Richmond, instantly accepting the challenge, had gone off with him, his quick flush betraying his gratification. The rest of the male company had gone upstairs to join the ladies in the long drawing-room, his lordship having apparently decided that even an evening spent amongst females was preferable to one spent alone, or closeted with his son in the library. Only two females were discovered in the drawing-room. Mrs. Darracott, inviting Hugo to a chair beside her own, explained, a little nervously, that Anthea had the head-ache, and had gone to bed. It seemed for an instant as though my lord would have uttered some blistering censure, but although his brow was black he refrained, with what was plainly an effort, from making any comment. Seating himself in a wing-chair, he fell into conversation with his son, while Lady Aurelia, who had abandoned her tatting for some tapestry-work, handed Claud a tangle of coloured wools, and desired him, with much the air of one providing a child with a simple puzzle, to unravel the various strands. He was perfectly ready to oblige her, and even, having subjected her work to a critical scrutiny, to offer her some very good advice on the accomplishment of the design.

Mrs. Darracott, meanwhile, was doing what lay within her power to make Hugo feel at home, considerably hampered by the knowledge that his lordship, lending only half an ear to Matthew, was listening to all that was said.

What my lord had learned by this means had not been very much, but one piece of information he had gleaned which had put him into a better temper: Hugo seemed to have no maternal relations living—or, at all events, none of whom he took account. His grandfather, he told Mrs. Darracott, in reply to her sympathetic question, had been dead for several years; he supposed, rather vaguely, that there were those who could call cousins with him, but the connection must of necessity be remote. No, he didn't think he had ever met them; the only member of his mother's family whom he remembered was Great-aunt Susan, who had been used to live with them when he was a child. She had been a spinster, but he thought Grandfather had had other sisters.

Lord Darracott was so much cheered by this that he had presently asked Hugo if he played chess. Upon Hugo's replying doubtfully that he knew what the moves were but hadn't played since he was a boy, he had said bluntly: "You couldn't give me a game, then. What can you play? Piquet? Backgammon?"

"Ay, or whist," offered Hugo.

"Play whist, do you?" said his lordship. "Very well, I'll try you in a rubber or two. Aurelia, you won't object to making up a table? Ring the bell, Hugh!"

The Major, with an uneasy apprehension that the form of whist played by a number of generally impecunious young officers belonging to a regiment that boasted very few bucks and blades of Society was likely to fall considerably short of his lordship's standard, tried to draw back from the engagement; but his suggestion that he should watch, while Mrs. Darracott, or Claud, took his place, found no favour at all. His lordship said that Mrs. Darracott was fit for nothing but casino, and that he would be damned if he played with Claud, who had no head for cards, or, indeed, anything else. So Hugo had been obliged to take his seat at the card-table, with his grandfather for partner. They played only for chicken-stakes, and it was not long before Hugo found that his apprehension had been well-grounded. He was forced to endure many sharp scolds for stupidity; and later, when the billiard-players came into the drawing-room, the severe imposition of having his hand overlooked by Vincent. He seized the earliest opportunity of relinquishing his seat to Vincent. No opposition had been raised, my lord merely saying "Well, you're no card-player!" and recommending him to watch his cousin's play. He had preferred, however, to slip away when my lord's attention was devoted to the play of a difficult hand, and to enjoy the solace of one of his cigars on the terrace. Here he had presently been joined by Richmond. "I thought you had come out to blow a cloud!" Richmond had said.

"Now, if you're framing to squeak beef on me——!" he had responded.

Richmond had chuckled. "You'd be in the suds, cousin! So would I be, if you were to squeak beef on me! Grandpapa thinks I've gone to bed. He wouldn't like it above half if he knew——That is, he don't want me to ask you about the war in the Peninsula, or——But never mind that! I wanted to tell you—you might not know—he—he doesn't *understand!*" He had raised his handsome young face, pallid in the moonlight, and had blurted out: "About

65

the Light Division, I mean! He—he only thinks of the Guards, and the Cavalry! He may say—oh, I don't know, but *pray* don't take it amiss!"

"Nay," Hugo had said reassuringly. "I won't take it amiss! Why should I? I've nothing to say against the Gentlemen's Sons, or the Cavalry either—some of 'em!"

"No. Well, I wanted just to warn you!" Richmond had confided. "He's quite antiquated, you know, and, of course, he does ride devilish rusty—though not with me, so perhaps I ought not to say it, only——"

"There's no need for you to be fatched, lad: my Grandfather Bray was just such a cobby old fellow!"

"Oh!" Richmond had sounded rather taken-aback. "*Was* he? I mean——Yes, I see! But there's Vincent, too, and——" He paused, knitting his brows. "I don't know why he was in such a bad skin tonight, but in general he—he is a bang-up fellow, you know! What they call Top-of-the-Trees! A regular out-and-outer! You should see him with a four-in-hand!"

"Happen I will."

"Yes, of course. Do you drive yourself, cousin?"

"Nay, I'm no Nonesuch!"

Richmond had been disappointed, but he had said quickly: "No, you haven't had the opportunity——" He had broken off short, and although no colour could live in the moonlight, Hugo had known that a vivid flush had flooded his cheeks. He had stammered: "I don't mean—I meant only that you have been doing other things! Things m-more worth the doing! I wish you will tell me, if it isn't a dead bore, about your campaigns!"

Yes, Hugo thought, reviewing that interlude, a nice lad, young Richmond; but what such an ardent colt was doing hobbled at Darracott Place was a puzzle. If ever a lad was mad after a pair of colours! He had said that his grandfather had set his face against the granting of this desire, but he didn't look to be the sort of lad to submit docilely to the decree of even so absolute an autocrat as old Darracott. If my lord didn't take care, thought Hugo, casting off the bedclothes, and swinging his feet to the ground, he would have the lad chin-deep in mischief.

Dismissing Richmond from his mind, he strode to the window, and pulled back the curtains, and stood for a minute or two, leaning his hands on the sill, and looking out. The sprawling house was built on a slight elevation, in parkland which stretched for a considerable distance to the south and east, but merged rapidly into thick woods on the northern and western fronts. Below Hugo's window, a part of the gardens, which appeared to be extensive though not in very trim order, lay between the house and the park; and the Military Canal and, beyond it, the Welland Marsh stretched into a distance still shrouded in morning mist. The day was fresh but fair; it beckoned compellingly; and within a very short space of time Hugo, fortified by a thick ham sandwich and a pint of Kentish ale, supplied to him by a pleasantly fluttered kitchenmaid, had set out for an exploratory ramble round the park.

He returned by way of the stables, which were situated to the west of the house. They had been built to accomodate many more horses than now stood in the stalls, and were ranged round several cobbled yards. Only two of these seemed to be in use; in the others weeds were pushing up between the cobbles, and rows of shut doors, the paint on them blistered and cracked with age, lent a melancholy air of decay to the scene.

The Major found his groom, a middle-aged Yorkshireman of stocky build and dour countenance, severely repelling the mischievous advances of a plump damsel in a print frock and a mob cap. To judge by the grin on the face of one of the stableboys, who had paused, bucket in hand, to listen to her sallies, she was full of liveliness and wit; but when she saw Hugo coming across the yard she fell into a twitter of embarrassment, dropped a hasty curtsy, and ran away.

"Set up a flirt already, have you?" remarked Hugo. "I'm surprised at you, John Joseph, at your time of life!"

"That giglet!" snorted his servitor. "I' bahn to take t'gray to the stithy, Mester Hugo: he's got a shoe loose, like I told you."

"How's Rufus?"

"Champion!"

"Good! I'll take a look at him. All well with you, John Joseph?"

"I'm suited," responded John Joseph stolidly. He cast an upward sidelong glance at his master's face, and added in a rougher tone: "Tha knows we mun be suited, Mester Hugo, choose how!"

The blue eyes gave nothing away, but there was a hint of mulishness about the Major's firm lips. "Maybe! We'll see!"

"Tha's quality-make, like t'gaffer used to say," urged John Joseph. "Nay then, sir——! If tha's bahn to be a lord, think on——"

"I am thinking," Hugo answered. He smiled. "Hold thy gab John Joseph!"

"*Mester Hugo!* If t'gaffer could hear thee——!"

"I'd get a bang on the lug. But——"

"Sneck up!" commanded his henchman. "Here comes his lordship, and Mester Richmond! I mun fettle t'tits."

With these words he withdrew into the stable, just as Lord Darracott and Richmond, who had been out at exercise, dismounted.

"Ha! Glad to see you're up and about!" said his lordship. "I've no patience with young fellows who lie abed till all hours. Another morning you may come out with me: no use suggesting it to you last night: you'll need to rest your horses. I'll take a look at 'em."

"Ay, sir, do! They're neither of them the equal of this fellow," said Hugo, patting the neck of Richmond's colt, "but the bay's a prime fencer, and strong in work. He has need to be!"

"H'm! Pity you're so big!" commented his lordship. "What do you ride? Seventeen stone?"

"All of that," admitted Hugo. "Eh, lad, you've got a proper high-bred 'un here!"

"Do you like him?" Richmond asked eagerly. "He's young—pretty green still, but a perfect mover! I broke him myself."

Lord Darracott, leaving Richmond to show off his treasure, went into the stable, and was soon heard putting curt questions to John Joseph. It seemed doubtful that he would find John Joseph's answers intelligible, but he apparently understood enough to satisfy him, for when he presently emerged he rather surprisingly told Hugo that he had a good man there, who knew his work. He bestowed moderate praise on Rufus, the big bay, but dismissed the Andalusian with the loose shoe as a clumsy-looking brute, high in flesh. Richmond having gone off to confer with his groom, his lordship commanded Hugo to accompany him back to the house. "I've a good deal

68

to say to you," he informed him. "I'll see you in the library after breakfast."

Few members of his family would have sat down to breakfast with much appetite after such a pronouncement as this, but although a slightly wary expression came into Hugo's eyes his appetite remained unimpaired, and he was soon consuming an extremely hearty meal. The fact that his cousin Anthea had chosen to seat herself on the opposite side of the table troubled him not at all. Glancing dispassionately at her, he was able to verify his first impression that she was a pretty girl, with remarkably fine eyes, and a good deal of countenance. It seemed a pity that she should be so cold and inanimate when a little vivacity would have done so much to improve her.

Neither Vincent nor Claud was an early riser, and each incurred censure for walking into the breakfast parlour when the meal was nearly over. Vincent, never in his sunniest mood before breakfast, furiously resented the scold he received, but betrayed this only by his thinned lips and a certain glitter in his eyes. Claud, on the other hand, was unwise enough to excuse himself. Owing to the stupidity of his man, the carelessness of the laundress, and the inexplicable whims of Fate, which decreed that although one might sometimes achieve a desired result at the first attempt, at others success would elude one until one was exhausted, it had taken him three quarters of an hour to tie his neckcloth. The style he had chosen was the Mailcoach, and as it was as bulky as it was wide, he bore all the appearance of having bound a compress round a sore throat, as his brother took care to inform him.

"Jack-at-warts!" said his lordship bitterly.

Everyone waited for him to develop this theme, but he said no more, merely staring fixedly at Claud under such lowering brows that that unfortunate exquisite became so much discomposed that he took an unwary gulp of tea and scalded his mouth.

"I have it!" suddenly announced his lordship, grimly triumphant. "I'll set you to work!"

"Eh?" ejaculated Claud, alarmed.

"You are a Bartholomew baby, a park-saunterer, a good-for-nothing Jack Straw!" said his fond grandfather.

"Well, I shouldn't put it like that myself, sir," said Claud, "but I daresay you're right. Well, what I mean is, no use setting me to work: I couldn't!"

"A smock-faced wag-feather!" pursued my lord inexorably. "Your only talent is for àlamodality!"

"Well, there you are, sir!" Claud pointed out.

"A certain sort of something!" mocked Vincent.

"*That's* what I'll turn to good account!" said his lordship. "You can teach Hugh how to pass himself off with credit! Give him a new touch! Rid him of that damned brogue! You don't know much, but you've moved in the first circles all your life, and you do know the established mode!"

"Father! Really——!" Matthew exclaimed.

"Cousin Hugo doesn't need any touch that Claud could give him!" declared Richmond, scarlet-faced.

Hugo, who had continued throughout this embarrassing dialogue to eat his way through several slices of cold beef, looked up from his plate to smile amiably, and to say, with a marked Yorkshire drawl: "Nay, I'd be fain to learn how to support the character of a gentleman. I've a fancy to be up to the knocker, and I'll be well-suited to be put in the way of it. And I should think," he added handsomely, "that our Claud could teach me better nor most."

"Exactly so!" said Vincent. "*An assinego may tutor thee!*"

"To support the character of a gentleman!" exclaimed Anthea, unexpectedly entering the lists. "In this house, cousin, unless you will be content with my brother, you will search in vain for a model!"

"You keep your tongue, miss!" said his lordship, without any particular animosity.

"Anthea, *pray*——!" whispered Mrs. Darracott.

"Oh, have you changed your mind?" asked Vincent, levelling his quizzing-glass at Anthea. A provocative smile curled his lip; he said silkily: "*Shall the elephant Ajax carry it thus*, my sweet life?"

Her eyes blazed, and Hugo, considerably surprised, intervened, saying in his deep, slow voice: "Nay then! Don't fratch over me! I don't know what I'm to carry, but I'm agreeable to be called an elephant: it won't be for the first time! They call me Gog Darracott in the regiment, but when I was a lad it was more often *that great lump!*

70

There's no need for any fuss and clart on my account: I've a broad back."

"It must at all events be acknowledged that you have an amiable temper," said Matthew, pushing back his chair. "You will excuse me, Elvira, if you please! I must go up to see how her ladyship does. She passed an indifferent night, and has the head-ache this morning."

Mrs. Darracott replied suitably, and Matthew left the room. He was shortly followed by Lord Darracott, who went away, commanding Hugo not to keep him waiting. Hugh, who had just received his third cup of tea from Mrs. Darracott, said that he would follow him when he had finished his breakfast, a reply which struck Claud as being so foolhardy that he was moved to utter an earnest warning. "Better go at once!" he said. "No sense in putting him in a bad skin, coz! Very likely to regret it!"

"Nay, what could he do to me?" said Hugo, dropping sugar into his cup.

"That you will discover," said Vincent dryly. "You will also discover the pains and penalties that attach to the position of heir."

"Happen I've discovered a few already," drawled Hugo.

Claud coughed delicately. "Rather fancy you mean *perhaps*, coz!"

"Ay, so I do!" agreed Hugo. "I'm much obliged to you."

"The spectacle of Claud entering upon his new duties, though not unamusing, is not one which I can support at this hour of the day," said Vincent. "Do you mind postponing any further tuition until I have withdrawn from the room?"

"Ah!" retorted Claud, with an odious smirk. "You're piqued because m'grandfather didn't ask *you* to hint Hugh into the proper mode!"

This quite failed to ruffle Vincent. "He did," he answered. "I was persuaded, however, that it would prove to be a task beyond my poor power, and declined the office." He saw that, while his target remained unmoved, Richmond was looking at him with a troubled frown between his eyes. He smiled slightly at the boy, and said, as he rose from the table: "What I *am* going to do is to teach Richmond how to point his leaders."

71

Richmond had been shocked by Vincent's conduct, but this was an invitation not to be resisted. His brow cleared; he jumped up, exclaiming: "No! Do you mean it? You're not hoaxing me, are you?"

"No, but perhaps I should have said I mean to *try* to teach you."

"Brute!" Richmond said, laughing. He thought he saw how to turn this cut to good account, and said ingenuously: "Vincent is always out of reason cross before breakfast, Cousin Hugo! Snaps all our noses off!"

"Well, if you ask me," said Claud, as soon as the door was shut again, "he's got a devilish nasty tongue in his head any hour of the day! Takes after the old gentleman." He looked at his large cousin, and shook his head. "*You* may think it's a fine thing to be the heir: got a strong notion m'father liked it pretty well, too. All I can say is, I'm dashed glad *I'm* not. Y'know, coz, if you've finished your tea, I'd as lief you went off to see what m'grandfather wants. There's no saying but what he may blame me for it if you keep him waiting."

Thus adjured, Hugo went in search of Lord Darracott, and found him (after peeping into three empty saloons) seated at his desk in the library. There was a pen in his hand, but the ink had dried on it, and he was staring absently out of the bay window. He turned his head when he heard the door open, and said: "Oh, so here you are! Shut the door, and come over here! You can take that chair, if it will bear you!"

It cracked, but gave no sign of immediate collapse under Hugo's weight, so he disposed himself comfortably in it, crossed one booted leg over the other, and awaited his grandfather's pleasure with every outward semblance of placidity.

For several moments his lordship said nothing; but sat looking at him morosely. "You don't favour your father!" he said at last.

"No," agreed the Major.

"Well, I daresay you're none the worse for that! You are his son: there's no doubt about it!" He put down his pen, and pushed aside the papers on his desk, something in the gesture seeming to indicate that with them he was pushing aside his memories. "Got to make the best of it!" he said. "When I'm booked, you'll step into my shoes. I don't mean to wrap the matter up in clean linen, and I'll tell you to your head that that's not what I wanted, or ever dreamed would come to pass!"

"No," said the Major again, sympathetically. "It's been a facer to the both of us."

Lord Darracott stared at him. "A facer for me, but a honey-fall for you, young man!"

The Major preserved a stolid silence.

"And don't tell me you'd as lief not step into your uncle's shoes!" said Lord Darracott. "You'll find me a hard man to bridge, so cut no wheedles for my edification!" He paused, but the Major still had nothing to say. His lordship gave a short laugh. "If you thought you'd turn me up sweet by writing that flim-flam to Lissett you mistook your man! I detest maw-worms, and that's what you sounded like to me! I do you the justice to say you haven't the look of a maw-worm, so maybe it was your notion of civility. Let me have no more of it!" He waited again for any answer the Major might like to make, but, getting none, snapped: "Well, have you a tongue in your head?"

"I have," responded Hugo, "but I was never one to give my head for washing."

"You're not such a fool as you look," commented his lordship. "Whether you've enough sense to learn what every other Darracott has known from the cradle we shall see. That's why I sent for you."

"It's why I came, think on," said Hugo reflectively. "My father being killed almost before I was out of long coats, there was no one to tell me anything about my family, and barring I'd a lord for grandfather I didn't know anything."

"You're blaming me, are you? Very well! If I had known that there would ever have been the smallest need for you to know anything about me, or mine, I should have sent for you when your father died, and had you reared under my eye."

"Happen my mother would have had something to say to that," remarked Hugo.

"There's nothing to be gained by discussing the matter now. When your father married against my wish he cut himself off from his family. I don't scruple to tell you, for you must be well aware of it, that in marrying a weaver's daughter—however virtuous she may have been!—he did

73

what he knew must ruin him with me!"

"Ay, they were pluck to the backbone, the pair of 'em,"
nodded Hugo. "What with you on the one hand, and
Granddad on t'other, they must have had good bottom,
seemingly." He smiled affably upon his lordship. "I never
heard that they regretted it, though Granddad always held
to it that no good would come of the match. Like to like
and Nan to Nicholas was *his* motto."

"Are you telling me, sir, that the fellow *objected* to his
daughter's marrying my son?" demanded Lord Darracott.

"Oh! he wasn't at all suited with it!" replied Hugo.
"Let alone my father was Quality-make, he was too much
of a care-for-nobody for Granddad: caper-witted, he called
him. Shutful with his brass, too, which used to put Granddad, by what I'm told, into a rare passion. But Granddad's
bark was worse than his bite, and he came round to the
marriage in the end. It's a pity you never met him: you'd
have agreed together better nor you think."

Lord Darracott, almost stunned, sought in vain for
words with which to dispel this illusion. Before he could
find them, Hugo had added thoughtfully: "You put me in
mind of him now-and-now, particularly when you start
ringing a peal over someone. However, you didn't send
for me to talk about Granddad, so likely I'm wasting your
time, sir."

"I wish to hear nothing about your granddad, as you
call him, or your mother, or the life you led when you
were a boy!" declared his lordship, his face still alarm-
ingly suffused with colour. "Understand me, that period
is never to be mentioned! I recommend you to put it out
of your mind! It shouldn't be difficult; you've been a serv-
ing officer for the past ten years, and must have other
things to talk of. I collect that there are no longer any ties
binding you to Yorkshire, and that circumstance I cannot
but regard as fortunate. I'll be plain with you: since I can't
keep you from succeeding me I mean to see you licked
into shape before I stick *my* spoon in the wall."

"Nay, we can't tell but what I'll break my neck over
a rasper, or go off in the smallpox," interposed Hugo, in
a heartening tone.

"Where the devil did you learn to hunt?" exclaimed
his lordship.

"In Portugal."

"Oh!" His lordship sat for a minute or two digesting this. "Well, that's more than I hoped for!" he said presently. "You'll be able to hunt from here: it's humbug country, but you'll see plenty of sport. *I* used to hunt in the shires, but I'm getting too old for it now. Sold my lodge in Leicestershire some years ago. Just as well I did! I should have had that nick-or-nothing boy of mine coming to grief over those fences, sure as a gun!"

"I've a fancy to hunt in the shires myself," confessed Hugo. "In fact——"

"Oh, you have, have you? Then you'd best rid yourself of it!" interrupted his lordship sardonically. "Behave yourself, and I'll make you a respectable allowance, but it won't run to the Quorn or the Pytchley, so don't think it!"

"Nay, I wasn't thinking it!" replied Hugo, looking a little startled. "Nor of your making me an allowance neither, sir. I'm much obliged to you, but I don't want that: I've plenty of brass."

Lord Darracott was amused. "Ay, your pockets are well-lined because you've just had the prize-money for the Peninsula and Waterloo paid to you. I know all about that, and no doubt it seems a fortune to you. You'll change your ideas a little when you've learnt the ways of *my* world."

"My grandfather left me some brass too," said Hugo diffidently.

"What you choose to do with your grandfather's savings is no concern of mine: spend them as you wish! For your support, you'll look to me—and you'll be glad enough to do so before you're much older! You are going to live in a different style to any you've been accustomed to, and you wouldn't find yourself able to strike a balance on a weaver's savings, however thrifty he may have been. Let me hear no more on that subject!"

"No," said Hugo meekly.

"Well, that brings me to what I have to say to you," said his lordship. "You're my heir, and you've all to learn, and I choose that you shall learn it under my roof. For the present you'll remain here—at all events until you've lost that damned, north-country accent! Later I'll let your uncle introduce you into Society, but the time for that's not yet. This is your home, and here you'll stay. Which reminds me that you must sell out, if you haven't already done so."

"I have," said Hugo.

The craggy brows drew together. "Taking a lot for granted, weren't you?"

"Well," Hugo drawled, "there was a lot I *could* take for granted, sir."

"What if I hadn't chosen to acknowledge you?"

"Nay, I hadn't thought of that," confessed Hugo.

"Don't be too pot-sure!" said his lordship, by no means pleased. "I could still send you packing! And make no mistake about it: if I find you intolerable I'll do it!"

A flicker of relief shone for an instant in the Major's eyes, but he said nothing.

"However, you're better than I expected," said his lordship, mollified by this docility. "I daresay something can be made of you. Watch your cousins, and take your tone from them! I don't mean Claud—though no one would ever mistake him for other than a gentleman, mooncalf though he is!—but the other three. Vincent's an idle, extravagant dog, but his ton is excellent—what they call nowadays top-of-the-trees! You may take him for your model—and I'll see to it you don't copy his extravagance! No use looking to him to set you right when you make mistakes, however: he won't do it, because he's as sulky as a bear over the whole business. I could force him to take you in hand, but I shan't. I don't want the pair of you coming to cuffs. That's why I've told Claud to give you a new touch. Between 'em, he and Anthea can teach you pretty well all you need to know. *She* was born and bred here, knows all the ways of the place, all our history, every inch of my land! Not married, are you?"

"Married!" ejaculated Hugo, taken-aback. "Lord, no, sir!"

"No, I didn't think you could be," said his lordship. "I recommend you get on terms with your cousin Anthea. She doesn't want for sense, and she's a spirited, lively girl, and would make you an excellent wife, if she took a fancy to you. I shall say no more on that head at present, however. Time enough to be looking to the future when you're better acquainted. What you can do at the moment is to go over the house with her: get her to tell you about the family! Ring the bell!"

The Major rose, and obeyed this peremptory behest. He also mopped his brow.

"I'm going to send for her," said his lordship. "She can take you up to the picture-gallery for a start."

The Major, showing alarm for the first time, tried to protest, but was cut short. "Ay, I know that throws you into a stew! You haven't been the way of doing the pretty, and you're as shy as be-damned: you needn't tell me! You'll have to get the better of that, and you may as well begin at once. Chollacombe, desire Miss Darracott to come to me here immediately!"

The Major, attempting no further remonstrance, ran a finger inside a neckcloth grown suddenly too tight, and awaited in considerable trepidation the arrival of his cousin Anthea.

6

∾∾∾∾∾∾∾∾∾∾∾∾∾∾∾∾∾

It was some little time before Anthea obeyed the summons to the library, but Lord Darracott, contrary to the Major's expectation, showed no sign of putting himself in a passion. He occupied himself with giving his grandson a few hints on the best ways of fixing his interest with females in general and his cousin in particular; and when Anthea did at last enter the room, greeted her quite genially, saying: "Ah, here you are, my dear! Where the devil have you been hiding yourself?"

She put up her brows. "I have merely been with my mother, sir. We are rather busy this morning."

"Well, never mind that!" said his lordship. "I want you to show your cousin round the house. Tell him its history! He don't know anything about the family, and that won't do. You can take him up to the picture-gallery, and let him see a few of his ancestors."

"I am persuaded, sir, that that is a task Chollacombe is longing to perform. He would be delighted to instruct my cousin."

"Don't argue with me, girl, but do as I bid you!" snapped his lordship.

"Nay, if my cousin's throng——"

"And don't you think you can argue with me either!" said his lordship. "You'll do as you're told, the pair of you!"

The Major hesitated, but Anthea said coolly: "Very well, Grandpapa. Will you come with me, if you please, Cousin Hugo?"

The Major, with something of the air of one nerving himself to lead a forlorn hope, bowed, and accompanied her out of the room. But once beyond Lord Darracott's sight and hearing he said apologetically: "There's no sense in fratching with the old gentleman, but if you're throng this morning I can look after myself well-enough, cousin."

"When you have lived in this house for a few days you will have discovered that it is wisest to obey Grandpapa," she returned, leading the way towards the staircase. "Certainly in small matters. Unless, of course, you have a fancy for the sort of brangling *he* delights in?"

"Nay, I'm a peaceable man."

"So I have observed," she said. "I don't know how you contrived to keep your temper at the breakfast-table. I could have wished that you hadn't."

"Well, it wouldn't be proper for me to start a fight with my grandfather."

"It would be very proper for you to start one with Vincent, however!"

He smiled, but shook his head. "Hard words break no bones. Seemingly, I've put Vincent's nose out of joint, so it's natural he should be nattered. Happen he'll come about."

She did not speak again until they had reached the upper hall. She paused then, at the head of the stairs, and asked abruptly: "Has Grandpapa told you that he means to keep you here?"

"Ay, but chance it happens that he can't abide me he'll send me packing," he replied cheerfully.

"Do you—are you going to submit to his tyranny?"

"Well, there you have me," he said, rubbing his nose with a large forefinger, and slightly wrinkling his brow. "It won't do for me to be at outs with him, so it's likely I'll have to submit to him."

She glanced up at him rather searchingly. "I see!"

"While I'm under his roof," added Hugo. "The odds are that won't be for long."

She walked across the hall, and into a large saloon, whose chairs and pendant chandelier were all muffled in holland covers. "The State apartments," she announced. "So-called because Queen Elizabeth once occupied them for a sennight. Tradition has it that she contrived, hunting in *forse* and in the chase, to denude the park of deer. I've forgotten what it cost our noble ancestor to entertain her:

79

some fabulous sum, and all to no avail, for she quarrelled violently with his lady, and is said to have left Darracott Place in a dudgeon. That, by the way, is a portrait of our noble ancestor," she added, nodding to the picture over the fireplace. "Very Friday-faced, not to say hangdog, but that might have been because of the Queen's visit."

"I should say myself that the poor fellow suffered from a colicky disorder," replied Hugo. "He has the look of it. Sallow as a Nabob!"

She laughed, and led him on into an antechamber. "Very likely! We are now approaching the Queen's Bedchamber. You will notice her cipher over the bedstead. The hangings are all original, but pray don't touch them! The silk is quite rotten."

The Major stood looking round at faded and tarnished magnificence. "Eh, but it's a shame!" he said. "Why has it all been let go to ruin? It queers me that a man as proud as his lordship shouldn't keep his house in better order!"

"Well, it won't *queer* you when you are rather better acquainted with him," she replied. "His pride is of a peculiar order, and is not in the least diminished by debts or encumbered estates. Did you suppose yourself to be inheriting fortune as well as title? You will be sadly disappointed!"

"I can see that. But that colt your brother has wasn't bought for a song, and here's the old gentleman wishing to make me an allowance!"

She stared at him. "He must do that, of course. As for Richmond's colt, there's always money to pay for what *he* has set his heart on. Vincent is another who can in general get what he wants from Grandpapa. Next to Richmond, he is Grandpapa's favourite. Have you looked your fill at our past grandeur? We have now only to go through the room allotted to the maids-of-honour—quite unremarkable, as you perceive—and we have reached the picture-gallery. There is a stairway at the far end which was originally the principal one. The present Grand Stairway is of later date."

"If ever I saw such a rabbit-warren!" he remarked.

"Exactly so, but I advise you not to say that within Grandpapa's hearing." She walked over to the first of six large window-embrasures, and stood looking out through the latticed panes, with her back turned to the Major. -

80

"Before I show you our forebears, cousin, there is something I wish to say. No, not that: something I feel myself obliged to say! You may think it odd of me—even improper!—but I have a notion you are not quite as stupid as you would like us to believe. I daresay you may understand why it is that I find myself in the very awkward position of being forced to put myself, and you too, to the blush. I know Grandpapa well enough to be tolerably certain that he has ordered you to make me an offer." She turned her head as she spoke, her colour a little heightened, but her eyes meeting the Major's squarely. "If he had not already done so, he will. But I think he has. Am I right?"

"He didn't precisely do that," replied Hugo cautiously.

"He will. I hope you will summon up the courage to refuse to obey that particular command. Pray believe that nothing would induce *me* to obey it! If that seems to you uncivil, I beg your pardon, but——"

"Nay, I'm reet glad to hear you say it!" he responded ingenuously.

Her eyes narrowed in sudden amusement. "I was persuaded you would be. I must warn you, however, of pressure brought to bear on you——! You don't know! He has ways of forcing us all to knock under: you may find yourself in a fix over it!"

"I may do that," he acknowledged, "but I'll be far if I make you an offer at his or any other man's bidding!" He added hastily, as she broke into laughter: "The thing is, I'm by way of being promised already! Othergates, of course, it would be different."

"Good God! Did you tell Grandpapa so?"

"I've not told him *yet*," owned Hugo sheepishly.

"You were afraid to!"

"Nay, it was just that it wasn't, seemingly, the reet moment for telling him!" he protested.

She was looking scornful. "It never will be the right moment. You *were* afraid!"

"Well, you weren't so brave yourself, not to tell him you wouldn't marry me," he pointed out.

"Yes, I was!" she retorted. "I would have told him so that instant I knew what he meant to do! I didn't do so because—oh, you don't understand! For me the case is quite otherwise!"

81

"Ay, it would be," he agreed.

"Well, it is, so you need not speak in that detestable way! Whenever I come to cuffs with Grandpapa it's Mama who suffers for it, and she has enough to bear without being blamed for my sins! That's why I asked you *not* to offer for me, so that Grandpapa couldn't say it was my fault, or bully Mama into urging me to accept you. Heaven knows your shoulders are big enough, but I see you are just like the rest, and dare not square up to him!"

The huge creature before her, looking the picture of guilt, said feebly: "It wasn't that-a-way. The thing is, I'm in a bit of a hobble. It wouldn't do for me to tell my grandfather I was promised, not before I was sure of it myself."

"But aren't you sure of it?" she asked, a good deal astonished.

"Well," he temporized, once more rubbing his nose, "I am and I'm not. There's been nothing *official* as you might say. It's—it's been kept secret betwixt the pair of us. It was just before the last campaign, you see, and I was recalled in such a bang that there was no time to do aught but get my baggage together, and be off. What's more there was no knowing but what I might have been killed, so it was thought best to keep it secret. And I haven't been home since."

"Good God, have you been engaged for two years?" she exclaimed.

"Better nor that," he said. "It was in the spring of '15 that it happened, and now we're in September. It seems to me I ought to make sure she hasn't changed her mind before I speak to the old gentleman, and so far I haven't been home."

"But she must have written to you!"

"Er—no," said Hugo, much discomposed. "She—well, there were reasons why she couldn't do that!"

A dreadful suspicion occurred to Anthea. "Cousin do you mean—is she a—a lady of Quality?"

The Major shook a miserable head.

"*Can't* she write?" Anthea asked, in a hushed voice.

"No," confessed the Major.

Feeling a trifle weak, Anthea sat down on the window-seat. "Cousin, this is—this is positively *terrible!* You can have no notion——! What's to be done?"

"If you think I *ought* to tell the old gentleman—"

"No, no!" she said quickly. "On no account in the world! Of course, I see now why you didn't say you wouldn't offer for me! He would have been bound to have asked you why not, and—I beg your pardon for being so uncivil about that! *No one* could be brave enough to make *that* disclosure to him! But what are you going to do?"

The Major had the grace to look a little conscience-stricken. He said vaguely that he hadn't yet made up his mind.

"I can't think how you dared to come here at all," said Anthea, knitting her brows. "To be sure, you didn't know what Grandpapa was like, but you *must* have known that he would never tolerate *that* sort of marriage! In fact, it was because he is afraid that you might wish to marry someone he would think unworthy that he made this odious scheme to marry you to me. Cousin, you're not in a hobble! you're in the *suds!*"

The Major, who, by this time, had had the satisfaction of seeing that his judgment had not been at fault when he had decided that animation would greatly improve Miss Darracott, ventured to approach her, and to sit down. "I am and-all!" he agreed ruefully.

"He won't receive her, you know," Anthea said. "It is useless to think he might come about. He never forgave your father, and *he* was his favourite son."

"Nay, I wouldn't bring her here."

"That's all very well, but you can't expect the poor girl to wait for years and years to be married!" objected Anthea. "Besides, surely you would not like that yourself! If you're thinking that Grandpapa may die soon, I must tell you that I don't think there's the least chance of it: he's old, but not at all decrepit, you know!"

"Oh, no, I should think he's good for a piece yet!" Hugo agreed. "But I'm not going to stay here for years and years."

"He thinks you are," she said doubtfully.

"Ay, but that's just one of the daft notions he takes into his head. There's no sense in stirring coals, so I didn't tell him he'd got the wrong sow by the ear. Happen he'll think it a good shuttance when I do tell him I'm off."

"But how will you do?" she asked. "It's he who holds the purse-strings, remember! I assure you he wouldn't hesitate to draw them tight."

He laughed. "Nay, he doesn't hold my purse-strings!"

"Ah, no! How stupid of me! You have your profession, and can afford to snap your fingers under his nose! Oh, how much I envy you!" She heaved a short sigh, but smiled immediately after, and said: "Did you come to look us over only? How long do you mean to stay?"

"Well, that depends," he said. "When I got the letter that told me the way things had fallen out, it fairly sent me to grass, for, not knowing anything about my family, I'd no notion how close to the succession I stood. Nothing will persuade my grandfather I wasn't happy as a grig to be succeeding him—though why he should have thought anyone would want to inherit a house that's falling to ruin, let alone encumbered estates, and a sackful of debts, has me fairly capped—but the truth is I wasn't at all suited, and the first thing that came into my head was to see if there wasn't a way out. That wouldn't fadge, however, so——" He paused, considering. "Well, I made up my mind to it that I'd have to come here, whether or no."

"I can understand that you didn't wish to do that while Grandpapa was alive."

"No," he admitted. "But if I've to step into the old gentleman's shoes, soon or late, it'll be as well I shouldn't be strange to the place, or the people. So when Lissett wrote to tell me I was to come here I did come. I don't say I wouldn't as lief have sent word his lordship might go to hell—eh, that slipped out! I'm reet sorry!"

"Don't give it a thought!" said Anthea cordially. "I never before heard such beautiful words, I promise you!"

He smiled, but shook his head. "I'd have caught cold at that. What's more, if his lordship and my father were at outs, that's no concern of mine. My other grandfather had more rumgumption than any man I've ever known, and he always would have it that my father came by his deserts. He didn't hold with a man's marrying out of his own order, and, taking it by and large, I'd say he was in the reet of it. What with him on the one side, hammering it into me I was Quality-born, and Grandfather Darracott here looking at me as if I was a porriwiggle, I don't know *what* I am!"

84

She went into a peal of laughter. "Oh, what is it? Por-riwiggle?"

He grinned. "It's what we call a tadpole."

That made her laugh more than ever. She said, wiping her eyes: "No, I don't think anyone would liken you to a tadpole, cousin! Tell me about the girl you are going to marry! Is she pretty?"

"I don't know if you'd say she was pretty. She—she has golden hair—corn-gold, you know—and blue eyes, with long lashes that curl. She has a straight little nose, and a mouth like a bow, and—and a complexion like straw-berries and cream!" replied Hugo rhapsodically.

"I should say she was a beauty!" Anthea said, slightly taken-aback.

"She has a good figure too," added Hugo, dwelling with obvious pleasure on the vision he had conjured up.

"In that case I think you should lose no time in posting north—though it is probably too late already. Such a par-agon *cannot* be wearing the willow!"

"I'm not afraid of that. I forgot to tell you that she's not one to break her promise."

She eyed him suspiciously. "What is her name?"

"Amelia," responded Hugo, adding after a reflective moment: "Melkinthorpe."

Anthea rose. "Well, I wish you very happy. Meanwhile, we haven't yet looked at the ancestors. We must do so, you know, for Grandpapa is quite likely to ask you search-ing questions about them. Chiefly you must study the Van Dyck: here it is! Ralph Darracott, who was killed at Naseby; his wife, Penelope—she was pretty, wasn't she?—holding Charles Darracott in her lap. There's an-other one of Charles in later life, a Lely, over here."

The Major, having subjected Charles Darracott to a critical scrutiny, remarked that he knew what he thought of him.

"Very likely," said Anthea. "His son, however, was extremely virtuous, as you may see for yourself. He was succeeded by his nephew, Ralph II. I daresay you may have been thinking that our ancestors were rather com-monplace, but Ralph II, I assure you, made quite a noise in the world."

"He would," said Hugo, regarding Ralph with disfa-vour.

"Yes, he was a beau of the first stare. His waistcoats were copied by all the smarts of his day; he had fought three duels, and killed his man, before he was five-and-twenty; and he is generally supposed to have murdered his first wife, either by throwing her out of the window, or by driving her to throw herself out of the window. Grandpapa, of course, holds by the latter theory, but the country-people know better. Her ghost walks, you know."

"What, here?"

Anthea laughed. "No, don't be alarmed! This stirring event took place before Ralph became Lord Darracott. When he came into the country, which was seldom, he resided at the Dower House. He is said to have incarcerated his wife there, and to have ridden all the way from London one stormy night, and murdered her. Then he galloped away again, and shortly afterwards married his second wife. There can really be *no* doubt of the truth of this legend, for the sound of his horse's hooves are frequently heard in the dead of night. He came to a violent end, like so many of our illustrious family."

"I should think he ended on the gallows, that road," observed the Major.

"Nothing so vulgar!" replied Anthea. "He was murdered."

"Who murdered him?"

"They never discovered that. His body was found in the Home Wood, and from some cause or another he had so many enemies that it was thought the deed might have been committed by almost anyone."

"And does his ghost walk?"

"No, happily it doesn't: we are quite free of spectres here at the Place! The portrait you are looking at now is of Lucinda Darracott. She married an Attlebridge, but that likeness was taken when she was eighteen. Several minor poets made her the subject of lyrics, but in later life she grew sadly stout. And here, cousin, we have my grandfather, surrounded by his progeny, his wife, and two dogs. The urchin leaning against his chair is your papa; mine is the infant being dandled by Grandmama. The coy damsel with the posy is Aunt Mary—Lady Chudleigh; beside her, Aunt Sarah, now Mrs. Wenlock; and the pretty one admiring my papa is Aunt Caroline, Lady Haddon. Your uncle Granville is the youth with one hand on his hip, and his riding-whip in the other; and the chubby lad is my uncle Matthew."

Hugo dutifully gazed upon this conversation piece, but made no comment. His eye was attracted by a kit-kat hanging beside it, and he exclaimed: "That's good!"

"Richmond? Yes, it's very like," she agreed. "Mr. Lonsdale painted it a year ago. There's a miniature of him also, but Grandpapa keeps that in his own room."

He stood looking up at the portrait. "Eh, he's a handsome lad!" he remarked. "Full of gig, too. What does the old gentleman mean to do with him?"

"I don't know."

He glanced down at her, and saw that the amusement had faded from her face. "Seemingly, the lad's army-mad?"

"My grandfather will never permit him to join, however."

"That's a pity. I never knew any good to come of setting a lad's nose to the wrong grindstone."

"Oh, that won't happen either!" she answered. "The likelihood is that he will be kept kicking his heels here. My grandfather dotes on him, you see."

"Nay, if he dotes on him he'll let him have his way!"

"How little you know Grandpapa! His affection for Richmond is perfectly selfish: he likes to have Richmond with him, and so it will be. The excuse is that Richmond's constitution is sickly. He is as tough as whitleather, in fact, but his childhood was sickly, and that is enough for Grandpapa. Do you wish to look at any more portraits, or have you had your fill?"

"I was forgetting that you're throng this morning," he apologized. "I've had my fill, and I'm reet grateful to you."

"I'll take you down the old stairway," she said, moving towards the door at the end of the gallery. "This end of the house is not used nowadays, but when the third Granville Darracott started building he added so much that the earlier part became nothing more than a wing. Take care how you tread on these stairs! Much of the thimber is rotten."

He came down cautiously behind her, but paused on the half-landing to look about him, at damp-stained walls, dry wood, and crumbling plaster. "It'll take some brass to put this in order!" he remarked.

"Money? Oh, it would cost a fortune, if it could be done at all! I daresay no one would think it worth it, for none of the rooms are handsome, and most of the panelling is sadly worm-eaten. It has been going to rack for nearly a hundred years." She showed him one or two of the parlours bare save for lumber, and he shook his head, pursing his lips in a silent whistle. She smiled. "Does it throw you into gloom? The only time anyone gives it a thought is when the windows are all cleaned. We can get back to the main part of the house through this door, if you don't object to going past the kitchens and the scullery."

When they reached the main hall of the house again, their arrival coincided with that of Vincent and Richmond, who had just come in from the stables. Richmond was looking pleased, for although he had had to endure some stringent criticisms on his handling of the ribbons, his Corinthian cousin had said that at least he had good light hands. Vincent, wearing a blue Bird's Eye neckcloth, and a coat with shoulder-capes past counting, rarely looked pleased, and just now looked bored. He was bored. He was quite fond of Richmond, but teaching a stripling how to drive a team in style was a task he found wearisome. He had offered the lesson on impulse, because it had nettled him to see Richmond so much inclined to take Hugo's part against himself; and it annoyed him still more to know that he could be nettled by such a trivial matter. There was a pronounced crease between his brows as he set his hat down on a table, and began to draw off his gloves, and it deepened as he looked at Hugo and Anthea.

"How did you acquit yourself?" Anthea asked her brother. "Was your teacher odious or kind?"

"Oh, odious!" replied Richmond, laughing. "I'm a mere whipster, with no more precision of eye than a farm-hand, but at least I didn't overturn the phaeton!"

Vincent, whose penetrating glance little escaped, put up his glass and levelled it at the hem of Anthea's dress. "It seems unlikely," he said, "but one might almost be led to infer that you had been sweeping the carpets, dear Anthea, or even clearing ash out of the grates."

She looked down, and gave an exclamation of annoyance. "How vexatious! I thought I had taken such pains to hold my skirt up, too! No, we have not yet been reduced quite to that: I have been showing the East Wing to our cousin here, and the floors are filthy."

"The East Wing?" said Richmond. "What the devil for? There's nothing to be seen there!"

"Oh, Grandpapa desired me to take him to the picture-gallery, and when we had reached the end of it I thought it a good opportunity to show him the original part of the house. He certainly ought to see it, but I'm sorry I did take him there now, for I must change my dress again."

"You don't mean to say you dragged poor cousin Hugo all over the tumbledown barrack?"

"No, of course not. I let him see the parlours, that's all—and quite enough to bring on a fit of the dismals, wasn't it, cousin?"

"Well, it's melancholy to see the place falling into ruin," Hugo admitted. "Still, I'd like to go all over it one day."

"You had better not," Richmond advised him. "The last time I went to rummage amongst the lumber for something I wanted I nearly put my leg through a rotten floor-board in one of the attics. At all events, don't venture without me! I'll show you over, if you're set on it. Then, if you go through the floor, and break a limb, I can summon all the able-bodied men on the estate to come and carry you to your room!"

"It 'ud take a tidy few," agreed Hugo, grinning.

"Why this desire to inspect a ruin?" enquired Vincent. "Pride of prospective possession, or do you perhaps mean to restore it, in due course?"

"Nay, I don't know," Hugo said vaguely.

"Obviously you don't. The cost of restoring it—a singularly useless thing to do, by the by!—would very soon run you off your legs."

"Happen you're reet," said Hugo amicably. "I'm just by way of being interested in out first-ends. It's early days to be making plays."

"Just so!" said Vincent, with so much meaning in his voice that Richmond intervened quickly, asking Hugo if he had seen the Van Dyck.

"He means the portrait of the first Ralph Darracott," explained Vincent smoothly.

"An unnecessary piece of information, Vincent!" said Anthea.

89

"Ay, so it is," nodded Hugo. "Now, wait a piece, while I cast my mind back! Ay, I have it! That was the picture of the gentleman with the long curls. What's more," he added, with naïve pride in this feat of memory, "it's the one my cousin told me I must look at particularly. Van Dyck would be the man who painted it. I've heard of him before, think on."

Richmond hurried into speech. "I don't know much about pictures myself, or care for them, but I like Ralph I. He was a great gun! Most of our ancestors were either ramshackle fellows, or dead bores. Did Anthea tell you about the second Ralph? Not that she knows the half of it! If ever there was a loose fish——! A regular thatch-gallows!"

"Yes!" Anthea interrupted. "And isn't it *mortifying* to reflect on the number of Darracotts who look like him? *You* favour the first Ralph, and so did Oliver, a little; but Uncle Granville, and Papa, and Aunt Caroline, and Grandpapa himself are clearly descended from Ralph II, while as for Vincent——"

"——you have only to place a powdered wig on his head and no one would know them apart," supplied Vincent. "Thank you, my love! I must derive what consolation I may from the knowledge that at least I resemble *one* of my forebears!"

At this point a welcome interruption occurred. Claud, hearing voices in the hall, came out of one of the saloons, and, addressing himself to Hugo, said severely: "Been looking for you all over!"

"What's amiss?" Hugo asked.

"Just what I expected!" said Claud. "Didn't I tell you the odds were my grandfather would blame me if you was to vex him? Dash it if he hasn't told me he shall hold me responsible for you!"

"Ee, that's bad!" said Hugo, shaking his head. "If I were you, I'd make off back to London as fast as ever I could, lad."

Claud looked a little doubtful. "Well, I *could* do that," he admitted. "A least——No, it wouldn't fadge. Don't want my father to take a pet, and he would, because *he* don't want to offend the old man. There's another thing, too."

He paused, and it was evident from his darkling brow

90

that he was brooding over a serious affront. His brother, halfway up the stairs, stood looking down at him contemptuously. "Don't keep us in suspense!" he begged. "What inducement has been held out to you?"

"He didn't hold out any inducement. No inducement he could hold out. *I* haven't swallowed a spider! *I* don't haunt Pontius Pilate's doorstep! *I* don't have to hang on my grandfather's sleeve!" He perceived that Vincent had turned and was about to descend the stairs again, and temporized. "Well, what I mean is, I haven't yet! No saying when I *might* have to, of course!"

"Fighting shy, brother?" said Vincent.

"I'm not fighting at all," replied Claud frankly. "I don't say I wouldn't like to see someone plant you a facer because I would, but I don't care for boxing myself, never did! Besides, I'm not up to your weight."

"Remember that, and don't crow so loudly, little dunghill-cock!" said Vincent, resuming his progress upstairs.

"One of these days," said Claud, as soon as Vincent was out of earshot, "somebody will do Vincent a mischief!"

"Gammon!" retorted Richmond. "It was you who stirred the coals, not Vincent! Cutting at him like that!"

"Well, I've been vexed to death!" said Claud. "I don't mind it when my grandfather comes the ugly. I don't mind his cursing me. I don't mind it when he says I've got no brains. I don't mind his calling me a fribble, or a popinjay, or a Bartholomew baby. But when he tells me I look like a demi-beau—*a demi-beau!*——"

"Claud!" breathed Anthea, deeply shocked. "He did not say *that?*"

"Oh, yes, he did! To my face! Said he didn't want Hugh tricked out to look like me, too. Said I could mend Hugh's speech, but he wouldn't have me teaching him to look like a counter-coxcomb! That to *me!* He must be queer in his attic!"

"Depend upon it, that's it!" she said. "If I were you I wouldn't stay another day where you have been so insulted!"

"Well, I am going to stay!" replied Claud. "I'll make him eat it, dashed if I won't! *He* wants Hugo to model himself on Vincent. A nice cake Hugo would make of himself if he started aping the Corinthian set!"

"I would and-all," said Hugo, who was listening to this with his shoulders propped against the wall, his arms folded across his great chest, and an appreciative grin on his face.

"Of course you would! You can't wear a Bird's Eye Wipe, and fifteen capes, and a Bit-of-Blood hat unless you're a top-sawyer, and you ain't! Told us you weren't! What's more, you couldn't wear a coat like that one of Vincent's even if you were, because you're a dashed sight too big already. You'd have all the street-urchins clamouring to know where the Fair was going to be held. You put yourself in my hands! *I'll* turn you out in new trim—show you the proper mode—all in print—no finery, but up to the nines!"

Hugo shook his head. "Nay," he said mournfully, "you can't make a silk purse out of a sow's ear, lad."

"Dashed if I don't have a touch at it! Yes, and don't say *nay*, or call me *lad!*"

"Nay then!" expostulated Hugo, opening his innocent eyes wide.

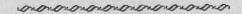

If the Major nursed a hope that his elegant cousin's determination to give him a new touch would not survive his wrath, he was soon obliged to abandon it. A crusading spirit had entered Claud's bosom, and before the day was out he had succeeded in cornering the Major, whom he found writing a letter in one of the smaller saloons. He had given much thought to a difficult problem, and he had decided that the first step must be a bolt to the village, where he would himself superintend the choice of hats, boots, gloves, knee-smalls, neckcloths, waistcoat, and shirts; and summon his own tailor to bring his pattern-card to his lodging in Duke Street. Gathering from this programme that a bolt to the village signified a visit to the Metropolis, the Major declined the threat. He was of the opinion that Lord Darracott would cup up extremely stiff if such a plan were even mooted.

"Thought of that too," countered Claud. "Say you have the toothache! I'll offer to drive to London with you, and take you to a good tooth-drawer. No need to tell the old gentleman I'm going to rig you out in style."

The Major said that he thought his lordship had too much know to be bamboozled; and Claud made the disheartening discovery that his pupil was as obstinate as he was amiable, and so woodheaded that although he listened to what was said to him he seemed to be incapable of taking it in. He agreed that to present a good appearance was of the first importance; when it was pointed out to him that the points of his shirt-collars were so moderate as to be positively dowdy he said he had been afraid that was so from the start; when told that Nugee or Stultz would turn him out in smarter style than Scott, he nodded; but whenever he had been worked up to the point (as Claud thought) of making the necessary alterations to his attire it became apparent that either he had not been attending, or had failed to grasp, the meaning of what had been said to him.

"Cast your ogles over me!" Claud adjured. "Don't want to boast, but I assure you this rig of mine is precise to a pin!"

"Ay, you're as fine as five pence," said Hugo, obediently looking him over.

"Well, I flatter myself this coat is an excellent hit. I don't say it would do for you, because you haven't the figure for it. Not but what you could wear a Cumberland corset, you know. Just to nip you in at the waist!"

"That 'ud be the thing," agreed Hugo.

"No need to broaden the shoulders, but a bit of wadding at the top of the sleeve would give 'em a modish peak."

"So it would!"

"The sleeves must be gathered at the shoulder, too."

"Ay, they'd have to be."

"And the tails made longer. Then, with a set of silver buttons—basket-work, I think; a natty waistcoat, and pantaloons of stockinette—*not* nankeen, or Angola—well, you see what I mean, coz?"

"I'd look champion."

"You look as neat as wax," said Claud. "Or trim as a trencher. *Not* champion!"

"I'd look as neat as wax," said Hugo tractably.

"Take my advice, and let Nugee make your coats! Vincent goes to Schweitzer and Davidson for his sporting toggery, and I rather fancy Weston made the coat he wore last night, but Nugee is the man for my money. Or Stultz. I'll tell you what! Have a coat from each of 'em!"

"Nay, I've enough coats already," said Hugo.

"Dash it, haven't I been telling you for ever that they won't do?" demanded Claud, in pardonable exasperation.

"Ay, you have, and I'm fairly nappered I didn't meet you before I let Scott take my measurements," said Hugo sadly.

A worse set-back was in store for the Pink of the Ton. When he pointed out to the Major that two cloak-bags and

94

a portmanteau could not, by any stretch of the imagination, provide adequate accomodation for the number of shirts any aspirant to fashion must carry with him, he was, in his own phrase, floored by his pupil's simple rejoinder that he had been informed that when staying in the country he might with perfect propriety make good the deficiencies of bucolic launderers with a Tommy.

"A Tommy?" gasped Claud, his eyes starting from their sockets. "A *false shirt-front?*"

"Ay, that's it," nodded Hugo. "Only in the country, of course!"

A shudder ran through Claud's frame. "No, no! Well, what I mean is——Dash it, coz!—*No!*"

Encountering only a blank stare from the Major, Claud was moved to order Richmond's man, Wellow, who was looking after Hugo, to render up to him any Tommies he might have found. Wellow naturally repeated this extraordinary command to his own master, with the result that when Richmond rode out with Anthea and Hugo next morning he warmly congratulated Hugo on having successfully bubbled Claud.

"Bubbled Claud? How did I do that?" asked Hugo.

"No, no, cousin, you won't bubble *me!* Telling him you meant to eke out your skirts with Tommies! The silly gudgeon bade Wellow hand 'em over to him. Wellow thought he must be touched, for of course you have none."

"There, now, I knew there was something I'd forgotten to pack!" said Hugo.

"Yes, and you have also forgotten that since Grooby unpacked your luggage, and Wellow is waiting on you, everyone in the house knows that the Major's linen is of the finest," remarked Anthea.

"Now, that I *am* glad to hear, because I took care to buy the best," confided Hugo.

She cast a somewhat amused glance at him, but said nothing. Riding on the other side of the big bay, Richmond said diffidently: "You don't mean to let Claud rig you out, do you?"

"Eh, but I'm sorely tempted!" said Hugo. "I'd look gradely! That is, I would if I wore some kind of a corset, and that's where the water sticks, for I'm one who likes to be comfortable."

"A corset?" exclaimed both his companions in chorus.

"To nip me in round the waist," he explained.

"Of all the impudence!" said Richmond. "You've a better figure than Claud!" He hesitated, and then said, with a slight stammer: "As a matter of fact—if you won't take it amiss!—my grandfather says you look more the gentleman then Claud does!"

The Major showed no signs of offence, but he did not seem to be much elated either. "Well, if he said our Claud looked like a counter-coxcomb that's not praising me to the skies," he observed.

"Praising one to the skies is not one of Grandpapa's weaknesses," said Anthea. "You look what you are, cousin: a soldier! I don't know how it is, but there is always a certain neatness that distinguishes them."

"That's due to Scott," he replied. "There wasn't much neatness about me, or any of us, barring poor Cadoux, in my Peninsular days. You'll hear people talk about our jack-a-dandy green uniforms, but, Lord, you should have seen 'em by the time we got to Madrid!"

That was quite enough for Richmond, who at once began to ply his cousin with questions about his campaigns. The Major replied to them in his goodnatured way, but either because he was not a loquacious person, or because he had been forbidden to encourage Richmond's interest in military matters, he was not as forthcoming as his young cousin had hoped he might be. Sometimes he was even a little disappointing, for when he was begged to describe the march to Talavera, or the battle of Salamanca, the only things he seemed to remember about the march were one or two ludicrous incidents in which he cut a comical but unheroic figure; and all he had to say about the battle was that the Light Bobs had had very little to do in it. Richmond, persevering, asked him if it had always been his ambition to become a soldier. His own romantic ardour glared in his eyes, but the Major's reply was again disappointing. "Nay, I never thought of it when I was a lad. All I ever wanted to do was to get under everyone's feet in the mill, or to run off up to the moors instead of minding my book."

"What made you join?" enquired Anthea. "Was it because your father had been a soldier, perhaps?"

"There wasn't much else I *could* do," he explained. "It was this road, you see: I never framed to be a scholar,

96

so it was no use thinking of the Church, or the Law; and as for tewing in the mill, my grandfather wouldn't hear of it, because I was a gentleman's son. So, as I'd no fancy for the navy, it had to be the army."

It was evident that this prosaic speech daunted Richmond. He said "Oh!" in a flattened tone, and relapsed for some time into silence.

He had accompanied the Major and his sister on their ride at Anthea's request. Lord Darracott had told her at the breakfast-table that she might usefully employ herself in making her cousin acquainted with the Darracott land: an attempt to throw them together so blatant that she could only be thankful that she had had the resolution to declare herself to the Major. More from a desire to be revenged on her grandfather than from reluctance to be tête-à-tête with Hugo, she had instantly invited Richmond to accompany her. In this she had been supported by Mrs. Darracott, whose notions of propriety, though constantly outraged by the careless Darracotts, were too nice to allow her to regard with complaisance the spectacle of her daughter's jauntering about the countryside with a strange man (be he never so much her cousin) for her only escort. Richmond, hoping to be regaled with stirring tales of war, had agreed willingly to go; and although the Major had disappointed him, he was too well-mannered a boy to make an excuse to leave the small party, or to betray that he thought talk about boundaries, enclosures, right-of-way, advowsons, leases, and crops a dead bore. He had never had much interest in such matters, and knew far less about them than his sister; so his contributions to the task of instructing the heir were largely confined to a description of the various forms of sport to be obtained in the neighbourhood.

The northern boundary to the estates being considerably nearer to the house than any other, they had set out in that direction. A nursery joke had had to be explained to Hugo. "And after that, which?" Richmond had asked his sister. "Kent or Sussex?"

"Kent," she had decided; and then, flashing a smile at Hugo: "We have a foot in each county, you know. Here, we are in Kent, and it was here that the first Darracott— well, the first that was ever in England!—settled. There's nothing left of the old Saxon manor, but it was certainly

on the site of the present house. Darracott tradition has
it that he was a person of consequence, but *we*—Richmond, and Vincent, and I—take leave to doubt that, because the original manor was quite small. That's why the
house lies so close to the northern boundary. It was much
later that the family crept over into Sussex. Today, that
part of Grandpapa's lands is the most important, because
of the rents, you know; but although Darracott Place has
been pulled down, and rebuilt, and enlarged a great many
times, no reigning Darracott has ever had the temerity to
remove the original site. *That* would be flying in the face
of tradition!—an unpardonable crime!"

So they had ridden towards the Weald, into more
wooded country, and then eastward, above the Rother
levels, for a little way, before dropping down again to the
Marsh, and crossing the Military Canal at Appledore. The
Marsh stretched before them, smiling and lush in the September sunshine, yet with a suggestion of eery loneliness
about it which made the Major exclaim, under his breath:
"Eh, it's a queer place!"

Just beyond Fairford, a cluster of alleys round a church,
they had reined in their horses, so that the few landmarks
could be more easily pointed out. Anthea had directed
Hugo's attention to the tower of Lydd Church, visible
some six miles to the south-east, but although he bestowed
a cursory glance on it his interest was claimed by the
expanse of reclaimed land that lay between Lydd and
Rye. Seen from the slight elevation on which Darracott
Place had been built, the Marsh had appeared to be quite
flat, with nothing but intersecting dykes, and, here and
there, a few willows and thornbushes to relieve its tame
monotony. His eye had been attracted by Rye, perched
so unexpectedly high above the Marsh, and reminding
him, in the distance, of the Point of Cassilhas, near Lisbon,
where there had been a military hospital (in which he had
languished for several painful weeks); and on the top of
just such another steep, isolated hill a convent had been
built. Now, standing on the edge of the Marsh, he perceived that it was not quite flat, but sloped slightly upwards towards the dunes that hid the sea from his sight.
A road meandered erratically across it, but there was no
traffic to be seen, and not so much as a shepherd's cot
afforded any sign of human habitation. There seemed to

be no living things on the Marsh but sheep, gulls, a moor-hen seeking safety in the rushes, and somewhere, sounding its unmistakable note, a peewit. The scene was peaceful, but it was not tame. As Anthea looked enquiringly at Hugo, he spoke the thought that came into his mind: "Do you meet flay-boggards, if you venture out when the light goes?"

"I don't *think* so," replied Anthea cautiously.

He glanced down at her, and laughed. "Where's our Claud to set me right? Hobgoblins is what I should have said! This is just where I'd look for them."

To Anthea and Richmond, born and bred on the edge of the Marsh, this was ridiculous. Richmond said: "Hobgoblins? You don't believe in them, do you, cousin?"

"Nay, I'm not so sure I don't since I've come into these parts," said Hugo, shaking his head. "I'll take care to turn my coat inside out, if ever I come here after nightfall, for fear of being pixie-led."

Richmond laughed; but Anthea said: "Does it seem to you an uncanny place? My Aunt Anne hated it: she used to say it was sullen land, full of evil sea-spirits, but she was very fanciful! It isn't uncanny—not a bit!—even though it was once at the bottom of the sea! Innings have been made all along this stretch of coast, you know, as far as Saxon times. People say it's unhealthy—aguish—and I own that those who live on the Marsh are peculiarly subject to fits of ague. That's why Darracott Place is almost the last of the great houses still remaining here: in general, the lords of the district removed to the uplands. Not the Darracotts, however! You may depend on that!"

"Unless *you* do so, Cousin Hugo?" interpolated Richmond. "My uncle Granville was used to say that he would leave Darracott Place, and live in one of the manors on the Sussex side. Northiamway."

"Yes! When he was at outs with Grandpapa!" retorted Anthea. "He would never have done it! Even had he really wished to abandon the Place, only think of the cost!" She smiled at Hugo, dancing lights in her eyes. "Did you fancy, cousin, that you had seen the worst of your family? I assure you, you have seen it at its best! When my uncle was alive, and he lived here, with all his family, brangles and brawls between him and my grandfather were the rule rather than the exception. He was inclined to be sickly, which Grandpapa took as an affront; and no matter what ailed him he always said that it was due to the horrid, marish situation of the house. You may imagine Grandpapa's wrath!"

"Well, what slum it was!" said Richmond scornfully. "Grandpapa knew he only got the notion out of an old book my aunt found, and was for ever quoting! It was enough to put anyone out of temper, for there wasn't a word of truth in it! Something about the Marsh being grievous in winter——"

"*Evil* in winter, grievous in *summer*, and never good," Anthea amended. "Also that Kent has three steps, Wealth without health—that's our part! Wealth *and* health—which is the Weald; and the third which *affordeth health only, and no Wealth.*"

"Which proves it was a fudge!" said Richmond. "*We* haven't wealth!"

"Ay, but there's wealth here right enough," said Hugo, his gaze roving over the scene before him. "The land's carrying more sheep to the acre than I ever saw. How many do you reckon on?"

"From six to twelve—but that's over Romney Marsh too," Anthea replied. "The farmers think it a bad year if the Marshes don't yield four thousand packs. I believe it's good wool, but I don't know much about it, because we don't keep sheep ourselves, of course. The pasturage and the arable lands are leased."

"I don't know much about it either," said Hugo, "but I've seen the fleeces in grease, in the market, and listened to a deal of talk. It's short-staple wool, isn't it? Carding wool, that is?"

"I haven't the least notion," replied Anthea frankly. "In fact, I don't know what carding wool is. Tell me!"

"Nay, I'd likely tell you wrong, for I was never very sure in my own mind between wools and worsteds. Long-staple makes the worsteds: combing wool, they call it. Lincoln and Leicestershire is where it mostly comes from. The Southdown is the best of the carding wools: it mills well. I know that much, but when it comes to qualities I'm at a stand. Pitlock's the first of the wools, and Fine of the worsteds, and Abb's pretty well the last of 'em both, but I'd be done up if you were to ask me what comes betwixt the first and the last. As for stapling, if I pored over the lot for a sennight as like as not I'd mistake Breech for Prime at the back-end of the week!"

She was interested, and would have questioned him further, but Richmond, attending with only half an ear, interrupted her to say: "Oh, never mind the sheep! I'll tell you what's to be had in abundance here besides those silly creatures, and that's hares! Only wait until January—from then until March is when they run strongest—and we'll show you some famous sport! There's excellent duck-shooting, too, if you care for it."

"Do you course your hares?" Hugo asked. "I've done a lot of that in the Peninsula."

"No, we hunt them with harriers. You'll soon see! The young hounds will be entered in a week or two. They hunt leverets at this season, of course: it teaches them their business, but the real sport is after Christmas. Do you know, an old Jack will give you almost as good a run as a fox? The doe doubles and turns shorter, but a Jack will very likely travel a four or even five mile point."

There was no more talk of wool or agriculture after that. As they rode gently along the track, Anthea let her mare drop behind a little, well-aware that once two gentlemen were fairly launched into sporting-talk neither would have a word to spare for a mere female. She occasionally rode to hounds herself, but she was by no means hunting-mad, and descriptions of great runs, of the wiles by which hares would baffle hounds, of the rival merits of the big Sussex-bred hound, and the fast, rough-coated harrier, very soon bored her. She preferred to follow the gentlemen at her leisure, and to occupy herself with her own thoughts.

These were largely concerned with her new cousin. She found him baffling. At first sight, he had appeared to her to be stupid: an overgrown gapeseed, slow of speech, and short of wit; either too wood-headed to understand the malicious shafts that had been aimed at him, or too meek to resent them. When she had first taken up the cudgels in his defence, she had yielded to the promptings, not of pity for a humble creature unable to defend himself, but of exasperation. High-spirited herself, and never afraid to answer a challenge, it had vexed her that Hugo should allow Vincent to make a butt of him. Her swift retort had been intended to furnish him with an example;

it had won no response from him: he had merely looked surprised; but just as she had decided that he was too blockish to be worth a thought, she had seen the twinkle in his eye, and had realized that however meek and yielding his disposition might be he was not lacking in intelligence. Her curiosity roused, she had been covertly studying him ever since. By the time she had conducted him through the picture-gallery she had revised her first opinion of his character, and given free room in her brain to the suspicion that her ox-like cousin had a strong (and possibly reprehensible) sense of humour. Final judgment was suspended, but of one thing there was no doubt: Major Darracott was as kind as he was goodtempered. As she rode behind him and Richmond, catching snatches of their talk, her heart warmed to him. In his place, Vincent, after a very short space of time, would have grown bored with the outpourings of a stripling; he would never have taken the trouble to draw Richmond out, as Hugo was doing. It would be no bad thing, Anthea thought, if Richmond were to transfer his allegiance from Vincent to Hugo. The Corinthian might prove dangerous to a worshipful young cousin; the Major, her instinct told her, could be trusted to do him no harm.

By the time she had arrived at this conclusion, the road that zig-zagged through the Marsh on its way to New Romney and Hythe had been reached. She called out laughingly: "Whoa there! How much farther do you mean to go in this direction, you wool-gatherers?"

They halted; and Hugo, turning Rufus about, walked him back a few paces to meet Anthea. He said, smilingly, as she came up to him: "We've been chewing the bacon so hard we forgot you! I'm sorry!"

His simplicity pleased her; she smiled back at him, saying: "Odious creatures! Do you wish to go on, or shall we turn back?"

"I'll do as you bid me," he replied. "Richmond has been telling me about his boat. He wants to show her to me, but he may do that another day."

"No, why?" said Richmond. "I've got her beached only a mile from here. We have plenty of time to take a look at her."

"Perhaps your sister's tired," suggested Hugo.

"Not she! Come along, Anthea!"

"Very well, but you'll swear a solemn oath that you will *only* take a look! *I* know you!"

"Nonsense! I'll just make sure all's snug. We shan't be late for dinner, if that's what's in your mind. Now, coz, over the ditch and into Sussex!"

He led the way at a brisk canter. The pastures were poor near the coast, with furze bushes growing out of the sand, and the grass giving place to marrams. The dunes were soon reached; the horses scrambled up, the sand sliding away under their hooves; and the sea (as it seemed to Hugo) burst suddenly into view.

Big Rufus, checking at the top of the path between two towering dunes, snorted, and put his ears forward. "Nay then!" the Major admonished him reproachfully. "Pluck up, lad! Tha's seen the sea afore, think on!"

Anthea, already awaiting him on the shore, said, as the bay came slithering down the steep slope: "Ah, York-shirebred, I collect?"

He met her quizzical look with one of his most guileless stares. "Nay, it's this road," he explained confidentially. "He was nobbut a young 'un when I came by him, and a smattering of Spanish was all he knew. He learned his English from John Joseph, sithee!"

"I must make John Joseph's acquaintance," she said. "How useful he must be to you!"

He eyed her speculatively. "Ay, he is and-all!"

"I daresay he has been with you for a great many years?"

"Since I was a lad," he corroborated.

"I thought as much. You'd be at a loss without him, wouldn't you, cousin?"

There was a dancing mockery in her eyes, a lurking smile in his. Before he could reply, Richmond, who had been listening impatiently to this passage, said: "This is the place I told you about, Cousin Hugo. Look, you may see the stakes holding the nets quite plainly! The season's drawing to a close now, but at its height, when they pull in the Keddle nets, the whole of the foreshore is covered with mackerel. But don't let's stand dawdling here! The Gap where I've got the *Seamew* beached is a little way along, towards Camber."

"Lead on, then!" said Hugo. "It seems to me an unhandy place, though. How do you get to your boat?"

103

"I ride, of course: it's a mile closer than Rye, you know."

"What happens to your horse while you're at sea?" asked Hugo, slightly mystified.

"Oh, I stable him in Camber! There's an inn," said Richmond briefly. "As a matter of fact, it's handier for me to run the *Seamew* into Mackerel Gap during the summer, when I might want to take her out any day, because Jem Hordle lives at Camber. He's my crew! When I have her moored in Rye harbour, someone must take a message to Jem before I can set sail: she's too big for one man to sail."

He had turned his head, to answer Hugo over his shoulder, but Anthea, looking ahead, said suddenly: "Good God, here comes that tiresome Preventive officer! I never knew anyone so ubiquitous! What on earth is he doing here, I wonder?"

"The Lord only knows!" replied Richmond, watching the approach of the Customs' Riding-officer with disfavour.

"Well, for heaven's sake be civil to the poor man!" she begged. "The last time I encountered him was when I was with Grandpapa, and he was so ill-advised as to accost us. He got so badly snubbed that I'm persuaded he thinks now that we are all of us in league with the free-traders."

"I wish I had been there!" Richmond said, grinning.

"I would have yielded my place to you with pleasure. Grandpapa is never more embarrassing than when he becomes high in the instep.—Good-day to you, Mr. Ottershaw!"

The Riding-officer, a rather tight-lipped young man, with eyes of a hard, shallow grey, pulled his horse up, and raised his hand in a stiff salute. "Good-day, ma'am."

"Whither away, Lieutenant?" enquired Richmond. "Not looking for tubs amongst the sandhills, are you? *I've* never come upon any there!"

The Lieutenant replied in a flat tone that matched his rigid back and unsmiling countenance: "No, sir. I am riding to Lydd. I see you have your boat beached in Mackerel Gap."

"Yes, I'm taking my cousin down to see her. Lieutenant Ottershaw—Major Darracott, of the 95th!"

"Sir!" said the Lieutenant, bringing his hand up again to the salute.

Hugo touched his hat in acknowledgment, and said, with a smile: "Land-guard?" The Lieutenant bowed slightly. "I'm told that's no sinecure on this coast."

"No, sir," said the Lieutenant, with a good deal of emphasis. "But we may see a change presently!"

"Yes, you've established a famous blockade, haven't you?" remarked Richmond. "What with Customs' cruisers, and Revenue cutters you should have the Channel swept clear before the year's out."

"The task of stamping out the illicit trade, sir, would be rendered easier if the rascals who engage in it met with less sympathy from those who live in these counties."

"And if the duties were less extortionate there would be no trade to be stamped out!" retorted Richmond. "It's all the fault of the Government—and a pretty set of leatherheads they are! The remedy is under their noses, but instead of cutting the duties they squander fortunes on Preventive measures!"

"Nay, that's no answer," interposed Hugo. "The law may be daft, but it has to be obeyed." He looked at Ottershaw, and said pleasantly: "I'm from the West Riding myself. They used to say there was plenty of smuggling went on at the ports, but I never knew much about it."

"If it were only the ports!" said Ottershaw bitterly.

"Ay, you've a job on here, with the French coast so near. I wouldn't want it—with the countryside hostile. I know what *that* means."

"Why, were the Spaniards hostile?" asked Richmond. "I thought——"

"They weren't hostile to us, but to the French they were." He nodded at the Riding-officer. "What you need is a Division here, and I doubt if that would answer either. Myself, I'd say it was a job for the navy."

"The Admiralty, sir, is now in control of the coast blockade, and the force patrolling the Channel is under the command of a very able and zealous officer. I am happy to say that running the blockade is becoming every night a more dangerous enterprise."

"Lord, yes!" said Richmond. "It's getting to be dangerous to put out to sea at all! I was overhauled myself last week by one of the sloops. What the commander
105

thought I was doing, God knows! For two pins, I daresay, he'd have fired a shot across my bows. He wanted to know who I was, where I came from, where I was bound for, why I didn't heave-to at once—which I thought I had done, but it turned out that I hadn't obeyed his signal. The only wonder is I wasn't put in irons."

"A strict watch is being kept on all vessels, sir, and it is the duty of those engaged on the coastal guard to pay particular heed to any vessel that appears to be behaving suspiciously. Failing to obey a naval signal would naturally give rise to grave suspicion—though in your case, as I collect the officer soon realized, this was groundless."

Having uttered this severe speech, the Lieutenant took his leave, punctiliously saluting, and then riding off without a word or a smile.

"Did you ever see such a pompous whipstraw?" said Richmond scornfully.

The Major looked meditatively at him. "Happen he's nattered," he drawled. "Seemingly, he doesn't like you, lad."

"I don't think he likes any of us," said Anthea. "That's Grandpapa's fault! He was odiously haughty to the poor man—and you may depend upon it that the Preventives have a pretty shrewd notion that all the brandy we have at the Place is run."

"It is, is it?" said Hugo. "That would account for it, then."

8

There was not very much time left for as minute an in-
spection of Richmond's boat as its owner would have liked.
He would certainly have made the whole party late for
dinner had he found a kindred spirit in Hugo; but Hugo,
although he uttered suitable comments when the vessel's
various perfections were pointed out to him, knew little
about boats or sailing, and was quite ready to leave the
shore as soon as Anthea grew impatient. Richmond was
again disappointed. It would have been unreasonable to
have expected a man brought up in an inland town to be
as knowledgeable as he was himself, but he detected a
lack of enthusiasm in his cousin which was hard to understand, until Hugo disclosed that whenever he went to
sea he was sick. Richmond, like most excellent sailors,
was much inclined to think seasickness largely imagina-
tive: no one need be ill who did not think he would be.
He responded with a sympathy as spurious as Hugo's
admiration of the *Seamew*'s lines, and tried not to think
the worse of him.

Hugo was not deceived. When he set off for home with
Anthea, Richmond having left them to visit his boatman
in Camber, he shook his head, saying sadly: "I've sunk
myself beneath reproach."

Anthea laughed. "Yes, but you may easily make a recover, you know! You have only to unbutton a trifle, and
tell him about your adventures in the Peninsula, to win
his worship."

"Nay, I'm no figure for worship!"

"You are a soldier, however, and he's army-mad. Do
you dislike talking about your campaigns? I wished you

would have told us more, but it seemed as if you didn't care to."

"I'll tell him anything he wants to know, but it wouldn't be the right thing for me to do, when your mother and his lordship don't wish it."

"I wondered if that was why you said so little. Grandpapa you need not heed; and Mama—well, I think you shouldn't heed her either! Poor love, she would be quite dismayed if Richmond should succeed in winning Grandpapa over, but she would soon become reconciled, I promise you. She has the happiest disposition! For myself, I believe nothing else will do for Richmond. I wish it were not so, but we have *none* of us the right to push him into some occupation he doesn't care for! You said that yourself, cousin!"

"Ay, so I did, but that's just my opinion. If his lordship asked me for it, I'd give it to him, but he won't, and I've no business to encourage Richmond to go against him, nor to offer advice that's not wanted." He smiled ruefully, and added: "It's bad enough for him to have me foisted on to him without my meddling in what's no concern of mine! A fine trimming he would give me, if I was to be so presumptuous, and small blame to him! From what I can see, Vincent is the only one he might listen to. If the lad wants someone to help him, why doesn't he ask Vincent? Seemingly Vincent's fond of him, so it's likely he'd be willing to try what he could do."

"Nothing is more *un*likely!" replied Anthea. "Vincent, my dear Hugo, is fond of no one but himself. As for thinking that he would run the risk of offending Grandpapa, merely to oblige Richmond, he would stare at such a notion!"

He offered no comment on this, but said, after a short pause: "It queers me to know why Richmond's so set on the army. I should have thought he'd be mad for the navy, with his liking for sailing."

"Yes, so should I," she agreed. "But it has always been the army with him, and if you ask him why he doesn't wish to become a sailor he says that it's a nonsensical question, and that being partial to sailing is not at all the same as wishing to embrace the navy as a profession."

"Happen he's right. Though to hear him talk about that boat of his——What did he call it? a yawl?"

108

"Yes, or a yacht, though she's too big for a yacht, I think."

"What did he want with a boat that size?" asked Hugo curiously. "I should have thought a little one he could handle himself would have been more to his taste."

"I daresay it would, in some ways, but it wouldn't have been to Grandpapa's taste," she explained. "And I must do him the justice to own that if he gave Richmond a yacht at all he was right to give him one he couldn't handle alone! I don't mean he doesn't know how, but you can never tell when he will take it into his head to run some foolish risk. You see, he *enjoys* doing dangerous things. You can't think what agonies of apprehension we have had to suffer!"

"Ay, no doubt he'd be prime for any lark, and the more risk the better. It would be well if he were put into harness."

"Yes," she agreed. "Yet sometimes I wonder—you see, he has never been in harness, as you call it. Papa died when he was very young, and Grandpapa has always indulged him so much that there has never been anyone to say him nay. He had two tutors, but only the first of them tried to make him obedient. His reign was consequently short, and his successor, speedily perceiving how things were, prudently acquiesced in all Grandpapa's ideas. It was a fortunate circumstance that Richmond liked him well enough not to wish for another in his place, so he was never so naughty with him as he had been with Mr. Crewe. I'm afraid he didn't learn very much, however!"

"Well, I was never bookish myself," Hugo said. "It's a pity the lad wasn't bridled when he was a little chap, but there's no need that I can see for you to be much worried. His lordship may indulge him, but he snaps out his orders to him just as he does to everyone else. I'd say myself that the lad is remarkably docile: there's many that would kick in his shoes."

"Richmond never argues with Grandpapa. He—yes, I suppose he *is* docile. He always does what Grandpapa wishes, and it is perfectly true, what Mama says: that he is sweet-tempered, never gets into a miff, or the sulks! Only—you may *think* he has yielded, but all the time, I believe, he means to have his own way, and, in general, he gets it!"

109

"Then maybe he'll get his way, over this business of a pair of colours," said Hugo, in a comfortably matter-of-fact voice.

She shook her head. "Not over that. He told me so himself. He said that there was nothing he could do or say to make Grandpapa change his mind. I wish——" She stopped, surprised and a little vexed to find herself talking so unguardedly to one who was a stranger. "But I must not run on! If we don't make haste, cousin, we shall have a peal rung over us for being late for dinner!"

She urged her mare into a canter, and the Major followed suit, saying, however: "Ay, so we shall. What's more, there's no knowing but what I might repeat what you say to me."

She blushed vividly. "Oh——! No, I'm persuaded you would not!"

"You can't tell that. If I was to have a fit of gabbing——"

"I should be much astonished!" she retorted. "You are not precisely *garrulous*, you know!"

"The thing is that I have to mind my tongue," he explained. "It's what you might call a handicap to conversation."

"Ah, to be sure! How stupid of me! But you have been minding it so well that I must be forgiven for not remembering how hard it is for you to speak the King's English!"

"Ay!" he said, with simple pride. "I have and-all, haven't I? I was taking pains, you see."

They had reached one of the gates that led into the park, and she waited for him to open it for her, eyeing him with a little speculation and a good deal of amusement. "Just as you did when you first arrived! You managed beautifully, and for such a long time, too! You deserve the greatest credit, for, I assure you, no one would have guessed you came from Yorkshire until we were halfway through dinner, when you suffered a sudden relapse—and grew rapidly worse."

He heaved a dejected sigh. "Came all-a-bits, didn't I? It's that road with me when I'm scared."

"But you contrived to conceal *that* from us," said Anthea encouragingly. "You didn't look to be in the least scared."

110

"You don't know how I looked: you never lifted your eyes from your plate!" he retorted.

"Nevertheless I was very well able to see how you looked," she said firmly. "I must tell you that you don't look scared *now*, though I realize, of course, that you must be. You haven't caught sight of a—a flay-boggard, have you?"

"It's not that," he said. "I'm thinking what a hirdum-durdum there'll be if the old gentleman is kept waiting for his dinner. It has me in fair sweat, so just you leave quizzing me, lass, and come through this gate!"

She obeyed, but said: "*What* did you call me?"

"It slipped out!" he said hastily. He shut the gate, and added, with all the air of one extricating himself neatly from a difficult situation: "We always call a cousin lass in Yorkshire—if she's a female. Of course, it would be lad, if I was talking to Richmond."

"That," said Anthea, with severity, "is a shocking bouncer, sir!"

"You're reet: it is!" he said, stricken.

She could not help laughing, but she said, as they fell into a canter again: "Instead of trying to bamboozle me, cousin, you had better consider how to get out of the fix you're in. You cannot talk broad Yorkshire for ever!"

"Nay, it wouldn't be seemly," he agreed. "I'll have to get shut of it, won't I?"

"Exactly so!"

"Happen our Claud will bring the thing off!" he said hopefully.

Since her feelings threatened to overcome her, it was perhaps fortunate that a peremptory hail at that moment interrupted them. Lord Darracott, accompanied by Vincent, was also riding home through the park. He came at a brisk trot, as erect in the saddle as his grandson, and demanded to be told where Anthea and Hugo had been. His manner would not have led the uninitiated to suppose that his humour was benign, but Anthea saw at once that he was pleased; and whatever timidity assailed Hugo at having questions barked at him he seemed well able to conceal. Not all of his answers were satisfactory, since he knew very little about the subjects that were of paramount importance to landowners; but although his ignorance

111

made Lord Darracott impatient, and he asked several questions which were naïve enough to exasperate his irascible progenitor, his lordship was not wholly dissatisfied. Indeed, it was generally felt, when he later announced that something might yet be made of Hugh, that he had begun to look upon his heir with an almost approving eye.

Escaping from his rigorous grandparent, the Major went upstairs to change his dress. Sounds of altercation assailed his ears as he approached his bedchamber, and when he reached it, and stood in the open doorway, he found that it had suffered an invasion.

Two gentlemen of the same calling, but of different cut, were confronting one another in a manner strongly suggestive of tomcats about to join battle. Each wore the habit of a private servant; but whereas the elder of the two, a middle-aged man of stocky build and rigid countenance, was meticulous in his avoidance of any ornament or touch of colour to relieve the sobriety of his raiment, the younger not only sported a pin in his neckcloth, but added an even more daring note to his appearance by wearing a striped waist-coat which only the most indulgent of masters would have tolerated. As the Major paused, in some astonishment, on the threshold, he said, in mincing accents: "Vastly obliging of you, Mr. Crimplesham, I am sure! Quite a condescension indeed!"

"Do not name it, Mr. Polyphant!" begged Crimplesham. "We are all put on this earth to help one another, and knowing as I do what a labour it is to you to get a gloss on to a pair of boots—something that *passes* for a gloss, I should say—it quite went to my heart to think of you wearing yourself out over a task that wouldn't take up more than a couple of minutes of *my* time. It is just a knack, Mr. Polyphant, which some of us have and others don't."

"And very right you were to cultivate it, Mr. Crimplesham! I vow and declare I would have done the same if I'd had only the one talent!" said Polyphant. "For, as I have often and often remarked, an over-polished boot may present a flash appearance, but it *does* draw the eye away from badly got-up linen!"

"As to that, Mr. Polyphant, I'm sure I can't say, but *nothing*, I do promise you, will distract the attention from a spot of iron-mould on a neckcloth!"

"I will have you know, Mr. Crimplesham," said Polyphant, trembling violently, "that it was a spot of soup!"

"Well, Mr. Polyphant, you should know best, and whatever it was no one feels for your mortification more than I do, for, as I said to Mr. Chollacombe, when the matter was being talked of in the Room, if *I* had been so careless as to let Mr. Vincent Darracott go down to dinner wearing a neckcloth that wasn't perfectly fresh I could never have held up my head again."

"When Mr. Claud Darracott left my hands, Mr. Crimplesham, that neckcloth was spotless!" declared Polyphant, pale with fury. "If Mr. Chollacombe says other, which I do not credit, being as only a perjured snake would utter those lying words——"

"What the devil are you doing in my quarters?" demanded the Major, bringing the altercation to an abrupt end.

This deep-voiced interruption was productive of a sudden transformation. The disputants turned quickly towards the door, guilt and dismay in their countenances, but only for an instant was the Major permitted a glimpse of these, or any other, emotions. Before he had advanced one step into the room, all trace of human passion had vanished, and he was confronted by two very correct gentlemen's gentlemen, who received him with calm and dignity, and, after bowing in a manner that paid deference to his quality without diminishing their own consequence, deftly relieved him of his hat, his whip, and his gloves.

"If you will permit me, sir!" said Crimplesham, nipping the hat from the Major's hand. "Having been informed that you have not brought your man with you, I ventured, sir, to give your boots a touch, young Wellow, though a painstaking lad, being but a rustic, and quite ignorant of the requirements of military gentlemen."

"If you will permit *me*, sir!" said Polyphant, possessing himself of the whip and the gloves. "You will pardon the intrusion, sir, I trust, being as my master, Mr. Claud Darracott, desired me to offer my services to you."

"I'm much obliged to you both, but I don't need either of you," said the Major, pleasantly, but in a tone that was unmistakeably dismissive.

113

There was nothing for his would-be attendants to do but to bow in acceptance of his decree, and leave the room. Crimplesham held the door, and made a polite gesture to his rival to precede him. Before he had time to consider what devilish stratagem might lie beneath the courtesy from one whose position in the hierarchy of the servants' hall was superior to his own, Polyphant had tripped out of the room, bestowing on Crimplesham, as he passed him, a gracious bow, and a smile of such condescension as was calculated to arouse the bitterest passions in his breast.

But herein he showed himself to be of lesser calibre than Crimplesham, who returned his smile with one of quiet triumph, and gently closed the door on his heels.

"Shall I pull off your boots before I go, sir?" he asked, coming back into the centre of the room, and drawing forward a chair for the Major to sit in. "Wellow, I fancy, is laying out Mr. Richmond's evening-dress, and you would hardly wish to make use of the jack."

The Major, having, indeed, no desire to use the jack, submitted, wondering, as he watched Crimplesham take a pair of gloves from his pocket and put them on, what was at the back of this very superior valet's determination to wait on him.

Two circumstances had in fact combined to overcome Crimplesham's regard for his own dignity: he had a score to pay off, and a nephew to establish suitably. Of these, the first operated the more powerfully upon him, but it was only the second which he disclosed to the Major. Whatever might be the differences between himself and his master, no living soul would ever learn from his lips that the smallest disharmony marred their relationship. To complain, as less lofty valets might, that his employer was exacting, impatient, often impossible to please, and always inconsiderate, would serve only to lower his own consequence. The truth was that he was frequently at silent loggerheads with Vincent, who neither tried nor wished to endear himself to his servants. When a suitable opportunity offered, Crimplesham had every intention of changing masters; but this was not a step to be taken lightly. Vacancies in the ranks of those who ministered to the leaders of high fashion occurred infrequently, and nothing could more fatally damage a valet's reputation

114

than to leave the service of a noted Corinthian for that of a kinder but less worthy master. Vincent was as thankless as he was exacting, but he did Crimplesham great credit, and through him Crimplesham was steadily acquiring the renown he craved. He had not yet attained the ultimate peak, when (he allowed himself to hope) aspirants to fashion would employ every sort of wile to lure him away from his master; but he was already well-known for his unequalled skill with a boot. The fantasies Vincent performed on his neckcloths sprang from his own genius, but the high gloss on his Hessians that excited the envy of his acquaintance he owed to Crimplesham, and not willingly would he part with him. Crimplesham was perfectly well-aware of that, so when any serious affront was offered him he was able to punish Vincent without fear of dismissal. He was not in Vincent's confidence, but he had no doubt at all that it would very much annoy him to learn that his cousin's footwear had received treatment at the hands of his own expert.

"A beautiful pair, sir," he said, tenderly setting them down. "Hoby, of course, as anyone that *knows* a boot can see at a glance. It quite goes to one's heart to see them mishandled. Not that Wellow doesn't do his best, according to his lights, but I fear he will never rise above Bayly's Blacking."

"What do you use?" enquired Hugo. "Champagne? Above my touch!"

"I have a recipe of my own, sir," replied Crimplesham, putting him in his place. "The care of a gentleman's boots is quite an Art, as I don't doubt you are aware." He picked up one of the stretchers and inserted it carefully into the boot. "You are, if I may be permitted to say it, sir, particular as to your boots. It occurs to me—but possibly you have made your arrangements already!"

For a surprised moment Hugo wondered whether Crimplesham was about to offer him his services, but in this he showed his ignorance of the world of ton: had he been the heir to a dukedom Crimplesham would not for an instant have contemplated an engagement so prejudicial to his career. Nothing that even the great Robinson, who had been Mr. Brummell's valet, could do would avail to turn a man of the Major's size and powerful build into a Tulip of Fashion.

"If you haven't yet engaged a valet, sir, I venture to think that I might be able to put my hand on just such a one as might suit you," Crimplesham said. "A nephew of my own, sir, whose name occurs to me because he has previously been employed by a military gentleman like yourself. A conscientious young man, sir, and one for whom I can vouch. Should you desire to interview him I should be happy to arrange it—without, of course, wishing to put myself forward unbecomingly."

"I'll think about it," promised Hugo, adding, as a discreet knock sounded on the door: "Yes, come in!"

The door opened to admit Polyphant, profuse in apologies for intruding upon the Major, but imperfectly concealing the jubilation that filled his soul. Mr. Vincent had rung his bell three times, he explained, with spurious concern, and was now demanding to have Crimplesham sent instantly to his room. "So I ventured to inform him of it, sir, feeling sure you would pardon me. *Very* put-out, Mr. Vincent is, though, of course, I explained to him that Crimplesham was assisting *you* with your toilet, sir!"

"Well, you'd better make haste and go to him," Hugo advised Crimplesham. "You can tell him I kept you."

"It will not be necessary sir," replied Crimplesham calmly. He rose unhurriedly from his knees, and carried the top-boots over to the wall, setting them down very precisely. "You need not wait, Polyphant," he said, to that gentleman's speechless fury. "Since you have been so kind as to bring me Mr. Vincent's message, perhaps you will inform him that I shall be with him directly." He met Polyphant's goggling stare with a faint, bland smile before nodding dismissal to him, and turning away.

It was almost more than flesh and blood could bear. A severe struggle took place in Polyphant's breast before his more primitive self yielded to the dictates of propriety, and he withdrew again from the room.

Crimplesham then satisfied himself that the Major's evening attire was correctly laid out for him, begged him to give his shoes a final rub with a handkerchief, to remove any possible fingermarks, and bowed himself out in good order.

This episode had seen more than one repercussion, for not only did it make Vincent late for dinner, which all concerned in it had foreseen, but it very much vexed

Claud, and decided Hugo to lose no more time in engaging a valet of his own.

Claud, learning from Polyphant that Crimplesham's services had been preferred, was deeply mortified, and took a pet, for which, as he was all too ready to explain, there was every justification. He had taken on himself the onerous task of giving his cousin a new touch; he had devoted the whole of one afternoon to the problem of how best to achieve a respectable result when confronted by a subject who refused to purchase a new coat; and when, having reached the decision that a more modish style in neckcloths would make a vast improvement to Hugo's appearance, he had gone his length, giving up several of his own neckcloths for Hugo's use, and changing his dress for dinner hours too early, so that Polyphant might be free to instruct Hugo in the art of arranging these, his only reward had been to have his self-sacrificing flung in his face.

"Nay, I never did that!" protested Hugo.

"Flung in my face!" repeated Claud. "I dashed well exhausted myself trying to think how to do the trick. Yes, and I was ready to go through stitch with it, even when I realized I should have to lend you some of my own neckcloths, because yours are all too paltry! I made Polyphant take three of my new muslin ones, so that he could turn you out in a Mathematical tie, for it can't be done with a cloth less than two foot wide, and I know dashed well you've nothing except what serves for that miserable Osbaldeston which you keep on wearing! And even so," he added, somewhat inconsequently, but with immense bitterness, "it couldn't have been anything but a shabby affair, because your shirt-points ain't high enough."

"Happen it's all for the best!" suggested Hugo.

"I'll be damned if it is! And don't say happen when you mean perhaps! Best, indeed! When you've put Polyphant into the hips, sending him off and letting that impudent fellow of Vincent's wait on you!"

That made the Major laugh. "Nay, that's doing it much too brown! You're not going to tell me that that niminy-piminy fribble was pining to waste his talents on me!"

"I should rather think not!" retorted Claud. "Why, it took me the better part of an hour to coax him into it! And

117

the chances are I shouldn't have done it then if I hadn't hit on the idea of telling him it didn't signify, because not even he could make you look elegant! Naturally that put him on his mettle. Well, he saw what a triumph it would be! I'm not surprised he's got a fit of the blue-devils, but I'll tell you this, coz!—I resent it! *You* may think it a chuck-farthing matter, but that's just what it ain't! When Polyphant gets moped there's no saying what he may do. Why, the last time he fell into a fit of dejection he handed me a Joliffe Shallow to wear in the Park! I've a dashed good mind to wash my hands of you!"

"Perhaps you should," agreed Hugo sympathetically. "It's plain I'm a hopeless case. You know, I warned you you couldn't make a silk purse out of a sow's ear."

But a gleam had come into Claud's lack-lustre eye. His frown lifted; he ejaculated: "By Jupiter, I will, though! Well, what I mean is, it *can* be done! Just proved it!"

"Who has?" asked Hugo, all at sea.

"You have! You said *perhaps!* Said it to the manner born, what's more! In the very nick of time, because I don't mind telling you I'd lost heart. Well, if it don't all go to *show!*"

"Ee, I was always a great gowk!" said Hugo, suffering another bad relapse.

When Vincent entered the saloon it was ten minutes past six, and he was greeted, inevitably, by a demand from his grandfather to know what the devil had been keeping him. There was a deep cleft between his brows, but he replied languidly: "Accept my apologies, sir! I regret infinitely that I have been obliged to keep you waiting, but I cannot—I really *cannot!*—be expected to scramble into my clothes, under any circumstances whatsoever. Certainly not to suit my cousin's convenience, which, I must own, is not an object with me."

"I don't know what the devil you're talking about!" said his lordship irritably. "I'll thank you to——"

"Nay, but I do," intervened Hugo guiltily. "I'm reet sorry, lad!"

"Not *reet*, and not *lad!*" begged Claud.

"You have your uses, brother," observed Vincent.

"Now, that will do!" said Matthew sharply. "Let us have one evening free from bickering between you two!"

118

"You are mistaken, sir: I am profoundly grateful to Claud."

"Profoundly ill-tempered!" said Matthew.

"It's my blame," said Hugo remorsefully. "You can't wonder at his being kickish, for he's been ringing and ringing for his man, and all the time the silly fellow was letting me keep him by me to pull off my boots."

"What, the great Crimplesham?" cried Richmond incredulously. "No! What the deuce can have possessed him?"

"Overweening conceit, I imagine: a desire to impress me with his skill in creating something out of nothing." Vincent's hard, insolent eyes flickered over Hugo's person. "*Vaulting ambition...*!"

"You are offensive, Vincent," said Anthea, in a low voice, and with a look of contempt. "If you had as much elegance of mind as of person——!"

"Impossible, dearest cousin!" he retorted.

"It is a severe mortification to reflect how often I am put to the blush by your want of conduct, Vincent," said Lady Aurelia, in a tone of dispassionate censure.

"You are too unkind, Mama! My dear Hugh, pray make the fullest use of Crimplesham! Your need, after all, is greater than mine. How could I be so selfish as to grudge him to you?"

"Nay, I don't know," drawled Hugo amiably.

Lord Darracott put a summary end to the discussion, as Chollacombe came into the room to announce dinner. "I've had enough of this damned folly!" he said. "One of you—you, Richmond!—may write to Lissett for me by tomorrow's post, and tell him to send down a valet for your cousin. Let me hear no more about it!"

"I'm much obliged to you," said Hugh mildly, "but there is no need for our Richmond to trouble himself."

Lord Darracott paused on his way to the door to glare at him. "I say you are to have a valet, and a valet you will have!"

"Oh, I'll do that, sir!" replied Hugo. "It's just that I've a fancy to engage one for myself."

"You should have done so before you came here!"

"I should, of course," Hugo agreed.

"You're a fool." snapped his lordship. "Where do you

119

imagine you will find one here?"

"Well, I think I'll give Crimplesham's nephew a trial," said Hugo. "That is, if my cousin Vincent's got no objection."

"It is a matter of indifference to me," shrugged Vincent.

It was not, however, a matter of indifference to Claud. Waiting only until his grandfather had walked out of the room behind the ladies of the party, he said indignantly: "Well, if that's not the outside of enough! *Crimplesham's nephew!*"

"Why, what's wrong with him?" enquired Hugo.

"Everything's wrong with him! For one thing, we don't know anything about the fellow, and for another thing, Polyphant won't like it. Yes, and now I come to think of it I'm dashed if *I* like it! Here am I, fagging myself to death with thinking how to bring you up to the knocker, lending you some of my best neckcloths, let alone Polyphant to put you in the way of arranging them, and first you set Polyphant's back up by sending him off, and allowing Crimplesham to help you to dress, and now you've settled to hire a valet without a word to me! Dashed well tipping me a rise!"

"No, no, I never settled it until a minute ago!" protested Hugo. "Now, don't flusk at me! I'm engaging in no flights with you, or anyone, if I can avoid it. Come in to dinner before the old gentleman starts putting himself in a passion!"

They entered the dining-room in time to forestall this disaster. My lord, just about to take his seat at the head of the table, had indeed turned his frowning eyes towards the door, but he made no comment. To Mrs. Darracott's relief, he seemed to be in one of his more mellow moods, which was surprising, since he had undergone the unusual experience of having his will crossed. She had quaked for Hugo, knowing how intolerant of opposition my lord was; she had even shaken her head warningly at him, but the poor young man had not grasped the meaning of her signal, merely smiling at her in a childlike way that showed how far he was from appreciating the perils of his situation. It was a thousand pities, she thought, that he should be so very slow-witted, and so prone to allow his origins to show themselves in his speech, for in all other respects he seemed to be an excellent person. Mrs. Dar-

120

racott, in fact, was developing a marked kindness for the hapless heir. Her mettlesome daughter might say what she chose in condemnation of what she called his want of spirit, but for her part Mrs. Darracott had no fault to find with an amiable temper and a docile disposition. In her view there were already far too many persons at Darracott Place endowed with spirit. No good had ever yet come from thwarting the head of the house, she thought, remembering with an inward shudder the devastating battles that had been fought when Granville and Rupert had been alive. Nor would any good that she could perceive come from Hugo's joining issue with Vincent. In wit, he was no match for Vincent; and if it came to blows (as she had the liveliest apprehension that it would) the resulting situation, whichever of them won the encounter, would be such as she preferred not to contemplate.

It was surprising that my lord had allowed Hugo to countermand his order to Richmond, for although the matter might have been thought too trivial for argument, his autocracy was becoming every day more absolute, and his temper more irritable. Lady Aurelia said that these were signs of senility, but Mrs. Darracott was unable to draw much comfort from this pronouncement. His lordship was certainly eighty years of age, but anyone less senile would have been hard to find. His energy would have shamed many a younger man; and no one, seeing him ride in after a hard day's hunting, would have supposed him to be a day over fifty.

Perhaps it was Hugo's horsemanship which had saved him from having his nose snapped off. My lord had watched him riding home across the park with Anthea, and there was no doubt that he had been agreeably surprised, for he had told Matthew that at all events the fellow had an excellent seat, and (unless he much mistook the matter) good, even hands. Mrs. Darracott recognised this as praise of a high order, and ventured to indulge the hope that Hugo was beginning to insinuate himself into his grandsire's good graces. She saw my lord look at Hugo several times as he sat talking to Anthea; it would have been too much to have said that there was kindness in his expression, but she fancied that there was a certain measure of approval.

Unfortunately this was short-lived. With the withdrawal of the ladies, and the removal of the cloth from the table, Hugo's fortunes fell once more into eclipse. "I can let you have some cognac, if you want it," my lord said to Matthew, who had moved round the table to take his wife's vacated chair. "Tell Chollacombe to put some up for you!"

"Take care, sir!" said Vincent warningly. "I feel reasonably sure that what you are offering my father paid no duty at any port."

"Of course it didn't!" replied his lordship. "Do you take me for a slow-top?"

"Far from it!" smiled Vincent. "You are awake upon every suit, sir. I apprehend, however, that there is an enemy in our midst." He turned his head to look at Hugo, a mocking challenge in his eyes. "You are opposed to the trade, are you not, coz?"

It was Richmond who betrayed discomfiture, not Hugo. Richmond flushed hotly, and kept his eyes lowered, wishing that he had not confided in Vincent; Hugo replied cheerfully: "If you mean the free trade, yes: I am."

Lord Darracott, bending a fierce stare upon him, barked: "Oh, you are, are you? And what the devil do you think you know about it?"

"Not much," Hugo answered.

"Then keep your tongue between your teeth!"

"Oh, I'll do that reet enough!" Hugo said reassuringly. He bestowed an affable smile upon Vincent, and added: "Chance it happens you were thinking I might inform against you——"

"Inform!" exclaimed Matthew. "Good God, what maggot have you got into your head? You don't, I trust, imagine that your grandfather—any of us!—is in league with smugglers?"

"Nay, I'd never think such a thing of you, sir!" said Hugo, shocked.

Matthew's colour mounted a little. "You may be very sure——My department has nothing to do with the Customs: I daresay I know as little about smuggling as you do!"

"Now, don't you start shamming it!" interrupted his father. "I'm not in league with the free-traders, and I'm not in league with the tidesman either, but by God, sir, if I had to choose between 'em I'd support the Gentlemen! That's the name they go by here: more worthy of it, too, than these damned Excisemen! A shuffling set! Mawworms, most of 'em, feathering their nests! I can tell you this; for every petty seizure that's made there are a dozen cargoes winked at!"

"Oh, well, no, Father!" said Matthew uneasily. "It's not as bad as that! I don't deny that there have been cases, perhaps——The pay is bad, and the rewards not large enough, you see, Hugh."

"I thought you knew nothing about it?" jeered his lordship.

"Some things are common knowledge, sir."

"Yes, and everyone knows that at many of the regular ports they bring the cargoes in as openly as you please, and how much is declared and how much is slipped through is just a matter of—oh, arrangement between the Revenue officer and the captains of the vessels!" said Richmond.

"Nay, lad, what difference does that make?" said Hugo. "Dishonesty amongst the Preventives doesn't alter the case."

"Of course it doesn't!" Matthew said, rather shortly. "Freetrading is to be deplored—no one denies that!—but while the duties remain at their present level, particularly on such commodities as tea and tobacco and spirits, the temptation to evade——"

"While duties remain at their present level," interrupted his lordship grimly, "the Board of Customs will get precious little support for its land-guard. Land-guard! Much hope they have of stopping the trade! By God, it puts me out of all patience when I heard that more and more money is being squandered on so-called Prevention! Now we are to have special coastguards, or some such tomfoolery! I'll lay you any odds the rascals will run the goods in under their noses."

"Oh, I should think undoubtedly," agreed Vincent. "I am not personally acquainted with any of the Gentlemen—at least, not to my knowledge—but I have the greatest admiration for persons so full of spunk. I am unhappily aware that they have more pluck than I have."

Richmond laughed, but Matthew said in a displeased

voice: "I wish you will not talk in that nonsensical style! A very odd idea of you Hugh will have!"

"Oh, no, do you think so, Papa? *Have* you an odd idea of me, cousin? Or any idea of me?"

Hugo shook his head. "Nay, I'm not judging you," he said gently.

Matthew stared at him for a moment, and then gave a reluctant laugh. "Well, there's for you, Vincent!"

"As you say, sir. Something in the nature of a half-armed stop. Do enlighten my ignorance, cousin! Does your very proper dislike of the Gentlemen arise from—er—an innate respectability, or from some particular cause, connected, perhaps, with the wool-trade?"

"There's no owling done now!" Richmond objected.

"What's owling?" asked Claud, with a flicker of interest.

"Oh, smuggling wool out of the country! But that was when there was a law against exporting wool, and ages ago, wasn't it, Grandpapa? There used to be a great deal of it done all along the coast."

"I wasn't thinking of that," said Hugo. "There were two things smuggled out of the country, and into France, while we were at war with Boney, that did more harm than owling."

"Why, what?" demanded Richmond, frowning.

"Guineas and information. Did you never hear tell of the guinea boats that were built in Calais? It was before your time, and before mine too, but it was English gold that kept the First Empire above hatches. Boney used to encourage English smugglers. He came by a deal of information that didn't make our task any the easier."

Richmond looked rather daunted; but Lord Darracott said testily: "No doubt! Possibly we too came by information through the same channel. Do you imagine yourself to be the only person here who thinks smuggling a bad thing? We all think it! It sprang from a damned bad cause, and until that's removed it will go on, and so it may for anything I'll do to stop it! Don't you talk to me about the rights and wrongs of it! Bad laws were made to be broken!"

He stopped, his hands clenching on the arms of his chair, for a chuckle had escaped Hugo. Vincent put up his glass, and eyed his cousin through it. "I do trust you mean to share the joke with us?" he said.

"I was just thinking what a pudder we'd be in, if every Jack rag of us set about breaking all the laws we weren't suited with," explained Hugo, broadly grinning. "Donnybrook Fair would be nothing to it, that road!"

9

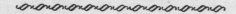

Richmond, knowing that his indiscreet confidence to Vincent was largely to blame for Hugo's fall from grace, tried gallantly to intervene; but it was Claud who saved Hugo from annihilation. To everyone's surprise, he suddenly said: "Well, Hugo's right! No question about it!" He looked up to discover that a singularly baleful stare from his grandfather's hard eyes was bent upon him, and blanched a little. "Well, what I mean is," he said manfully, though in a less decided tone, "no harm in buying run brandy, though I shouldn't do it myself, because I don't like brandy above half. The thing is you don't know where it's going to stop. Not the brandy. Running it."

"I collect that *some* meaning lies behind these cryptic utterances," remarked Vincent. "Or am I indulging optimism too far?"

"Much too far!" said Lord Darracott gratingly.

"No, you ain't!" retorted Claud, stung. "What's more, if you'd as much know as you think you have, you wouldn't ask me what I mean, because it's as plain as a pikestaff!"

"Is that to my address?" demanded his lordship ominously.

"No, no, sir! Good God, no!" said Claud hastily. "Talking to my brother! Besides, you *do* know what I mean: you told us all about it yourself! Hawkhurst Gang!"

"The Hawkhurst Gang!" ejaculated his lordship, and fell suddenly into silence.

"Yes, of course no one wants——But that was *years* ago!" Richmond said. "Nothing like that happens nowadays!"

"It could, though," said Claud. "Never thought about

126

it much before, but now I do come to think about it, I'm dashed if I don't think it's bound to happen!"

"Nonsense!" snapped his lordship.

"Well, Father——" said Matthew hesitantly, "one must hope, of course—but I own that there is a great deal of sense in what Claud says." He looked across the table at Hugo, and said: "The Hawkhurst Gang was a pernicious set of ruffians—smugglers, you understand—that held a rule of terror over the countryside when your grandfather was a boy. They committed every sort of atrocity, and were so strung in numbers—how many men was it they were able to muster within an hour, Father?"

"I forget," returned his lordship shortly.

"Five hundred," supplied Richmond. "And they used to have regular battles with rival gangs!"

"They indulged in far worse practices than that, my boy," said Matthew dryly.

"Yes, I know—murdering people, and torturing any they thought had informed against them—horrid! It went on for years, too. I wish I had been alive then!"

"Wish you'd been alive then?" echoed Claud. The height of his collar made it impossible for him to turn his head, so he was obliged to slew his body round in his chair to obtain a view of Richmond, seated beside him. "Well, of all the jingle-brained things to say!"

"No, because only think what sport it would have been! None of us—I don't mean only ourselves, but everyone like us!—seems to have made the least push to get the better of the gang, and of course the Government did nothing but what was paltry, but I'll swear the country people only wanted someone to lead them! Arms, too, but we could have supplied them with arms, and made them into—what do you call those irregular troops that fought in Spain, Hugo?"

"Guerrilleros," Hugo responded, regarding him with a lurking twinkle. "So that's what you'd have enjoyed, is it?"

Richmond blushed, but his eyes still glowed. "Well, you must own it—it would have been something like!"

Hugo shook his head. "Nay, lad, what it would have been like is something you've never seen."

"Oh, you mean burning ricks, and laying the country waste, but *that* wouldn't happen! I daresay the gang would have tried to burn our houses, but we should have kept watch—yes, and laid ambushes, too!"

"Well, if that's your notion of comfort it ain't mine!" said Claud. "Dashed if I don't think you've got windmills in your head!"

Lord Darracott thrust back his chair, and rose. "I wish to hear no more from any of you!" he said harshly. "I don't know which puts me the more out of patience, Hugh's damned morality, or your nonsense, Richmond! Matthew, I want a word with you! The rest of you may join the ladies."

He then stalked out of the room, and Vincent, getting up, said: "That I take to be a command. Shall we go?"

His lordship was not seen again that evening, but shortly before the tea-tray was brought in Matthew joined the drawing-room party, all of whom, with the exception of Vincent, who was absent, were gathered round a card-table. As Matthew entered the room, his wife laid her hand face upwards on the table, to the accompaniment of a chorus of indignant protests, which she acknowledged with a small, triumphant smile.

"Dash it, Mama, that makes it five times you've looed the board!"

"Oh, Aurelia, you *wretch!*"

"Aunt! That was my forlorn hope! You've left me without a feather to fly with!"

"Well! you are all very merry!" said Matthew. "Silver-loo, eh?"

"No, *copper*-loo, sir," replied Richmond. "We were too fly to be hooked in to play silver-loo with my aunt!"

"Aha! so you have been physicking them, have you, my dear?"

"I should rather think she has!" said Claud. "If she don't loo the board outright, you may depend upon it she holds Pam!"

"Except when Hugo has it! Hugo, if you've saved your groats *again*——!"

"No, not this time. My luck is nothing to her ladyship's. Do you always hold such cards, ma'am?"

"I am, in general, very fortunate," said Lady Aurelia. She gathered up her fan and her reticule, and said graciously: "Well, that was very diverting! You would have stared, I daresay, Matthew, had you seen us being so

128

foolish, and cutting such jokes!"

Matthew had never known his wife to cut jokes, or to behave foolishly, but he accepted this without a blink, saying that he was glad she had been so well entertained. He then looked round the room, and asked, with a slight frown, what had become of Vincent. To this she replied with majestic unconcern that she had no notion, but it was to be inferred from the subsequent folding of her lips that she was displeased.

"Begged to be excused," said Claud. "Beneath his touch to play copper-loo."

"Stupid fellow!" Matthew said, his frown deepening.

He did not mention Vincent again until he was alone with Lady Aurelia. He found her ladyship attired in a voluminous dressing-gown, reading a volume of sermons, as was her invariable custom, while her maid brushed her hair. She raised her eyes, and after a moment's dispassionate study of his face, placed a marker in her book, laid it down, and dismissed the maid.

"Well, Matthew?"

He was fidgeting about the room, and at first seemed to have nothing of much moment to say; but after making several desultory remarks, to which she responded with accustomed patience, he disclosed the real purpose of his visit by saying that he wished she would speak to Vincent.

"It would be useless," she replied.

"He is behaving abominably!" Matthew said angrily. "I am vexed to death! If anyone has a right to resent Hugh's presence it is I—though I trust I have too much dignity to conduct myself towards him as Vincent does! It is a fortunate circumstance that Hugh is a muttonhead, and doesn't know when Vincent is cutting at him, but sooner or later Vincent will go too far, and a pretty uproar there will be!"

"I do not consider Hugh a muttonhead, nor do I think he is unaware of Vincent's hostility."

He stared at her. "I cannot imagine why you should say so, ma'am! For my part, he seems to me little better than a dummy! It is always so with these clumsy giants: beefwitted! When I think of the future—that oaf in my father's shoes!—I declare I don't know how to support my spirits! But as for coming the ugly, as Vincent does——Upon my word, he will be well served if Hugh does take offence! That is——" he paused, looking harassed, but Lady Aurelia said nothing, and after a minute he burst out with the true cause of his anxiety. "I do not conceal from you, Aurelia, that my mind misgives me! There is no saying what might come of it, if a quarrel were to spring up between those two! Vincent is capable of anything: he is my father over again!"

She considered this calmly, before saying: "There is a want of conduct in him that vexes me very much, but I cannot suppose that he would go so far as to force such a quarrel upon his cousin as I collect you have in mind, my dear Matthew."

It was what he had in mind, but he exclaimed instantly: "Good God, I hope not indeed! It does not bear thinking of!" He took a hasty turn about the room. "I wish I knew what to do for the best! I don't understand Vincent: I have frequently been shocked by the reckless things he will do. His temper, too! Then the feeling he seems to have for this place: one would imagine he had always expected to inherit it, but that is absurd! And——But I will not say all I feel upon this occasion!"

"You are afraid that Vincent may force a duel on his cousin," she said relentlessly. "I cannot think it possible. If he did so, it could only be with the intention of putting a period to Hugh's life, and that, my dear sir, would be such an infamous act as I am persuaded no son of ours would be capable of performing."

"No, no, of course not!" he said. "Good God, I should hope—Aurelia, my father told me this evening that he wishes Vincent to remain here for a week or two! I had had no notion that anything like that was in the air, and I cannot like it. I ventured to suggest to my father that it would be wiser to let Vincent go, but you know what he is! He will never listen to one word of advice. Indeed, he is becoming so——However, I do not mean to discuss *that!* But I don't deny that I am excessively uneasy, and could almost wish it were not necessary for me to be in London next week. However little *intention* Vincent may have of bringing things to a—a fatal conclusion, I cannot rid myself of the apprehension that a quarrel might flare up; and I do not scruple to tell *you*, ma'am, that I do not feel that any dependence may be placed on my father's nipping anything of that nature in the bud. In fact, the suspicion flashed across my mind——But that's nonsense. of course! You will not regard it, I beg!"

"Certainly not," she replied. "I believe you are overanxious, and although I place no more reliance than you do upon your father's behaving as he ought I am strongly of the opinion that we may place every reliance on Major Hugh Darracott's good sense. Of the amiability of his disposition even you can have no doubt. I have observed him narrowly, and have been agreeably surprised. He is a man of principle; his temper is equable; his manners perfectly gentlemanlike and unaffected. The only fault I perceive in him is a tendency to levity, but——"

"*Levity?*" broke in Matthew.

"If it escaped your notice, my dear sir, that his atrocious brogue overcame him only when it had been made deplorably plain to him that his family held him in contempt, I can only say that it did not escape mine."

"You mean to tell me——No, I don't believe it! He slips into it when he forgets to guard his tongue! If he *is* shamming it——Well, upon my word, what infernal impudence!"

"I am no friend to levity, but I cannot but acknowledge that in taking his family's hostility in good part he showed himself to be a man of considerable forbearance," said her ladyship repressively.

He coloured, and looked discomfited. Lady Aurelia, satisfied that her words had gone home, continued in precisely the same composed tone: "As to Vincent, though I do not anticipate any such issue as you have suggested, I daresay it would be wiser for me to remain at Darracott Place, instead of returning with you to Mount Street."

His expression changed to one of relief. "Should you dislike it, ma'am? I own, *I* should be easier in my mind, for although you may say Vincent does not listen to you, I am tolerably certain that while you are at hand he will take care to keep within bounds. But I don't mean to press you: it is not an object with my father to make his guests comfortable!"

"My dear sir, I hope my mind is stronger than you believe it to be! I do not suffer from an excess of sensibility. I have never allowed your father's odd humours to sink my spirits, and it would be a strange thing if I did so now, after nearly thirty years. I am perfectly willing to remain, particularly so because Elvira has twice expressed her wish that I should stay to support her through this very awkward time."

"Ay, no doubt she must be dreading your departure! I hadn't thought of that, but I promise you I pity her with all my heart! She is thrown into high fidgets by no more than a rough word from my father. If she could school herself to be a little less in alt she would go on better with him, but her understanding I have never thought superior. I only wish you may not find it a bore to be continually with her!"

"You may be easy on that head. We have the habit of easy intercourse, and if she has little force of mind she is always so good-natured and attentive that you need entertain no fears that I shall not be comfortable."

With these words, Lady Aurelia picked up her book again, and Matthew, interpreting this as a sign that the audience was at an end, imprinted a salute upon her cheek, and took himself off to his own room.

Hugo, meanwhile, had been strolling up and down the terrace, and enjoying the solace of one of his forbidden cigars. His countenance was thoughtful; and when he presently sat down on the parapet there was the hint of a crease between his brows. He remained there for some little time, staring abstractedly before him; but presently some small sound caught his attention, and he turned his head to look searchingly across the shadowed garden below. The moonlight was faint, obscured by broken clouds, but he was able to discern a vague figure striding across the lawn towards the house. He remained motionless, and in another minute or two recognized Vincent. It was not until Vincent had reached the foot of the shallow stone steps that he perceived his cousin. He paused, looking up, and said: "Ah! Ajax! Taking the air, or is it possible you were waiting for me?"

"Just blowing a cloud," replied Hugo, lifting his hand to show the butt of the cigar between his fingers.

"A filthy habit—if you don't object to my saying so?"

"Nay, why should I?"

Vincent mounted the steps leisurely. "Who am I to instruct you? I daresay you know why you should *not*, at all events."

"Oh, yes, I know that!" Hugo said serenely.

"Your compliance is only equalled by your amiability—and I find both insupportable."

"There's no need to tell me that. I'm sorry for it, but happen you'd find me insupportable whatever I did."

"Almost undoubtedly. I find virtue a dead bore. I have very little myself. I don't know how it is, but the virtuous are invariably dull, which I can't bring myself to pardon."

Hugo's deep chuckle sounded. "Nay then! You're trying to hoax me! To think of you calling me virtuous! You'll have me blushing like a lass!" He pitched the butt of his cigar into one of the flowerbeds below. When he turned again towards Vincent he spoke in a different tone, and with less than his usual drawl. "Sithee, Vincent! Squaring with me won't help either of us. I'd be very well suited if you were in my shoes, but there's no way of bringing that about, and naught for either of us to do but make the best of it."

"Yes, you wrote as much to my grandfather, didn't you?" Vincent said. "A mistake! It didn't turn him up sweet at all. He's a hard man to gammon, and that, you know, was doing it much too brown."

Hugo heaved a despairing sigh. "You're as daft as he is! I can understand that you should think it a grand thing to inherit all this, for you've known it your life long, and I don't doubt it's home to you. It's not home to me, and why any of you should have got it stuck in your heads that I'd want to be saddled with a place that's falling to ruin I'll be damned if I know!"

"To *you*, I feel sure, it must seem a sad, rubbishing place—almost a hovel, in fact!"

"Nay, I didn't mean to offend you! It's a fine old house, but it's like everything else I've seen: there's been no brass spent on it for many a day, and it'll take a mountain of brass to set it to rights. As for the land, I've a notion there's something more than brass needed, and that's better management. I can see I'll have a hard job on, and one to which I wasn't bred. Eh, it's more like a mill-stone tied round my neck than a honey-fall!"

"And the title, of course, means nothing to you!"

"I'd as lief be without it," admitted Hugo.

"Humdudgeon! Are you really such a Jack Adams as to think I'll swallow that?"

"Suit yourself!" Hugo answered. "If that's the way it

133

is with you, there's no good talking."

"None whatsoever—for you would certainly be unable to understand what it means to be Darracott of Darracott Place! You do not appear to me even to understand that I dislike you!"

"Oh, I understand that!" Hugo said, with another chuckle. "If there were any cliffs here you'd be ettling to push me over the edge, wouldn't you?"

"The temptation would be almost irresistible, but I hardly think I should go to those lengths. Let us say that if you tottered on the verge I shouldn't pull you back from it!" Vincent retorted.

"It 'ud be a daft thing for you to do, think on," said Hugo reflectively. "You'd go over with me, choose how!"

134

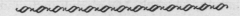

Major Darracott spent the next week acquainting himself as best he might with his future inheritance. He received no assistance and very little encouragement from his grandfather, his tentative suggestion that my lord enlighten his ignorance being met with a crushing snub. My lord had not enjoyed the novel experience of being left without a word to say, nor was he accustomed to meet with disagreement in the bosom of his family. His sons and his grandsons, and even his spirited granddaughter, had learnt the wisdom of refraining from argument, in general receiving his more dogmatic utterances in silence, and never forcing him into the position of being obliged to defend the indefensible. Such divergent opinions as they might have held remained unuttered, under which arrangement they were at liberty, for anything his lordship cared, to differ from him as much as they chose. It had come, therefore, as a shock to him when Hugo (an upstart, as near to being misbegotten as made no odds), instead of keeping to himself his shabby-genteel notions of morality had not only owned to them without hesitation when challenged, but had had the effrontery to maintain them in the teeth of his grandfather's disapprobation. That he had taken little part in the resultant argument in no way alleviated my lord's anger. What he had said had served to compel Matthew, uneasily conscious of his office, to support him. My lord was indifferent to Claud's revolt, but Matthew's defection had infuriated him. Forgetting that it was not Hugo, but Vincent, who had tossed the bone of dissension into their midst, he saw Hugo as an impudent make-bait, too full of north-country bumptious-

135

ness to realize that he had nothing to do but to hold his peace amongst the relatives who had magnanimously admitted him to a place within their ranks. Far from conducting himself with becoming humility he had, in his maddeningly simple way, exposed the weakness of his grandfather's case; and, to crown his iniquity, he had recognized and laughed at the absurdity of an aphorism hastily uttered as a clincher to a losing argument.

The hostility which the Major's style in the saddle had done something to diminish flamed up again; and when he expressed a desire to be instructed in the extent and management of the estates, he was seen as an encroaching mushroom, a burr, and an irreclaimable commoner, and was informed that his cousin Anthea would tell him as much as it was needful for him to know. My lord added that if he thought he would be allowed to put a finger in a pie not yet his own, he would soon learn his mistake.

It had not been Anthea's intention to gratify her grandsire by devoting any appreciable part of her time to the entertainment or the education of Major Darracott. She had not disliked her one expedition in his company: indeed, she had enjoyed it, for she had discovered him to be likeable and amusing. But she had detected in him a certain audacity which set her on her guard, and made her determined to keep him (in a perfectly friendly way) at arm's length. Had he tried to advance himself in her good graces, or to coax her to ride with him, she would have hardened her heart, and abandoned him to Claud; but the Major committed neither of these imprudences. When Mrs. Darracott, her earlier scruples forgotten, suggested that Anthea should take him to see some view, or picturesque village, he said that he did not wish to be a nuisance to his cousin, who must not feel it to be her duty to entertain him when, no doubt, she had many more important tasks on hand.

Unlike her mother, who thought the Major's meekness very touching, Anthea regarded him with a good deal of suspicion. She could detect nothing but humble deference in his smile, but she was finding it increasingly difficult to believe that he was either meek or biddable. His countenance was certainly goodhumoured, and his blue eyes guileless, but about his firm-lipped mouth and decided chin there was not a trace of weakness or of humility; and although he was unassertive, making no attempt to force his way into the family circle, or to take an uninvited part in any conversation, this modesty carried with it very little suggestion of bashfulness. It had more than once occurred to Anthea that he had a good deal of quiet assurance. He could scarcely be unaware of the hostility with which he was regarded by at least three members of the household; a shy man, she thought, must have been flustered by the knowledge that his every word and movement came under critical survey; but she had yet to see him betray any sign of nervousness. It was significant, too, that the servants, usually quick to take their tone from their betters, treated him with respect, and served him with every appearance of willingness. It might have been expected that he should have the habit of command, but Anthea could not discover that he did command: he merely requested.

"The servants all like him," Mrs. Darracott told her. "Mrs. Flitwick was saying so to me only this morning, and I am not at all surprised, for I am sure everyone must like him—except, of course, your grandfather and Vincent, which doesn't signify, because they never like anyone! He is the kindest creature!"

"I can see that you like him, at all events, Mama!"

"Yes, my love, I do like him. I should be a positive monster if I didn't, for I don't think I ever met anyone so considerate. Only think of his mending the casement in my bedchamber, just because I told him how disobliging and cross old Rudge is, saying he will do it when he has time to spare, and never making the least push to do anything except what Glossop, or your grandfather, orders him to do!"

"If he borrowed Rudge's tools, there is *one* servant who doesn't like him!"

"Nothing of the sort!" said Mrs. Darracott. "I own, I was very much afraid Rudge would take a pet, but—would you believe it, love?—he came up to my room while Hugo was at work on the window, and actually apologized to me! He wanted to finish the job, but Hugo wouldn't have it, so, to my amazement, he stayed to help Hugo, telling him all the time what he *ought* to do, and shaking his head over it, but not in the least disagreeably! And he asked me if there was anything else that needed attention, so I mentioned the loose board in your room, and he has promised he will nail it down this very afternoon! Say what you will, Anthea, he never would have done so for *me:* he didn't want Hugo to think he was disobliging, which, of course, he *is!*" She looked a little anxiously at her daughter, and ventured to say: "I wish you will take pity on him, my dear! Poor boy, he must feel quite wretched, with your grandfather treating him so unkindly, and Matthew very little better, while as for Vincent—— Well, I only hope he comes by his deserts!"

So Anthea took pity on her cousin. He did not look at all wretched, although he admitted that he was in disgrace with his grandfather, and, to some extent, he thought, with his uncle.

"Yes, we heard all about it," she said. "You put my uncle in a fix, you know, for while, on the one hand, he did not wish to vex Grandpapa, on the other, he felt himself to be obliged, as a member of the Government, to condemn the free-traders. My aunt, however, considers that you feel just as you ought, and honours you for it!"

"Now, if you're going to roast me——!"

"Nothing of the sort! She says you are pretty-behaved, and don't want for sense. High praise, I assure you!"

"She frightens me to death," he confided.

She turned her head, and surveyed him thoughtfully. "Will you think me very uncivil if I say that I don't believe you, cousin?"

"Ay, I shall and-all!" he replied promptly.

Her eyes laughed, but she said: "Then I will merely say that you are what Richmond calls a complete hand. Does Vincent frighten you too?"

"He has me all of a twitter."

"I shouldn't wonder at it if he thinks so!" she said, with some tartness. "I wish you will stop shamming it, and tell me how much longer you mean to endure his insolence!"

"Nay, it doesn't worry me," he said, smiling.

"It should! It puts me in such a rage when he cuts at you, and you do *nothing* to stop him!"

"Now, why?"

"Because he would be all the better for a sharp set-down!"

"Happen he'll get one, but it won't be from me."

She rode on in silence for a few moments, but presently

said: "It—it is so *spiritless* of you!"

"I know it is," he said, with a mournful shake of his head. "Downright malten-hearted, that's me!"

"Yes, but I don't think you are! Well, how could you be? You are a soldier!"

"Ay, and a terrible time I had of it, keeping in the rear," he said falling into reminiscent vein. "When I wasn't being a Belem-ranger—that's what we—*they!*—used to call the fellows who were always going off to hospital in Lisbon, you know——"

"No doubt that's how you became a Major!" she interrupted.

"No, you're out there: I had my majority by purchase, of course. Mind you, if it hadn't been for the losses we suffered at Waterloo——"

"If you mean to continue in this style," she exclaimed, reining in her mare, "I shall go home immediately!"

"I was being modest," he explained. "It wouldn't become me to tell you what a devil of a fellow I was. However, since I see you've guessed it, I'll own that Hector was nothing to me. You'd have thought I was one of the Death or Glory boys!"

"Well, what I think now is that you are the most shameless prevaricator I ever encountered!" retorted Anthea.

"Eh, there's no pleasing you!" he said, heaving a despondent sigh. "Now, I've perjured myself to no purpose at all!"

"You are perfectly ridiculous!" she told him, choking on a laugh. "It would please me—though what you do is quite your own affair, and no concern of mine!—to see Vincent taken at fault for once in his life!"

He rubbed his nose meditatively. "Ay, I can see it would, and that's where the water sticks, lass! Now, just you tell me what you'd have me do!"

"Good heavens, make it plain to him you'll stand no more of it!"

"And how will I do that?"

"You have a tongue in your head! If I were in your shoes, I'd give as good as I got!"

He smiled. "I don't doubt you would. But, setting aside I've no taste for fratching, if that didn't answer I'd be in a bit of a hobble, wouldn't I?" She looked frowningly at him, and his smile broadened. "Ay, I know what's in your

139

head. I'd look champion, coming to handyblows with a man two or three stone lighter than I am, and a good three inches shorter!"

"I hadn't thought of that," she admitted. "What a dead bore it must be to you, being so very large!"

"Ay, it's a reet handicap," he agreed gravely. "If I'd been a reasonable size I could have kicked up all sorts of riot and rumpus. I daresay I'd have been a prime favourite with everyone by this time."

She laughed. "Well, I must own I, at least, shouldn't blame you if you knocked Vincent down! I see, of course, that you won't do it—unless, perhaps, he hit you first? I believe he is a very good boxer."

He grinned at the hopeful note in her voice. "Nay, why should he? If you're thinking I might provoke him to it, I'm sorry to disoblige you, but my name's Darracott—not Captain Hackum!"

"No, no, of course I wouldn't wish you to do that! In fact, I trust you won't, because there's no saying, with Vincent——Well, never mind! Let us go on, shall we?"

"Where are you taking me?" he asked, trotting beside her down the narrow lane.

"Into Sussex. We extend for some way across the county border. I'll make you known to one or two of Grandpapa's tenants. You may depend upon it they are all agog to see you! They won't show it, however, so don't be dismayed if they seem unfriendly. Sussex people are suspicious of *foreigners!* Your father was well liked, though: that will stand you in good stead! My uncle Granville was not, and nor is Grandpapa—for reasons that will become apparent to you if they are not so already."

It had been apparent to the Major for several days that his grandfather was a bad landlord; by the time they turned their horses' heads homewards, after a tour that had included visits to two tenant-farmers of long-standing, and a brief survey of two farms leased on short tenancies, he had a more exact knowledge of the condition of his inheritance.

Wondering what he made of it (for his countenance was inscrutable), Anthea said, breaking a long silence: "Well?"

He glanced down at her, and smiled. "I'm sorry: I was in the clouds!"

"What were you thinking, Hugo?"

"I was wishing I knew more about husbandry—and wondering what the deuce I'm going to do."

"I doubt if you'll be permitted to do anything," she said frankly. "Unless you can contrive to bring Grandpapa round your thumb, and I never knew anyone do that except Richmond. Besides, what could you do?"

"It wouldn't be a question of bringing him round my thumb, though the Lord knows it would be a ticklish business to do the thing without setting up his back. I'd be loth to do that, for he's an old man, and my grandfather besides."

"Do you wish to manage the estates?" she asked, in a little perplexity. "I thought—something you said made me think you didn't mean to remain here while Grandpapa is alive."

"I don't know what I mean to do," he said. "I didn't think to stay, but there's work crying out to be done here, and though I'm not the man to do it I can't hoax myself into believing that it isn't a matter of duty to make a push to set things to rights."

"Hugo," she said earnestly, "to set things to rights will mean putting money into the land instead of wringing the last groat out of it, and that you'll never persuade Grandpapa to do! Do, pray, talk to Glossop before you do anything rash!"

"Is he your steward? I can't talk to him behind my grandfather's back, but I shan't do anything rash, I promise you. It's too soon for me to do aught but feel my way, at any hand." He saw that she was looking rather anxious, and smiled reassuringly down at her. "Nay, lass, I'm not one to go full-fling at anything! If I *don't* feel my way, I'll be off!"

"But I thought—that is, Grandpapa told us that you had sold out? How will you do, if you don't remain here?"

"I'll do well-enough," he replied, with a chuckle. "I've some brass of my own. My grandfather Bray left me what he had—his savings, you might call it. That's what his lordship calls it, at all events."

Her brow cleared. "Oh, in that case——! I didn't know, and was afraid you might, having sold out, be dependent upon Grandpapa. Hugo, take my advice, and don't let yourself be bullied into staying at the Place! I've lived

141

here all my life, and I've seen what it *does* to people! There's never any peace, there never was! Grandpapa quarrels with everyone: I think he enjoys it. Not only with the family, you understand, but with *everyone!* That's why you'll rarely see a guest at the Place, and never a morning visitor. He is not on terms even with the Vicar! When you have lived with us for a little longer, you'll understand. We are all so fretted and rubbed that our tempers will be as bad as Grandpapa's in the end: I know mine will! Not Mama's, but it is worse for her, because she has more sensibility than I have, poor love and is very nervous. But if you had known the family when my father and uncle Granville were alive——! I assure you, you would take care not take up residence under the same roof as Grandpapa, for even *your* temper would crack under the strain!"

He smiled, but said: "I daresay it would. I haven't been here many days yet, but I know already that I couldn't live with his lordship, and I don't mean to try. And that puts me in mind of something! Who lives in the Dower House?"

"No one, at present. No one but Spurstow, that is. He was Great-aunt Matty's butler, and when she died Grandpapa said he might remain at the Dower House, to look after it until it should be inhabited again."

"And who was Great-aunt Matty?" he enquired.

"Oh, she was Grandpapa's sister! When Grandpapa was married, she and our *great*-grandmother removed to the Dower House. Great-grandmother died before I was born, and Aunt Matty continued there until *she* died—oh, nearly two years ago now! She was very eccentric, and she looked exactly like a witch, and was used to mutter to herself. Richmond and I were terrified of her, when we were children, but fortunately she hated to be visited, so that it was only very occasionally that we were obliged to go to the Dower House. She always sat in one room, and kept the blinds drawn in the others, and had *dozens* of the most odious cats. It used to be one of Richmond's worst nightmares, that he was shut up in that dark house, with cats' eyes staring at him wherever he looked, and poor Jane Darracott's ghost creeping up behind him!"

"I'd forgotten the ghost. Is that why the house stands empty?"

"Well, yes, in a way it is. My Uncle Granville wished

to live there, after Aunt Matty died, but Aunt Anne said that she would as lief do anything in the world as set foot inside the house. She's very fanciful, suffers nervous disorders—distempered freaks, Grandpapa calls them! But I believe the real cause of the scheme's coming to nothing was that the house was found to be in shocking repair, and, of course, Grandpapa refused to waste any money on it. When Grandpapa practises economy it is always at the expense of his family, never his own! Are you thinking that you might live there? I warn you, it is rat-ridden, ghost-ridden, and damp into the bargain! Spurstow says the roof leaks in several places."

"It sounds champion!" he remarked. "Don't tell me it hasn't dry rots as well, for I wouldn't believe you!"

"Very likely, I should think." She threw him a mischievous glance. "And to add to your comfort, there is said to be an underground passage, leading from the cellars to the Place, in which (could you but find it) you would discover the bones of several persons who were so unfortunate as to have fallen out with one—or possibly more—of our ancestors."

"That adds a cosy touch," he agreed. "Ralph II?"

"No, we were obliged to abandon that notion," she said regretfully. "It seems to be established that the passage was walled up long before his time. However, the son of the Darracott who came over with the Conqueror we understand to have been a *shockingly* loose screw, so we are much inclined to think it was he who hid the bodies of his enemies in it."

"Ay, a passage would be just the place anyone would choose," he nodded. "And, if you've done trying to make an April-gowk out of me, I'd be glad to know why you're so set on holding me off from the house?"

She laughed. "Oh, I'm not! I merely thought it right to warn you!"

"Eh, that was kind!" he said appreciatively. "Of course, I'd be wasting my time if I tried to find the passage, wouldn't I?"

"Well, we wasted ours, when we were children," she admitted, "but if you mean to say that you don't believe there is a passage I shall take in very bad part. Its existence is one of our more cherished traditions! There's a reference to it somewhere in our archives. Unfortunately, no

143

hint of its precise locality is vouchsafed, and when Oliver ventured to suggest to Grandpapa that we might discover it with the aid of a pickaxe or two, the notion, from some cause or another, found no favour with him! He did own that in ancient times there had been a passage, but although we—that, Oliver, and Caro, and Eliza, and Vincent, and Claud, and I—thought it could be put to *excellent* use, he quite failed to enter into our sentiments!"

"I'm not so sure that I blame him!"

She gurgled. "I wish you might have seen his face when Claud and I said that it was his duty to find the bones of our murdered foes, and give them decent burial! You see, we were the youngest, and we became wholly confused by the tales the others made up! I think the bones were Oliver's contribution to the legend, and to this day I'm not perfectly sure how much belongs to the original legend, and how much was added by the boys. I must say I wish you may persuade Grandpapa to let you have the Dower House (although I fear you won't!), so that you might do a little excavation, and confirm our ancient tradition! I'll take you to see it tomorrow, if you would like it."

The Dower House was situated only some four hundred yards to the north-east of Darracott Place, from which it was hidden by a belt of trees, and a tangle of overgrown bushes. A carriage-drive gave access to it from a narrow lane, but Anthea took the Major there by way of a footpath through the wood, and entered the garden at the side of the house. A ditch surmounted by a black-thorn hedge enclosed the grounds, which seemed, at first glance, to consist almost wholly of a shrubbery run riot. Holding open a wicket-gate, which squeaked on its rusty hinges, Hugo glanced round, remarking that it looked a likely place for a ghost. Anthea, disentangling the fringe of her shawl from the encroaching hedge, agreed to this, and at once took him to see what she called the fatal window. It was at the back of the house, and faced south-east, on to what Hugo took to be a wilderness but which was, she assured him, a delightful pleasure-garden. "If you look closely, you will see that there are several rose-beds, and a sundial," she said severely. "The lawn, perhaps, needs mowing."

"It does, doesn't it?" said Hugo, eyeing the rank grass

with disfavour. "Myself, I'd have it ploughed up and re-sown, but I daresay it's in keeping with the rest as it is."

"Well, I warned you how it would be. *That* is the window. The room was originally the best bedchamber, but after the accident—if it wasn't a murder—none of the subsequent tenants cared to sleep in it, so it was reserved for the accommodation of guests."

"Ay, it would be. It must go to his lordship's heart to think he hasn't a haunted room at the Place: I don't doubt I'd have found myself in it if there had been one. Is this where the lady walks?"

"Oh, she walks all round the house, and in it, too, according to some! Very few of Aunt Matty's servants ever stayed for long with her, but I never heard that they *saw* the ghost. They used to complain that they heard strange noises, but I fancy they wouldn't have made anything of that if they hadn't been warned by the villagers. None of *them* would dream of coming near the house after dark, of course."

She led the way, as she spoke, towards the front of the house. Here the trees grew so close to the building that a branch of one giant elm almost brushed the roof, seeing which, Hugo said decidedly: "I'd have that down for a start. Eh, but it's a fine old house!"

"I suppose it is," Anthea replied, with a certain lack of enthusiasm. "It is older than the Place, I know, and said to be a good example of that style of ancient stone-building, but it has always seemed to me a dreadfully gloomy house."

"If all that ivy were stripped away, and the bushes uprooted, and some of the trees felled, it wouldn't be gloomy. I allow there's no prospect on this side, but there should be as good a one, or better, as there is from the Place, on the garden side, once a clearance was made."

"Is that what you would do?"

He nodded. "I would, if I meant to live here. I've a strong notion that we have only to let in some light and air to lay that ghost of yours."

"But this is iconoclasm!" she exclaimed. "Lay the Darracott spectre? For shame! Have you no respect for tradition?"

He looked quizzically down at her. "Nay, that's a matter of up-bringing," he said. "I wasn't reared to respect Darracott tradition. Come to think of it, I doubt if I'd respect a ghost that scared the servants out of my house, whatever way I'd been reared. Can we go inside?"

"Certainly—unless Spurstow has gone out, and left the doors locked," she responded. "If he is in, he won't accord us a very warm welcome, but don't be dismayed! He has grown to be as eccentric as ever Aunt Matty was, and regards all visitors in the light of hostile invaders, but he won't repel us with violence! He has lived for thirty years here, so you can't wonder at it that he should be a trifle crusty."

"So he's not afraid of the ghost?"

"Oh, no! He holds poor Jane in great contempt—like you!"

"Do *you* believe she haunts the place?" Hugo asked, walking beside her up the weed-grown drive towards the house.

She hesitated. "N-no. At least—I don't believe it at this moment, in broad sunlight, but—no, I shouldn't care to come here at night! It isn't only the villagers who have seen things: Richmond has, too."

"Has he, indeed? What did he see?"

"A female form. He couldn't imagine who it was at first. He says he went towards her, and suddenly she vanished. Ugh!"

"Well, if that's all she does she's welcome to haunt the place," said the Major prosaically.

They trod up two worn stone steps into the flagged porch; but as Anthea grasped the rusted iron bellpull the door was opened by a grizzled man in a frieze coat. He looked the visitors over morosely, bade Anthea a grudging good-morning, and said that he had seen her coming up the drive, and supposed that she must be wanting something.

"Yes, I want to show the house to Major Darracott," she replied cheerfully.

"If you'd have sent me word, Miss Anthea, you were coming here this day-morning I'd have had it ready to be shown," said Spurstow, with considerable severity. "The rooms are all shut up, as well you know. You'll have to bide while I get my keys."

With these quelling words, he admitted them into the hall, and left them there while he went off, grumbling

146

under his breath, to his own quarters. When he presently returned he found that the Major, having opened the shutters covering the windows at the back of the hall, was standing in rapt contemplation of the Cromwellian staircase, while Miss Darracott, holding her flounced skirt gathered in one hand, looked with a wry face at the dusty floor.

"It's not my fault, miss," said Spurstow, forestalling criticism. "You shouldn't ought to have come without you gave me warning."

"I can see I shouldn't!" she retorted. "But I have come, and I mean to take Major Darracott over the house, even though it be *knee*-deep in dust, so you may as well make up your mind to it."

This forthright speech appeared rather to please than to exacerbate the retainer. He gave a sour smile, and, with only a passing reference to the troublesome characteristics displayed by Miss Darracott in childhood, unlocked the door leading into the dining-parlour, and opened the shutters.

It would not have surprised Anthea if the Major's wish to inspect the Dower House had deserted him long before their tour of the ground-floor had been completed. Dirty panes and encroaching ivy darkened the rooms; there were several patches of damp on the walls; most of the ceilings were ominously blackened above the old-fashioned fireplaces; every room smelled of must; and a final touch of melancholy was added by the furniture, which had been huddled together in the middle of each room, and covered with newspapers, old sheets, and scraps of sackcloth.

"I warned you what it would be like!" she told Hugo.

"Ay, it's in bad repair, but it could be put to rights," he answered.

"That could be done, but it will always be a dark, gloomy house."

"Nay, if the ivy were stripped from it, and all those bushes cleared away, you'd never recognize it," he said. "The best of the rooms face to the south-east, but the sun's shut out by trees and shrubs."

"Miss Matty, sir," observed Spurstow, in hostile accents, "wouldn't have the sun shining in, and fading the carpets."

147

"Maybe she wouldn't, but she wasn't reared on the edge of the moors," returned Hugo. "I'm not used to be shut in: I want room to breathe, and never mind the carpets!"

A disapproving sniff was the only answer vouchsafed to this. Spurstow then conducted the unwelcome visitors to the upper floor, and volunteered no further remark until Anthea, showing Hugo Jane Darracott's bedchamber, asked whether her ghost had been seen there. He said repressively that he took no account of ghosts.

"The Major takes no account of them either," said Anthea. "He thinks I'm telling him a Banbury story, but the house *is* haunted, isn't it?"

"Folks say so," Spurstow replied. "I never did, miss. I'm not one to talk, and I don't scare easy. I've lived here thirty years and more, and it's done me no harm. I don't take any notice."

Anthea gave an involuntary shiver, but the Major said: "Any notice of what?"

Spurstow looked at him under his brows. "Aught I hear," he said.

"What *do* you hear?" enquired Anthea.

"Nothing, miss. It doesn't worry me," he said. "Time was when I'd get up out of my bed, thinking there was someone got into the house, but it was all foolishness: you can search from the cellars to the attics, but you'll see naught. Leastways, I never did. It's only footsteps, when all's said."

"Oh!" said Anthea rather faintly. "Only footsteps!"

"Now, you don't want to listen to the silly stories folks tell, Miss Anthea!" said Spurstow roughly. "The rest's naught but the wind in the trees, or an owl, maybe. There are nights when it sounds like someone was moaning outside here pitiful, but lor' bless you, miss, the wind can make queer noises! *I* don't heed it!"

Repressing an impulse to glance over her shoulder, Anthea moved rather closer to the Major, unexpectedly grateful for the presence of so large and solid a body. He looked down at her, and smiled reassuringly. "That makes another good reason for pushing the woodland back from the house," he remarked. "As for the footsteps, I'd have in the rat-catcher!"

His eyes were on Spurstow as he spoke, but that worthy

said nothing. There was nothing acquiescent in his silence, however; his expression was that of one who might, had he chosen to do so, have made further and more alarming disclosures; and Anthea could only be glad that nothing more remained to be seen of the house than the cellars and the servants' quarters. The Major obligingly disclaimed any interest in these, so they went downstairs again, followed by Spurstow, who broke his silence to inform them that whenever it rained the roof leaked in a dozen places. If they had gone up into the attics, he said, they would have seen the buckets placed there to catch the drips.

On this depressing note they departed, Spurstow, slightly mellowed by the *douceur* bestowed upon him by the Major, holding open the door for them, and even going so far as to say that they would always be welcome.

"If we were welcome, I'd be sorry for anyone that was unwelcome," remarked Hugo, as they retraced their steps to the wicket-gate. "Did you say he'd been the old lady's butler?"

"Yes, but he was never trained to be a butler. Aunt took him out of the stables, because none of the butlers she hired from London ever stayed with her above a month. She didn't care about his manners, and I must own that he was amazingly faithful to her, and, I think, fond of her, in his rough way. She let him do just as he pleased, and, of course, when she took to living in one room he managed everything, and never cheated her out of a groat, what's more. He was born and bred on the estate, and his father and grandfather before him, but even Grandpapa wouldn't have wondered at it if he had feathered his nest at Aunt Matty's expense. She left him an annuity, but only quite a small one, which was why, I suppose, he was willing to stay on alone in the Dower House. I wouldn't have done so for a fortune! Didn't he make your blood run cold when he said it was *only footsteps?* Just as though that made everything right! *I* thought it made everything ten times eerier, didn't you?"

"Ay, he did it very well," agreed Hugo.

She looked quickly up at him. "Did it very well? Do you mean he was trying to frighten us? It didn't seem so to me. He made so little of it! He even said the wind was to blame for the moaning noise."

Hugo chuckled. "So he did! If you could have seen your own face, lass! Not that I think it was you he was trying to scare away. What I did think was that as soon as he suspected I'd a notion of living in the Dower House myself he did all he could to set me against it."

She knit her brows. "Yes, I suppose that's possible," she said, after considering for a minute or two. "Unless you hired him with the house, which is not very likely, he would be obliged to leave, and I daresay——No, it can't be that! The house was known to be haunted long before he came to it!"

"If it was half as badly haunted as he'd have us believe, our great-grandmother wouldn't have gone to live there in the first place, let alone have stayed there till she died!" replied Hugo. "Nay, lass! Spurstow wants to keep people away from it. That might be because he's afraid of being turned out: I'm not saying it isn't, but what I suspect is that he's got some other reason—and a havey-cavey one at that!—for scaring the people roundabout here with his talk of footsteps and pitiful moanings!"

"But Richmond *saw* the ghost!" she argued. "One or two of the villagers have seen it, too, though not as clearly as he did. Old Buttermere said it was a white *thing*, that glided over the ground, and vanished into the shrubbery."

"And a very good place for it to vanish, too," said Hugo, wholly unimpressed. "Give me a sheet, and a night without too much moonlight, and I'll engage to do the same!"

"And the form Richmond mistook for a living person?"

"If Richmond came up here expecting to see the ghost of Jane Darracott," he suggested, after a moment, "and in fact saw that old rascal, draped in a sheet, the likelihood is that his imagination took hold of him, and made him ready to swear he'd seen a deal more than he *did* see. It's a queer thing, imagination—and I'd say Richmond's was a lively one."

She thought this over, saying at the end of her cogitations: "Well, if you are right, Hugo, I daresay I can guess why Spurstow wishes to keep everyone away from the Dower House. Indeed, I wonder that it shouldn't have occurred to any of us! Depend upon it, the house is being used by free-traders!"

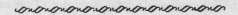

The Major received this suggestion without any visible signs of surprise or disapproval; but after turning it over in his mind, he said: "I don't know much about smuggling, but I should have thought the Dower House would have been too far from the coast to be of use."

"No, why? It's not much more than ten miles, and you may be sure that those who carry the run goods inland know the Marsh so well that they can find their way on the darkest of nights. They must wish to store the goods as far from the shore as they may, because the land-guard keep their strictest watch on the dwellings nearest to the coast, but they can't go very far, on account of the darkness. The goods are landed on moonless nights, you see: the *darks* is what they call them."

"Ay, they'd have to be. Do the smuggling vessels sail close in to the shore, or do the landsmen row out to them?"

"Well, I don't know precisely. I think they very often land their cargoes in creeks, and gaps, but sometimes, I believe, they cast the goods overboard at high tide. I remember once, when I was a child, that the tide-waiters captured a cargo of tea which had been thrown overboard. It was packed in oilskin bags, made to look like mackerel pots, my nurse told me. She knew a great deal about the trade: I expect her brothers had to do with it."

He could not help grinning at her cheerful unconcern, but he was somewhat startled, and said incredulously: "You nurse's brothers were smugglers?"

"Not *master*-smugglers, but hired to help carry the goods up from the shore," she explained. "They worked

151

on their father's farm, and were perfectly respectable, I assure you!"

"Nay!" he protested.

She smiled. "Well, quite as respectable as their fellows at all events. You don't understand, Hugo! In Kent and Sussex almost everyone has to do with smuggling in some way or another. The farm labourers hire themselves out as porters, and the farmers themselves sometimes lend their horses, and nearly always allow their barns to be used as hiding-places. We, of course, don't have any dealings with smugglers, but if we found ankers in one of our outhouses we shouldn't say a word about it. No one would! *Why*, Grandpapa told us once how a cargo of brandy was stored in Guldeford Church, with the Vicar knowing all about it, and saying from the pulpit that there would be no service on the following Sunday because the roof needed repair! Grandpapa could tell you hundreds of stories about smuggling: he used to do so when we were children, and he was in a good humour: we thought it a high treat!"

"I'll be bound you did," Hugo said.

She detected a little dryness in his voice, and said, with a touch of impatience: "I collect you think it very shocking! I daresay it may be, but it is not so regarded in Kent. When Grandpapa was a young man, he says there was scarcely a magistrate to be found who would commit a man charged with smuggling."

"So that made all right," he nodded.

"No, of course it didn't! I only meant—well, to show you why we don't think it such a dreadful crime as you do!"

"Nay, you don't know what I think," he said, smiling down at her.

"You will not be much liked here if you show yourself to be at enmity with the Gentlemen," she warned him.

"That's bad," he said, gravely shaking his head.

She said no more then, but the subject came up again later in the day, when Richmond asked Hugo how he had fared at the Dower House. It was Anthea who answered, exclaiming: "Richmond, do you think that odious old man is trying to keep everyone away from the house?"

"Yes, of course he is!" he replied, laughing. "You know he hates visitors! Besides, if we took to paying him visits,

152

he'd be obliged to bestir himself, and scrub the floors. Was he crusty?"

"Yes, and worse! He made my blood run cold, with his talk of footsteps, and moaning, and *paying no heed to the things he hears!* I began to have that horrid feeling that there was something behind me. If Hugo hadn't been there, I should have picked up my skirts and fled!"

"Humdudgeon!" scoffed Richmond. "In broad daylight?"

"Well, it ain't humdudgeon," intervened Claud. "I know just what she means, and a dashed nasty feeling it is! It happened to me once, walking up the lane here. Couldn't get it out of my head there was something following me. Made my flesh creep, because it was getting dark, and not a soul about."

"Did you run?" asked Anthea, quizzing him.

"I should dashed well think I did run!" he replied. "It was a devilish great black boar that had got loose. Never had such a fright in my life! Yes, it's all very well for you to laugh, but they're dangerous things, boars."

"I'd prefer to have a boar behind me than a ghost," said Anthea. "At least it would be a *live* thing!"

"Well, if you think a live boar behind you would be better than a dead one, it's easy to see you've never been chased by one!" said Claud, with some feeling. "And as for ghosts, you ought to know better than to believe in 'em! They don't exist."

"Oh, don't they?" struck in Richmond. "Would you be willing to spend the night in the grounds of Dower House?"

"You know, Richmond, you've got the most uncomfortable notions of anyone I ever met," said Claud. "Dashed if I don't think you're a trifle queer in your attic! A nice cake I'd make of myself, prowling round the Dower House all night!"

"But wouldn't you be afraid to, Claud?" Anthea asked. "*Truly*, wouldn't you?"

"Of course I'd be afraid to! I'd be bound to catch a chill, for it stands to reason I couldn't keep on walking for ever, and I'd be lucky if it didn't turn to an inflammation of the lung. I'm not afraid of seeing a ghost, if that's what you mean. I know dashed well I shouldn't."

"Don't be too sure of that!"

Claud bent a sapient eye upon his young cousin. "Well, I am sure of it. And don't you take a notion into your head that I ain't up to slum, my boy, because I am! What I should see, if I was such a nodcock as to spend the night at the Dower House, would be you, capering about in your nightshirt, with a pillowcase over your head. I don't doubt I'd see *that!*"

Richmond laughed, but said emphatically: "Not I! Anywhere else I'd be happy to try if I couldn't hoax you, but not at the Dower House! Once is enough, thank you!"

Hugo, who had been glancing through the latest edition of the *Morning Post* to reach Darracott Place, lowered the journal at this, and looked at Richmond with a twinkle in his eye. "Seemingly you're the only person who ever saw the poor lady plainly," he remarked. "What did she look like, lad?"

"I didn't see her plainly enough to be able to answer that," Richmond returned. "Besides, she was gone in a flash."

"But you did see a female form, didn't you?" Anthea asked.

"Yes, I thought it was someone from the village, when I first caught sight of it, but there wasn't much light, of course, and——"

"A misty form?" interrupted Claud.

"Yes. That is——"

"Did it shimmer?"

"Lord, I don't know! There was no time to see whether it did or not: one moment it was there, and the next it had melted into the shrubbery."

"Thought as much!" said Claud, with a satisfied air. "I get it myself. In fact, it runs in the family. There's only one thing for it, and that's mercury. You take my advice, young Richmond, and the next time you see things slipping away when you look at them ask my Aunt Elvira for a Blue Pill! Surprised she doesn't give 'em to you, because it's as plain as a pikestaff you're as liverish as Vincent!"

Vincent, entering the room in time to hear his comparison, interrupted Richmond's indignant refutal, saying, as he shut the door: "Am I liverish? I wonder if you could be right? I thought it was boredom. What have you been doing to earn this stigma, bantam?"

The matter was explained to him by Richmond and

154

Anthea in chorus. Hugo had returned to the *Morning Post*, and Claud had lost interest, his mind being occupied suddenly by a more important matter. As Vincent strolled forward, Claud's gaze was dragged irresistibly to his gleaming Hessians, and he fell into a brown study, wondering if their magical gloss could have been produced by a mixture of brandy and beeswax, and if it had ever occurred to Polyphant to experiment with this entirely original recipe. He tore his eyes away from the Hessians, and found that Vincent was looking mockingly down at him.

"Even I do not know, brother," Vincent said gently. "I hope you haven't wasted any blunt on champagne? It isn't that."

Claud was pardonably annoyed. "If you want to know what I was thinking——"

"I do know," interpolated Vincent. "I beg your pardon, Anthea! You were saying?"

"I was saying—no, Claud, don't answer him! it's precisely what he wants you to do!—I was saying that whatever Richmond may, or may not, have seen, I think the Dower House *is* haunted," stated Anthea. "I had the horridest feeling, all the time I was there!"

Hugo, who was seated sideways on the window seat, with the *Morning Post* spread before him, raised his head, and said, with a grin: "No wonder, if you let that old humbug bamboozle you into believing him!"

"You're not going to tell me that Spurstow said the place was haunted?" demanded Richmond. "Because I'll swear he never did so! He doesn't give a rush for any ghost! I happen to know, too, that when they ask him questions about it, down at the Blue Lion, he turns surly, and won't answer. Why should he take it into his head to start talking about it to you?"

"Hugo thought he was trying to frighten him. And I must say, Hugo, it does seem as though you might be right!"

"Fiddle!" said Richmond. "Why should he want to frighten Hugo?"

"Happen he thought I'd too much interest in the place," suggested Hugo, turning a sheet of his journal.

"Hugo said that he would like to strip all the ivy off, and clear away those thick shrubs," explained Anthea.

155

"I wonder? You know, it's perfectly true that he tries to keep everyone away. It hadn't previously occurred to me that he might be hiding something, because Aunt Matty never would see visitors either, but when Hugo put it into my head—Richmond, could he be using the Dower House as a hiding-place for run cargoes?"

"He *could* be," Richmond replied, "but I don't advise you to accuse him of it. He'll take it very unkind, and start prosing about having been thirty years in service and never a stain on his reputation. Ash told me he went right up in the bows when that clunch, Ottershaw, set a watch on the Dower House."

"Good God, did he do so?" exclaimed Anthea. "I never knew that! When was it?"

"Oh, soon after Ottershaw was sent here! Just after Christmas, wasn't it?"

"Dear me, what stirring events seem to take place when I am not here to be beguiled by them!" remarked Vincent. "What made Ottershaw suspect Spurstow?"

"His face, I should think," said Claud. "Anyone would!"

"The Preventives always suspect haunted houses," said Richmond, ignoring the interruption. "Ottershaw's a bigger sapskull than the man we had before! He came up to see my grandfather about it!" He grinned at Vincent, his eyes alight with mischief. "You ask Chollacombe how Grandpapa liked it!"

"I am sure he disliked it very much," said Vincent, flicking open his snuff-box. "I have every sympathy with him. A gross impertinence: Spurstow has been in Grandpapa's service all his life."

"But was that all the reason Ottershaw had?" demanded Anthea. "Merely that the Dower House is haunted?"

Richmond shrugged. "No use asking me: *I'm* not in the fellow's confidence. All I know is that he had the place watched. Spurstow discovered it, of course, and nabbed the rust. He went off to Rye, ran Ottershaw to earth in the Ship, and asked him what the devil he meant by it. I wasn't there myself, but I'm told there was a rare kick-up. Ottershaw lost his temper, because Spurstow challenged him to go back with him and search the Dower house, and of course, he dared not do it without a warrant, unless he had Grandpapa's permission, which he most certainly had *not!*"

"And did Spurstow's display of righteous indignation allay suspicion?" enquired Vincent, restoring his snuffbox to his pocket, and dusting his sleeve with his handkerchief.

"Well, it wouldn't allay my suspicion!" said Claud. "If any such gallows-faced cove came and talked to me about his spotless reputation, I'd give him in charge! Too smoky by half! Depend upon it, he's got run goods hidden all over the house!"

"If that's so, how did he get them there?" retorted Richmond. "Each time the Preventives have got wind of a big run, Ottershaw has posted dragoons in the lane, and they've never seen or heard a thing! There's no other way of getting to the house, except by the gate that leads out of the shrubbery into our grounds, and that couldn't possibly be used. For one thing, it squeaks loud enough to be heard half-a-mile away, and, for another, a man posted outside the main-gate, in the lane, couldn't help but see if anyone came out of the shrubbery."

"True," agreed Vincent. "Assuming, of course, that he was a stout-hearted fellow, and maintained his post—which I doubt. From what I know of the inhabitants of this unregenerate locality, I should suppose that they could be counted on to fortify the dragoon for his vigil with some pretty choice ghost-stories."

"Yes, of course they do," grinned Richmond. "Ash—he's the buffer at the Blue Lion, you know—says the men hate that duty like the devil. According to him, they've seen more ghosts at the Dower House than we ever dreamed of! I don't suppose they do stay too close to the gate, but it makes no odds as long as they keep the lane covered: any pack-train would have to come that way. The best of it is that while Ottershaw concentrated his forces there, the night of a big run, the train was miles to the west, and got through without catching so much as a whiff of a Preventive!"

Vincent looked rather amused. "You are remarkably well-informed! Where do you come by all this information, little cousin?"

Richmond laughed. "My boatman, of course! Lord, you don't imagine anything happens along the coast that Jem Hordle doesn't know about, do you?"

"I had forgotten your boatman. Is he one of the fraternity?"

"I haven't asked him. You should know better than to think one puts *that* sort of a question to one's boatman!"

"To be sure I do! How could I be so stupid?"

"I'll tell you something, young Richmond!" said Claud suddenly. "You're a dashed sight too caper-witted! If you don't take care you'll be made to look no-how. Ought to be sure of your boatman! What's more, you oughtn't to beach that yawl of yours where anyone could launch her, and not a soul the wiser. A rare mess you'd find yourself in if she was caught bringing in run goods, and it's all the world to a handsaw that that's just what *will* happen one of these nights!"

"I fail to see why Richmond should find himself in a rare mess because his boat was stolen and put to improper purposes, even though I'm spell-bound by your eloquence," said Vincent. "Have you undertaken to bear-lead him as well as Hugo, by the way?"

"You needn't be anxious, Claud!" Richmond interposed, a confident little smile playing about his mouth. "Jem would no more take my boat out without my leave than he'd rob me of my watch, and he wouldn't let anyone else do so either."

Claud, an expression of deep scepticism on his face, looked as though he had more to say, but as his father came into the room at that moment, the subject was allowed to drop.

Matthew, on the eve of his departure from Darracott Place, made another attempt to persuade Vincent to follow his example. He failed, for the very simple reason that Vincent's financial embarrassments made it desirable not only that he should oblige his grandfather, but that he should be put to no living-expenditure until quarter-day came to relieve his situation. But as Vincent was well aware that Matthew strongly resented Lord Darracott's capricious custom of bestowing on his grandsons handsome sums which he grudged to his own son, he did not present Matthew with this explanation to remain where he was plainly bored to death. In fact, he presented him with no explanation at all, a circumstance which sent Matthew back to London in a mood of anxious foreboding only partially allayed by his dependence on his lady's ability to control what he felt to be an increasingly dangerous situation. "My dear sir," Vincent said, "it would

158

be so unkind—really quite barbarous!—to leave my grandfather without support in this hour of trial. I could not think of it! But do, I beg of you, remove Claud!"

But Matthew very properly ignored this request, and Claud too remained at Darracott Place. He received no encouragement from his host, nor could anyone feel that a rural existence held the slightest charm for him. Still less was it felt that he entertained any very real hope of reforming his large cousin, for his first enthusiasm had not survived the several checks he had received, and although he frequently censured Hugo's dialectical lapses, and occasionally made an attempt to coax him into a more fashionable mode, it was certainly not to educate him that he remained in Kent. The truth was that his grandfather's summons had made it necessary for him to refuse an invitation to make one of a very agreeable houseparty in quite another part of the country, so that he found himself in the position of having nowhere to go for several weeks, a return to his lodgings in Duke Street at this season being clearly ineligible. He would not have chosen to stay for any length of time at Darracott Place, but he was not bored, as was his more energetic and very much more dashing brother. Notwithstanding his sartorial ambition, Claud's tastes were simple; and since the self-imposed strain of cutting a notable figure in the world of fashion was extremely exhausting he was really quite glad to spend a few weeks in the country, on what he referred to as a repairing lease. He was able to try the effect of various daring new quirks of fashion without having his pleasure marred by the dread of being thought by the high sticklers to have gone a little too far; for although he met with much adverse criticism in the bosom of his family, this was so ill-informed as to have no power to discompose him. His grandfather's notions were Gothic; his father had never aspired to a place amongst the smarts; Richmond was a callow youth, knowing nothing whatsoever about matters of taste and ton; and Vincent's contempt sprang so obviously from jealousy that he was able to ignore it. Criticism from Hugo would naturally have been beneath contempt, but Hugo never criticized his appearance: he regarded each new extravagance with awe and admiration, only once being betrayed into the expression of something in the nature of a protest. "Eh, lad,

159

you're never going to Rye in that rig?" he exclaimed involuntarily, when Claud came down the stairs wonderfully attired for this projected expedition.

"Certainly he is," said Vincent, who had unfortunately come out of the library at that moment. "Claud, my dear coz, likes nothing better than to preen himself under the admiring gaze of the local population. Don't try to deter him! So much endeavour deserves *some* recognition, after all, and when he goes on the strut in London he can never be perfectly sure that the attention he attracts is as admiring as he hoped it would be."

Since he had, with his usual acumen, stated the exact truth, Claud was roused to fury, and would have favoured him with some pithy criticisms of the style he had chosen to affect that morning had not Hugo intervened, saying, as he gently but irresistibly thrust him out of the house: "Nay, if you start a flight we shan't get to Rye at all!"

Fuming, Claud climbed up into the waiting curricle, the reins gathered in one elegantly gloved hand; Hugo got up beside him; Claud told the groom to stand away from the heads of the staid pair of horses borrowed from his grandfather's stable; and drove off, sped on his way by an earnest entreaty from Vincent, who had strolled out of the house to watch his departure, not to put his cousin in the ditch. This shaft, however, fell wide of the target, for Claud, though by no means a Nonesuch, was well-able to handle the reins in form. He instantly proved this by taking the first bend in the avenue in style, a feat which quite restored him to good-humour, since he knew Vincent to be watching him.

The road to Rye was rough, the post-road being in almost as bad a state of repair as the lane which led to it, but the journey was accomplished without mishap; and in rather less than an hour the curricle-and-pair had passed through the massive Land gate, climbed the East Cliff, and was proceeding circumspectly along the narrow, cobbled High Street to the George Inn. Here Claud gave the equipage into the charge of an ostler, for although Vincent would have unerringly negotiated the difficult turn into the yard, he wisely preferred to run no risk either of scraping his grandfather's curricle or of creating a bad impression on those inhabitants of the town who happened to be passing at the time.

Having bespoken a luncheon at the George, he led Hugo off to show him the town, but it rapidly became apparent to Hugo that his chief object was to give the town every opportunity to see him. It was also apparent that his was a known and welcome figure in Rye, for his dawdling progress down the High Street was attended by much doffing of hats, many bobbed curtsies, and as many awed stares as would have been bent upon the Prince Regent. He responded with great affability to greetings, acknowledged respectful bows graciously, magnificently ignored a following of less respectful small boys, and ogled every passable female through his quizzing-glass. It was evident that the citizens of Rye regarded him in the light of a raree-show, but if broad grins decorated male countenances, it was seldom that the female population failed to gratify him by taking in every detail of his attire with rapt eyes of admiration. Long before the bottom of The Mint had been reached, Hugo was moved to protest, which he did in blunt terms, informing Claud that he was not one who liked to be stared at, and would part company with his cousin unless he stopped behaving as though he were the chief exhibit in a procession.

"Why, I thought you wanted to see the town!" said Claud, rather hurt.

"Ay, so I do, but at this rate it will be time to have the horses put to before we've seen aught but one street. Nay then, lad, stop making an April-gowk of yourself, or we'll have all the boys in the town at our heels!"

Claud, perceiving that the Major had every intention of propelling him along the street, averted the danger of having his coat-sleeve crushed by the grip of that large hand by quickening his pace. He complained, in an injured tone, that he would never have come down The Mint at all if he had not thought it his duty to show his cousin the Strand Gate; but when they reached the bottom of The Mint there was no gate to be seen, and, after a surprised moment, he suddenly remembered that it had been demolished a couple of years previously.

"Pity, because I daresay you'd have liked it," he said. "Don't come down here often myself, which accounts for my having forgotten they'd pulled it down. However, it don't signify! We'll stroll up Mermaid Street, and I'll show you the old coaching-house. Shouldn't think they've pulled that down, though it ain't used any longer. Do you remember what we were saying t'other night, about the Hawkhurst Gang? Well, they'll tell you here it was one of their kens. Used to stamp in, as bold as Beauchamp, and sit there, boozing and sluicing, with their pistols and cutlasses on the table in front of them. Enough to put up the shutters then and there, you'd think, but I rather fancy it went on being an inn for a good few years. Yes, and I'll tell you another interesting thing about Mermaid Street," he added, after a moment's mental research. "At least, I think it was in Mermaid Street. House at the top, anyway. Fellow had a knife stuck into him. Seems to have made the devil of a stir at the time." He paused, frowning. "Now I come to think of it, I fancy it happened in the churchyard, but I'm pretty sure they found the poor fellow in the house. Bled to death."

"Who was it? Did they discover the murderer?"

"Yes, they did all right and tight. I rather fancy he was a butcher, or some such thing, who had a grudge against the Mayor."

"No wonder it made a stir!" remarked Hugo.

"Yes, but I've a notion it wasn't the Mayor who was stabbed, but some other fellow. I've forgotten just how it was, but I do know they hanged the butcher on Gibbet Marsh, above the Tillingham Sluice. Kept his body in an iron cage there for a matter of fifty years. I never saw it myself, because they took it down before I was born, but m'father says it used to be quite a landmark."

This engaging anecdote ended his account of Rye's history, the rest of his conversation, as he picked his way between the ruts and channels of Mermaid Street, being confined to bitter animad-versions on the shocking condition of the road. None of the streets that led up to the top of the hill were paved, and as they were very steep, every heavy fall of rain played havoc with their surfaces. By the time he had reached the Mermaid Inn, Claud, whose beautiful Hessians were not meant for rough walking, was a good deal ruffled; and when he discovered a serious scratch on the shining leather he came near to losing his temper. "It's no use asking me how old the place is, because I don't know, and what's more I dashed well don't care!" he said testily. "Don't stand there gaping at it! Just look at this boot of mine! Do you realize I've only had this pair a couple of months? Now they're ruined, all because nothing will do for you but to go prowling about this ramshackle town!"

"I shouldn't worry," said Hugo, with only the most cursory glance at the damaged boot. "I daresay Polyphant will know what to do. Can we get into this place?"

"No, we can't, and as for not worrying, anyone can see *you* wouldn't, but I'll have you to know——" He stopped, suddenly, and, as Hugo turned his head to look enquiringly at him, ejaculated in an altered tone: "By Jupiter, I believe that's——No, it ain't, though!—Yes, by Jupiter, it *is!*"

With this disjointed utterance he made his way across the street, sweeping off his hat, and executing a superb bow to a blushing damsel in a print dress, and a straw bonnet tied over a mop of yellow curls, who was coming down the street with a basket over one mittened arm. "La, Mr. Darracott, to think of meeting you!" she said coyly, dropping him a curtsy. "And me on my way to the chandler's, never dreaming you was in the town! Well, I do declare!"

"Allow me to carry your basket!" begged Claud gallantly.

"How can you, Mr. Darracott? As though I'd think of such a thing!"

"At least you won't refuse me the pleasure of escorting you!" said Claud.

Perceiving that the lady had no intention of refusing him this pleasure, the Major seized the opportunity to make good his escape, tolerably confident that Claud would be happily engaged in flirtation for some time to come. The yellow-haired charmer spoke in far from refined accents, but the Major felt no surprise at his elegant cousin's effusive behaviour, for he had discovered Claud two days previously, trysting with the blacksmith's pretty daughter. Claud's disposition was mildly amorous, but as he was terrified of falling a victim to a matchmaking mama, he rarely attempted to flirt with girls of his own order, indulging instead in a form of innocuous dalliance (which made his more robust brother feel very unwell) with chambermaids, milliners' apprentices, village maidens, or, in fact, any personable young female of humble origin who was ready to encourage his attentions without for a

163

moment imagining that those were serious.

So the Major deserted him with a clear conscience, and explored the town by himself. At the end of Watchbell Street he fell into conversation with a venerable citizen, who gave him much interesting information about Rye's history, not all of which was apocryphal, and directed him to the Flushing Inn, which was the scene of the murderous butcher's last drink before his execution. The Major thanked him, but preferred to visit the church, after which he wandered on until he found himself at the end of the town, in front of the ancient Ypres Tower, which provided Rye with its jail. Close by it the town-wall had been breached to allow those wishing to reach the quay below to do so by way of the Baddyng Steps. The Major walked towards the steps, and reached them just as Lieutenant Ottershaw arrived, somewhat out of breath, at the top of them.

The Lieutenant stared for a moment, and then saluted the Major, who greeted him pleasantly, and said, looking over the low wall at the precipitous slope of the hill: "A stiff climb!"

The Lieutenant agreed to this monosyllabically, and hesitated, as though he were in two minds whether to continue on his way, or to linger. Hugo settled the matter for him by nodding towards the rugged jail, and saying: "I take it that must have been a mediaeval Martello Tower. I've been talking to one of the inhabitants of the town, and from what I could gather—but my ear's not used yet to the Sussex tongue!—the Frogs made a habit of raiding Rye."

"Yes, sir, I believe they did land here on more than one occasion. Is it your first visit?"

"Ay, it is. I was never in Sussex, think on, before I came to stay with my grandfather. I don't know Kent either, beyond what I saw when I was at Shorncliffe, and that wasn't much. Are you a native of these parts?"

"No, sir. I was born in London, but my father's people were from Yorkshire," disclosed the Lieutenant.

"No, is that so? Ee, lad, that's gradely! Is ta from t'West Riding?" exclaimed Hugo broadly.

The Lieutenant's severe countenance relaxed into a reluctant grin. "No, sir—North Riding, not far from York. I was never in Yorkshire myself, though."

Hugo shook his head over this, and by dint of a few friendly questions succeeded in thawing some of the ice in which the Riding officer seemed to wish to encase himself. Ottershaw ventured, in his turn, to enquire after Hugo's military service; and in a very short while had relaxed sufficiently to perch beside him on the wall, listening with keen interest to what he had to say about the war in the Peninsula, and allowing himself to be beguiled into talking a little about his own career. It was evident that he had chosen his profession as the next best to joining the army; he spoke of it in a defensive manner, as though he suspected Hugo of despising it; whereupon Hugo said, with his slow smile: "From all I can discover, yours is a harder job than any I ever met with, and a thankless one, too."

Ottershaw gave a short laugh. "It's thankless enough! I don't care for that, but these people—in Kent and Sussex both: there's nothing to choose between 'em!—well, sir, they say Cornish folk are double-faced, but I'll swear they're nothing to what I've met with here! You saw that barrel-bellied fellow who doffed his hat to me a minute ago, and smiled all over his oily face? To hear him talk you'd think he ought to have been a Preventive himself, while as for the way he begs me to come and take my pot-luck at his house whenever I choose——" He broke off, his jaw hardening. "One of these days that's what I will do—when I'm sure I'll find pot-luck there!" he said. He jerked his thumb over his shoulder. "There's a tavern down there, on the quay—the Ypres: I was coming away from it when I met you. I *know* it's a smugglers' haunt, and I'll take my affidavit there's no one they want to see inside it less than me, but I've never been there yet but what the rascally ale-draper that owns it is all smiles and welcome! He thinks he's tipping me a rise, but I'll catch him redhanded if it's the last thing I do! I'll tell you this, sir: the whole town's abandoned to smuggling! Ay, and the Mayor, and the jurat, winking at what goes on under their noses!"

"Where does the stuff come from?" asked the Major.

Ottershaw shrugged. "Most of it from Guernsey: that's the biggest *entrepôt;* but some of it is run straight over from roundabout Calais."

"Don't they get intercepted at sea?"

"Sometimes, but, to make the naval patrol effective, double—three times!—the number of vessels is needed. Even then—with the whole coast to be watched, and the tricks that are employed being past counting—I doubt if it could be done. It's not only a matter of false bulkheads, and suchlike, sir. There's no question but that the smuggling craft slip through time and again because they get signals warning them where there's a Revenue cruiser or a sloop lurking, from vessels no one would suspect." He nodded to where a fishing smack was drawing clear of the harbour. "That craft, for instance. She may be innocent, but the chances are that if she sights a patrol-boat some damned hoverer will have her bearings before nightfall." He paused, as though deliberating, and then said: "You can't signal every craft you see to heave-to, sir, let alone board them. People don't like it—very naturally, if they're going about an honest business, such as that smack out there may be, or perhaps cruising for pleasure, as Mr. Richmond Darracott does."

"They wouldn't, of course," agreed the Major.

"However, there's one thing you can be sure of," said Ottershaw. "The blockade's in charge of a man who means to stamp out smuggling, no matter how many people he offends. Ay, and so does the Government! Time was when they were pretty lukewarm in London, but since the war ended there's been so much smuggling done that if it isn't stopped things will get to be as bad as ever they were when the Hawkhurst Gang was ruling Sussex. That's something that those who protect the *Gentlemen*, as they call them, maybe don't realize, but it'll be as well for them—and I name no names!—if they——"

His voice died in mid-sentence, and the Major saw his jaw drop, and his gaze become fixed, a sort of fascinated awe in his eyes. Considerably surprised, the Major looked round to discover what he had seen to strike him to sudden silence, and beheld his cousin Claud advancing towards him.

12

∽∾∽∾∽∾∽∾∽∾∽∾∽∾∽∾

Since he had parted from Hugo, Claud had acquired a buttonhole of enormous size, which added the final touch to an appearance startling enough to excuse Lieutenant Ottershaw's stupefaction. It was seldom that any gentleman honoured Rye by sauntering through its streets in the long-tailed coat, the pantaloons, and the Hessians that were fashionable for a lounge down Bond Street, or a promenade in Hyde Park; and even in these modish haunts Claud's costumes must have been remarkable, for his pantaloons (with which he hoped to set a fashion) were neither of a sober biscuit hue, nor of a more dashing yellow, but of a clear and delicate lilac; his neckcloth was of inordinate size, and had a large amethyst pin stuck in its folds; his hat, the very latest product of Baxter's inventive genius, was so revolutionary in design as to cause even its wearer to feel some qualms, for instead of being the bell-topped and rough beaver favoured by town-dwellers, or the more countrified shallow, it bore a marked resemblance to a tapering chimneypot. But even more stunning than his hat, or his pantaloons, was the long cloak of white drab, lined with lilac silk, which hung in graceful folds from his shoulders. It was not the custom of gentlemen to wear cloaks over anything but evening-dress; but it had occurred to Claud, studying his reflection once before setting out for Almack's Assembly Rooms, that there was something peculiarly becoming in a well-cut and silk-lined cloak. The idea of designing one suitable for day-wear had flashed into his mind, and he had instantly suggested it to Polyphant. Polyphant had not seemed to care for it, but although he usually allowed

Polyphant to guide his taste, he had been so much taken with this flower of his own brain that after brooding over it for several weeks he laid it before the more adventurous of his tailors. "Yes, sir. For a masquerade?" had said Mr. Stultz, rather dauntingly.

But Claud had not allowed himself to be daunted; and when he subsequently showed his cloak to two of his particular friends they were loud in their expressions of envy and approval. He had not yet worn it in London, but its effect on Rye had been very encouraging, and he rather thought he would venture to try it on the ton at the start of the Little Season.

Lieutenant Ottershaw found his voice. "Is that—is that Mr. *Claud* Darracott, sir?" he asked.

"Yes," replied the Major. "It is!"

The Lieutenant drew a long breath. "I'm glad I've seen him," he said simply. "I've heard a lot about him, but I didn't believe the half of it."

Having come within range, Claud put up his glass, the better to scrutinize his cousin's companion. The Lieutenant, fascinated by an eye thus hideously magnified, could not drag his gaze from it, and was only released from its spell when Claud let the glass fall, and addressed himself to Hugo, in fretful accents. "Dash it, coz! Been searching for you all over! Even took a look-in at the church. If I hadn't thought to ask pretty well everyone I met if they'd seen a mountain moving about on legs, I might be hunting for you still!"

"I've been chewing the bacon with Lieutenant Ottershaw here," replied Hugo.

"How-de-do?" murmured Claud, groping for his glass again. He raised it, a puzzled frown on his brow, and levelled it at the Lieutenant's blue and white uniform. "Naval?" he said doubtfully.

"Customs' Land-Guard, sir," said the Lieutenant stiffly.

"Thought you wasn't wearing naval rig," said Claud. "Never know one uniform from another, but those breeches didn't seem right. Well, what I mean is, don't wear 'em in the navy, do they? Silly thing to do, because it stands to reason—*Customs' Land-Guard*, did you say?"

The Lieutenant, growing stiffer every minute, made him a slight bow. "I am a Riding-officer, sir."

"That accounts for the breeches," said Claud, glad to

have this point cleared up. "Had me in a puzzle. Very happy to have met you, but trust you'll forgive me if I drag my cousin away: got a nuncheon waiting for us at the George!"

"You remind me that I also must be on my way, sir," responded Ottershaw. He then bowed again, saluted Hugo, and strode off.

"If ever I met such a ramshackle fellow!" said Claud severely. "Hobnobbing with a dashed tidesman! Next you'll be arm-in-arm with the beadle!"

"You're mighty high in the instep all at once!" remarked Hugo.

"No, I ain't: no all at once about it! Never rubbed shoulders with a Preventive in my life! Not the thing! I'll tell you what, coz: if you don't take care you'll have people wondering if you're hand-in-glove with the fellow, and you'll be in bad loaf. Take my word for it!"

"And if I were thought to be hand-in-glove with the free-traders? I collect that would be all right and regular?"

"Nothing of the sort!" retorted Claud crossly. "What you ought to do is to have nothing to say to any of 'em. I don't wish that tidesman of yours any harm—in fact, I hope he may prosper, though I shouldn't think he would, because he looked like a clunch to me. The point is, catching free-traders ain't my business, and it ain't yours either. And another thing! If my grandfather knew you'd formed that sort of an acquaintance he'd very likely go off in an apoplexy!"

Having uttered this warning, and even enlarged on it over the excellent ham pie provided for nuncheon at the George, it was with considerable exasperation that Claud heard his incorrigible cousin, some hours later, describing his encounter with Lieutenant Ottershaw to an audience that included not only Lord Darracott, but Vincent as well. This foolish lapse took place at the dinner-table, and just when everything, in Claud's judgment, was going on particularly well. When the port had been set on the mahogany, his lordship had bethought him of his heir's expedition to Rye, and had asked him, in a mood of rare geniality, if he had been pleased with the town. Upon Hugo's responding that he had been both pleased and interested, and would like to know much more about its history than he had been able to glean in one visit, he had

169

nodded approvingly; and it had needed only one question from Hugo to set him talking about the town. As far as Claud was concerned, it was a dead bore, but he was glad to see Hugo getting on terms with his grandfather, feeling vaguely that a great deal of credit was due to himself; and he did his best to promote further discussion by requesting my lord to tell Hugo the true facts about the murderous butcher. Happily unaware of having irritated my lord, who had been describing the original island-town, he then retired into his own thoughts, and paid no more heed to the conversation until his attention was recalled by Vincent's saying idly: "Didn't you tell me once, sir, that one of the cottages in Trader's Passage has a secret way down to the Strand, or some such thing?"

"That's what Ottershaw is trying to find, I daresay," remarked Richmond. "He's supposed to be stationed at Lydd, but he's for ever prowling about Rye. You didn't see him there, did you, Cousin Hugo?"

"Oh, yes, I saw him!" Hugo replied. He refilled his glass, and passed the decanter on to Vincent, and added: "I met him at the top of the steps by the Ypres Tower."

Beginning to feel a trifle uneasy, Claud directed a look at him that was meant to convey a warning that any further disclosure should be sedulously avoided. He succeeded in catching his cousin's eye, and so was startled and exacerbated when Hugo said, quite unnecessarily: "He said he had been at the Ypres Tavern."

"Accosted you, did he?" said his lordship. "Intolerable Jack Straw! I hope you gave him a sharp set-down?"

"Nay, he didn't accost me: I accosted him," said Hugo. "I wouldn't call him a Jack Straw, either."

"What the devil possessed you to do so?" demanded his lordship, a frown gathering. "I wish you will remember that you're a Darracott, sir, and learn to keep a proper distance! The fellow's an infernal coxcomb!"

"I expect my cousin didn't realize that," said Vincent suavely.

"You're right: I didn't," replied Hugo. "I'd say myself that he's a stiff-necked lad, and devilish punctilious."

"Full of starch, and muttonheaded into the bargain!" said Richmond.

"Nay, I wouldn't run away with that notion," said Hugo, meeting Richmond's eyes, and holding them. "He's

170

not as muttonheaded as you think, lad."

"What makes you say so?"

"Some of the things he told me," Hugo replied. He lowered his eyes to the glass in his hand, contemplating the play of the candlelight on the port. "There's not much he doesn't know about smuggling ways, seemingly, and not much that escapes him. I've met his sort before: I'd take care how I tried to cut a wheedle with him."

"I feel sure you are right," said Vincent. "I cannot believe that you would cut a successful wheedle with anyone."

A little chuckle shook the Major, but he said regretfully: "Nay, I'm too gaumless."

"Can none of you find anything of more interest to discuss?" demanded his lordship contemptuously. "I wish you will inform me what you find to interest you in an Exciseman?"

"Speaking for myself," answered Vincent, "nothing whatsoever, sir. Should you object to it if I were to take that sprig——" he nodded at Richmond—"to see how Cribb's latest pupil shapes in the ring? He's matched to fight Tom Bugle at Sevenoaks, for twenty guineas a side, and shows off, Cribb tells me, in excellent style. If he's not levelled in the first round, it should be a good contest: stopping and hitting the order of the day—no hugging, or hauling, and nothing shy."

"You may take him, if he cares to go," replied his lordship. "*I've* no objection, though no doubt your aunt will raise a dust."

"No, she won't, Grandpapa! Not if I have *your* leave!" Richmond said impetuously. "Besides, I'm not a child! When is it to be, Vincent? How shall we do? I've never seen a real match—only a few turnups, with tremendous milling, but no science."

He could talk of nothing else. His grandfather listened to him indulgently, Vincent with weary resignation, and Claud not at all. It seemed to occur to no one but Hugo, watching him curiously, that his eager excitement was that of a schoolboy rather than a youth on the threshold of manhood. He was transformed, his big, expressive eyes sparkling, his cheeks a little flushed; and it was evident that he looked forward as much to spending two nights away from his home as to the treat of watching a fight under the aegis of a patron of the Fancy. As soon as his grandfather left the dining-room, he went off to cajole his mother into viewing the project with complaisance, reminding Hugo of a spirited colt kicking up his heels in sheer exuberance.

"I wonder what can have possessed me?" said Vincent, a look of ineffable boredom on his face. "My only hope now is that my Aunt Elvira may be moved to beg me not to take her nestling to watch such a horrid, brutal exhibition: I should not dream of doing so against her wishes."

"Well, it beats me why he should be so devilish full of gig about it, but I call it dashed shabby if you run sly, when you've cast him into transports!" said Claud disapprovingly.

"Yes, that reflection quite sinks my spirits," agreed Vincent. "If only I had known that he *would* be cast into transports!"

"Didn't you? And you so all-alive!" said Hugo.

Vincent looked at him, his brows lifting haughtily.

"No saying what Richmond will do!" said Claud, intervening in some haste. "Odd sort of a boy. Often thought so!"

"There's not one of you that has thought about him at all," said Hugo. "Eh, Vincent, can't you see that what's cast him into transports is being let off his chain for a piece? The only odd thing about him is that he's much too biddable for such a high-couraged lad!"

"The subject holds very little more interest for me than that of Excisemen, but I feel sure you are right."

"You'd have more hair than wit if you didn't," replied Hugo, smiling. "I've had to do with a score of lads of Richmond's age! You may take it that I know what I'm saying when I tell you that if he's kept for much longer dancing attendance on his grandfather he'll be getting up to mischief."

"How very dreadful!" said Vincent sardonically.

"That's what I'm thinking," replied Hugo. "He's got a deal of energy, and no more worldly sense than a lass not out of the schoolroom. He wants always to be *doing*, but what he's got his heart set on he's been forbidden to think of, and the chances are there'll be the devil to pay, because you're brewing trouble when you try to keep randy, hey-go-mad lads of his cut in leading-strings."

"May I suggest that instead of wasting your eloquence on me you should bestow your advice—no doubt excellent!—on my grandfather?"

"Good God, no!" exclaimed Claud, horrified. "Don't you do any such thing, Hugo! Assure you—wouldn't answer the purpose at all! In fact, far otherwise!"

"Nay, what right have I to interfere?" Hugo said.

"For once, cousin, I am entirely in accord with you," remarked Vincent.

"Happen we've neither of us any right, but if I'd known the lad from his cradle, and he looked up to me, as he does to you, I'd make a push to help him. Why don't you do it, instead of throwing your tongue at me in a way that'll do you no good nor me any harm?"

"*Happen*," Vincent retorted, "I lack the effrontery!"

"Nay, you don't lack that!" said Hugo, with his deep chuckle.

Vincent stiffened, his eyes narrowing; for a moment the issue seemed to be in the balance; and then he shrugged, and walked out of the room.

As had been foreseen, Mrs. Darracott was strongly opposed to the projected scheme for her son's entertainment. She held prize-fighting in abhorrence, and seemed to be equally divided in her mind between dislike of Richmond's being taken into low, vulgar company, and fear that he had only to witness an encounter to be fired with emulation. It was useless for Lady Aurelia to tell her that she need be under no apprehension, since gentlemen did not engage in prize-fighting: between prize-fighting and boxing she was unable to perceive the least difference; and, in any event, he had been subject, as a child, to severe nose-bleedings, which would very likely be brought on again if he were to sustain a blow in the face.

"But, Mama, indeed, I don't think he has the least wish to be a boxer!" Anthea said coaxingly. "After all, Oliver didn't box, did he? And he was for ever going off to see a fight!"

She broke off suddenly, with a comical look of dismay, as it occurred to her that this comparison was not entirely felicitous.

"*Well!*" uttered Mrs. Darracott, her plump bosom

swelling with indignation. "If you wish to see your brother—your *only* brother!—return in the perfectly *disgusting* condition——"

"I don't, I don't!" interrupted Anthea, trying not to laugh. "Now, Mama——!"

"I am no friend to the sport in any form," announced Lady Aurelia, "but in this instance, my dear Elvira, you need not fidget yourself. Recollect that Richmond will be in his cousin's charge! Depend upon it, Vincent will take good care of him."

Good manners compelled Mrs. Darracott to hold her peace, but it was with difficulty that she refrained from retort, as Anthea presently explained to Hugo.

"I daresay she wouldn't have cared so very much, if Richmond had not been going with Vincent," she said. "Not that she would have *liked* it, for she never could. Indeed, I don't see how *anyone* could, except that men seem to like the most peculiar things. There is no understanding it at all!"

"That's true," he agreed. "Time and again I've wondered what maggots gets into lasses' heads to make them wild after summat that seems to me plain daft!"

"Very possibly! But at least *we* don't like cocking, and prize-fighting, and wrestling, and getting odiously foxed!" she countered, with spirit.

"We're a terrible set!" he said, much struck.

"Yes, but some of you, I own, are worse than others," she conceded handsomely. "I was used to think you were all detestable, but that, of course, was because I had only met the men of my own family. I still think *them* detestable—well, perhaps not Claud, and certainly not Richmond, though he's only a boy—but the rest of them—ugh!"

"Well, that's sent me to grass, choose how!" said Hugo, in a dejected voice.

She stared at him for a moment, and then burst out laughing. "I didn't mean you! You know I didn't! I never think of you as one of the family."

"That's the worst you've said yet!"

"On the contrary! Not but what you are detestable too, but in your own fashion!" said Anthea. "Now, do, pray, be serious! Do you think there can be any harm in Richmond's going to this horrid fight with Vincent?"

174

"None at all," he replied.

"No, nor do I, but Mama has it fixed in her head that Vincent may lead Richmond into his own way of life. I am not very sure I know what that is, precisely, but Mama seems to think it quite shocking, which I can readily believe. But, in fairness to Vincent, I should perhaps tell you that Mama is *not* to be depended on when she speaks of him, for she holds him in the greatest aversion."

"She needn't be in a worry," he said, smiling a little. "Vincent won't lead Richmond into any way of life at all!"

"Well, I wish you will tell Mama so!" she said. "She is in such a fret over it! Since Grandpapa has said he may go, I don't think Richmond will attend to her, but it must spoil his pleasure if he knows he is making her unhappy! At least——" She paused, considering this. "Well, I should think it would, wouldn't you?"

"No," he replied frankly. "But if you wish me to do so I'll talk to your mama, and gladly! Eh, lass, what nonsense it is! All this uproar about Richmond's going to watch a prize-fight, as though he were eight years old instead of past eighteen! There's not one lad in a hundred would have thought he must have his grandfathers permission, and none at all that would have breathed a word about it to his mother! Lord, by the time I was Richmond's age I'd fought my first campaign in South America, and was on my way to Sweden, with Sir John Moore! I wasn't thought to be so very young when I joined, either."

She looked up into his face, her eyes searching it rather anxiously. "It *is* unnatural, isn't it, the life Richmond leads? I didn't question it at first: you see, I know very little about the world! Except for one Season in London, and going to stay now and then with one or other of my aunts, I've hardly ever been away from this place. Of course I knew that Oliver wasn't brought up as Richmond has been, but that only made me think how fortunate it was that Grandpapa loved Richmond too much to part with him, because Oliver was for ever getting into trouble! I don't know what he did, except that it was always very expensive, and put my Uncle Granville into a passion, as well as Grandpapa, but I *do* know that he was a *loose* fish, because I once heard my uncle tell him so, and I daresay you know what *that* means!"

"Yes, love," said Hugo, smiling very kindly at her. "I

175

know right enough but happen you'd better not say it!"

"Oh, no! It sounds most improper! I wouldn't say it to anyone but—Hugo, how dare you call me *love?*"

"Did I do that?" he asked incredulously.

"You know very well you did! What is more, it is by far more improper than anything *I* said!"

"It must have slipped out," said Hugo feebly. "It's a common expression in the north!"

"Like *lass*, no doubt! And if you think, sir, that just because I grew fagged to death with telling you not to call me that, you are at liberty to call me anything else that comes into your head——"

"No, ma'am!" he intervened hastily. He shook his head in self-condemnation. "I wasn't minding my tongue. The instant our Claud's not by to give me a nudge, it's down with my apple-cart again! Eh, but it's downright disheartening!"

"And d-don't call me m-ma'am either!" said Anthea, in a hopelessly unsteady voice.

He heaved a disconsolate sigh. "I thought it would please you—Cousin Anthea!"

"You did *not!* You are an abominable person, Hugo! You've done nothing but make a May-game of us all ever since you set foot inside the house, while as for the whiskers you tell——!"

"Not *whiskers*, Cousin Anthea!" he pleaded.

"Whiskers!" she repeated firmly. "Besides acting the dunce——"

"Nay, I was always terribly gawky!"

"—and talking broad Yorkshire on the least provocation!"

"But I told you how it is with me!"

"You did! You said you couldn't help but do so whenever you are scared, and if that wasn't a whisker I never heard one! Well! If you spent your time hoaxing them all in your regiment I shouldn't wonder at it if you were *compelled* to sell out!" said Anthea, nodding darkly.

"Worse!" said the woebegone sinner before her. "I was hoping you wouldn't discover it, but there! I might have known——"

"*Hugo*——! You—you———"

He laughed. "Yes, Cousin Anthea?"

"Where did you go to school?" demanded Anthea sternly.

"That's a long time ago," he objected. "There's so much has happened to me since then——"

"More whiskers!" said Anthea, casting up her eyes.

"Well, it was—it was a school not so very far from London," he disclosed, looking sheepish.

"Eton?"

"Nay, lass!" he exclaimed shocked. "What would I have been doing at a place like that?"

"Wearing your tutor to death, I should think. But now I come to think of it I know you can't have been at Eton, for you must have met Vincent there. Harrow?"

He looked at her for a moment, and then grinned, and nodded.

"And why have you told no one that you were there?"

"Well, no one asked me," he replied. "If it comes to that, Claud hasn't told me he was at Eton!"

"No, but he hasn't done his best to make you think he was educated at a charity school!"

"Now, what have I ever said——"

"Hugo, you deliberately tried to talk like your groom! They *cannot* have allowed you to do so at Harrow!"

He smiled. "No, but I was very broad in my speech before I went there, and I had it in my ears in the holidays, so that I've never really lost it. My grandfather—not this one!——"

"*I* know!" she interpolated. "T'gaffer!"

There was an appreciative twinkle in his eye. "Ay, t'gaffer! Well, he spoke good Yorkshire all his life, but I got skelped for doing it—being Quality-make! But I do use Yorkshire expressions now-and-now—when the occasion calls for them! And in the regiment—cutting a joke, you know!"

"Yes, I understand *that!* Like Richmond saying things in the broadest Sussex—he does it beautifully, and so did Oliver! Only Grandpapa disliked it, and made them stop doing it. He said it would get to be a habit, and I must own it became very tedious. But *you*, Hugo, talked Yorkshire to hoax us!"

"It wasn't exactly that," he said. "I'd no notion of hoaxing anybody when I came here, but when I saw the way

177

you were all of you pretty well expecting me to eat with my knife—eh, lass, I couldn't resist!"

"How anyone who looks as you do can be so mad-brained——!" she marvelled. "If ever I hear of you in Newgate I shall know you owed your downfall to a prank you couldn't resist going into full-fling!"

"I'll be lucky if it's no worse," he said pessimistically. "Granddad was used to say I'd end on the gallows, all for the sake of cutting a joke. Mind you, I didn't think to find myself in the suds over this, because I hadn't been in the house above an hour before I was wondering how soon I could escape! I'd no more notion of remaining here than of flying to the moon."

"What will you do?" she asked.

"Oh, I'll bring myself home!" he said cheerfully.

"You do mean to remain, then?"

"If I get what I want."

"The Dower House?"

"Nay, that's a small matter! I'll tell you what it is one of these days, but I'm not so very sure I can get it yet, so happen I'll do best to keep it to myself."

"Well, I wouldn't tell anyone!" she exclaimed.

"The thing is you might say I'd no hope of getting it," he explained. An odd little smile came into his eyes as he saw her puzzled frown. "I'd be all dashed down in a minute," he said, shaking his head. "That would never do!"

If the Major did not succeed in wholly reconciling Mrs.
Darracott to Richmond's expedition, he did contrive, with
the aid of much tact and patience, to convince her that to
protest against it would only serve to make Richmond feel
that he was tied to her apron-strings. Perceiving from her
suddenly thoughtful expression that he had struck home,
he enlarged gently upon this theme; but it soon became
apparent that while she could be persuaded to agree (with
a sigh) that Richmond must be allowed to spread his
wings, any suggestion that she should support his ambition to enter upon a military career threw her instantly on
the defensive. In a rush of volubility, she explained why
this was not to be thought of, her reasons ranging over a
wide field which began with the delicacy of Richmond's
constitution, and ended with the clinching statement that
Lord Darracott would not hear of it. Not being one (as he
himself phrased it) to fling his cap after lost causes, he let
the matter rest, devoting his energies instead to the task
of soothing her fear that Vincent was imbued with a sinister determination to corrupt the morals of his young
cousin. To do this without setting up her back by the least
hint that few things would bore Vincent more than to be
obliged to sponsor Richmond into his own or any other
social circle called for no little ingenuity; and it spoke
volumes for Hugo's adroit handling of the situation that
Mrs. Darracott should later have told her daughter that
no one would ever know what a comfort dear Hugo was
to her. She added that he was like a son to her; and, upon
Anthea's objecting that only fifteen years lay between
them, replied, with great dignity, that in mediaeval times

it would not have been considered remarkable had she become a mother at an even earlier age.

So Richmond was allowed to set forth for Sevenoaks with no other manifestation of maternal concern than a few injunctions to be sure that his bed at the Crown had been well aired before he got between possibly damp sheets; to wrap himself up while watching the fight (because however warm he might suppose himself to be nothing could be more depended upon to give him a chill than sitting about in the open air); to go to bed in good time; to remember that buttered crab and roast pork were alike fatal to his digestion; to resist any attempts made by persons unnamed to lead him into excess; to be careful always to have a clean handkerchief in his pocket; and, finally, not to forget to thank his cousin for the treat.

Blithely promising to bear all these sensible instructions in mind, Richmond kissed his anxious parent farewell, climbed up into the phaeton, and proceeded without loss of time to forget all about them. However, as he returned two days later not a penny the worse for his hazardous adventure, Mrs. Darracott remained in ignorance of his perfidy, and was even able (though with the utmost reluctance) to give Vincent credit for having taken every care of the delicate treasure entrusted to his charge.

Meanwhile, the absence of his two favourites left Lord Darracott with no other male companion (for Claud could not be said to count) than his heir: a circumstance which prevailed upon him not only to take Hugo on a tour of his estates, but also to embark on the disagreeable task of putting him in possession of a great many financial details which he would have preferred to have kept to himself. Treading warily, Hugo listened, and made few comments. His lordship would have been furious had he demanded explanations, which, since the estate was settled, he had every right to do; but when Hugo asked no questions that could be construed as criticism he was not in the least grateful for this forbearance, but bitterly contemptuous, informing Lady Aurelia later that he did not know what he had done to be cursed with a blubberheaded commoner for his heir. She could have furnished him with several reasons, but she remained true to her traditions, hearing him out in high-bred silence, and merely remarking, at the end of his tirade, that for her part she did not consider Major Darracott to be at all deficient in understanding, however meagre might be his scholastic attainments.

The Major emerged from these sessions with his grandsire undismayed, and with one object attained: my lord's steward had been formally presented to him, and he had been advised to ask this melancholy individual to furnish him with such further information as he might desire.

Glossop, regarding the neophyte without enthusiasm, said, with mechanical civility, that he would be happy to be of service to him. Hugo responded with equal civility and even less enthusiasm, his own observations having given him the poorest opinion of Mr. Glossop's capability. It was not long, however, before each discovered that he had done the other less than justice. The steward's laodicean attitude rose not from ineptitude but from despair; and the Major's ignorance was offset by a shrewdness which awoke in Glossop's breast a faint gleam of hope that the repairs and improvements he had long since ceased to urge upon Lord Darracott might some day be undertaken.

The return of Vincent and Richmond from Sevenoaks coincided with the arrival at Darracott Place of Crimplesham's nephew. He was a solemn-eyed and conscientious young man, the eldest of a numerous family. His mother, a widow of long-standing, sped him on his way with anxious exhortations to prove himself worthy of her dear brother's exceeding kindness; his uncle received him with rather stronger exhortations to the same effect; and by the time he was conducted to his new master's presence he was so nervous that he could hardly speak. The Major's size did nothing to soothe his alarm, nor did his uncle's introductory speech add to his self-esteem. No one could have gathered from it that he had the smallest pretension to call himself a valet. His uncle trusted that the Major would make allowance for his lack of experience; and the best he seemed able to say of him was that he believed him to be honest and hardworking. It would not have surprised the unhappy young man if the Major had then and there dismissed him; but the Major dismissed Crimplesham instead, which did something to restore his sinking spirits. Upon being asked his name, he said: "Ferring, sir," and ventured to raise his eyes to his employer's face. The Major smiled kindly, and said: "Eh, don't look so dejected! If your uncle's spoken the truth about you, we'll deal very well together. I don't want a valet who will try to turn me into a Bond Street Beau, and I don't want a dry-nurse either. You'll keep my gear in good order, and make yourself useful in a general way, but you won't shave me, or brush my hair for me, and if I find you waiting to put me to bed we'll fall out!"

Ferring grinned shyly at him, and said that he would do his best to give satisfaction. By the time he had laid out the Major's evening-dress, hauled off his boots, helped him out of his coat, and rendered him as much assistance in dressing as he would accept, he had registered a silent vow to exert himself to the utmost in his determination to make himself indispensable to a master who seemed to him to approach very nearly to the ideal. When he went down to the Servants' Hall he was blissfully looking forward to an honourable and comfortable future; and when his formidable uncle yielded precedence to him at the table, his cup almost overflowed. He was a modest young man, and would willingly have taken the lowliest place, but when Mrs. Flitwick invited him to a seat beside her, opposite no less a personage than Grooby, his lordship's own valet, he realized that he had leapt magically into a position of consequence, and his elation was only tempered by regret that his mother was not present to see his triumph.

He would have been distressed had he known what heart-burnings his elevation had caused his uncle to suffer, for he was deeply grateful to him. It had not occurred to Crimplesham, when he recommended Ferring to the Major, that he was placing his nephew above himself; and when the odious Polyphant had maliciously pointed this circumstance out to him his first impulse had been to claim precedence over Ferring on the score of their relationship. But however lax they might be in the dining-room, in the Hall the hierarchy was strictly observed. There could be no question that the heir's valet ranked above Mr. Vincent's and Crimplesham was a stickler on points of etiquette. Moreover, although he had no doubt that Ferring would yield precedence to him, he had also no doubt that he would yield it to Polyphant too. Having weighed the matter carefully, he decided that the most dignified course for him to pursue, and the one that would most annoy his rival, would be to insist on Ferring's going before him, with a smile that would indicate at once appreciation of a humorous situation, and sublime indifference to his own position at the board. Having carried out this programme, he had the consolation of knowing that he had not only annoyed Polyphant, but had disappointed him as well. This was satisfactory, and even more so was the very proper way Ferring responded to several spiteful remarks addressed to him by Polyphant. He was civil, as became his years, but his smile was abstracted, conveying the irritating impression that his mind was otherwise. This happened to be the exact truth, but as Crimplesham did not know it, he continued to be very well pleased with him, and even suspected that the boy had more intelligence than he had hitherto supposed.

By the end of the week, Ferring had completely identified himself with the Major's interests, and had consolidated his position by winning the qualified approval of John Joseph, who informed his master somewhat grudgingly that the lad was better nor like, and (although born south of the Trent, which was to be deplored) certainly preferable to the Major's late bâtman: a hapless creature, to whom John Joseph referred as *that gauming, clouterly gobbin we had wi' us in Spain.*

The Major let this pass. He was seated on a horseblock, smoking a cigarillo, a circumstance that prompted John Joseph to inform him that it was a favourite perch of Miss Anthy's. "Ee, she's a floutersome lass!" he said, with a dry chuckle, and a wag of his grizzled head. "Eyeable, too," he added, with a sidelong glance at Hugo.

The Major let this pass too, his countenance immovable. After a pause, John Joseph asked bluntly: "What's tha bahn to do, Mester Hugo? Tha knows I'm not one to frump, but chance it happens tha's framing to bide here I winna be so very well suited."

"No, I'm thinking I might set up for myself at the Dower House," said the Major.

"Nay then! By what that slamtrash that lives there tells me, it's flue-full of boggarts!"

"Oh, so he's been telling you ghost-stories too, has he? Tell me now, John Joseph, what do you think of him?"

"He's a reet hellion!" replied John Joseph promptly.

"Ee, Mester Hugo, what gaes on here? Seck a meedless set they are in these parts as I never saw! Ay, and not to take pack-thread, sir, t'gaffer up yonder——" He jerked his thumb in direction of the house—"nigh as bad as the rest! Sithee, tha knows t'Blue Lion, Mester Hugo?"

Hugo nodded. "Yes, I know it: it's the inn in the village. Well?"

"I've been there whiles, playing off my dust, and neighbouring wi' t'tapper. Seemingly there's some kind of scuggery afoot at that Dower House."

"Smuggling?"

"Ay, that's what I think mysen, nor it wouldn't surprise me. There's nowt 'ud surprise me in these flappy, slibber-slabber south-country folk! I'd be reet fain to be shut of every Jack rag of 'em! Hooseever, that's not to be, so no use naffing. Mester Hugo, if tha's shaping to wink at smuggling, like t'rest o' t'gentry hereabouts——"

"Don't be a clodhead, John Joseph! Are the Preventives still suspicious of Spurstow? I know they had dragoons watching the Dower House, but I was told they never had sight or sound of run goods being carried into it."

"Nor they hadn't, sir, but when t'new young gadger came into these ungodly parts he got it into his head, seemingly, that uncustomed goods were being brung up from t'coast and stored in t'Dower House. They run t'boats in pick-nights, and mun store t'goods until t'moon's up. They carry 'em on to London then. By what t'tapper's let fall—and a reet clash-me-saunter he is when he gets to be nazy, which he does at-after he's swallowed nobbut a driver's pint!—there's hidden ways hereabouts. Least-ways, that's what they call 'em, but they're nobbut t'owd roads, sunk-like."

"Is there a watch kept on moonlight nights, to see if anything is taken *out* of the house?"

"Nay, that 'ud be sackless, Mester Hugo! Hark-ye-but, if there's nowt carried in there'll be nowt carried out! There's nobbut a half-squadron o' dragoons quartered twixt here and t'North Foreland, besides t'gadgers—and noan so many of them, by what I learn—and there's plenty of other places need a watch kept on 'em. But I'll tell you summat, sir!"

He paused, nodding. Hugo waited patiently, and after

a few moments, during which he seemed to be chewing the cud of his own reflections, John Joseph said: "T'young Riding-officer's more frack than t'owd one, and since t'last run, when him and them dragoons was made April-gowks of, chasing after nobbut a few loads o' faggots, Peasmarsh way, while t'run was carried off, it were rumoured, not so very far from here, I'll take my accidavy he's got his eye fixed on Spurstow again. Happen he's not so sickened on watching the Dower House as he makes out, for there's them as is ready to swear they seen him up t'lane now-and-now. There's been no dragoons stationed thereabouts this while back, and no manner o' good gin there had been, for Clotton—him as is his lordship's head groom—tells me they'd got so that they took every bush for a boggart, and reet laughable it was one night when a couple of 'em—nobbut ignorant lads!—came sticklebutt into t'Blue Lion, frining and faffling that there was a flaysome thing jangling round t'Dower House, and wailing fit to freeze t'blood in a body's veins. At-after that t'sergeant went up there, wi' another chap, neither of 'em being flaid o'boggarts." He smiled dourly. "They say in t'village t'sergeant weren't very well suited wi' what he saw and heard. Hooseever, he challenged t'boggart, but it vanished into t'shrubbery, and he didna care to gae after it, chance it happened Spurstow went frumping to t'owd lord that he'd been trespassing."

"Spurstow himself, with a sheet draped round him!" said Hugo. "Well, I thought as much."

"Nay, hold thee a minute, Mester Hugo! Tha's out there: it weren't Spurstow. That's sure, because Spurstow stuck his head out o' t'window, calling out to know who was there, and tha knows there's no road he could have got back into t'house from t'shrubbery without t'sergeant would have seen him, let alone he'd no time to do it."

"Oh!" said Hugo slowly. He was silent for a minute, and then looked thoughtfully at John Joseph, and said: "Keep your eyes and your ears open, will you, John Joseph?"

"Ay—and my tongue between my teeth. Happen it's nob-but a silly lad playing tricks, Mester Hugo."

"Happens it is," Hugo agreed. "I think I'll go up to the Dower House myself one night."

John Joseph grunted. "Tha'll need to bide a spirt, till

185

t'moon's up a bit. I'll gae wi' ye."

"The devil you'll not! Do you think I'm afraid of ghosts?"

"Nay, it's no ghost, sir!"

"I'll go alone, thank you, John Joseph."

Several days elapsed before the waxing moon afforded enough light to make a midnight visit to the grounds of the Dower House practicable, and when the Major did go he saw nothing more alarming than Spurstow, who came out of the house (he said) to discover who was prowling about the gardens. As the Major had strolled all round the house in full view of its windows, and knew that even in the dim light his great size made him easily recognizable, he doubted this statement, but he replied in his pleasant way that he was sorry if he had alarmed Spurstow. "I came up to see this ghost of yours, but it seems to be shy of me."

"You shouldn't ought to listen to what they'll tell you in the village, sir. It's all foolishment! Leastways, *I've* never seen it!" Spurstow said, in a surly tone.

"I'll go bail, you haven't!" replied the Major, amused.

He mentioned his expedition to none but Anthea. She regarded him in frank admiration, exclaiming: "All by yourself? Weren't you nervous? Just the *least* bit nervous?"

"Nay, I was as brave as a lion!" he assured her.

She laughed, but said: "Well, I must own I think you were! And you didn't see or hear anything horrid?"

"No, but I wasn't expected," he said. "Another time maybe I might see something."

"You mean you believe that there's no ghost, only Spurstow? If it is so, he'll never dare to try to hoax *you*—not when he knows you weren't afraid to walk all round the house in the middle of the night! What are you hoping to do? To find if smugglers do use the Dower House, or to lay the ghost?"

"Well, I'd like to do that," he answered.

"To be sure! Miss Melkinthorpe would wish it laid, of course!"

"Who's she?" asked Hugo, taken off his guard.

She opened her eyes at him. "But, my dear cousin——! Miss *Amelia* Melkinthorpe!"

"Miss Amel——" He broke off abruptly, and Anthea was glad to perceive that he had the grace to blush. "Oh! *Her!*"

She said, in a shocked voice: "You cannot, surely, have forgotten her?"

"Ay, but I had," he confessed, rubbing his nose. "I'm that road, you see: out of sight, out of mind!"

Miss Darracott realized, with considerable indignation, that the Major had yielded once more to the promptings of his worser self, and said, somewhat ominously: "Indeed?"

He nodded, meeting her smouldering gaze with one of his blandest looks. "Ay. Mind you, I wouldn't forget a lass I'd formed a *lasting* passion for!" He sighed. "The trouble is I mistook my own heart. Of course, she being so beautiful, it's no wonder I was carried away."

"I should suppose her to have all Yorkshire at her feet," said Anthea. "I remember thinking, when you described her to me, that she must be the loveliest creature imaginable! Almost too lovely to be true, in fact. There is something so particularly ravishing about brown eyes, and black curls, isn't there?"

"Nay!" he said reproachfully. "That was another one! Amelia's got *blue* eyes, and *golden* curls."

She choked.

"The thing is, she wouldn't be the right kind of wife for me when I get to be a peer. She wouldn't wish to leave Huddersfield, either—on account of her mother."

"Her mother," said Anthea encouragingly, "could come to live with you."

"No, that won't fit. She's bedfast," explained the Major, ever-fertile.

Anthea strove with herself.

"Besides, we shouldn't suit. And there's no use thinking his lordship would take to her, because he wouldn't."

"*Surely*, cousin, you cannot mean to *jilt* her?" said Anthea, in accents of reprobation.

"Nay, it wouldn't be seemly," he agreed. "I'll just have to dispose of her, as you might say."

"Good God! *Murder* her?"

"There's no need to be in a quake," he said reassuringly. "No one will ever know!"

"If only—oh, if *only* I could do to you what I *long* to do!" exclaimed Anthea. "If you were but a *few* inches shorter——!"

He said hopefully: "Nay, don't let that fatch you, love! It'll be no trouble at all to lift you up: in fact, there's nothing I'd like better!"

Furiously blushing, she retorted: "I didn't mean that I wished to *kiss* you!"

He heaved a despondent sigh. "I was afraid you didn't," he said, sadly shaking his head. "I was reet taken-aback, but I thought to myself: Come now, lad! She'd never raise your hopes only to cast you down! So——"

"Cousin Hugo, you are *outrageous!*" said Anthea, in a shaking voice.

Horrified, he replied: "You're reet; I am, love! I need someone to take me in hand, and that's the truth! Of course, if Amelia had been a different sort of a lass—more after your style!—she'd have been just the one to undertake me, but——"

"Cousin Hugo!" interrupted Anthea, feeling that it was high time he was brought to book, "you may bamboozle everyone else, but you won't bamboozle me!"

"Do you think I don't know that, love?" he said, smiling at her in a very disturbing way.

"You invented Amelia Melkinthorpe because you were afraid you might find yourself obliged to offer for me!" continued Anthea, prudently ignoring this interpolation. "And if you think——"

"Nay, you're fair and far off, lass!"

"Am I? Then perhaps, cousin, you will tell me why you *did* invent her? Not," she added scathingly, "that I shall believe a word of it!"

"Are you telling me I'm a liar?" demanded Hugo, insulted.

"Yes!" responded Anthea doggedly.

"I thought you were," said Hugo, relapsing with disconcerting suddenness into dejection.

Miss Darracott, realizing with bitter resentment that she was quite unable to control her own voice, averted her gaze, and took her quivering underlip firmly between her teeth.

Much encouraged, the abandoned creature before her

188

said confidentially: "It was this road, love! By the time you took me up to the picture-gallery my spirits were so low and oppressed by all the black looks I'd had cast on me, and I was feeling that lonely—eh, I was never more miserable in my life!"

"F-Fiddle!" uttered Anthea, shaken but staunch.

"I won't deny the old gentleman threw me into a terrible quake when he told me the scheme he had in his mind," pursued Hugo, making a clean breast of it. "It seemed to me there was only one thing for it: to shab off as fast I could before I found myself gapped! For of all the proud, disagreeable females——"

"Yes, but I——You know v-very well why I——"

"The way you sat there beside me at the dinner-table, never so much as looking at me!" he said reminiscently. "And not a word to be got from you but *Yes*, and *No*, except once, when you said *Indeed!* I thought you were reet cruel. There I was, scared out of my wits——"

"You weren't! You were *not!*"

"—scared out of my wits," he repeated firmly, "and my heart in my shoes, and you weren't even civil to me, let alone friendly!"

"You need not th-think I don't know you are m-merely trying to overset me! You didn't care a rush for any of us!"

"However, when you told me how it was," he continued, still lost in reminiscence, "I saw I'd been mistaken in you. That was the first time you smiled at me. Ee, lass, you've got a lovely smile! Happen you don't know the way it starts in your eyes, giving them such a mischievous look as——"

"That will do!" interposed Anthea, rigorously suppressing a strong desire to encourage him to develop this agreeable theme.

"I was only trying to explain how I came to invent Amelia!" he said in an injured voice. "The thing was that when you smiled at me it set me cudgelling my brains to hit on some way I could get you to stop thinking you had to keep me at a distance, which I could see you'd be bound to do, the way his lordship was trying to throw us together, unless I could put it into your head that there was no reason why you should."

"It is possible that you have the—the *audacity* to sup-

189

pose that you can make me believe that I had only to smile to make you wish to marry me?" demanded Anthea, justly incensed.

"Nay, I never said that!" he protested. "All I wanted was a friend! In fact," he added, with the air of one brilliantly inspired, "it was Hobson's Choice! I don't say I wouldn't liefer have made up to my Aunt Aurelia, mind, but——"

"*Will* you stop behaving in this odious fashion?" begged Anthea, in sore straits. "You are *utterly* without conduct, or—or propriety of taste! You would be very well-served if you did find yourself riveted to me! I promise you, you'd come home by weeping cross!"

"Ay, I know I would," he agreed. "A dog's life I'd lead, with you riding rough-shod over me, as I don't doubt you would, seeing that you're such a shrew, but——"

"Exactly so! So why, pray, do you wish to be married to me?" said Anthea, pouncing on opportunity.

"Eh, lass, I thought you knew!" he answered, his eyes round with surprise. "To please his lordship, of course!"

Miss Darracott's feelings threatened to overcome her. None of the rejoinders that rose to her lips seemed adequate to the occasion; she stared up in seething impotence at her tormentor; saw that he was watching her with an appreciative and extremely reprehensible twinkle in his eyes; and decided that the only way to deal with him was to pay him back in his own coin. So she said, with really very creditable calm: "I need scarcely tell you that that is an object with me too, but try as I will I can't bring myself to the sticking-point."

"Come now, love, never say that!" he responded, in heartening accents. "To be sure, there's a lot of me to swallow but you're too game to be beaten on any suit!"

She shook her head. "There's not *enough* of you to swallow," she said. "I must tell you that my disposition, besides being shrewish, is mercenary. I am determined to marry a man of fortune. *Large* fortune!"

"Oh, I've plenty of brass!" he assured her.

"I am only interested in gold," she said loftily. "Furthermore, I have no fancy for living in the Dower House."

"Well, I can offer you a house in Yorkshire, if you think you could fancy that. I was meaning to see it, but——"

"Have you really a house in Yorkshire?" she asked suspiciously.

"Of course I have!"

"There's no *of course* about it!" she said, with asperity. "You tell such shocking whiskers that not the slightest dependence can be placed on anything you say! Where is this house?"

"On the edge of the moor, by Huddersfield. That's the trouble. When my grandfather gave up the old house, next to the mill, and we went to live at Axby House, it was right in the country, but the town's been growing and growing, and it will grow still faster now the war's over, and more and more machines are being invented, and put to use. I hardly recognized the place when I came home at the end of the war in the Peninsula. I don't think you'd like it, love."

"No, not at all. I should want a house in London—in the best part, of course!"

"Oh, we'll have *that!*" he replied cheerfully.

"We shan't have anything of the sort—I mean, we *shouldn't*—because my Uncle Matthew has the town-house!"

"Well, there's more than one house to be had in town!"

"Dear me, yes! How could I be so stupid? I might have known you meant to purchase a handsome establishment!"

"I was thinking of hiring one, myself."

"No, no, only think how shabby! Next you will say that you don't intend to have more than one house in the country!"

"Nay, I shan't say that! I want one in Leicestershire."

"Oh, in that case there's no more to be said, for I've set *my* heart on one in the moon!"

"You don't mean that, love! Nay then, you can't have thought!" he expostulated. "It's much too far from town!"

An involuntary laugh escaped her, but she said: "I might have known you'd have an answer! Do you think we have now talked enough nonsense?"

"I'm not talking nonsense, lass. I'd give you the whole moon if I could, and throw in the stars for good measure," he said, taking her hand, and kissing it. "You couldn't be content with less?"

191

"You—you *are* talking nonsense!" she said, feeling suddenly breathless, and more than a little startled. She was inexperienced in the art of flirtation, but it had certainly occurred to her on various occasions that in this her large cousin had the advantage of her. His methods (judged by such knowledge as she had acquired during one London Season) were original, but that he might be entertaining serious intentions she had not consciously considered. Nor had she looked into her own heart. She had accepted him, after her first mistrust, as a delightfully easy companion who had kept her in a ripple of amusement: not the hero of her vague imaginings, but a simple solid creature, wholly to be trusted. She now realized, with a sense of shock, that this enormous and apparently guileless intruder had taken the grossest advantage of her innocence, advancing by imperceptible but rapid stages from the position of a stranger to be treated with circumspection to that of the close friend in whom she could safely confide, and who was, for some obscure reason, indispensable to her comfort. Any belief she might have had in the existence of the beautiful Miss Melkinthorpe had admittedly been of short duration, but the thought of marrying the Major herself had not, until this moment, entered her head. It was clearly necessary to temporize. Withdrawing her hand from his, she said, in a rallying tone: "Recollect that we have been acquainted for less than a month! You cannot, cousin, have fallen—formed an attachment in so short a time!"

"Nay, love, don't be so daft!" he expostulated. "There's no sense in saying I can't do what I *have* done!"

Miss Darracott, an intelligent girl, now perceived that in harbouring for as much as an instant the notion of marrying a man who fell so lamentably short of the ideal lover she was an irreclaimable ninnyhammer. Ideal lovers might differ in certain respects, but in whatever mould were cast not one of them was so unhandsome as to make it extremely difficult for one not to giggle at their utterances. This hopelessly overgrown and unromantic idiot must be given a firm set-down. Resolutely lifting her eyes to his face, and summoning to her aid a smile which was (she hoped) satirical, but not so unkind as to wound him, she said: "You are being quite absurd, my dear cousin! Pray say no more!"

"Never?"

She transferred her gaze to the topmost button of his coat. If anything had been wanting to convince her that he was quite unworthy of her regard, he had supplied it by putting a pistol to her head in this unchivalrous way. She wished very much that she had not committed the imprudence of looking up into his face, but how, she wondered indignantly, could she have guessed that anyone so incurably frivolous would look so anxious? Any female of sensibility must shrink from inflicting pain upon a fellow-creature, but how did one depress pretension without hurting the sinner, or rendering him unnecessarily despondent?

On the whole, she could only be thankful that the Major, apparently realizing that he had fallen into error, spared her the necessity of answering him. He said ruefully: "If ever there was a cod's head, his name is Hugo Darracott! Don't look so fatched, love! Forget I said it! I know it was too soon!"

Grateful to him for his quick understanding of her dilemma, Miss Darracott decided, with rare forbearance, to overlook the impropriety of his putting his arm round her, as she spoke, and giving her a hug. "*Much* too soon!" she answered.

His arm tightened momentarily; he dropped a kiss on the top of her head, but this she was also able to ignore, for he then said, in a thoughtful voice which conveyed to her the reassuring intelligence that he had reverted to his usual manner: "Now, where will I come by a book on etiquette! You wouldn't know if his lordship's got one in the library, would you, love?"

Her colour somewhat heightened, she disengaged herself from his embrace, saying: "No, but I shouldn't think so. He has one about ranks and dignities and orders of precedency: is that what you mean?"

"Nay, that's no use to me! I want one that'll tell me how to behave correctly."

"I am well-aware that you are trying to roast me," said Anthea, resigned to this fate, "and also that you don't stand in any need of a book on etiquette—though one on *propriety* wouldn't come amiss!"

"I'm not trying to roast you!" declared Hugo. "I want to know how long you must be acquainted with a lass before it's polite to propose to her!"

Any fears lurking in Anthea's mind that the Major's premature declaration might be productive of some awk-
wardness between them were very swiftly put to rout.
Except for a certain warmth in his eyes, when they rested
on her, she could detect no change in his demeanour. She
was devoutly thankful, for she knew that her grandfather
was closely watching the progress of a courtship he had
instigated.

It was perhaps fortunate that his lordship's attention
should have been diverted by the repercussions of quite
another sort of courtship. The blacksmith, a brawny individual, imbued with what his lordship considered revolutionary notions, had not only taken exception to
Claud's elegant trifling with his daughter, but had seized
the opportunity afforded by that rather too accomodating
damsel to pay off an old score against his lordship. To
Claud's startled dismay, the elder Ackleton waylaid my
lord when he was riding home through the village, and
lodged an accusation against his least favourite grandson,
referring to him darkly as a serpent, who had stung his
daughter, and hinting (without, however, much conviction) at reprisals of an obscure but dreadful nature. My
lord, whose native shrewdness had earned for him the
reputation in the neighbourhood of being a deep old file,
was neither credulous of the story, nor alarmed by the
threats. He might be eighty years of age, and considered
by his family to be verging on senility, but he was perfectly capable of dealing with far more determined efforts
at blackmail, and he disposed of the blacksmith in a few
forceful and well-chosen words, which included a rec-

ommendation to that disconcerted gentleman to take care the fair Eliza did not end her adventurous career in the nearest Magdelen. Since this interview took place in the middle of the village street it very soon became common property, and was the occasion of much merriment, and many exchanges, when neither the elder Ackleton nor his even more formidable son was damaging rumours about Eliza's way of life. His lordship was not popular, but the Ackletons were cordially disliked by all but their few cronies, Eliza being thought by the respectable to be a disgrace to the community, and the two male members of the family not only scandalizing decent folk with their hazy but seditious political opinions, but alienating all sorts by their invariable pugnacity when they had had a cup too much. No one was hardly enough to betray the least knowledge of the encounter outside the forge, but the sudden silence that fell on the company in the taproom of the Blue Lion, when the father and son walked in that evening left neither of them in any doubt of what the subject of the interrupted discussion had been. The elder Ackleton, after vainly trying to pick out a quarrel with anyone willing to oblige him, was bowled out by a toothless and decrepit Ancient, who took infuriating advantage of his years and infirmity, and asked the raging blacksmith, with a shrill cackle of mirth, if he had had comely speech with his lordship that morning. Encouraged by a smothered guffaw, he wagged his hoary head and stated his readiness to back the old lord to make the smith and a dozen like him look lamentable blue.

The smith, realizing that the weight of public opinion was against him, stayed only to inform the Ancient what his fate would have been had he been some seventy years younger before slamming his tankard down, and departing. It would have been as well if he had taken his son with him, instead of leaving him to drink himself into a potvaliant condition, in the company of a like-minded young man, whose reckless statements of what he would do if he stood in Ned's shoes strengthened his resolve to draw Mr. Claud Darracott's cork at the earliest opportunity. By the time an astonishing quantity of heavy wet and several glasses of jackey had been drunk, the propensity of the entire aristocracy and gentry for grinding the faces of the poor under their heels discussed, and the

195

date of a revolution modelled after the French pattern settled, Ned Ackleton was determined to seek out Mr. Claud Darracott immediately, and Jim Booley, applauding this bold decision, announced his intention of accompanying him. The landlord, contemptuously watching the manner of their departure, gave it as his opinion that the courage of neither would be sufficient to carry him beyond the gates of Darracott Place. In uttering this prophecy, however, he failed to make allowance for the invigorating effect of companionship. The harbingers of the revolution reached the house itself before Booley realized that it would be improper for him to take any active part in a quarrel which was no concern of his. He began to feel that it might, perhaps, be wiser if Ned were to postpone drawing Mr. Claud Darracott's cork until such time as he should meet him in some rather more suitable locality. But Ned was made of sterner stuff; and although the effects of liquor had to some extent worn off he had ranted himself into a state of mental intoxication which made him even more belligerent. Rejecting with scorn his friend's uneasy suggestion that it might be wiser to seek an entrance at the scullery-door, he tugged violently at the bell hanging beside the main door, and followed this up by hammering the great iron knocker in a ferocious style that caused Mr. Booley to retreat several paces, urgently advising him to *adone-do!*

This craven attitude, far from damping Ned's ardour, whipped up his courage, which had faltered a little for a moment and gave him an added incentive to force his way into the house. Booley should see that he was a man of his word; and Booley was not going to be given a chance to undermine his friend's prestige by spreading through the village a story of flight at the last moment.

Charles, the footman, opened the door. Startled by so thunderous a demand for admittance, he did so rather cautiously, which incensed Ned. Commanding him to get out of the way, he barged his way into the house, demanding, in stentorian accents, to be led immediately to Claud, whose character, appearance, and licentious villainy he described in terms which made Charle's eyes start from their sockets. Charles was of unheroic stature, but he knew his duty, and he was no coward. He did his best to hustle Ned out of the house, and was sent reeling backwards, bringing down a chair in his fall.

All this commotion brought Chollacombe and James hurrying to the scene. Ned, his appetite whetted, invited them to come on, promising them some home-brewed as a reward, but before either could accept the invitation three more persons entered on the stage. The first was Lord Darracott, who came stalking out of the library, demanding to know what the devil was going on; the second was Major Darracott, in his shirtsleeves; and the third, also in his shirtsleeves, and still holding a billiard-cue in his hand, was the hapless cause of the whole affair.

Ned put up his fists menacingly as Lord Darracott advanced towards him, but there was something about that tall, gaunt figure which made him give ground, even though he uttered a blustering threat to mill his lordship down if he tried to interfere with him.

"You drunken scum!" said his lordship, with awful deliberation. "How dare you bring your filthy carcase into my house? Outside!"

Ned spat a foul epithet at him.

"That's enough! You've had your marching orders! I'll give you precisely fifteen seconds to get yourself through that door."

Ned jumped, and looked round, but he was hardly more startled than the rest of the company. No one at Darracott Place had heard the Major speak in that voice before. It brought a gleam into Lord Darracott's eyes, and a grim smile to his lips, and it made Ned drop his fists instinctively. But just as he was about to retreat he caught sight of Claud, and he threw caution to the winds. Before he could wreak his vengeance on Claud's willowy person, Major Darracott must be swept from his path. The Major was large, but large men were notoriously slow, and could be bustled. Ned, himself a big man, and with thews of iron, went in with a rush, to mill him down before he could get upon his guard, and was sent crashing to the floor by a nicely delivered punch from something more nearly resembling a sledge-hammer than a human fist.

The Major, standing over him, waited with unruffled calm for him to recover sufficiently from the stupefying effect of this punch to struggle to his feet again. When Ned got upon his hands and knees he apparently judged it to be necessary to assist him to leave the premises, which he did in an expeditious fashion that struck terror into the heart of Mr. Booley, faithfully awaiting the return of his friend from his punitive expedition.

The Major, having hurled the unbidden guest forth, turned, and came back into the hall, nodding to James, who was holding open the door, and saying with his customary amiability: "That's all: shut the door now!"

Lord Darracott, surveying him with something approaching approval, said: "I'm obliged to you!" and went back into the library.

He was better pleased than he chose to betray, for without supposing that there was anything very remarkable in the Major's ability to floor Ned Ackleton he liked the neatness with which he had done it, and was agreeably surprised to see that for all his great size Hugo could move with unexpected swiftness. When Vincent presently came in he described the episode to him, saying: "Well, he's not such a clumsy oaf as I'd thought: I'll say that for him. Showed to advantage. Good foot-work, too."

Vincent was not much impressed, but he congratulated Hugo on his exploit with an air of exaggerated admiration. "I wish I had been privileged to witness the encounter," he said. "I hear you rattled in, game as a pebble, coz; stopped your opponent's plunge in first-rate style; and ended by throwing in a classic hit."

"Wonderful, it was!" replied Hugo, shaking his head. "Ay, you missed a high treat! He was no more than half-sprung, mind you, and not very much more than a couple of stone lighter than I am, so I did well, didn't I?"

That drew a reluctant laugh from Vincent. "My grandfather seems to think so. I'm told the fellow is much fancied as a fighter in these parts, but I collect you're not yourself a novice?"

"I can box," Hugo admitted, "but it's not often I do. I'm too big."

Everyone was pleased with Hugo's conduct except the Ackletons, both of whom were popularly held to be planning a hideous revenge; and Claud, who had no doubt on whom such a revenge would be wreaked, and considered that Hugo would have done better to have detained Ned at Darracott Place until he could have been induced to have listened to reason. Claud knew himself to be innocent of the charge brought against him, and great was his indignation when he discovered that his grandfather not only believed in his innocence on no grounds at all, but thought the worse of him for it. In high dudgeon he declared his intention of leaving Darracott Place immediately, and might actually have done so had not his lordship said, crashing his fist down on the table before him, that, by God, he should do no such thing!

"No grandson of mine shall turn-tail while I'm in the saddle!" he announced. "I wouldn't let you shab off, you pudding-headed fribble, if you *had* given that light-skirt a slip on the shoulder!"

What Lady Aurelia thought about it no one knew, for she never mentioned the matter, and nothing could be learned from her countenance or her demeanour. One or two jibes addressed to her by Lord Darracott were met with such blank stares of incomprehension that even he seemed to be daunted; and Mrs. Darracott confessed to her daughter that she for one doubted whether her ladyship knew anything at all about the affair.

Several days passed before Hugo paid his second nocturnal visit to the Dower House, wet weather making the sky too cloudy for observation. But on the first clear evening he strolled up the path to the wicket-gate into the shrubbery shortly before midnight, a cigar between his teeth. The gate shrieked on its rusty hinges; the beaten track that led to the house was sodden; and the leaves of the bushes were very wet, damping the Major's coat as he brushed past them.

A slight reconnaissance showed him that the shrubbery was intersected by several paths, once, no doubt, when the hedges were clipped, and gravel strewn underfoot, furnishing the inhabitants of the Dower House with an agreeable promenade on windy days. The hedges had not been trimmed for years, however, and the place had become a wilderness, the various paths so overgrown as sometimes to be difficult to follow. The Major, making his way out of it to the path at the side of the house, thought it would afford an excellent retreat for any ghost finding itself hard-pressed.

The moon was not yet half-full, and its light was a little fitful, clouds occasionally obscuring its face; but it was possible to make out the way, and even to discern objects at some distance. The house showed no light at any win-

199

dow, so it was to be inferred that Spurstow was either in bed and asleep or had put up the shutters in the kitchen-quarters as well as everywhere else in the house. Having walked round the building, Hugo trod across the rank grass that had once been a shaven lawn and took up his position in the shadow of a tree standing on the edge of the carriage-drive.

He had not very long to wait. The wind that fretted the tree-tops was hardly more than a whisper, but the stillness was broken after a short time by the screech of an owl in the woods, followed almost immediately by a long drawn-out wail that rose to a shriek, and died away in a sobbing moan, eerie in the night-silence. The next instant a vague, misty figure appeared round the angle of the house, and flitted into the shrubbery.

The Major, unperturbed by these manifestations, threw away the butt of his cigar, and strode towards the shrubbery. A hasty movement behind him made him check, and turn quickly, searching with narrowed eyes the deep shadows cast by the bushes by the gates. Someone, who had been concealed by these, started forward. The Major saw the moonlight gleam on the barrel of a pistol, and, a moment later, recognized Lieutenant Ottershaw. Ottershaw, paying no heed to him, began to run across the grass, with the obvious intention of plunging into the shrubbery, but two long strides brought the Major between him and his goal, and obliged him to check.

"Nay, lad, I wouldn't do that if I were you," Hugo said placidly.

"Did you see?" Ottershaw shot at him. "After that ghastly—that damned scream—someone in a sheet! Well, I'm going to discover who it is!"

"I saw," Hugo said. "But happen you'd best take care what you're about. You can't go ghost-hunting in a private garden, you know."

"That was no ghost!" Ottershaw said violently. "*You* know that, sir! I watched you: you never so much as jumped when that scream sounded! If you'd believed it was a ghost——"

"Oh, no! I didn't, of course."

"No! And why did you come here if it wasn't to discover who's playing tricks to keep people away from this place? I don't believe you're in it, but——"

200

"In what?" interposed Hugo.

The Lieutenant hesitated. "In what I know to be an attempt to drive *me* off!" he answered rather defiantly. "I've had my suspicions of this house ever since I came here, and I'm as sure as any man may be that it's one of the smugglers' chief storehouses!"

"No I'm not in anything like that," said Hugo.

"No, sir, I never supposed you could be. But——"

"If I were you, I'd put up that pistol, Mr. Ottershaw," said Hugo. "Were you meaning to challenge the ghost with it? You'd catch cold if you did, you know. It's no crime that I ever heard of to caper about rigged up as a boggard."

The Lieutenant did restore the pistol to its holster, but he was angry, and said very stiffly: "Very well, sir! But I will tell you plainly that I believe that—apparition!—to have been none other than Mr. Richmond Darracott!"

"Ay, so do I," agreed Hugo.

Ottershaw peered up at his face, trying in the uncertain light to read its expression. He sounded a little nonplussed: "*You* think that?"

"Why, yes!" Hugo said. "I think he's trying to make a May-game of you, and, if you want to know, I also think there's little he'd like better than for you to hold him up. Eh, lad, don't be so daft! It would be all over the county before the cat could lick her ear! Your commander wouldn't thank you for making a laughing-stock of yourself, and if you were to interfere with Richmond the dust you'd raise would be nothing to the dust his lordship would kick up!"

"Oh, I'm well aware of that!" replied Ottershaw bitterly. "I look for nothing but obstruction from *that* quarter! I may say—from any member of your family, sir! I'd risk being made a laughing-stock if I could catch Richmond Darracott at his tricks—as I might have done, but for you!"

"Now, what good would that do you?" asked the Major. "I daresay you'd like to give him a sharp lesson not to get up to this kind of bobbery at your expense, but you'd regret it if you did. You'd be better advised to pay no heed to him: he'd soon tire of the sport if you laughed at him—and got your men to do the same!"

"So you think he does it for sport, do you, sir?"

"Of course I do!" said the Major. "It's just the sort of

201

thing a mischievous lad would do—particularly if he thought you were a trifle over-zealous."

Ottershaw was silent for a moment. Then he said curtly: "I'll say goodnight to you, sir. I should not have spoken so freely, perhaps, but since I have done so there can be little point in concealing what I make no doubt you have guessed: I believe Mr. Richmond Darracott to be hand-in-glove with these pernicious smugglers! I have no wish—it is not the wish of the Board of Customs—to incur the ill-will of persons of Lord Darracott's consequence, but I shall take leave to warn you that no such consideration would deter me—or, I should add, would be expected to deter me!—in the performance of what I might consider to be my duty!"

"Very proper," approved the Major, a note of amusement in his voice. "But, if you don't despise a word of advice from one who's older than you, and maybe more experienced, you'll make very sure you're right in your suspicions before you go tail over top into action. It's one thing to sympathize with smuggling, but quite another to be engaged in the trade, if that's what you're suggesting. You've been having the devil of a time of it here, and seemingly it's made you think that everyone who don't help you must be mixed up in the business himself. You'll end with windmills in your head that road—if you haven't 'em already!—let alone finding yourself in bad loaf with that Board of yours."

"Is that a threat, sir?" demanded Ottershaw, standing very erect.

"Nay, it's a friendly warning," replied Hugo. "Don't you make a pigeon of yourself! Goodnight!"

The Lieutenant clicked his heels together, bowed, and strode off. Hugo watched him go, and then began to retrace his own footsteps. When he reached the wicket-gate, he studied it thoughtfully for a moment. It would have been no difficult feat to have vaulted over it, but having satisfied himself on this head he merely opened it, and walked through, impervious to its protesting shriek.

He had left his bedroom candle and his tinder-box on a table by the side-door through which he had left the house, and after kindling a light, and bolting the door, he made his way up one of the secondary staircases with which Darracott Place was lavishly provided. This one served the wing in which his own and Richmond's bed-chambers were situated; and when he reached the head of it he went without hesitation to Richmond's door, and knocked on it. Eliciting no response, he turned the handle, only to find that the door was locked. He knocked again, this time imperatively, and was rewarded by hearing Richmond call out: "Who is it?"

"Hugo. I want to speak to you," he replied.

There was the sound of an impatient exclamation, followed by the rattle of curtain-rings along a rod, and a creak which indicated that Richmond had got out of bed. The key turned in the well-oiled lock, and the door was pulled open.

"What the devil do you want?" Richmond said crossly. "I thought you knew I hate to be disturbed at night!"

"I do," said Hugo. "It had me in a bit of a puzzle to understand why, too. Nay, don't stand there holding the door! I'm coming in, and it's not a bit of use scowling at me. You can get back into bed, and we're going to have a talk, you and I."

"At this hour?" Richmond ejaculated. "I'll be damned if I do!"

"I don't know about that, but I do know that I'll toss you into bed if you don't do as you're bid," responded Hugo, wresting the door from his hold and shutting it. He held up the candlestick, and looked round. The room was a large one, with a four-poster bed standing out into it. A glance showed Hugo that the curtains had been thrust back from one side, and the bedclothes flung off. Not far from it, a chair stood, with a coat thrown carelessly on to it. Hugo's gaze alighted on this, and travelled to where a pair of breeches and a shirt lay untidily on the floor. "You did undress in a hurry, didn't you?" he said.

Richmond, climbing into bed again, linked his hands behind his head, and said, with a yawn: "I wish you will say what you want, and go away! I shan't get a wink of sleep now: I never can, if I'm wakened."

Hugo set his candle down on the table beside the bed, and lightly clasped the other which stood there. He said, smiling: "Nay, lad, I don't think you were asleep: your candle's still warm."

"I suppose I had just dropped off. That's worse! O God, *must* you sit on the bed?"

Hugo paid no heed to this complaint (for which there was some justification, as his weight bore the springs down ominously), but said: "Richmond, my lad, you've not been to sleep at all, and those clothes you've just stripped off weren't the ones you were wearing at dinner, so let's have no more humbug! Not half an hour ago you were playing hide-and-seek over at the Dower House! And from the hasty way you got between sheets I think you'd a shrewd notion you'd be receiving a visit from me."

Richmond's eyes gleamed under his down-dropped lids. "Oh, have you seen the ghost, cousin?"

"No."

Richmond chuckled. "Didn't I hoax you? I made sure I should! What made you suspect——Oh, I suppose it was what Claud said!"

"You didn't hoax anyone, and it wasn't me you were trying to hoax, was it?"

"Of course it was! I saw you set out, and guessed what you meant to do, so I followed you. Didn't you think I made a good ghost? *I* think I did!"

"Nay, you didn't follow me. You were there before me," replied Hugo. "You came round the corner of the house, and you couldn't have crossed the path between the shrubbery and the house unbeknownst to me."

"But I could get into the garden from the shrubbery, and keep under cover there until the house shut me from your view."

"Ay, you could have done that," agreed Hugo. "Did Spurstow tell you that I visited the place before, on the same errand?"

Richmond laughed. "Of course!"

"And that Ottershaw was watching the house himself?"

"No, *is* he?"

"Come, lad, you knew that!"

"How should I know it?" Richmond countered.

"Probably because Spurstow told you; and if it wasn't he I've a notion you've other sources of information. Between the pair of you, you've scared Ottershaw's men, but when you set out to scare him you made a back-cast, Richmond: he wasn't scared, and he wasn't deceived. If I hadn't stopped him he might well have caught you."

"Not he! Much good would it have done him if he had, too!"

204

"So I told him," said Hugo. "It would have done him no good, but it would have done you no good either."

"Why, is there a law against bamboozling Excisemen?" asked Richmond, opening his eyes wider.

Hugo looked rather gravely down at him. "For what purpose?"

"Oh, just kicking up a lark!"

"Is that why you did it?"

"Yes, of course: why else should I do it?" Richmond said impatiently.

"That's what I don't know, lad, but I think you're too old to be kicking up that sort of a lark."

The impish gleam had faded from Richmond's dark eyes; the look he shot at Hugo was one of smouldering resentment. "Maybe! What the devil else have I to do? In any event, what concern is it of yours? I wish you will go away!"

"Happen I will, when you stop trying to stall me off, and give me a plain answer," Hugo replied, a little sternly. "I've a notion you're in dangerous mischief. If I'm right, you're likely to find yourself floored at all points, for Ottershaw's not the clodhead you think him. Don't play off your cajolery on me, but tell me the truth! Have you embroiled yourself in the smuggling trade?"

Richmond sat up with a jerk. "Well, upon my word ! What next will you ask me? Just because I cut a lark with that stiff-rumped Exciseman you seem to think I'm as good as rope-ripe! Why should *I* take to free-trading, pray?"

"For sport," replied Hugo, smiling faintly. "Because it's a dead bore to have nothing to do but mind your book— which I've yet to see you do!—and dance attendance on your grandfather. I own, the life you're made to lead would be out of cry to me, as it is to you. If you're helping to run contraband goods, it's because you like the adventure, not for gain." His smile broadened as he saw Richmond glance strangely at him. "Well, has that hit the needle?"

Richmond lay down again, this time on his side, pillowing his cheek on his hand. "Lord, no! I played ghost for sport. Famous sport it was, too! You should have seen those cowhearted dragoons huddling together! I made 'em take to their heels once. However, if Ottershaw's rum-

205

bled me there's no sense in continuing. I won't do it again: are you satisfied?"

Hugo shook his head. "Not quite. What makes you lock your door every night?"

"How do you know that I do?" Richmond countered quickly, up in arms.

"Eh, there's no secret about it! Everyone in the house knows it. You take precious good care no one should come near you once you've gone to bed, don't you?"

"Yes, and you've been told why!"

"I've been told that if you're roused you don't drop off to sleep again, and I think—not to take packthread, you young gull-catcher!—that that's humdudgeon!"

Richmond gave a little chuckle. "Oh, no! Not wholly! But there are nights when I don't sleep much. If you must know, when that happens I can't lie counting the minutes: I get up, and go out, if there's moonlight. And sometimes I go out with Jem Hordle, fishing. Well, that's why I take care no one shall come tapping at my door! If my mother knew, or Grandpapa—Lord, what a clutter there would be! They want to keep me wrapped in lambswool: you know that! As for taking the *Seamew* out at night—particularly since my uncle and Oliver were drowned!—if either of them so much as suspected I did that—oh, I'd be so watched and guarded I should run mad!"

Hugo said nothing for a moment or two, but sat looking down at Richmond with a slight frown in his eyes. The explanation was reasonable, but he thought the boy was on the defensive, watching him from under his lashes, a guarded look on his face, a hint of tautness about him.

It was Richmond who broke the silence, saying sweetly: "May I try now if I can go to sleep, cousin?"

"I suppose so," Hugo answered, getting up. He hesitated, and then said: "You've told me you're not meddling in contraband, and I hope that was the truth, because if it wasn't you won't be the only one to fall all-a-bits. You've listened to a deal of loose talk about free-trading, lad, but if it were to come out that you'd had a hand in such dealings there's no one who would be more over-powered than your grandfather."

"Oh, go to the devil!" snapped Richmond, with a spurt of temper. "You needn't be afraid! Do you mean to tell him that you think I'm a free-trader? I wish I may be

206

present! No, I don't, though: I hate brangles! As for what I choose to do when I can't sleep, you've no right to scold: you're not my guardian, or—or even head of the family—yet!"

"Nay, did I do that?" asked Hugo, mildly surprised.

There was an angry flush on Richmond's cheek, but it faded. He muttered: "No—I beg pardon! But I can't endure—oh, well, it's no matter!"

Hugo picked up his candlestick saying, with his slow grin: "Can't endure to be interfered with, eh? It's high time you learned discipline, you meedless colt—military discipline! I'm not the head of the family, but happen I'll help you to that pair of colours, if you don't bring yourself to ruin before I've a chance to do it."

Richmond smiled wryly. "Thank you! You can't do it, however. When I'm of age—oh, talking pays no toll! I shall be at Oxford then, I daresay."

"I doubt it! In the meantime, lad, tread the lineway, and never mind if it's a bore. I mislike the cut of that Riding-officer. He's mighty suspicious of you, and though I wouldn't say he was down to every move on the board, he's by no means the sapskull you think him."

A little, confident smile curled Richmond's mouth. "He's been outjockeyed again and again—by what I've heard."

"Ay, and he's not the man to cry craven," said Hugo significantly. "He don't love you, Richmond, and if he thought he could bowl you out he'd do it."

"But he can't."

"I hope he can't, but chance it happens that you find yourself in a hobble, don't throw your cap after it, but come to me! I've been in more than one tight squeeze in my time."

"Much obliged to you!" Richmond murmured. "It's midsummer moon with you, you know, but I'm persuaded you mean it kindly! *Do* go to bed, Hugo! I'm so *very* sleepy!"

15

Richmond did not look, on the following morning, as
though he could have been as sleepy as he said he was
when Hugo left him. He went riding as usual before
breakfast, but when his mother and his grandfather saw
him each perceived immediately that he was heavy-eyed,
and a little pale. He was subjected to a cross-fire of anxious
solicitude on the one hand and rigorous interrogation on
the other, and bore it with such patience that Hugo marvelled at his restraint. His eyes met Hugo's once, in a look
ridiculously compound of defiance and entreaty. He won
no response, but derived considerable reassurance from
his large cousin's expression, which was one of bovine
stupidity. Since he did not think that Hugo was at all
stupid, he interpreted this as a sign that he had no immediate intention of disclosing the previous night's
events to Lord Darracott, and did not again glance in his
direction.

That swift, challenging look had not, however, escaped
his sister's notice, and at the earliest opportunity she commanded Hugo to explain its meaning. Even less than
Richmond was she beguiled by his air of childlike incomprehension. She said severely: "And pray don't stare at
me as though you were a moonling!"

"Nay, love, that's not kind!" protested the Major, much
hurt. "I know I'm not needle-witted, but I'm not a *moonling!*"

"You're the slyest thing in nature!" his love informed
him with great frankness. "But I myself am pretty well up
to snuff, so don't think to tip *me* a rise, if you please!
You'll make wretched work of it."

Shocked by this forthright speech, he said: "Eh, you mustn't talk like that, lass! You'll be setting folks in a regular bustle! That's a very ungenteel thing to say: even *I* know that!"

"Forgive me, cousin!" she begged, primming up her mouth. "I meant, of course, that it is useless to think you can *deceive* me!"

"That's much more seemly," he said approvingly.

"Yes, but I now find myself at a loss to know how to advise you, in polite language, not to draw herrings across the track in the vain hope that you'll persuade me to run counter!" she retorted.

"Oh, I'd never be able to do that!"

"Well, I'm happy to know you're awake upon *that* suit, at all events!" She looked up into his face, smiling a little wistfully. "Don't quiz me, Hugo! Why did Richmond look at you like that? As if he was afraid of you—afraid you were going to say something he didn't wish you to! Tell me what it was—*pray* tell me, Hugo!"

He possessed himself of her hands, and held them clasped together against his chest. Smiling reassuringly down at her, he said: "Now, what's made you so hot in the spur, love? And just what sort of a queer nabs do you think I am?"

"Oh, no, no, I don't think that!" she said quickly.

"Well, I'd be a *very* queer nabs if I'd a secret with Richmond, and blabbed it to you!" he replied. "Nay then! don't look so fatched! All Richmond was afraid of was that I might say something, in my clumpish way, which he'd as lief wasn't said before his mother and the old gentleman. And I can't say I blame him," he added reflectively. "To hear the pair of them talk you'd think he was eight years old instead of eighteen!"

She nodded. "Yes, I know that. Do I seem a dreadful pea-goose? I daresay I am!"

"You do and-all!" he told her lovingly.

"What a truly detestable creature you are!" she remarked. "I collect Richmond was not tossing restless in his bed, but was not, in fact, in his bed at all, but I promise you I don't mean to enquire where he was, because from anything I have ever heard one should never, if one wishes to retain the least respect for them, enquire what

209

gentlemen do when they have contrived to escape from their female relatives."

Charmed by this large-mindedness, the Major said, with simple fervour: "I *knew* you'd make a champion wife, love!"

"On the contrary! My husband will live under the cat's foot."

"I'm very partial to cats," offered the Major hopefully.

She smiled, but drew her hands away, shaking her head at him. "My own belief is that you are a gazetted flirt!"

"Oh, is it?" he retorted. "If that's so I'll be off and ask my Aunt Elvira's leave to pay my addresses to you without any more ado!"

"I shall warn her to hint you away—not that I have much hope that a mere hint will serve, because you are quite without conduct or delicacy, and altogether a most improper person!"

Cordially agreeing with this reading of his character, the Major ventured to remind her that it was her duty, as seen by her grandfather, to reclaim him.

"I am persuaded it would be a hopeless task," she replied firmly. "What's more, I know very well that all this nonsensical talk is what Richmond calls a *fling*, to lead me away from what I wish to say to you. Don't joke me any more, but tell me——" She broke off, knitting her brows.

"Tell you what, love?"

"I don't know. That is, it is so hard to put it into words! Lately—before you came here—I have felt uneasy about Richmond. I can't precisely tell why, except that he was in such flat despair when Grandpapa ordered him to put the thought of a military career out of his head. He wasn't sullen, or rebellious—he never is, you know!—but dawdling, and languid, not caring for anything very much, his spirits low, and depressed—Mama was afraid he would fall into a lethargy! And then, all at once, and for no reason that I could perceive, he became *alive* again. He has a great deal of reserve, but one can always tell by his eyes: they are so very speaking! Mama says that when they are bright it is a sign that he is in good health, but it's not so—not wholly! When he was a little boy, and in dangerous mischief, they used to look alight, just as I've seen them again and again in these past months. Once, when

210

I went for a sail with him and Jem in the *Seamew*, a gale blew up, and we had the narrowest of escapes from foundering. *I* was never so frightened in my life—well, it was the *horridest* thing!—but Richmond *enjoyed* it! He had that look: his eyes positively blazing—smiling, too, in the most *inhuman* way! It was as though he liked fighting the waves, and being in the greatest peril, which Jem afterwards told me we were!"

Hugo nodded. "Ay, he would: he's that road. It's excitement he likes, and it leads him into daredevilry, because he's bored, and too full of energy for the loitering life he leads. I've met his like before. Don't fret, lass! He's only a colt yet—a resty, high-couraged colt that needs exercise, and breaking to bridle. He puts me in mind of a friend of mine: just such a wiry, craze care-for-nobody, but the best duty-officer I ever knew. By hedge or by stile we must bring his lordship round to the notion of a Hussar regiment for the lad."

"If one could!" she sighed. "He thinks Richmond will out-grow that ambition—has done so already, perhaps."

"He'll learn his mistake," the Major said dryly. "If he won't yield now, with a good-grace, he'll suffer a bad back-cast the moment the lad comes of age, and joins as a volunteer. You may lay your life that's what he'll do, and his lordship wouldn't be very well suited with *that*!"

"No, indeed! Or any of us!" she exclaimed. "But he's not nineteen yet, and sometimes I feel such an apprehension that he may do something reckless, or even outrageous, because he's not used to being crossed, besides never counting the cost before he plunges into the most hare-brained scrapes! You may say I'm indulging crotchets, but when he looked at you today it flashed across my mind that he is in a scrape, and that you know what it is. Do you, Hugo?"

"Nay, I'm not in his confidence," he replied.

She scanned his face searchingly but to no avail. "When he shot that look at you I knew that he didn't go to bed when he said goodnight to us, and it was plain that you knew *that* at least."

He laughed. "Don't fidget yourself, love! He took it into his head to try if he could play a prank on me, young varmint!"

She looked relieved, but not wholly convinced. After

211

thinking it over for a moment, she said: "I think he does sometimes slip out of the house when we believe him to be in bed. I went to his room once, in the middle of the night, because Mama had the tooth-ache, and remembered that she had given her bottle of laudanum to him when he had a bad tic. I knocked and knocked on his door, and even called to him, but he didn't answer me, and I thought then that he wasn't there. But when I told him about it in the morning he said that he had taken a few drops of laudanum himself, which had made him sleep like the dead."

"Well, that's very possible," Hugo answered.

"Yes, only—one can't but own that the Darracotts all have a—a certain unsteadiness of character—if you know what I mean!"

"I know just what you mean, and the Darracotts have not *all* that particular unsteadiness of character!"

She smiled. "Well, I *hope* not! But after Claud's escapade——"

"So that's what's put you into the hips!" he interrupted. "You may be easy! I fancy we'll receive no drunken invasion on our Richmond's account. I'd a notion myself he might be in mischief, but he's told me it's not so. Think no more of it, love!"

She said gratefully: "If Richmond knows your eye is on him I shouldn't think he'd dare plunge into a scrape. I am *very* much obliged to you!"

He had the satisfaction of seeing the worried look vanish from her face; but the reassurance he had conveyed to her was no reflection of his own state of mind. He found himself in a quandary; for while, on the one hand, the task of informing Lord Darracott of his discovery and his suspicion was naturally repugnant to him, and certainly fatal to his future relationship with Richmond, on the other, he was unable to persuade himself that Richmond's word might be accepted without reservation. He had come away from his interview with the boy considerably disquieted, and at a loss to know what course to pursue. He was too much a stranger to be able to win Richmond's confidence, and even doubted whether Richmond gave his confidence to anyone. He had thought from the outset that Richmond was oddly aloof. The reason had not been far to seek, but it had not been until he came to grips with him that he realized how impenetrable was the barrier behind which Richmond dwelled. An impulse to encourage Anthea to question him herself had no sooner occurred to him than he had rejected it. Richmond, in his judgment, was neither young enough nor old enough to tolerate the interference of a sister. There seemed to be nothing for it (since his uneasy suspicion rested on no solid foundation) but to watch Richmond unobtrusively, and to hope that the knowledge that there was one member of the household at least who was on the alert would make him chary of pursuing any unlawful form of amusement.

A third course swiftly presented itself. Vincent, encountering him on his way home from one of his tours of the estate with my lord's bailiff, elected to ride back to the house with him, and said as soon as Glossop had parted company with the cousins: "I hear you've laid the Darracott ghost, coz. Poor Richmond! But I think he should have known better than to have entertained the least hope of shaking your stolidity."

"So he told you, did he?" Hugo said slowly.

"But of course!" Vincent returned, his brows lifting in mockery. "He may have misjudged *you*, but he knows *me* well enough not to dream of withholding such an excellent story from me."

"I should have thought of that before," said Hugo. He turned his head, the hint of his disarming grin on his countenance. "You were in the right of it: *dull, brainless Ajax* fairly hits me off! Happen you're the only one amongst us with the power to bring that lad to his senses. Did he tell you all that passed between us last night?"

"He didn't withhold the cream of the jest from me, if that's what you mean," replied Vincent, with his glinting smile.

"Remember I'm blockish!" said Hugo. "What was the cream of it, by your reckoning?"

"Do you know, dear cousin, there have been moments when I have wondered whether I was a trifle out in my first judgment of you? How comforting it is to meet with reassurance on this head! The cream of the jest was the conclusion you jumped to, in your somewhat ingenuous fashion—if I may be permitted so to describe it!"

Quite unmoved by the studied offensiveness of this

answer, Hugo asked straitly: "Has it never occurred to you that there's something devilish smoky about that half-ling's docility? He doesn't want for spirit: he's full of spunk, and as meedless as be-damned besides!"

"I am afraid I have never given the matter a thought," said Vincent, smothering a yawn.

"Give it one now, then! You may be too well-accus-tomed to the state of affairs here to be struck by what must fairly stagger anyone coming, as I did, as a stranger amongst you. I told you once that I've had more experi-ence of lads than you, and I'll tell you now that I hadn't been here above a sennight before I hadn't a doubt but that our Richmond was playing some kind of double game, though what it might be I hadn't a notion, until I got into conversation with that Riding-officer. I'd have had to be twice as blockish as I am not to have realized that there was more behind his hostility to Richmond than resent-ment at the treatment he'd met with at his lordship's hands. I'm bound to own that the suspicion that gave me seemed too cock-brained to be entertained—until I'd added one thing to another, and, in particular, the sort of loose talk the lad had listened to all his life: not one of you, seemingly, having enough sense to see the daft risk you were running! The blame's to be laid chiefly at his lordship's door, but you're no floss-head, and you've known the lad from his cradle! Nay then, Vincent! Did it never occur to you he was touchwood, needing no more than a spark to set him ablaze?"

"No," said Vincent, very gently. "But do, pray, con-tinue! You mustn't think I'm not enjoying it. I am, in fact, *much rapt in this*, and—er—apprehend *immediately The unknown Ajax*. The passage, which I've mauled a little, continues: *Heavens, what a man is there!*—But perhaps it would be uncivil to complete the line, and for me to be uncivil to the future head of my family would not do at all."

The Major regarded him with tolerant amusement, re-marking placidly: "For one who doesn't want for sense you waste a mort of time milking the pigeon! You'll pick no quarrel with me, so you may as well stop trying to make me nab the rust, and attend to what's of much more moment. Richmond wasn't playing ghost last night for my benefit: he wanted to scare Ottershaw away from the

214

Dower House, if he could do it. He knows now he can't, and I believe him when he says he won't cut the caper again. If I didn't, I'd have no choice but to lay the whole matter before his lordship, which is the last thing I want to do. Ottershaw had his pistol in his hand when I halted him. Whether he'd have used it is another pair of shoes: I think not, but it won't do to run the risk of it."

"If it comforts you, you may know that I have already told Richmond that, however amusing the repercussion of his exploit may have been, such pranks are really quite unworthy of him," said Vincent languidly.

"It would comfort me much more if I felt I could leave the matter in your hands. Richmond won't confide in me: it's not to be expected he should."

"But he has—unless I have misinformed—given you his assurance that he is not engaged in any such nefarious occupation as smuggling," interpolated Vincent, in a voice of silk.

"Ay, he's done that," admitted Hugo. He was silent for a moment, gazing meditatively ahead, between his horse's ears. A rather rueful smile crept into his eyes. "I've no reason to doubt his word, and the Lord knows it goes against the pluck with me to do so, but I think he lied to me."

"I cannot supply you with any reason for doubting him, but I can, and will, supply you with one—possibly incomprehensible to you, but nevertheless to be relied on—for accepting his word," said Vincent, his eyes hard and contemptuous. "Richmond, my dear coz, was born into, and reared in, an order of society whose members do not commonly give lying assurances, or engage in criminal pursuits. However much *you* may have been misled by what you term the *loose talk* so reprehensibly indulged in by my grandfather, it is as inconceivable that Richmond should confuse *sympathy* with *participation* as that he, a Darracott, would entertain for one instant the thought that he might join a gang of such vulgar persons as free-traders. I trust I have made myself plain?"

"You've done that, right enough," Hugo replied. "I don't know if you believe what you say, or if you say it because you dislike me too much to think of aught else; and any road it doesn't make a ha'porth of odds: you don't mean to lift a finger to save a lad who thinks the world

215

and-all of you from bringing himself to ruin! You've made me a fine, top-lofty speech about Richmond's birth and rearing: his birth's well-enough, but his rearing was as bad as it could be! Sithee, Vincent, you know that! I know it too. When you were at Eton, I was at Harrow, and what hadn't been clouted into me by my granddad I learned there." He paused, and the twinkle came back into his eyes. "And there wasn't so very much to learn either!" he added. "Reet vulgar he was, my granddad, but worth a score of any Darracott I've yet laid eyes on!"

"Harrow——!" murmured Vincent, in the grip of cold fury. "To be sure, our opinion of Harrow was never very high, but—ah, well!"

Hugo chuckled. "Nor ours of Eton, think on! Ee, if you haven't got me talking as you do yourself! Sneck up, and ask yourself how much you'd have learnt if you'd been reared as Richmond was!"

They had ridden into the stable yard by this time, and as their grooms had already come out to take charge of the horses Vincent's sense of ton prevented him from making any reply which he considered to be worthy of the occasion. He was silent therefore, but his groom, catching a glimpse of his face, would have given a month's pay to have been privileged to know what the Major had said to put him in the devil's own passion.

He strode out of the yard without vouchsafing a word either to his cousin or to his servant; and after exchanging a few observations with John Joseph, and, to that severe critic's disapproval and the grinning delight of several stableboys, admonishing Rufus in the broadest dialect for his want of manners in demanding with every sign of equine impatience the sugar he knew very well would be bestowed upon him, the Major followed him, in his leisurely way, to the house.

The post had been brought up from the receiving-office during his absence, and a thick letter, addressed to himself, and stamped Post Paid, lay on the table by the door. He had just broken the wafer that sealed it, and spread open three closely written sheets, when Chollacombe came into the hall to tell him that my lord desired to see him in the library as soon as might be convenient to him. The Major, already perusing the lengthy communication sent him by one who subscribed himself as his attached

216

friend and obedient servant, Jonas Henry Poulton, acknowledged this message with an abstracted grunt, neither looking up from the letter in his hand, nor evincing the smallest disposition to make all speed to his grandfather's presence. Any one of his cousins would have recognized the civil form in which the message was phrased as the cloak spread by Chollacombe over a peremptory (and possibly explosive) command; but nothing would ever avail, thought Chollacombe despairingly, to teach Mr. Hugh the wisdom of obeying such summonses with all possible dispatch. He coughed deprecatingly, and said: "His lordship, sir, is anxious to see you, I fancy."

The Major nodded. "Yes, very well! I heard you. I'll go to him as soon as I've changed my clothes. Send Ferring up to my room, will you, Chollacombe?"

Chollacombe sighed, but attempted no remonstrance. For his own part, the Major's invariable custom of putting off his riding-habit as soon as he came in from the stables met with his fullest approval, but my lord, he knew well, had no particular objection to the aroma inseparable from the horses, and every objection to being kept waiting for as long as five minutes. He went away, knowing from experience how useless it would be to remind the Major of this circumstance, or to hint to him that my lord was sadly out of temper.

The Major discovered this for himself when he walked into the library some twenty minutes later. When last seen by him my lord had been unusually amiable; his brow was now thunderous, and he showed, by the nervous twitch of his fingers, and the throb of the pulse beside his grim, thin-lipped mouth, that something had happened to cast him into the worst of ill-humours. He was standing with his back to the fireplace, and he greeted his huge grandson with a fierce scowl and a barked demand to know where the devil he had been.

"Over into Sussex, sir," replied the Major, shutting the door. "Was there something you wanted me to do? I'm sorry."

Lord Darracott seemed to be exerting himself to curb his temper. He did not answer the Major, but said abruptly: "I sent for you because I've had a letter from your uncle Matthew. I don't know what maggot's in his head, or where he came by the information he has sent

217

me. He's a damned fool, and always was! Anyone could gull him!"

The Major, though of the opinion that Matthew had rather more common-sense than any other member of the family, allowed this unflattering estimate to pass without comment, and waited with patience and equanimity for my lord to reach the kernel of whatever piece of information had raised his ire.

Lord Darracott, hungry for legitimate prey, glared more menacingly than before; and, failing to unnerve his grandson into committing the imprudence of answering him, snapped, with bitter loathing: "Dummy!" The gambit eliciting no more than a twinkle in the Major's guileless blue eyes, he expressed, not for the first time, his burning desire to be told why Fate had seen fit to afflict him with a grapeseed for his heir; and came, at last, to the meat of the matter. "My son writes to inform me that that fellow— your maternal grandfather!—was the head of some curst firm or other—*I* don't know anything about such things!— that goes by the name of Bray & Poulton. Is that so?"

The Major nodded. "Ay, that's so. He was its founder. Uncle Jonas Henry is the head of it now, but at the first-end, when he was a little lad, he was just one of the pieceners—they're the children that keep the frames filled, or join the cardlings for the slubbers——"

"*Uncle?*" interrupted his lordship. "You told me you had none!"

"Nay, he's no kith of mine," replied Hugo soothingly. "It was what I used to call him when I was a lad myself, and he the best weaver in the Valley. He was a prime favourite with my granddad, but it wasn't until near the back-end of his life that Granddad took him into partnership—having no one but me to succeed him, who hadn't been bred to the wool trade."

"Are you telling me, sir, that your maternal grandfather was a mill *owner?*" thundered my lord.

"Why, yes!" replied Hugo, smiling. "That's what he rose to be, though he started as a weaver, like his father before him. He was as shrewd as he could hold together, my granddad—a reet knowing one!"

Stunned by this disclosure, it was several moments before his lordship was able to command his voice enough to utter: "A man of *substance?*"

"Ay, he was well to pass," replied the Major. "You might say that he addled a mort of brass in his day, tewing and toiling—which he did to the end, think on! It wasn't often you wouldn't have found him at the mill, wearing his brat, even when he'd got to be one of the stiffest men in the whole of the West Riding. His brass wasn't come-by easily, either," he added. "It was make and scrape with him before he'd addled enough to get agate—not that he was what we call sneck-drawn, in the north. It was just that he knew how to hold household, like any good York-shireman." He paused, perceiving that my lord was staring at him in mingled incredulity and wrath, and added, in a tone of kindly explanation: "That wasn't the way he made his fortune, of course: it was only the start of it. He was flue-full of mother-wit: the longestheaded man I ever knew, and with a longsight to match it, what's more! Fly shuttles were invented before he was born, of course, but it wasn't until he was five years old that the first of the power-looms was put into use—and precious few liking it overly much! He saw it when he was a piecener himself: he told me once that that was the start of his life. Seemingly, he had never any other notion in his head from that time on but what was tied up with machines. He was one of the first to buy Cartwright's loom—not the one they use now: that didn't come till a matter of a dozen years later; but a queer old machine you'd think even-down antiquated today. All that was long before I was born or thought of: by the time I was out of short coats such things weren't considered newfangled any more, and the mill, which the better part of Huddersfield said Granddad had run mad to build, was doing fine!" He smiled, and said apologetically: "Nay, I might as well talk Spanish to you, sir, mightn't I?" His smile broadened to a grin. "And if any wool-man could hear me explaining the trade to you he'd laugh himself into stitches, think on! You could floor me with any one of a dozen questions, for all I know is little more than I picked up, running about the mill when my grandfather's back was turned. The thing was that in the old days there was no such thing as a mill, where the packs went in at one door, as you might say, and came out of another as cloths—serges, kerseymeres, friezes, and the like. Cartwright set up a factory in Doncaster, where weaving and spinning both were done; but Granddad went one better nor that—levelling at the moon, they used to say—until they saw that old, ramshackle mill growing and growing! Today, the name of Bray is known to the trade the world over."

This intelligence did not appear to afford Lord Darracott the smallest gratification. He said, in the voice of one goaded to exasperation: "I know nothing about mills, and care less! Answer me this, sir! Is it true, what your uncle writes me—that you inherited a *fortune* from Bray?"

"Well," replied the Major cautiously, "I don't know just what you'd call a fortune, sir. I'd say myself I was pretty well-inlaid."

"Don't come any niffy-naffy, shabby-genteel airs over me!" barked his lordship. "Tell me without any damned roundaboutation how much you're worth!"

The Major rubbed his nose. "Nay, that's what I can't do!" he confessed.

"You can't, eh? I guessed as much! Trust Matthew to exaggerate out of all recognition! *Why* can't you?"

"I don't know myself, sir," said Hugo, making a clean breast of it.

"What the devil do you mean by that, idiot?" demanded his lordship. "Presumably you know what your grandfather left you!"

"Oh, I know what his private fortune was, reet enough!" said Hugo. "It's invested mostly in the Funds, and brings in between fifteen and sixteen thousand pounds a year; but that's not the whole of it. I've a sizeable share in the mill over and above that. I can't tell you what they may be worth to me. Times have been bad lately, what with Luddite riots, and the depression that followed close on the Peace. The harvests were bad last year, too: my uncle Jonas Henry wrote me that in Yorkshire wheat rose to above a guinea the bushel. However, things seem to be on the mend now, so——"

"Are you telling me that Bray cut up to the tune of *half a million?*" said my lord, in a strange voice.

"It would be about that figure—apart from the mill," Hugo agreed.

Lord Darracott was shaken by a sudden gust of rage: "How dared you, sir, deceive me?" he exclaimed.

"Nay then! I never did so," Hugo reminded him. "It was in this very room that I told you I'd plenty of brass."

"I remember! I supposed you to be referring to prize-money—as you knew!"

Hugo smiled down at him. "And I told you that my other grandfather had left his brass to me. You said I might do what I pleased with my granddad's savings, but that you wanted to hear no more of them or him. So I didn't tell you any more, for, to own the truth, sir, I was better suited, at that time, to keep my tongue between my teeth until I'd had time to look about me. What's more," he added reminiscently, "I wasn't ettling to remain here above a sennight—particularly when you told me you had it all settled I was to wed my cousin Anthea. Eh, it was a wonder I didn't take to my heels there and then!"

Lord Darracott stared at him, his lips tightly gripped together, and his eyes smouldering. He did not speak, but after a moment went to the wing-chair on one side of the fireplace, and sat down, his hands grasping its arms. The Major sat down too, saying: "Happen it's as well my uncle wrote to you, for it's time we reached an understanding. It chances that I'd a letter myself by today's post, from Uncle Jonas Henry." He chuckled. "Seemingly he's as throng as he can be, and a trifle hackled with me for loitering here. I shall have to post off to Huddersfield next week, sir—and a bear-garden jaw I'll get when I arrive there, if I know Jonas Henry!"

Lord Darracott said, with an effort: "Have the goodness to tell me whether you mean to return, or to stay there!"

"Nay, that's for you to say, sir."

The fierce old eyes flashed. "It appears I have no hold over you!"

The Major considered him, not unsympathetically. "Well, that's true enough, of course, but don't fatch yourself over it, sir! If you're thinking of the brass, I'll tell you to your head it makes no difference: you'd have had no hold over me any road. But all the brass in the world wouldn't help me to cross this threshold if you didn't choose to let me."

His lordship gave a contemptuous snort of unmirthful laughter, but said in a milder tone: "Well, what do you mean to do?"

"Unless you dislike it, I'd choose, once I've settled my affairs, and talked things over with Jonas Henry—I'm by way of being his sleeping partner, you see—to come back.

221

I'd be very well suited if you'd let me have the Dower House. That's assuming you wish me to take up my quarters here. If not—well, there's my grandfather's house above Huddersfield, or I might buy a house in the Shires, perhaps. Time enough to decide what I'll do—and maybe it won't be for me to decide, either."

Lord Darracott looked intently at him. "Am I to understand you mean to marry Anthea?"

"If she'll have me," said the Major simply.

"She should be flattered! In these hurly-burly times I don't doubt your fortune will make you acceptable to any female. I dare swear every matchmaking mother in town will cast out lures to you: you have only to throw the handkerchief," said my lord sardonically.

"Well, as I'm doing no throwing of handkerchiefs we'll never know if you're right. Myself, I shouldn't think it, but there's no sense in breaking squares over what won't come to pass. If my cousin won't have me—eh, that doesn't bear thinking about!"

"H'm! You seem to have become wondrous great with her!" remarked his lordship. "Does she know what your circumstances are?"

"Well, I told her, but she didn't believe a word of it," replied Hugo. "And what she's going to say when she finds I wasn't trying to bamboozle her has me in the devil of a quake!" he confessed.

His lordship returned no answer to this, but said presently, keeping his eyes fixed on the Major's face: "What's your purpose in wishing to live here while I'm above ground?"

"Much what yours was, when you sent for me, sir. Since I must succeed you, it will be as well your people should know me, and I them. I've the devil of a lot to learn, too, about the management of estates, for that's something that's never come in my way." He paused, returning my lord's gaze very steadily. "All to one, they're in bad shape, sir, so happen it's a good thing I've plenty of brass."

"Ah!" My lord's hands clenched on the arms of his chair. "We come to it at last, do we? I don't need you to tell me my land's in bad heart! I know better by far than you what is crying out to be done, and what it would cost to do it! But if you think to make yourself master here in

222

my time, you may take your *brass*, as you call it, to hell with you!"

"Nay, that's foolishness, sir!" Hugo remonstrated. "I've no wish to be master here, for I'd make wretched work of it, as ignorant as I am. But soon or late it will be my fortune that sets matters to rights, and I'd liefer it was soon. If I put money into the place, I'll not be kept in the dark about any question that properly concerns me, so it's likely we'll fratch now and now; but I'll be no more master than Glossop is. I'd be the junior partner."

"I'll brook no interference from you or anyone with what's my own!" declared his lordship. "You'd like to make me your pensioner, wouldn't you? I'll see you damned first!"

"There's nothing I'd like less," replied Hugo. "And what you do with your own is none of my business. But what's done with settled estates you won't deny is very much my business." He saw his grandfather stiffen; and said, smiling a trifle wryly: "You bade me talk without roundaboutation, sir! I'm not such a dummy that I can't see for myself that there have been things done the trustees never knew of, for they'd not have consented to what's nothing more nor less than waste."

"Are you threatening me?" demanded his lordship.

Hugo shook his head. "Lord, no, sir! I don't doubt it was forced on you. I'm neither threatening, nor asking questions. I'll set things to rights—and keep 'em so! That's all."

"It is, is it?" said his lordship, eyeing him with grim humour. "I begin to think that you're a damned, encroaching, managing fellow, Hugh!"

Hugo chuckles. "Ay, but happen you'll grow accustomed to me, for you need someone to manage for you, other than your bailiff." He got up, and stood for a moment or two, looking down with a lurking twinkle at his lordship's brooding countenance. "You sent for me to lick me into shape, sir, because you couldn't stomach the thought that a regular rum 'un would step into your shoes, if naught was done to teach him how to support the character of a gentleman. Well, it may be that I'm not quite such a Jack Pudding as I let you think. I own, it was a ramshackle thing to do, but when I saw how there wasn't one amongst

223

you that didn't believe I'd been reared in a hovel I could no more resist trying how much I could make you swallow than I could stop drawing breath! But by what road you thought I came by a commission in such a regiment as mine, if I'd been an unlettered rustic, the lord only knows! I was no more bookish than Richmond, but I got my schooling at Harrow, sir! However, when it comes to the management of large estates, I'm no better than a raw recruit—and that's what I'm hoping you mean to teach me."

A gleam shone in his lordship's eyes. "At the end of which time you'll be ruling the roast, I collect!"

"Nay, if I'm here at all I'll be leg-shackled, and no spirit left in me!" replied the Major. "Never you fear, sir! A terrible shrew she is, the lass I've set my heart on!"

16

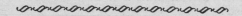

The first person to learn the news was Vincent, entering the library not ten minutes after Hugo had left it. His mood was far from sunny; and when his grandfather told him bluntly that so far from being a penniless weaver's brat his cousin was the grandson of a wealthy mill owner, and plump enough in the pocket to be able to buy an Abbey, he stared at him for a full minute, his eyes glittering, and his mouth thin with bitterness. When he at last spoke, it was with his usual languor, but in a voice that had a cutting edge to it. "So!" he said. He drew out his snuff-box, and took a pinch. "I felicitate you, sir!"

Lord Darracott gave a sardonic grunt, but said: "So you may! He's prepared to drop his blunt to bring the place about."

Vincent flicked a grain of snuff from his sleeve. "Handsome of him! Does he happen to have the smallest notion how much blunt he will be obliged to drop to restore the Darracott fortune, I wonder?"

"He seems to have a good many more notions than I knew!" replied his lordship harshly. "He may or he may not have that one, and he's not likely to care: he won't easily break his back! He's worth half a million at the least computation."

"Half a million——!" Vincent ejaculated. His mouth smiled unpleasantly. *"That mongrel cur, Ajax!"*

His lordship laughed shortly. "Ironic, ain't it? Damn his effrontery! He as good as told me I'd rendered myself open to an action at law!"

"You do not surprise me at all, sir: I always thought you were over-sanguine in believing he could be brought up to the rig."

"Oh, he was within his rights!" said his lordship un-expectedly. "It put me out of temper, but I'm sure I don't like him the better for showing fight. He needn't think he's going to rule the roast, however!"

"I devoutly trust you may be able to hold your own, sir, but I must confess that I find it difficult to perceive how, if he pays for it, he is to be prevented from ruling the roast."

"You'll perceive how soon enough, if I have any inch-ing attempts made to unsaddle me!" said his lordship tartly. "To do him justice, he told me he'd no such inten-tion. Said he'd prefer to be my junior partner, if you please!"

"*Timeo Danaos!*" Vincent murmured.

"Don't be a fool! He may have hoaxed us all, impudent dog! but he's no shuffler. It's a pity he was ever born, but I'll say this for him: he's the only one amongst you that ain't a blood-sucker!" He added, on a note of satisfaction: "He means to marry Anthea, too, so that takes *her* off my hands."

"Yes, that has been very obvious," answered Vincent. "I must certainly be the first to congratulate her on her good fortune!"

Since he encountered her in the hall, on her return from a carriage-drive with Mrs. Darracott, he was not only the first to congratulate her on her good fortune, but the first to inform her of it. She lifted her brows, asking him what he meant. He replied, with exaggerated surprise: "But, my dearest cousin, what could I possibly mean? How could you think I should be backward in offering you my felicitations on your forthcoming marriage?"

Her smile was quite as satirical as his. "Am I about to be married? I did not know it."

"Then I have been not backward but premature, which is much worse—quite unworthy of me, indeed! Between such old friends as we are, however, the *convenances* need not be too strictly regarded. Dear Anthea, *don't*, I do most earnestly counsel you, let such a prize slip through your fingers! Believe me, once he shows his front in town there will be girls past counting on the catch for him! I would not, on any account, play fast and loose, though I feel sure you do it charmingly. One does not— if one is a Darracott!—play fast and loose with a fortune!"

226

She began to look genuinely amused. "Ah, I understand you now! When do you mean to stop allowing Hugo to hoax you? I was used to think you the most knowing one in the family, too!"

"Did you, my sweet? That comforts me, for I was used to think so myself, until I discovered that I must yield priority to you."

"Vincent, what *are* you talking about?" she asked patiently.

"Why, Hugo's fortune, of course!" he said, opening his eyes at her.

She burst out laughing. "He hasn't got a fortune! Vincent, you goose!"

"What a day of surprises this is!" he remarked. "Do you know, I never dreamed you were possessed of such large ideas? For myself, I should be content with a *quarter* of a million pounds!"

"I should think you might indeed be! You don't imagine, surely, that Hugo has a quarter of a million pounds?"

"No, no, nothing so paltry! Half a million at the *least!*"

She was still amused, but a puzzled frown gathered on her brow. "I hope you mean to tell me why you are trying to gammon me!" she said. "In general, I understand you pretty well, but this fling is quite beyond me. If Hugo told you he had a huge fortune——"

"I shouldn't have believed him, of course," he interrupted. "The news, dear Anthea, came from my father, and I can't feel that he was gammoning us. It would be quite unlike him, you know."

The smile had vanished from her lips; she stared incredulously, growing a little pale. "It's not true!"

"Oh, weren't you aware of it? I am disappointed: I was thinking you the only provident member of the family! Yes: half a million, in the Funds. Quite a genteel fortune! Then there is his share in the mill—not, perhaps so genteel, but I daresay you won't despise it."

"I don't believe it!" she exclaimed impetuously. "My uncle must have been mistaken—or you are trying to roast me?"

He looked at her, his brows raised. "Do you know, I begin to think you really were unaware of your good fortune?" he said.

She returned no answer, but stood perfectly still, an

expression of shocked dismay in her eyes. He laughed, and sauntered away; and for a full minute she remained at the foot of the staircase, one gloved hand tightly gripping the carved baluster. Recovering slightly from her stupor, she set her foot on the first stair, and then, on a sudden impulse, turned back, determined to find the Major immediately, and to confront him with what she still suspected to be a hoax.

She ran him presently to earth in one of the smaller saloons, engaged in writing a soothing reply to his partner's letter. "So here you are!" she exclaimed. "I have been searching all over for you! You will please explain to me, *at once*, how Vincent came by this—this cock-and-bull story he has just told me!"

He looked round, his pen in hand, and said admiringly: "Eh, you do look pretty, love!"

Since the flower-trimmed silk bonnet tied under her chin with a broad satin ribbon was of her own making, this tribute would, at any other time, have been very acceptable. At the present moment, however, she had no thought to spare for such frivolities, and retorted with asperity: "Never mind how I look! Vincent says—Hugo, it isn't true, is it? You *haven't* a large fortune, have you?"

"Nay, lass!" he said, in a tone of pained remonstrance. "I *told* you I had!"

She gazed at him, flushed and horrified. "I thought you were funning! I never *dreamed*——! Oh, how *could* you?" she said passionately.

He laid the pen down, and got up, and went towards her. "Oh, it was none of my doing!" he assured her. "Granddad addled it, and, having no other chick or child, he just left it to me."

"*Half a million pounds?*" she said, in tones of revulsion.

"Something like that," he nodded.

"Oh, how—how *horrible!*" she uttered, putting out her hands to thrust him away.

"Nay, love, I thought you'd be pleased!" he expostulated.

"*Pleased?*"

"Of course I did! Why, you told me yourself you meant to marry a man of large fortune! Mind, I was a trifle shocked to find you were so mercenary, but——"

"You knew very well I was joking you! I would never have said such a thing if I'd had the least notion——Oh, how abominable you are!" she said indignantly.

"Now, how was I to know that? The way you stood there, telling me only a house in the best part of town would do for you, and saying I was sneck-drawn to be thinking of hiring one instead of buying it—well, I was fairly taken-aback!" he said, shaking his head.

"Then I marvel at it that you still wished to offer for me!" she said, quite unable to refrain from retort.

"Well," he confessed, looking sheepish, "I'd gone so far I couldn't for the life of me see how to hedge off."

After a moment's severe struggle with herself, Miss Darracott said bitterly: "I should have known better! I might have guessed you were only waiting for the chance to say something outrageous! Well, you can hedge off now, sir!"

"It's too late, lass," he said, with a heavy sigh. "I'd have everyone saying I'd conducted myself reet shabbily."

"That needn't trouble you! I will engage to make it very plain to all that I refused your obliging offer! As for people saying you had behaved shabbily, what, pray, do you think they would say of me, if I married you? Cream-pot love is what they'd say! Vincent is doing so already? He-he thinks I knew the truth from the start, and—and set my cap at you, just because I wished to be wealthy! And I don't!" declared Miss Darracott, much agitated.

Perceiving that she was having great difficulty in finding her handkerchief in the recesses of her reticule, the Major very kindly gave her his own. She took it, casting a wet but darkling glance at him, angrily dried her eyes, and informed him, in a slightly husky voice, that she never cried but when she was enraged.

"If ever I met such a naggy lass!" observed the Major, recovering his hankerchief, and contriving, at the same time, to put his arms round her. "Now, don't cry, love! We can soon set things to rights! How much money would you *like* to have?"

"Don't be absurd!" begged Anthea, making a half-hearted effort to push him away. "What I should like is of no consequence whatsoever!"

229

"Ay, but it is. It won't do for me to get rid of my fortune without knowing how much of it you want me to keep," he said reasonably.

"Get rid of it?" She lifted her head to stare at him. "Would you—if I asked you to?"

He smiled down at her. "Well, it wouldn't be a particle of use to me if you didn't marry me. The only thing that fatches me a trifle is that I've promised my grandfather to let him have what's needed to set this place in order. Of course, I *could* make him a present of it, to play at ducks and drakes with, which I don't doubt he would: but setting aside that it would drive me daft to see him doing it, if I've to step into his shoes one day it'll be just as well if I'm able to stand the nonsense. Besides, I'll have to support an establishment of my own—and it's no use asking me to set you up in a weaver's cottage, love, because there's reason in all things, and I won't do it! It would be well enough if I were a small man, but to be obliged to duck my head every time I went through the doorway wouldn't suit me at all. What's more," he added thoughtfully, "I'd be bound to fill the place up more than you'd like."

"Are you *never* serious?" asked Anthea despairingly.

"I was trying to hit on a way out of the difficulty," he explained, injured.

"You were trying to make me laugh—and don't waste your breath denying it!"

"I wouldn't call it a *laugh* exactly," said the Major diffidently. "It's more of a *gurgle*, if you know what I mean. Yes, *that's* it!"

"Any female who was so idiotish as to marry you would be driven to madness within one week!" declared Anthea.

"I know she would," he agreed. "That's why I'll not live in a cottage with you, love."

"Hugo, this is no laughing matter!" she said. "I feel quite *dreadfully* about it!"

"I can see you do, but why you should has me in a puzzle. If you're nattered by what Vincent says——"

"What Vincent says is what everyone else will say, or, at any rate, think!" she interrupted. "I daresay I should myself. They'll say I *caught* you before you'd had time to meet other, and far more eligible females! Indeed, I shouldn't wonder at it if they said you had been *entrapped* into marrying me—which is perfectly true, because Grandpapa sent for you with that end in view! Hugo, you might marry *anyone!* I think you should go to town, and—and look about you! At least no one could say then that you were allowed no opportunity to make your own choice."

"Nay, I can't do that!" he said hastily. "It would be downright foolhardy, and that's something we Light Bobs don't hold with. I'm not going next or nigh London till I'm safely wed."

"*Now* what are you going to say?" asked Anthea, in a resigned tone.

"I see I'll have to make a clean breast of it," said the Major, with every sign of shamefaced reluctance. "The thing is, love, that my grandfather tells me that the instant I show my front in town I'll have all the matchmaking mothers hunting me down. I wouldn't know what to do, for I'm not accustomed to that sort of thing, never having had lures cast out to me before, besides being a bashful kind of a man. It wouldn't be cousinly of you to abandon me. In fact," he added, rapidly developing a strong sense of illusage, "it would be reet cruel, seeing how I put myself in your hands, just as I was bid."

"I would give much to see you fleeing in terror from a matchmaking mother," remarked Anthea wistfully. "Or, indeed, from anyone. But as you are utterly brazen——"

"Nay!"

"—and *much* in need of a set-down——"

"I'm not in need of that, lass, for I'm getting one," he interpolated ruefully.

"No, no!——At least——Oh, dear, I daresay it sounds foolish to you, and I know I told you I was mercenary, but I'm *not*, Hugo! Only think how it would appear to everyone! As though I had been determined before ever I saw you not to let your odious fortune slip through my hands!"

He patted her consolingly. "You needn't worry about that, love. When people see you wearing the same bonnet for years on end they'll never think you married me for my fortune."

"As nothing would induce me to wear the same bonnet for years on end——"

"You'll have to," he said simply. "I'm a terrible nip-farthing. Sare-baned, we call it. It'll take a deal of coaxing to get as much as a groat out of me. I hadn't meant to tell you, but I wouldn't want to take advantage of you, and if you were thinking I'm not one to cut up stiff over the bills, or——"

"If you knew what I was thinking, you'd never hold up your head again!" she told him. "You seem to forget that you wished to purchase the moon for me!"

"Nay, I don't forget that! The thing is I can't purchase it, so there was no harm in saying it. Now, if I'd said I'd like to give you a diamond necklace, or some such thing, you might have taken me up on it. I remembered that just in time to stop myself," he explained, apparently priding himself on his forethought.

"I should like very much to have a diamond necklace," said Anthea pensively.

"Wouldn't a paste one do as well?" he asked, in a voice of great uneasiness.

She had been so sure that he would fall into the trap that she was taken, for an instant, off her guard, and looked up at him with such a startled expression on her face that his deep chuckle escaped him, and he lifted her quite to her feet, and kissed her.

Scandalized by such impropriety, Miss Darracott commanded him to set her down immediately, on pain of never being spoken to by her again. This threat cowed him into obedience, and Miss Darracott, considerably flushed and ruffled, was just about to favour him with her opinion of his conduct when Claud walked into the room, thus saving his large cousin from annihilation.

Claud had come in search of him, the news of his affluence having by this time reached him. He could scarcely have been more delighted had he himself suddenly inherited a fortune, for he instantly perceived that now more than ever would Hugo need a guiding hand, particularly in the choice of a suitable town residence, and its furnishings. He had a great turn for such matters, and had, indeed, so unerring an eye for colour, and such exquisite taste in decoration, that his advice was frequently sought by ladies of high fashion who desired to bestow a new touch on their drawing-rooms. Since he lived modestly in two rooms in Duke Street, there was little scope for his genius in his own abode: a circumstance which made him look forward with intense pleasure to the prospect of being able to lavish his skill not merely on a drawing-room or a saloon, but on an entire house, from attics to basement. "It'll be something like!" he assured Hugo. "Just you leave it to me, old fellow! No need for you to worry yourself over it! You dub up the possibles, and I'll lay 'em out to the best advantage. Yes, and don't, on any account, enter into a treaty for a house behind my back! You'd be diddled, as sure as check, because it stands to reason you can't know your way about in London. Anthea don't know either, so it's no use thinking you can leave it to her. As likely as not she'd land you in Russell Square, all amongs the Cits and the bankers, or Upper Grosvenor Street, miles from anywhere."

This was a little too much for Miss Darracott. "Have no fear!" she said coldly. "Indeed, I can't conceive why you should suppose I should wish to choose a house for Hugo!"

"Dash it, you're going to marry him, aren't you?" said Claud. "We all know *that!*"

"You know nothing of the sort!" she declared hotly. "The only thing you know is that Grandpapa desires it, and if you imagine that I care a rush for——"

"No, dash it!" interrupted Claud. "Never thought about the old gentleman at all! Well, what I mean is, it's as plain as a pikestaff! You can't go about smelling of April and May, the pair of you, and then expect to gull people into thinking you don't mean to get riveted! A pretty set of gudgeons you must think we are!"

"That's dished me!" said the Major fatalistically.

"I'll tell you what!" said Claud, engrossed in his vicarious schemes, "we'll take a holt to the village next week, and see what's to be had! No reason why you and my Aunt Elvira shouldn't come too, Anthea. You can put up at——"

"Nay, we'll do no such thing!" intervened Hugo, in some haste. "I'm off to Huddersfield next week."

Anthea, making a dignified exit, looked back involuntarily. "Going away! Oh—oh, are you? Will you be making a long stay at Yorkshire?"

"Not a day longer than I must," replied Hugo, smiling at her so warmly that she felt herself blushing, and retired in shaken order.

In all but one quarter, the news of Hugo's wealth was very well received, Ferring, in particular, becoming so puffed-up that his uncle felt obliged to snub him severely. My lord came to dinner in a mood of unprecedented amiability; and Mrs. Darracott told her affronted daughter that fortune was the one thing needed to make dear Hugo wholly acceptable.

"Mama, how can you!" exclaimed Anthea.

"Well, my love, it is a great piece of nonsense to pretend that life is not very much more comfortable when one can command its elegancies, and always be beforehand with the world, because it is!" replied Mrs. Darracott, with one of her disconcerting flashes of commonsense. "I liked Hugo from the outset, but although I very soon perceived that he was just the man to make you happy, I *could* not wish you to marry him when I believed it meant that you would be obliged to live here, dependent on your grandfather! But he has been telling me about his scheme to refurbish up the Dower House, if you should not dislike it—and I can't think why you should, dearest, for he says the ghost is nothing more than Spurstow, trying to keep everyone away, which wouldn't surprise me in the least, for I always disliked that man, and even if there is a ghost it cannot possibly be more disagreeable to live with than your grandfather! *I* should not find it so, at all events, and only think, Anthea! dear Hugo wishes me to live there too! Of course I said I should not, but I was very much affected: indeed, I cried a little!" She paused to dry the tears that were again rolling down her cheeks. "He couldn't have been kinder if he had been my own son!" she disclosed. "You must not suppose I wasn't *devoted* to your poor Papa, my dear, but no one could call him a *dependable* man, and oh, what a *comfort* it is to one to have a creature like Hugo to turn to! Say what you will, my love, there is something *about* very big, quiet men! So ridiculous, too!" she added, with a rather shaky laugh. "He says if you won't marry him he will want me more than ever to live at the Dower House, to keep house for him! I was obliged to laugh, though naturally I gave him a scold for talking such nonsense. And although I wouldn't press you for the world, my dearest child, I did tell him that nothing could make me happier than to see you married to him—and it is of no use to take a pet, because if you are not in love with him, all I can say is that you are a most shocking *flirt*, which I should be sorry to think of any child of mine! And as for not marrying him because he is much wealthier than we knew, I never heard anything so absurd in my life!"

Miss Darracott made no attempt to defend herself; but, revolted by the knowledge that the better part of her family was apparently waiting in hourly expectation of receiving the news of her betrothal, she roundly informed her suitor next day that nothing would induce her to gratify a set of persons whom she very improperly described as vulgar, prying busybodies.

The Major received this declaration with perfect equanimity, even going so far as to say that he would be very well suited to postpone the announcement of the engagement until (as he phrased it) they were shut of his Uncle Matthew's family. "That won't be long after I get back from Huddersfield, from what my Aunt Aurelia was saying t'other evening. I'll have to go there, love, because when I was recalled, before Waterloo, I'd no time to do more than pitch all my affairs back into Jonas Henry's lap, as you might say. Ay, and that puts me in mind of another thing! He hired Axby House from me when my grandfather died, and I've a notion he'd be glad if I'd sell it to him outright. Now, tell me, love: shall I do it, or have you a fancy for it?"

"I think you should do exactly as you wish."

"Nay, love!" expostulated the Major.

"I only meant that—well, how could I have a fancy for a house I've never seen?" said Anthea. "Though I own I *should* like to see that place where you were born."

"Well, I wasn't born at Axby House, so that settles it," said the Major cheerfully. "Tell me another thing! Do you think Richmond would care to go with me?"

She looked quickly at him. "Richmond! Why, Hugo?"

He said, with one of his most innocent stares: "Just for company. Happen he'd be interested to see something more of the country than he's yet had the chance to."

"I should think he would like very much to go, but I do *not* think that that's what you have in your head," she said shrewdly. "I know you don't mean to tell me what it is, so I shan't waste my breath in trying to persuade you to do so. I only wish you may prevail upon Grandpapa to

235

let Richmond go with you, but I very much doubt that you will. He is suspicious of you, Hugo: did you know that? He is afraid you may foster Richmond's military ambition."

He nodded. "Yes, I know that, and he's in the right of it, think on! I'm going to do more than that, odd-come-shortly—and that's another reason, love, why you should marry me!"

This was an opening not to be ignored. "You mean, I collect," said Anthea thoughtfully, "that you won't help Richmond unless I do marry you."

"No, love," responded the Major gently, "I'm not holding a pistol to your head. I'll do what I can for Richmond in any event, but I'd be standing in a far better position if I were his brother-in-law, and not merely one of his cousins."

She drew an audible breath. "What a delightful thing it is to know that if I'm such a wet-goose as to marry you I shall be able to depend on having a husband who won't hesitate to take the wind out of my eye every time I try to get a point the better of him!" she remarked. "And let me tell you," she added, with strong indignation, "that that wounded look doesn't move me in the least, because nothing will make me believe you didn't know very well that I was trying to roast you!"

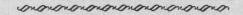

Richmond's first reaction to the invitation to accompany his cousin to Yorkshire was a sparkling look of surprised pleasure. This was followed almost immediately, however, by a slight withdrawal. He said, stammering a little: "Thank you! I should be very happy—I should like to—but—I don't know! It might not be possible: Grandpapa..."

"Nay, that won't fadge!" said Hugo, with a grin. "You can bring Grandpapa round your thumb if you wish to!"

Richmond laughed, but shook his head. "Not always! When do you mean to set out?"

"On Wednesday next, but if that doesn't do for you I could change the date," replied Hugo obligingly.

"Not till Wednesday! Oh!" Richmond said. He glanced up, feeling his cousin's inscrutable blue gaze to be fixed on him, and coloured, saying quickly: "That should give me time to bring him round my thumb! Thank you! I'd like to go with you—if I can do it."

It seemed to Hugo that his hesitation had its root in something other than doubt of winning Lord Darracott's consent, but what this could be was difficult to guess. Had the moon been on the wane, Hugo would have suspected that he had engaged himself to pick up, from the *Seamew*, a dropped cargo, but smuggling craft did not put to sea on moonlit nights, and it would be several days yet before the moon reached the full. If there was a run cargo lying concealed in the Dower House, it seemed improbable that Richmond should consider it necessary to take any part in its removal. The possibility that he might prefer the excitement of such a venture to an expedition into

Yorkshire did occur to the Major, but he discarded it: Richmond had been within ames-ace of jumping at the chance offered him, and his subsequent hesitation had clearly been due to an undisclosed afterthought.

The Major knew better than to question him. Richmond had made it plain that he was not going to confide in him; and to persist in interrogating him would serve no other purpose than to arouse his hostility. Hostility had certainly flickered for a minute in his eyes during the session in his bedchamber; and it seemed unpleasantly probable that Richmond, regarding his cousin as a foe to beware of, was only waiting until he should be out of the way to prosecute whatever illicit undertaking it was that he had on hand.

This unwelcome suspicion was not quite laid to rest by the discovery that Richmond had at least told Lord Darracott of the offered treat. Telling his lordship and coaxing him were two very different things: Richmond was bound to tell him, but in what manner he had done it Hugo could not know. If he had used any cajolery his efforts had not so far met with success. When his lordship was alone with his elder grandsons that evening, the ladies of the party, and also Richmond, who rarely kept late hours, having retired to bed, he bent one of his more intimidating stares upon the Major and demanded to be told what the devil he meant by inviting Richmond to go with him on a tedious journey that was certain to knock him up.

"I don't think it would knock him up, sir," replied Hugo, with the imperturbability which had by this time ceased to surprise his cousins.

"Much you know!" barked his lordship. "*Your* way of travel won't do for Richmond, let me tell you!"

"Never fear!" said Hugo, an appreciative twinkle in his eye. "I'll be travelling post, and it's no matter to me how many times I break the journey: I won't let the lad be knocked-up!"

Balked at this point, his lordship delivered himself of a diatribe against posting-houses, all of which, he appeared to believe made it their invariable custom to seek, by every means at their disposal, to render their patrons' visit not only uncomfortable, but generally fatal.

Listening in great astonishment to these strictures,

Claud was moved to protest. "No, no, sir!" he said earnestly. "Assure you——! Not a word of truth in it! Daresay it may have been like that in your day, but it ain't so now! Ask anyone! No reason at all to think young Richmond would be put between damp sheets, or given bad fish to eat! What's more, if you ask me, it would take more than a journey by stagecoach, let alone one in a post-chaise-and-four, to knock *him* up!"

"I don't ask you—fribble!" snapped his lordship, rounding on him, with the speed of a whiplash. "You may keep your tongue between your teeth!"

"Yes, sir—happy to!" uttered Claud dismayed. "No wish to offend you! Thought you might like to be set right!"

"Thought *I* might like to be set right?"

"No, no! Spoke without thinking!" said Claud hastily. "I know you don't!"

"There's no need for any fratching about it," interposed Hugo. "I'd be glad of the lad's company, I'll see he takes no harm, I think he'd enjoy it, and that's all there is to it."

His deep, unperturbed voice seemed to exercise a soothing effect upon Lord Darracott. After glaring at Claud for a moment he turned away from him, to inform Hugo, disagreeably, but in a milder tone, that Richmond would find nothing whatsoever to interest him in such a place as Huddersfield. Driven out of this position, as he very soon was, he once more lost his temper, and said, gripping the arms of his chair: "Very well, sir, if you will have it, you may! The less Richmond sees of you the better I shall be pleased! I've had trouble enough with him without wishing for more! Before you came here, to set him off again, he was in a fair way to forgetting a crack-brained notion he took into his head that nothing would do for him but to join the army. *I* knew it was merely a silly, boy's fancy he'd soon recover from, but I'm not running the risk of letting you stir him up, so don't think it!"

Hugo stood looking down at him impassively; but it was Vincent who spoke. He had been listening with an expression on his face of sardonic amusement, but at this point he said, unexpectedly: "I fear, sir, that such an attempt on my cousin's part would be a work of supererogation. To judge by the confidences made to me when I took Richmond to Sevenoaks he has by no means forgotten that crack-brained notion. He was, in fact, a dead bore on the subject."

Lord Darracott stared at him. "He was, was he? Well, if he hasn't recovered yet, he will presently! I'll never give my consent, do you hear me? Good God, *that* weakly boy? As well kill him outright!"

Forgetting caution, Claud said incredulously: "What, is Richmond weakly? I'd never have thought it! Well, what I mean is, he doesn't seem to me to be happy unless he's careering all over the county on one of his wild horses, or walking for miles after a few wretched pigeons, or tossing about in that boat of his! I should think the army would suit him down to the ground, for they always seem to be drilling, or manoeuvring, or doing something dashed unrestful, and that's just what Richmond is—unrestful!"

"*Will* you hold your tongue?" said his lordship violently.

"It goes against the grain with me to agree with Claud," drawled Vincent, "but honesty compels me to own that there is much in what he says, sir."

"So you're in this, are you?" said his lordship, dangerously. "What the devil do you imagine it has to do with you?"

"Nothing at all, sir: I am merely curious. Forgive me if the question is impertinent, but have you any other reason than Richmond's supposed sickliness for holding a military career in abhorrence?"

"One of them should be obvious to you!" flashed his lordship. "I had a son who embraced a military career!"

"Well, if that don't cap the globe!" gasped Claud. "No, dash it, sir——!"

"Nay, I've a broad back! Sneck up!" said Hugo, rather amused.

"Really, I had no intention of being so maladroit!" sighed Vincent. "I fancy—but I am wretchedly ignorant on the subject of military customs!—that it is seldom that junior officers ally themselves with the daughters of—er—wealthy mill owners." He smiled wryly at his grandfather. "Now, don't, I implore you, sir, put me under the obligation of apologizing to Hugo for drawing down your fire upon his head, for I should dislike it excessively! Is it

240

permissible to ask what you do mean to do with Richmond?"

"No! Nor need you trouble yourself over the boy!" said
his lordship curtly. "I'll take care of his future!"

"I am sure you will," said Vincent. "But the thought
that he might perhaps—er—take care of it himself, does
just faintly occur to me."

"Richmond is under age! By the time he's twenty-one
he will have forgotten he ever so much as thought of the
army! Depend upon it, it's nothing more than a trumpery,
boy's wish to peacock about in a jack-a-dandy Hussar regiment! I knew that as soon as he blurted out that it was
a Hussar regiment he had in his mind. Well, I'm not
squandering a thousand pounds, or whatever the sum is,
on a cornetcy which the silly boy would wish to God he'd
never asked me for by the time he'd spent a month in the
army!"

"It would be very expensive," agreed Vincent. "We
have one amongst us, however, so full of—er—juice, as
to be able to stand the nonsense, if he chose to do it." He
turned his head to survey Hugo. "*Would* you choose to
do it?" he enquired.

It was not the moment Hugo would have selected for
the broaching of so ticklish a subject, but he nodded. The
result was much what he had foreseen. Lord Darracott's
wrath boiled over. It was to Hugo that he addressed himself, but so menacing was his mien, and so unbridled his
tongue, that Claud, fearful that he might become the next
target, edged his way to the door and, opening it with
great stealth, made good his escape.

Hugo, reminding Vincent irresistibly of a rock battered
by the waves, waited, with an unmoved countenance, for
his lordship's eloquence to expend itself. All he said, at
the end of a comprehensive denunciation, was: "Well, it
wouldn't be seemly if I were to start a flight with you, sir,
so happen I'd best say goodnight! I'd buy a cornetcy for
Richmond tomorrow, if I were his guardian, but as I'm
not there's no reason that I can see why you should be
at the housetop." He then smiled amiably upon his seething grandsire, nodded to Vincent, and went unhurriedly
out of the room.

Lord Darracott, exhausted by his passion, remained

241

silent for several minutes, leaning back in his chair; but presently, as his breathing grew steadier, he turned his head to look at Vincent, still seated at his graceful ease on the sofa. "Since you've elected to remain here, you may tell me, you treacherous young hound, what the devil you meant by turning against me!" he said, in a rather spent voice. "How *dared* you, sir?"

"My dear sir, I have numerous vices, but no one has yet accused me of running shy!" replied Vincent coolly. "Nor have I turned against you. Far from it, in fact!"

"Don't lie to me! You know very well what my sentiments are on *that* subject! Why did you encourage that— that upstart to think his damned fortune gave him the right to meddle with Richmond?"

"I *was* maladroit, wasn't I? I can only set it down to inexperience: I can't recall that I ever before attempted to play the rôle of disinterested benevolence. I own I made sad work of it, but do acquit me, sir, of encouraging the elephant Ajax! My opinion of his intellect is not high, but he is not so blockish as to suppose that it is within his power to meddle with Richmond's future."

"So you were being benevolent, were you?" said his lordship, on a jeering note. "And since when have you cared the snap of your fingers for Richmond's future?"

A slight frown appeared between Vincent's brows. "I don't know that I do care for it, sir. I have a certain amount of affection for him, but, I confess, it wouldn't prompt me to concern myself in his affairs if I could be perfectly sure that frustrating the only ambition he appears to have would not lead to trouble."

"Balderdash!" said his lordship impatiently. "What put that rubbishing notion into your head?"

"It was put there by your damned upstart, and pray don't imagine that I accepted it readily! No one is more violently irritated by him than I am, believe me, sir!"

"I might have guessed it was he! Much he knows about it!"

Vincent's frown deepened. "Yes, that was more or less what I told him, but the disagreeable truth is that I have a reluctant suspicion that he may be right. He could scarcely have attained his present rank, one presumes, without acquiring considerable experience of striplings of Richmond's age."

242

"He knows nothing whatsoever about Richmond, whatever he may know of any other boy! I should like to know what trouble he thinks could possibly befall *my* grandson!" said his lordship contemptuously. "Damme, I thought you'd more wit than to be nose-led by Hugh! I know his cut! I'd be willing to lay you any odds that his notion of trouble is the sort of scrape I don't doubt Richmond will tumble into, just as you did, and I did, and every one of my sons did! It won't worry me, but I haven't any shabby-genteel moralities, as you may be sure he has! Damn his infernal impudence! I'll have him know that Richmond's a gentleman! Ay, and a grandson to be proud of, too! There's not one of you that can match him for pluck, for he don't know what fear is! He has the best disposition of any of you, too, *and* the best looks! Let me hear no more from you! *Hugh* to think he knows the boy better than I do——! By God, it passes the bounds of effrontery!"

"Certainly," said Vincent. "But I am afraid I have expressed myself inaccurately. It is only fair that I should tell you that Hugo cast no slur on Richmond's character. The trouble he has in mind is the sort of dangerous—mischief—a green and headstrong boy might plunge into because he was bored, reckless—as we all know Richmond is!—and too much disappointed to care what risks he ran." He glanced frowningly at Lord Darracott, and then lowered his eyes to the snuff box he was holding. "Rather a surprising youth, Richmond," he said slowly. "I collect *you* didn't know that he hasn't by any means forgotten his ambition; *I* certainly didn't, until I took him to watch that fight. I can only suppose that he was a trifle carried away, for he has never before favoured me with his confidence. I am quite sure he later regretted it, which makes me wonder how much any of us know about him."

"Well, don't wonder any more!" said his lordship brusquely. "Why the devil should he confide in you? I know all I need to about him, and I'll thank you to mind your own business!"

Vincent shrugged, and got up. "As you wish, sir. I am clearly unequal to the rôle I so foolishly assumed, but I do hope it may be chalked up somewhere to my credit that I did at least attempt it."

"Oh, don't talk such fustian!" exclaimed his lordship

irritably. "Go away before I lose my patience with you!"

"Consider me gone, sir!" Vincent replied.

He went out of the room as he spoke, and walked slowly across the hall to the staircase. Before he had reached it, Hugh came into the house through the still unbolted main door. At sight of him, a shade of annoyance came into Vincent's eyes, but he said lightly: "Ah, still indulging your lamentable taste for cigars, I collect!" He hesitated, and then, as Hugo said nothing, added, with a wry grimace: "I am afraid, coz, that I did more harm than good—or, at any rate, that you think so!"

"I do," said Hugo, just a trifle grimly. "And I'm wondering which of the two it was that you meant to do."

"Strange as it may seem to you—it seems very strange to me!—my intentions were admirable. I actually had not the smallest desire to set you at outs with my grandfather, and even less to thrust a spoke into your wheel, which is what I can't deny I have done."

"There's little chance he'll let Richmond go with me to Yorkshire, if that's what you mean," answered Hugo.

"It is precisely what I mean. I perceive that I shall be obliged, after all, to offer you an apology."

"Nay, I'll make shift to do without it. Will you keep your eye on that lad while I'm away?" said Hugo bluntly.

"Yes, coz, I will—if only to prove you wrong in your suspicion! By the way, I wouldn't, if I were you, mention it to my grandfather!"

"That's the last thing I'll do!" said Hugo.

"Very prudent! Goodnight!" said Vincent, beginning to mount the stairway. At the first landing, he paused, and looked down at Hugo, saying smoothly: "I wonder how it was that we contrived, before your arrival, to rub along tolerably well, and certainly without falling into disaster? I must confess myself to be wholly at a stand to account for it."

"Well, that's something that has me in a puzzle too!" retorted Hugo, a sudden grin putting the unusual gravity of his countenance to flight.

Vincent raised his brows in faint surprise. "Your trick, cousin!" he acknowledged, and went on up the stairs.

By the time a somewhat depleted breakfast-party met next morning, everyone at Darracott Place knew that the previous day had ended with a Scene of no common order,

244

for those, like Richmond, whose rooms were so remote from the library as to put them out of the reach of even such a powerful voice as Lord Darracott's had the pleasing intelligence conveyed to them with their cups of chocolate and cans of hot water. Mrs. Darracott, whose room was situated immediately above the library, carried the news to Lady Aurelia, together with a moving description of the nervous spasms which had subsequently made it impossible for her to close her eyes all night. Her appearance bore such eloquent testimony in support of her story that Lady Aurelia, though herself made of sterner stuff, said kindly: "Very disagreeable!"

"No one seems to know what provoked Lord Darracott, but my woman had it from Charles that Hugo *slammed* out of the house in a terrible rage—though that I do *not* believe, because I must have heard the door slam had he done so, and in any event Chollacombe told me himself that Hugo merely went out to smoke a cigar, which he always does—not that I knew it, and I own I wish he would not, for I *cannot* like smoking, even if it's dear Hugo! However, that has nothing to do with it, and for my part I don't believe that Hugo was in a rage, for there was never a sweeter-tempered, more truly amiable creature born, and when one considers—but I shall not speak of *that*, for I am sure we have talked it over often enough, and enter into each other's sentiments *exactly!* But what makes me quite ill with apprehension, Aurelia, is that there seems to be no doubt at all that it was Hugo Lord Darracott quarrelled with! But why? What, I ask you, can Hugo possibly have done or said to provoke my lord? There were just the three of them, when we had gone up to bed, and it can't have been Claud, because James told Mrs. Flitwick that he came out of the library *long* before the end of the quarrel; and it can't have been Vincent, because he stayed with my lord, after Hugo had left the room, and *after* my lord stopped shouting. So it *must* have been dear Hugo! And what utterly sinks my spirits is that my woman met Grooby coming away from Lord Darracott's room this morning, and knew, the instant she set eyes on him, that things are as bad as they could possibly be, instead of having blown over, as very often they do, and my lord in the *worst* of humours! So I sent for some coffee, and a slice of bread-and-butter, to my bed-chamber, not that I could swallow a morsel, for *nothing* will prevail upon me to go down to the breakfast-room while everyone is at outs! *But*," concluded the widow, with sudden resolution, "if Lord Darracott has dared to endanger my only daughter's happiness, he will have Me to reckon with, for where my children are concerned I can be as brave as a Lioness, Aurelia, even at the breakfast-table!"

Lady Aurelia, whose invariable custom it was to partake of a far more substantial breakfast in bed, saw nothing to object to in this, and nodded her head. After considering the matter she pronounced, in a very regal way: "I will see Claud."

But Claud, summoned to his august parent's room before he had finished dressing, was far too peevish to be of any material assistance. Attired in a dressing-gown of rich silk, he was much more concerned with the style of neckcloth most proper to be worn with a frock-coat, and a daring waistcoat of Polyphant's design, than with a quarrel from which he had managed to escape, and only wished to forget. He was inclined to be indignant with his mother for having sent for him on frivolous grounds; and, finding that she was determined to get to the bottom of what seemed to him a very trivial affair, extricated himself without hesitation or compunction by advising her to apply to Vincent for information, since he was the instigator of the quarrel. Before he could make good his retreat, however, he was incensed and appalled by a command to go immediately to Vincent's room, and to inform him that his mama desired to have speech with him before he went down to breakfast. Since it was the time-honoured practice of the brothers to sacrifice each other in such situations as now confronted Claud, it was not fear of Vincent's wrath at finding himself betrayed which prompted Claud to despatch Polyphant on the errand, but the knowledge that not even a messenger bearing gifts of great price would meet with anything but the rudest of receptions from Vincent at this hour of the morning.

The events of the previous evening having put Vincent in the worst of tempers, it was in anything but a propitious mood that he presently visited Lady Aurelia, nor did the measured speech with which she favoured him soften his humour. Her ladyship, disclaiming any desire either to know the gist of the quarrel, or to listen to excuses, informed him, without passion or waste of words, that if his cousin and his grandfather were set at loggerheads through his agency he would fall under her deepest displeasure. That, she said, was all she wished to say to him; and as Vincent was well-aware that her fortune, and not his father's humbler portion, was the source of his own allowance, it was quite unnecessary for her to say more. Pale with anger, he bowed stiffly, and replied in a voice of ice: "I do not propose to burden you, ma'am, with an account of what occurred last night, nor can I deny that some unfortunate words of mine were the cause of my grandfather's attack on my cousin. It was not, however, my intention to instigate a quarrel, as I trust I made plain to my cousin. I have only to add that you need be under no apprehension that my dislike of Hugo would, under any circumstances, prompt me to make mischief between him and my grandfather."

"Your character, Vincent, is in many ways unsatisfactory, but I have never found you untruthful," said her ladyship. "I have no hesitation in accepting your assurance, therefore. Pray close the door carefully behind you! the catch is defective."

After this, it was not surprising that Vincent, instead of putting in an appearance at the breakfast-table, strode off to the stables, and worked off the worst of his spleen by riding at a slapping pace to Rye, where the George provided him with a belated but excellent breakfast.

The breakfast-party at Darracott Place was thus reduced to four persons, Anthea having left the room before Claud entered it. Conversation did not flourish. Lord Darracott wore a forbidding scowl, and, beyond nodding curtly to Richmond, paid no attention to anyone; Richmond, as yet uninitiated into the cause of the quarrel, was looking anxious, and scarcely spoke; Claud, after one glance at his grandfather, confined his utterances to what was strictly necessary and Hugo, finding his companions disinclined for conversation, placidly consumed his customary and sustaining meal.

It was not until he was about to rise from the table that Lord Darracott broke his silence. Addressing himself to Richmond, he demanded to know how long it was since he had visited his tutor. Without waiting for an answer, he said that Richmond had been idle for weeks, and must now resume regular hours of study.

"Yes, Grandpapa. But am I not to go with Hugo?" Richmond asked.

"No, certainly not! You need not look glum, for you would find nothing to interest you in Huddersfield, and a great deal to disgust you!"

"The mills would interest me," Richmond said. "I know how sheep are sheared, but I don't know what is done to the fleeces to turn them into cloth, but Hugo says I may see every bit of it, if I like. *Pray* let me, go, Grandpapa!"

"I said no, and I meant it!" interrupted his lordship, more peremptorily than it was his custom to speak to Richmond. "I am astonished that you could wish to interest yourself in a cloth mill! You have nothing to do with mills, or any other such things, and you will oblige me by not mentioning the subject again!" He then turned towards Hugo, and said: "As for you, I do not know what your purpose is in travelling to Yorkshire, but I trust you mean to dispose of whatever may be your interest in your grandfather's business. It is extremely repugnant to me to think that a Darracott, and my heir, should owe any part of his subsistence to it!"

He did not wait for an answer, which was fortunate, since Hugo showed no sign of giving him one, but stalked out of the room.

Claud, who had listened to him in open-mouthed astonishment, exclaimed: "Dashed if I don't think he's begun to get queer in his attic! Well, what I mean is, hubble-bubble! I don't set up as one of these clever coves, but I've got more sense in my knowledge-box than to say such an addlebrained thing as that! Seems to me it don't make a ha'porth of difference whether you keep the dashed mill, or whether you don't, because that's where all your gingerbread came from, whichever way you look at it. And don't you tell me it's repugnant to him to have you coming down with the derbies, because all I've got to say to that is, *Gammon!*"

Hugo did not reply. He was watching Richmond, who had gone over to the window, and was staring out, his gaze unfocused. He looked dejected, and Hugo said: "I'm sorry, lad, but happen I'll be able to take you another time."

Richmond turned his head. "Yes, of course. I hope you will, for I should like very much to go with you. Was it that which made him angry last night? He didn't like it, when I told him you'd asked me to go, but he didn't rip up at me. Why did he fly into a passion all at once, and quarrel with you?"

"Nay, the Lord only knows!" said Hugo.

"Well, that's a hummer, if ever I heard one!" said Claud. "We all know what made him quarrel with you! It was Vincent's doing, of course. Sort of thing he would do, what's more!"

"*Vincent?*" Richmond said.

"That's it," nodded Claud. "If he hadn't stirred the coals, it wouldn't have happened, and I daresay the old gentleman would have let you go with Hugo, but once he'd flung the cat amongst the pigeons the trap was down."

"He didn't mean to stir the coals," interposed Hugo, seeing the look of bewildered chagrin on Richmond's face. "He certainly took the wrong sow by the ear, but what he wanted to do was to try whether he couldn't get his lordship to listen to reason about *you*, lad."

"Well, if that's what you think, you don't know Vincent!" said Claud. "Yes, I wish I may see Vincent trying to help Richmond, or anyone else, for that matter! A fine way to help him, asking you whether you'd be willing to purchase a cornetcy for him! Why, even a regular flat would have seen what he was trying to do!"

Richmond caught his breath, his eyes flying to Hugo's face. "Oh, no! You wouldn't—would you?"

Hugo smiled at him. "Yes, of course I would, but I may not be able to do it until you're of age. You needn't fear I won't make a push to bring his lordship round to the notion, but it'll be best if you, and Vincent, too, leave it to me to choose my own time for coming to grips with him."

Those ridiculously expressive eyes were fairly blazing; Richmond said impetuously: "I'll do anything you say! Hugo, do you *mean* it? If I'd *known*——*!* I didn't think there was the least hope, because even when I'm of age I

249

shan't be able to purchase it for myself, and all I thought I could do was to join as a volunteer, which I would, only I want a cavalry regiment m-more than anything else in the world! Hugo, will you *lend* me the purchase-price? I shan't be able to pay it back for years, because my father didn't leave anything but debts, and Mama's own fortune is very small, but in the end, of course it will come to me, so——"

"Whoa, lad!" begged Hugo, laughing at this tumbled entreaty. "You keep out of mischief, and I'll make you a present of it for your twenty-first birthday!"

Richmond tried to speak, failed, swallowed convulsively, and managed to jerk out: "Thank you! I c-can't—— You don't *know* what it means to me! Even if I have to wait—go to Oxford—it doesn't signify! It was thinking there wasn't any *hope*——! Well, I——Well, *thank you!*" he ended, in a rush. He bestowed a shy, tremulous smile upon his benefactor, and, his feelings threatening to overcome him, ran out of the room.

Claud, who had been regarding him with the sort of mild wonder he might have felt upon being confronted with a freak at Bartholomew Fair, sighed, and shook his head. "What did I tell you?" he said. "It wouldn't surprise me if it turns out *he's* a trifle queer in his attic too. I don't say he won't look bang-up to the knocker in Hussar rig, because, now I come to think of it, it's just the thing for him, but it's my belief he don't care a rush what kind of a uniform he'll have to sport."

"Nay, do you think *I'm* queer in my attic?" expostulated Hugo.

"*Think?* I dashed well know you are! In fact," said Claud frankly, "it's my belief you were *born* with rats in your upper storey!"

18

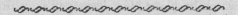

Lord Darracott's bleak mood lasted throughout the day, but since Richmond appeared to have accepted his harsh decree with perfect serenity, and neither repulsive looks nor snubbing replies produced any change whatsoever in Hugo's demeanour, he had become so far mollified, by the time he sat down to dinner on the following evening, as to be able to bring himself to address several remarks to Hugo, and even, once, to agree with what he said, besides demanding of Lady Aurelia, with a near approach to geniality, whether they were to enjoy their usual rubber or two of whist. This was generally felt to be a sign that the storm (provided that no one offered him any provocation) was over; and although Anthea could have thought of a more agreeable way of passing the evening, and Vincent considered that playing whist for chicken-stakes was a dead bore, neither hesitated to acquiesce in this scheme for his lordship's entertainment, though both wished heartily that it had not developed into a ritual. Lord Darracott had been a hardened gamester in his day, but, unlike Vincent, he cared as much for the play as for the stake, and all that was needed for his enjoyment was a reasonable degree of luck, and three other players who could be relied on not to provoke him by stupidity, inattention, slowness of wit, or, in fact, any of the faults that characterized such indifferent cardplayers as Mrs. Darracott, and Hugo.

Any apprehension that Richmond's unmistakeable air of elation would make his lordship suspicious the Major was soon able to banish from his mind. His lordship's egotism was of too sublime an order to allow of his having the smallest perception; and since a long and unquestioned reign over his family had convinced him that submission to his commands and prohibitions was inevitable, he saw nothing remarkable in a docility that anyone else must have deemed so unnatural as to give rise to serious alarm. If he thought at all of the warning Vincent had tried to convey to him, it was with contempt. No doubt of his infallibility troubled him; no misgiving that the high courage in which he gloried was incompatible with docility ever so much as occurred to him: Richmond was the product of his own, untrammelled training; he had perceived at the outset he was worthy of attention; so it would have seemed to him very extraordinary had the boy not grown up to be as near perfection as made no odds.

Vincent, perceiving more clearly than anyone the absolute nature of his lordship's belief, remarked to Hugo, with something of a snap: "It is devoutly to be hoped there's no truth in your suspicion, coz, for I shudder to think of what the consequences might be if Richmond were to tumble off the pedestal our misguided progenitor built for him to sit on!"

Hugo nodded.

"I tried to give him a hint, you know. I might as well have spared my breath."

"Eh, you shouldn't have done that!" Hugo said.

"Oh, have no fear! I seem to have made a slip-slop of the whole affair, but I am not quite chuckleheaded! I gave him no hint of the particular mischief I had in mind," replied Vincent, with a short laugh. "I collect, by the way, that you've promised Richmond that cornetcy. I trust it may give him something other to think of than smuggling—if he does think of smuggling!"

"That's what I trust, too," said Hugo. "I told him he should have it if he kept out of mischief, and I'm hopeful we'll have no more need to fatch ourselves, for there's no question at all about it: he was thrown into such transports he could hardly speak!"

"I am aware. You have certainly become his beau ideal!"

"Nay, there's no hope of that," said Hugo despondently. "I'll never be able to take the shine out of you, for I'm no top-sawyer, and I'm sick everytime I go to sea."

Vincent laughed, but a faint flush stained his cheeks, and he said sharply: "Good God, do you think I care? Not the snap of my fingers!"

Having had ample time to become acquainted with his demon of jealousy, Hugo heaved a profound sigh of relief, and said: "Eh, I'm glad to hear you say that! The way you're never happy but what you have the lad at your heels, let alone the pleasure it is to you to listen to his chatter, I thought you'd be reet miserable!"

This response succeeded as well as any could; but although Vincent smiled in genuine amusement, he was still furious with himself for that instant's self-betrayal, and his temper, already exacerbated, was not improved. He had never felt more than tolerance for Richmond; and the boy's admiration had amused rather than gratified him. Had he arrived at Darracott Place to find that Richmond had outgrown his youthful hero-worship it would not have troubled him in the least; but when he saw Richmond's eyes turn away from his towards Hugo, and realized that, instead of following his lead, Richmond had drawn a little aloof from him, he fell a prey to a jealousy which none knew better than he to be irrational. Between this bitter envy of his brother and cousin whose financial circumstances rendered them independent of Lord Darracott; resentment that his own, very different, circumstances made it necessary for him to serve his grandfather's caprice; and dislike of the usurper whose arrival on the scene had led to a great many disagreeable results, he was so much chafed that to keep his temper under control imposed a severe strain upon him. Pride, quite as much as prudence, demanded that he should preserve an attitude of languid indifference, but so coldly civil was his manner to Hugo that that usually immovable giant was considerably surprised when, two evenings later, he came quickly into the billiardroom, and said, in a voice from which all affection had vanished: "Hugo, where's Richmond? Have you seen him?"

Claud, startled into miscueing, exclaimed indignantly: "Damn you, Vincent, what the devil do you mean by bursting in here when you know dashed well we're playing? Anyone would take you for a cawker instead of the Go you think you are! *Look* what you've made me do!"

Vincent paid not the smallest heed to him; his frowning eyes remained fixed on the Major's face; he said: "He's not in his room."

The Major met that hard, anxious stare without any sign of emotion. He returned it, in fact, with a blankness that might well have led Vincent to suppose that he was wholly lacking in comprehension. After a moment, he said calmly: "Nay, it's too early."

"It's eleven o'clock."

"As late as that?" Hugo seemed to consider this, but shook his head. "No, I don't think it. Not while everyone's still up."

"Then where is he?"

Claud, who had been listening to this exchange with gathering wrath, demanded, in the voice of one goaded beyond endurance: "Who the devil cares where he is? Dash it, have you got a drop in the eye? Bouncing in when I'm in the middle of a break, just to ask Hugo where young Richmond is! If you want him, rub off, and find him for yourself! *I* don't want him, and Hugo don't want him either, and, what's more, we don't want you!"

"Oh, be quiet!" snapped Vincent impatiently.

"Well, if that don't beat the Dutch!" gasped Claud.

"Nay, keep your tongue, lad, will you?" Hugo interposed. "I've not seen Richmond since we left the dining-room. I thought he went up to the drawing-room with you."

"Yes, he did. He took up a book, when we began to play whist, but went off to bed very early. I don't know what the time may have been: it was considerably before Chollacombe brought in the tea-tray—possibly half-past nine, or thereabouts. I thought nothing of it: he'd been yawning his head off, and my aunt kept on urging him to go to bed. I can't say I paid much heed, beyond wishing that he *would* go, instead of insisting that he wasn't tired, for I found the pair of them extremely distracting. In fact, I was on the point of suggesting that he should either stop yawning or do what he was told, when my grandfather took the words out of my mouth, and ordered him off to bed."

He paused, knitting his brows. His incensed brother exclaimed: "*No!* Ordered him off to bed, did he? Never heard such an interesting story in my life—wouldn't have

254

missed it for a fortune! Well, if I were you, I'd go off to bed too, because if you're not top-heavy you're in pretty queer stirrups, take my word for it! Very likely you'll have thrown out a rash by tomorrow."

"Damn the young dry-boots!" Vincent said suddenly, ignoring the interruption. "I'll teach him to make a bleater of me!"

"You think it was a hoax?"

"Not at the time, but I do now. Rather more up to snuff than I knew, my little cousin Richmond! If he'd made an excuse to retire, I should have been suspicious, and he knew that. I asked him yesterday if he was in mischief—it's wonderful, the harm I do every time I try to do good!"

Hugo was slightly frowning. "It doesn't fit," he said. "Not at that hour! He couldn't be as crazy! Eh, Vincent, think of the risk he'd be running! Are you sure he wasn't in his room when you went to find him?"

"I am very sure he wasn't. His door was locked, and I must have wakened him, had he been asleep, but there wasn't a sound to be heard within the room. Why should Richmond hesitate to answer me?"

"Well, I can tell you that!" said Claud. "What's more, I wish I'd locked this door!"

Hugo laid down his cue, and strode over to one of the windows, and flung back the heavy curtain. "Cloudy. Looks like rain," he said, "He told me that he sometimes takes his boat out at night, fishing. You know more than I do about sea-fishing: would he be likely to do so tonight?"

"God knows!" replied Vincent, shrugging. "I shouldn't myself, because it doesn't amuse me to get soaked to the skin. Nor should I choose to go sailing when the light is uncertain. But I'm not Richmond. Does he sail at night? I wonder why he never told me?"

"He might have been afraid you'd put a stop to it."

"I should have supposed there was more fear that you would, but that didn't prevent his telling you."

"He told me when I asked him why he always locked his door. I didn't believe him, but it might have been true."

"It might, but—Hugo, I don't like the sound of it! What the devil is the confounded brat up to?"

"I'm damned if I know!" said Hugo.

"Well, if ever I met a more bufflehead pair of silly gudgeons——!" exclaimed Claud disgustedly. "Dash it, if young Richmond's gone out, it's as plain as a pikestaff what he's up to! And I must say it's coming to something if he can't slip off for a bit of fun and gig without you two trying to nose out what game he's flying at, and raising all this dust! Anyone would think, to listen to you, that he'd gone off to rob the Mail!" He found that he was being stared at by both his auditors, and added with considerable asperity: "And don't stand there goggling at me as if you'd never heard of a young club having a petticoat-affair, because that's doing it a dashed sight too brown!"

"Good God, I wonder if you could be right?" said Vincent. He looked at Hugo. "I didn't think—but it might be so, I suppose."

Hugo shook his head. "No. There's not a sign of it. He's not that road yet. You'd know it, if he'd started in the petticoat-line."

"Dashed if I can make out what's the matter with you both!" said Claud. "Why can't you leave the wretched boy alone? He won't come to any harm! Why should he?"

"Hugo thinks he's in a string with a gang of smugglers," said Vincent curtly.

"*What?*" gasped Claud. "Thinks *Richmond*——No, dash it! Of all the crack-brained notions I ever heard——! *You* don't believe that, Vincent!"

"I don't know what I believe!" said Vincent, jerking the curtain across the window again, in a way that betrayed his disquiet. "I do know *one* thing, and that's that I'll have the truth out of Richmond when he comes in!"

"Well, if you mean to ask him if he's joined a gang of smugglers, I hope he draws your cork! I call it a dashed insult! You can't go about saying things like that just because he's gone out on the spree!"

"There's more to it than that," Hugo said. "Ottershaw's watching him like a cat at a mouse-hole, and he'd not do that if he hadn't good reason to suspect him. He's got no proof yet, or we'd know it, but—eh, I wish the lad would come in!"

Claud's eyes started almost from their sockets. "Are you talking about that Riding-officer I found you gabbing to at Rye? Suspects Richmond? You can't mean that!"

"Ay, but I do mean it," replied Hugo grimly. "There's

little would suit him better than to catch the lad red-handed—make no mistake about that!"

"He wouldn't dare! No, no! Dash it, Hugo—a Darracott of Darracott?"

"That won't weigh with him, if Richmond walks into a trap he's set. Plague take the lad! I warned him that Ottershaw's not the clodhead he thinks him, but he's as pot-sure as he's meedless!" He checked himself, and said, after a moment. "Well, talking will pay no toll!"

"Just so!" said Vincent. "Perhaps you'll tell me what *will* pay toll!"

"Ask me that when I know where the lad is! There's only one thing I can think of to do at this present: I'll walk up to the Dower House—ghost-catching! Happen I might get some kind of a keening—and if I find the place is being watched, at the least we'll know they've not got wind of the lad yet, for it's there that they look for him!" He glanced at Vincent. "If I'm asked for here, you'll have to cut some kind of a wheedle for me: we don't want to raise a breeze! What are they doing, upstairs? Have my aunts gone to bed yet?"

"They hadn't, when I left the room, though my Aunt Elvira was about to go. She said something about a sore throat, and feeling a cold coming on, so no doubt she'll have retired by now. Anthea went off to find Mrs. Flitwick—something about a posset she knows how to brew!—so it's more than likely she's in the kitchen-quarters. Does she know?"

"No, and I don't mean she shall! Fob her off, if she should come in here! I take it his lordship's still up?"

"Since he and my mother were engaged in playing over again every hand about which they had—er—disagreed, you may take it that they will both be up for some time to come," replied Vincent sardonically.

"Well, if that's what they're doing, they won't be heeding aught else. I'll be off," Hugo said, turning to pick up his coat.

Even as he spoke, the door opened, and Anthea came hurriedly into the room, her face as white as paper. "Hugo!" she uttered breathlessly. "Please come—please come *quickly!* I—I *need* you!"

Two strides brought him to her. He saw that she was trembling, and grasped her shoulders. "Steady, lass! What is it? Nay, there's no need to fear your cousins! Out with it, now! Is it Richmond?"

She nodded, and said, trying to command her voice: "He's hurt—bleeding dreadfully! John Joseph says—not fatally, but I don't know! They were cutting his coat, when I came running to find you——"

"Who were?" he interrupted.

"John Joseph, and Polyphant. Chollacombe is there too, and Mrs. Flitwick. We—she and I—went to the pantry, you see, and that's how—John Joseph had carried him there. He w-wasn't conscious, and his face—his face was *black*, Hugo! At first, I—I couldn't think who it was! He had on a smock——"

"Oh, my God——!" exclaimed Vincent. "It's true, then! *Now* what do you propose we should do, cousin?"

"Find out how badly the lad's hurt!" Hugo answered. "Come, love! No vapours! We're not grassed yet!"

"No—oh, no!" she said, following him from the room. "I won't fail! It was only the shock of——Hugo, he—he must have been *smuggling!* I c-can't *believe* it! Richmond!"

"Keep mum for that just now, love!" he replied. "Happen we'll bring him about."

He was striding down the broad corridor that led from the hall to the kitchen-quarters, and she had almost to run to keep up with him. "We must, Hugo, we *must!* John Joseph says you'll know how to do it. He's washed the soot from Richmond's face, and Mrs. Flitwick bundled that dreadful smock up, and took it away under her apron, to burn it immediately. They were so *good*, Hugo! They did *everything*—even Polyphant!"

They had reached the door leading to the kitchen-wing, and as Hugo thrust it open, Vincent, hard on his heels, demanded: "How many of the servants know about this? Is the entire household attending to Richmond?"

"No, only those three—and Chollacombe, I think."

He uttered an impatient exclamation under his breath, but by this time Hugo had entered the pantry, and Anthea, squeezing her way in, between his massive form and the door-post, paid no heed.

Richmond, who was lying on the flagged floor, had come round. He was being supported by John Joseph, kneeling behind him, while Polyphant was waving some burnt feathers under his nose, and Chollacombe, looking very much shaken, stood rather helplessly behind Polyphant, holding a glass of brandy in his hand. Richmond's coat had been cut off, and his shirt ripped away from his left arm and shoulder. Claud, managing to obtain a glimpse into the room over Vincent's shoulder, recoiled, shuddering, from a scene which did, indeed, resemble a shambles. There seemed to be blood everywhere he looked, even on his valet's immaculate raiment, and as he invariably felt queasy if he only cut his finger, he could scarcely be blamed for his hasty retreat.

John Joseph looked up under his brows at the Major, saying dourly: "Tha'll do well to bestir thysen, Mester Hugo, if we bahn to bring t'lad out of this scuddle! Happen t'gadgers will be banging on t'door in a piece, so, if tha wants to be any hand afore, think quick!"

"How badly is he hit?" Hugo asked, putting Polyphant out of his way, and bending over Richmond.

"Nay, it's noan so bad, but seemingly t'bullet's lodged." He shifted Richmond slightly, and raised the folded dishcloth he was holding over an ugly wound high up on Richmond's shoulder. It began to bleed again, but sluggishly. Hugo saw that the blood was coming mostly from the torn flesh; and a brief scrutiny satisfied him that the bullet, which seemed to have ripped its way at an oblique angle into the shoulder, had not penetrated deeply enough to touch any vital parts. He said cheerfully: "Well, that's the first thing to be dealt with. But we'll have him where I can get to work on him. Nay, Anthea, a little blood-letting won't kill him! One of you bring lights in the morning-room—you, Polyphant! I'll want a bowl of hot water, plenty of lint, if you have it, and the brandy: take it along there, Chollacombe! Now then, you young good-like-naught!" He stooped, as he spoke, and, without apparent effort, lifted Richmond up in his arms.

Richmond, still dazed and faint, muttered: "Dragoons, I think. Two of them. Couldn't see clearly—light bad. In the Home Wood. Must have rumbled me."

"Out of the way, Vincent!" Hugo said, bearing his burden to the door.

"Wait, you fool!" Vincent said. "The boy's got to be hidden! You can't take him into the morning-room! If there were dragoons in our grounds they must have a warrant to search: we may have them upon us at any moment! They mustn't find him here, like this!"

"Nay, we'll have him in better shape to be looked at. Don't be a dafthead, man! If it's Richmond they want, the lad must be here, where he should be! There's no hiding him: you had as well hand him over to Ottershaw without more ado! We must think of a better way out of the mess than that. Nay, sneck up, Vincent! you're wasting time, and it may be we've very little of it at our disposal."

Vincent fell back, but said angrily: "What can we possibly do but hide him? He's led them straight to this house, dripping blood all the way, I don't doubt, the damned little idiot, and what can we do but get him away?—out of the country, if we can!"

"I'm sorry—they were guarding the Dower House," Richmond said, very faint still, but in a rather stronger voice. "No light in the window. That's Spurstow's signal. Hugo said come to him—in a tight squeeze. I was nearly caught, not far from Peasmarsh. *Very* tight squeeze!"

Hugo lowered him into a chair by the table in the middle of the morning-room, but kept a supporting arm round him, stretching out a hand for the brandy Chollacombe was still holding. He put the glass to Richmond's lips, and made him swallow the draught. His face was quite calm, but a little graver than usual; he glanced round, taking note of the bowl of water Anthea had set down on the table, of the lint, and the torn sheets Mrs. Flitwick was assembling; and said, his eyes coming to rest on his groom: "How do you come into this, John Joseph? Were you seen with Mr. Richmond?"

"Nay, I was nobbut taking a stroll, and smoking my pipe. I heard t'shot, but I never saw hair nor hide of any dragoon, nor gadger neither."

"I shook them off. Only got a glimpse of me," Richmond said, wincing under Hugo's hands. "Thought I could reach the house, but I suppose I was losing blood all the way. Found I couldn't see—began to feel too giddy——" He broke off, settling his teeth, as Hugo began to swab the wound.

"That's reet enough, Mester Hugo. I saw him come stackering round t'corner of t'ould barn up yonder, and I brung him in nighest-about, and washed t'soot off his face first thing."

"That's good; they'll search through the woods before they come here," said Hugo, not lifting his eyes from his task. "Get back to your own quarters now, John Joseph: I don't want you mixed up in this. Tell me, Richmond: why did they shoot at you?"

"I didn't halt, when one of them shouted out. Couldn't, because—no time to get rid of—the smock," Richmond gasped jerkily. "Blacked my face, too—*Hugo!*"

"I'm sorry, lad, but I've got to pack this wound as tight as I can, or we'll fall all-abits. There was no coming to cuffs?"

"No. I didn't know they were there, till I heard them shout. Then I ran for it, dodging—this way and that. Know the wood better than they do—didn't need much light."

"Ottershaw wasn't there," Hugo decided. "He'd have given no order for shooting, and he won't be suited when he knows you *were* shot at."

Vincent, who was holding Richmond's arm in a firm grip, glanced up at the Major, saying: "If they didn't catch the boy with smuggled goods, they've no case against him. As for shooting at him—in his own grounds, too!—we might use that to scotch the whole business, if it weren't for the smock, and the black face. You damned young fool, what possessed you to put on that rig?"

"Had to put myself out of twig—didn't want to be recognized. Before, I've always put off my disguise at the Dower House. Tonight, couldn't. I think—Ottershaw guessed it—some time ago. I knew he was on a hot scent. That's why I took the risk of getting the goods away as soon as it was dark. It seemed the only chance—hoped there'd be no watch so early. I didn't want to fall back on—my other plan—but—had to—because——"

"Hold him, Hugo! he's going off again!" Vincent said quickly, releasing Richmond's arm to snatch up the decanter of brandy.

"No wish to be troublesome," said Claud, in an ominously faint voice, "but I think I'll take a drop myself! Can't stand the sight of blood: never could! Willing to do any thing in my power, but I can't and I won't come near the table till you take that bowl away, so I'll be obliged to you if you'll bring a glass over to me, Vincent. Not you, Polyphant! There's blood all over your coat!"

Vincent glanced towards him, where he sat limply on

the sofa, his handkerchief pressed to his mouth, and exclaiming contemptuously: "For God's sake, don't be so lily-livered, you miserable man-milliner! Anyone would think, to look at you, that *you'd* been wounded! Hell and the devil, he *is* going faint!" He relinquished the glass he had just filled into Hugo's hand, and swiftly crossed the room to render rough and ready treatment to his younger brother, thrusting his head down between his knees, and holding it there despite protests from his victim, who tried feebly to free himself, but was only rescued by Anthea's intervention. She begged Vincent to let him go, so that he could lie flat on the sofa, and recover at leisure. "Take the smelling-salts, Claud, and shut your eyes! You *mustn't* faint!" she told him urgently. "Chollacombe, pray fetch another glass directly!"

Richmond, meanwhile, was recovering his colour a little. He swallowed some of the brandy, and murmured: "Not going to go off again. Better now. Give me a moment! It was only—hurts like the devil—what you're doing!"

"It's got to be done, lad, if I'm to bring you off. I've no time to do more than stop the bleeding the best way I can, and it's bound to hurt like the devil, for I'm packing it tightly, and you've a bullet lodged there, you know. Come, now, swallow another mouthful, and you'll be champion!"

Richmond obeyed. He was lying relaxed against Hugo's arm, and he looked up at him, saying: "I lied to you. I had to. It was *my* responsibility: I couldn't leave them in the lurch! I *had* to see all safe. I was in command, you see, because it was my scheme."

The Major looked down at him, slightly smiling. "Happen you'll shape to be a good officer, after all," he said. "Lean forward again now: I've nearly done."

"Go on! I've got him," Vincent said. "I'm damned if I know what we do next, though! You're not going to try to convince the Excisemen he's been with us all the evening, are you? If we could get rid of the bloodstains here, in the house, which we've no hope of doing, the tracks will lead them to the side-door, as soon as there's light enough for them to be followed." He felt Richmond writhe, and his hold on him tightened. "Keep still! You're very well-served if it does hurt: I've no sympathy to waste on you! How you can have been such a crass fool as to

262

have gone out on the damned disreputable business to-night, after all that Hugo said to you, after assuring me you weren't in mischief, inspires me with only one desire, and that's to wring your worthless neck!"

"I *had* to! The casks were still here!"

"Still *where?*" Vincent said sharply.

"Here. In the passage. Ever since the last run."

"*What* passage?" Vincent demanded, looking down at him in sudden, astonished suspicion. He could not see his face, however, for a pang of exquisite anguish had made Richmond gasp, and lean his forehead against his supporting arm. Vincent stared down at the top of his dark head. "Are you trying to tell me you've found the secret passage?"

Richmond managed to utter: "Yes. *This* end. Spurstow found—the other—ages ago."

He stopped, quite unable to continue speaking for several moments. Vincent glanced quickly up at Hugo, but Hugo's attention seemed to be fixed wholly on what he was doing. Vincent, violently irritated, was obliged to choke back an impatient demand to know whether he was listening.

He was certainly the only one of those present to remain unmoved. Mrs. Flitwick, letting the scissors fall from her fingers, ejaculated: "Lawk-a-mussy on us, whatever do you mean, Master Richmond?"

"Richmond, you didn't?" Anthea said, quite incredulous.

"The boy's raving! Doesn't know what he's saying!" pronounced Claud, who had sat up with a jerk.

"Yes, I do. Not difficult—once we'd cleared—the blockage," Richmond said thickly. "Roof had fallen in—not far from the other entrance. Think it must be—where there's that dip—in the ground——"

"Never mind that!" interrupted Vincent.

"No. Well—Spurstow only used it—to store—the run cargoes—till I found out—and knew—must be the passage—and made him—help to clear the blockage. Devil of a task, but managed to do it. Easy, after that. Only had to work out—where the other entrance must have been. In the old part of the house, of course. Cellars. Bricked up. Only fear was—might be heard when we broke through. Servants' quarters—too close to the old wing.

But bad thunderstorm one night—did it then!"

"Well, I'll be damned!" said Claud, who had been listening, open-mouthed, to these revelations. "You know, there's no getting away from it!—Young Richmond's a hell-born babe, all right and tight, but, by Jupiter, he's a bit of a dab!"

"A bit of a dab to use this house as a smuggler's store?" said Vincent, in a voice of scathing contempt.

"I'm not a hell-born babe!" Richmond lifted his head. "It's no worse than letting them use the barn by the Five Acre—which they're always done! *Grandpapa* wouldn't say so!"

"My God——!" Vincent's eyes again went to Hugo's face, but he was still not attending. "Listen, you young sapskull!" Vincent said harshly. "Can you see no difference between that and becoming yourself a smuggler?"

"Oh! Well—yes, but I didn't think it was so very bad. I only did it for the sport of it! I don't *benefit* by it—and in any event—when Grandpapa said he would never let me be a soldier—I didn't care about anything anymore! You wouldn't understand. It doesn't signify."

"Master Richmond, Master *Richmond!*" said Chollacombe, tears of dismay in his eyes. "*Never* did I think to hear——"

"No sense in talking like that!" snapped Mrs. Flitwick. "A judgment—that's what it is! A judgment on those as should have known better, and nothing will make me say different!"

"Sticking-plaster!" interrupted Hugo imperatively.

Polyphant, who had constituted himself his assistant, started, and said hurriedly: "Yes, sir—immediately! I beg pardon, I am sure! I allowed myself to be distracted, but it shall not occur again! And the scissors! Mrs. Flitwick, the scissors!—Good gracious me, ma'am——Ah, I have them!"

Richmond, wincing as Hugo began to cover his handiwork as tightly as he could with strips of the sticking-plaster, said: "Any way—I did it! Ottershaw was always suspicious of Spurstow. Began to watch the Dower House whenever he got word a run was expected. Made it devilish difficult—to use the place. That's how—I came into it. Saw how I could make Ottershaw look as blue as—as

264

megrim. I did, too. He don't know now—how the kegs were got into the Dower House. We ran them up here, from the coast, and took them the rest of the way through the passage. But I never had them *kept* at this end of the passage! Or let them be taken away from here—until to-night, when—nothing else I could do. Knew I might have to, so had it all—trig and trim. Ponies in the Park. Had the kegs carried there: too dangerous to bring 'em up to the house. Only thing was—knew Ottershaw was hot on my scent—couldn't be sure he wasn't keeping some kind of a watch on this place too, so—had to lay a false scent. That's why we did the thing—so early. Ottershaw's grown too—fly to the time of day. Had to make him think it *must* be the real run, and we'd hoped to get away before any watch was set on the place. He did." Richmond's head was up, and his sister, gazing at him in horror, saw the glow in his eyes. "It was the best chase of them all—my last!" he said, an exultant little smile on his pale lips. "You don't *know*——! If only I hadn't taken it for granted I was safe on our own ground!—I ought to have known, but I'd shaken off the pursuit, and never dreamed there'd be anyone watching for my return *here*. I've never come back before except by the passage. Jem said I'd be taken at fault one day, but he's got no stomach at all for a close-run thing. He didn't like it even when we took up the casks in broad daylight once—pulling in mackerel-nets! Swore he'd never go out with me again, but *I* knew no Exciseman would think anyone would dare do that, so it wasn't really very dangerous." A tiny laugh broke from him. "We were hailed by a naval cutter: you should have seen Jem's face! But the kegs were hidden under the mackerel—we'd got the *Seamew* spilling over with them! I offered to sell 'em to the lieutenant aboard the cutter: just joking him!—and of course we came off safe!"

Claud, who had been listening with his eyes starting from their sockets, drew a long breath. "When I think of the way we've been living here, never dreaming we'd be a dashed sight safer in a powder-magazine——! Well, at least there's *one* good thing! No need to be afraid he'll go to Newgate! Well, what I mean is, he's stark, staring mad! Ought to have put him into Bedlam years ago!"

"Not mad!" Vincent said. "Rope-ripe!"

"There!" said the Major, pressing down his last strip of sticking-plaster. "Cut, Polyphant! I fancy that will do the trick."

"*Beautiful*, sir!" said Polyphant, carefully snipping off the dangling end of the plaster. "A really *prime* piece of work, if I may be permitted to say so!"

"We'll hope it may hold, anyhow. If it doesn't, we shall all of us end in Newgate!"

"That," said Vincent acidly, "is extremely likely unless we are able to think what next is to be done! If you can drag your mind away from this damned young scoundrel's wound, perhaps you'll apply it to *that* problem, for it is quite beyond my poor capabilities to solve!"

"Then happen you'll find that *Ajax shall cope the best!*" retorted the Major, with a grin. "Now then! we must bustle about a little. The dragoons will have gone to report to Ottershaw, but for aught we know they may not have had to go far, so just do what I'm going to tell you, every one of you, without asking why, or arguing about it! Mrs. Flitwick, I want you out of the way until we're rid of Excisemen: the fewer people to be mixed up in this the better. So you may stay out of sight, and don't say a word to anyone about what's been happening! Chollacombe, I want a couple of packs of cards, another brandy-glass, and the clothes you stripped from Mr. Richmond—yes, I mean that, so off with you! Anthea, love, slip away to the billiard-room, and fetch Claud's and my coats, will you? Nay, pluck up, lass! We're going to save Richmond's groats, never you fear!"

She nodded, trying to smile, and hurried away.

"Claud," said the Major, a twinkle in his eye, "I want every stitch of clothing you've got on, except your drawers! Go on, lad, don't stand gauping at me, or we'll have Anthea back before we've made you respectable again! It's you that got fired at, not Richmond, and I want your clothes for him!"

"Here, I say, no!" exclaimed Claud, appalled. "If you think I'll put on Richmond's clothes—dash it, even if they weren't soaked in blood I wouldn't like it, and——"

"Get your shoes off, and be quick about it!" interrupted Vincent, advancing upon him. "If you don't, I'll knock you out and strip you myself! *Hurry!*"

The look on his face was so alarming that Claud sat

266

down hastily to untie his exquisitely ironed shoestrings. No sooner were his shoes and striped socks off than Vincent jerked him to his feet, ripped off his neckcloth, and began to unbutton his waistcoat, commanding him to do the same to his breeches. Over his shoulder, he said: "I make you my compliments, Hugo! But *why* was Claud skulking in the wood? I see that no Exciseman in his right senses could possibly think him engaged in smuggling but we must have some reason to account for his running away when challenged!"

"Nay, lay!" said the Major reproachfully, tossing Richmond's rent and blood-soaked shirt on to the floor. "You've got a short memory! He thought it was the Ackletons, lying in wait to rend him limb from limb, of course! Happen it gave him such a fright that he didn't hear just what they were shouting—nothing about halting in the name of the King, for instance!—and when they took to firing at him, what could he do but run for his life? Let alone he'd no weapon, he was in a very ticklish situation—having been trysting with that prime article of virtue the Ackletons forbade him ever to look at again!"

"I'll be *damned* if I have anything to do with a story like that!" declared Claud indignantly. "Why, I'd never be able to show my face here again!"

"Why should you want to?" said Vincent, who was shaking with laughter. "It's magnificent, Hugo! Here, Polyphant, take these, and give me Mr. Richmond's! claud, there's no need to *look* at Richmond's breeches: all you have to do is to step into them: I'll even pull 'em up for you! They'll be a tight fit, but you won't have to sit down in them: we'll stretch you out on the sofa!"

Claud, bullied and hustled into his cousin's obnoxious breeches, was so much incensed that he became quite scarlet in the face as he informed his relatives, in impassioned accents, that nothing would induce him to take part in the proposed drama. "I ain't handy with my fists, and I don't like turn-ups, but I ain't a rum 'un, and I'm damned if I'll have you two cooking up a story like that about me! Not if you were to offer me a fortune!"

"No one will offer you a fortune, brother," said Vincent, pushing him on to the sofa, and picking up one of Richmond's boots. "Pull this on!—all you will be offered, if you don't do as you're bid, is a facer heavy enough to send you to sleep while we exhibit you to the Excisemen."

"Think, lad!" Hugo interposed. "If we're to hoax Ottershaw, we must have a tale that's got some likelihood to it, for he'll not swallow it readily!"

"*Likelihood?*" gasped Claud. "Well, of all the——"

"Nay, how should he know whether you're a right one, or a pudding-heart?" said Hugo hastily. "What, you may depend upon it, he *does* know, is what happened to Ackleton, the night he came up here, and the silly way he's been blustering ever since about what he'll do to you, if he gets the chance. Knowing that much for truth, he'll find it hard to disbelieve the rest surely enough to put our tale to the test—for he knows well that if he were to make a false accusation against Richmond there'd be the devil to pay, and no pitch hot for him!" He paused, and then, as Claud still looked mutinous, added: "It's no matter if you're made to look foolish, Claud. If we can't conceal the truth from Ottershaw, it's not only Richmond who'll be laid low, but every Darracott amongst us."

Richmond said suddenly: "*No!* You can't ask Claud to do that! *I* wouldn't—I *couldn't!*"

"That we believe!" retorted Vincent. "It is possible, however, that Claud cares more for our name than you have given us reason to suppose *you* do! Come, Claud! what odds does it make to you if a parcel of hicks laughs at you?" He added, rather unfortunately: "They've been laughing at you for years!"

The astonished gratification with which Claud had listened to the first part of this speech changed rapidly. A mulish look came into his face, and he was just about to deliver himself of a flat refusal to sacrifice himself for the sake of any family of which his brother was a member, when Polyphant, engaged in tieing the neckcloth round Richmond's neck, saved the situation by saying: "If I may take the liberty, Mr. Vincent, I venture to say—with the greatest deference, sir!—that Mr. Claud is equal to *anything!*"

Claud wavered. Anthea came back into the room at that moment, and was not unnaturally staggered to find him sketchily attired in her brother's blood-stained breeches, and topboots. The reason for this peculiar transformation was briefly explained to her, whereupon she instantly threw herself into the obviously necessary task of persuading Claud to immolate himself. Without allowing him an opportunity to speak, she thanked him with so much warmth as to make it extremely hard for him to disabuse her mind of its apparent conviction that he had consented. By the time she had marvelled at his nobility, prophesied the reverence with which he would for ever afterwards be regarded by them all, and declared her positive belief in his ability to carry the thing off to admiration, Claud had become so far reconciled to the scheme as to raise no further objection to it.

Polyphant, who had come into his own with the necessity of arraying Richmond in his borrowed plumage, then called upon the Major to assist him in the task of getting him into Claud's coat. It was plain that he was revelling in the affair, but only he knew the cause of his elation; and none could have guessed that while his nimble fingers coped with shoestrings, buttons, and neckcloth, his mind was filled with the vision of himself triumphant beyond his wildest dreams over the odius Crimplesham. Crimplesham might never learn just what had taken place on this fateful evening, but Crimplesham would know, like everyone else, that there had been very strange goings-on from which he had been rigorously excluded, with such insignificant persons as the footmen, while his rival had been in the thick of it, the trusted confidant of even his own master. And if Crimplesham tried to discover what had happened, Polyphant had every intention of proving himself worthy of the trust reposed in him by replying that his lips were sealed, which would undoubtedly infuriate Crimplesham very much indeed.

"Now, sir!" he said, with the authority of one who knew himself to be an expert, "if you will be so obliging as to do precisely what I shall request you to do, I trust I shall be able to manage to put Mr. Richmond into both waistcoat and coat—you will observe that I have placed one within the other—without causing him to feel too much discomfort, and without disturbing *your* handiwork, sir. From you, Mr. Richmond, I wish for no assistance at all. Do not attempt, I most earnestly implore you, to shrug your sound shoulder into the garment! You will please to leave it *entirely* to me. Fortunately, you are of slighter build than Mr. Claud: indeed, we must hope that the Riding-officer is not a person of ton (if you will pardon the jest!), and so will not think your coat sadly ill-fitting, must we not?"

Talking chattily all the time, he began to ease Richmond into the coat. Claud, watching him with a jaundiced eye, expressed his conviction that he was going about it in quite the wrong way; but the Major meekly obeyed such instructions as he was given; and by the time Chollacombe came into the room the difficult feat had been performed with a competence that drew a *Well-done!* from the Major. Polyphant bowed his acknowledgment, saying that he would now slip upstairs to collect one of Mr. Claud's black silk socks. "For it occurs to me, sir, that a few snips with the scissors will make it a tolerable mask, and we must not forget, must we, that Mr. Richmond's face was blackened? So you will pardon me if I now absent myself for a very few moments!"

He then departed, sped on his way by a bitter recommendation from his master to ruin a few more of his garments while he was about it.

The Major picked up his own coat, and had just shrugged himself into it when Anthea, whose hearing was very acute, caught the sound of hoof-beats, and said sharply: "Listen! Hugo, they're coming!"

"Well, we could have done with another few minutes, but happen we'll make shift without them," he responded calmly. "Vincent, go up to the drawing-room before they start knocking on the door—or, if his lordship's come down to the library, join him there! You've been writing letters—anything you choose!—and you've not been next or nigh the rest of us. Keep Ottershaw brangling with the old gentleman: that oughtn't to be difficult! I must see Claud bandaged up, and the scene well set, and then I'll part, but *make me tell you* why I want to speak privately to you! Quick, man! Here they are!" He fairly thrust Vincent from the room, and turned to Chollacombe. "Not in too much of a hurry to open the door to them!" he warned him. "You're not expecting any such visitors, so you may look as surprised as you please, but take you you look affronted too! Treat them just as you would any vulgar person who came here asking impertinent questions—not that I think they'll ask you any. All I want of you is that you shall bear it in mind that Mr. *Claud* has met with an accident, which is no business of any Exciseman, and that

270

Mr. *Richmond* and I have been playing cards here all the evening. Don't take them straight to his lordship: shut them into the Green Saloon, and say you'll inform his lordship! Mr. Vincent will take care he don't refuse to see them. Once you've taken them to the drawing-room, don't show yourself again!"

"Have no fear, sir!" said Chollacombe. "I trust I know how to depress the pretensions of such persons who know no better than to hammer on the door of a gentleman's residence in *that* ill-mannered fashion!"

The knocker had certainly been somewhat violently plied, and the effect of this solecism on Chollacombe was all that the Major could have desired. At one moment a very shaken old man, he stiffened at the next into the personification of outraged dignity, and, with a slow and stately tread, left the room, and proceeded down the broad passage that led through an archway into the central hall.

Hugo shut the door, and cast a swift, measuring look at Richmond, seated at the table, and resting his left arm on it. Richmond was very pale, but his eyes were alert, and he met his cousin's searching glance with a confident smile. "I shall do!" he said.

"Ay, you'll do, you scamp! Give him some more brandy, love!" said the Major, picking up the bowl of reddened water, and setting it down on the floor beside the sofa.

"I shall be foxed if I drink any more," Richmond warned him.

"I want you to be foxed, lad—just about half-sprung! Not so drunk that you'll say what you shouldn't, but drunk enough to look as if you might be. That'll be reason enough why you should stay sprawling in your chair." He turned his head as the door opened, and for an instant it seemed to Anthea that he stiffened. But it was only Polyphant who entered the room, with his tripping gait, and delicately dropped a maltreated sock beside the horrid pile of Richmond's clothing. The Major said: "I'm more obliged to you than I can say, Polyphant. The moment the coast is clear, off with you! I don't want you to get tangled up in this business, so stand out now—and thank you!"

"Sir!" said Polyphant, exalted by the realization that his moment was upon him, "any other command you may see fit to give me I shall obey with alacrity, but never,

never shall it be said that a Polyphant deserted his master in his hour of need, or flinched in the face of danger!"

"Well, if that's how you feel, you can dashed well move that disgusting bowl out of my sight!" said his master tartly.

19

It was not quite fifteen minutes later that the Major entered the drawing-room; and he knew before he opened the door that the task of prolonging the interview between his grandfather and Lieutenant Ottershaw had imposed no very severe strain upon Vincent's ingenuity. It even seemed improbable that he had found it necessary to take any steps at all to achieve his aim, for his lordship had plainly taken instant umbrage when informed that the Lieutenant had come armed with a warrant, and was in fine fighting fettle.

The scene was not quite what the Major had hoped it might be. It included two persons with whom he could well have dispensed: Lady Aurelia was still seated at the card-table; and Mrs. Darracott, attired in a dressing-gown, was standing beside her chair, her pretty countenance flushed, and her expression one of strong indignation. Lord Darracott was also seated at the card-table, his chair pushed back a little from it, and one leg crossed over the other. Before him, very stiff, stood the Lieutenant; standing in front of the fireplace was Vincent; and a stalwart Sergeant of dragoons had taken up a discreet position in the background. His mien was one of stern stolidity, but although his appearance was formidable to the uninitiated the Major was not uninitiated, and one glance was enough to inform him that Sergeant Hoole, while doggedly determined to do his duty, was very far from sharing the Lieutenant's conviction that he had as good a right to force his way into a nobleman's house as into a common person's humbler dwelling.

The Sergeant was indeed wishing himself otherwhere.

At no time (as the Major well knew) did he relish being placed at the orders of the Board of Customs; and when it came to being obliged to accompany a mere Riding-officer into the presence of a fierce old gentleman who reminded him forcibly of his own Colonel, he disliked it very much indeed, for it was quite evident to him, if not to Lieutenant Ottershaw (who was not by any means *his* notion of an officer), that the old lord was not one with whom it was at all safe to take what he felt increasingly sure was a gross liberty.

The Lieutenant was not entirely at his ease either, but he was upheld by a Calvinistic sense of duty, and he was not so much awed by Lord Darracott's manner as resentful of it. He had convinced his superiors that an application for the warrant he had exhibited to his lordship was fully justified, but the attitude of the Board had been cautious and reluctant, and he knew that a mistake on his part would lead to consequences disastrous to his career. He was determined to execute the warrant, but how to do it, if Lord Darracott remained obstinate in opposing him, was unexpectedly difficult to decide. Nor had he been prepared for the presence of two ladies, one of whom was a Roman-nosed dowager of quelling aspect, and the other his quarry's mother.

Mrs. Darracott's entrance had followed hard upon his own, and was due, not to any apprehension that her son might stand in need of her protection, but to her conviction that the arrival of visitors at so late an hour could only mean that Matthew Darracott had returned to his ancestral home; and since this would entail such domestic duties as the making up of his bed, and the provision of a suitable supper, she very naturally wished to assure herself, before setting all these matters in train, that it was indeed he who had arrived. When she had entered the drawing-room to find her father-in-law berating a complete stranger, she would have retreated in haste, had his lordship not caught sight of her, and commanded her to come in, and listen to what the stranger (whom he described as an insolent whipstraw) was having the infernal impudence to say about her son. She seemed at first to be quite bewildered by the charge laid at Richmond's door, but by the time Hugo came into the room she had passed from bewilderment to sparkling indignation.

Hugo's entrance was a masterpiece of clumsy stealth. He opened the door cautiously, and having first looked round the edge of it, ventured to advance a few steps into the room, fixedly regarding his cousin Vincent. It was apparent to those who had observed his entrance that he wished to attract Vincent's attention, and also that he was in a condition generally described as a little bit on the go. His appearance was not quite as neat as it might have been, and a singularly foolish smile dwelled on his lips. The Sergeant surveyed him dispassionately; his aunts, both of whom were facing towards the door, in considerable surprise; and Vincent, putting up his quizzing-glass, with languid contempt. This had the effect of making his lordship and Lieutenant Ottershaw look round, at which moment the Major sought, by dint of a wink, and a tiny jerk of his head towards the door, to convey to his cousin the information that he desired private speech with him.

Ottershaw, instantly on the alert, watched him suspiciously; my lord, irritated by his peculiar behaviour, said impatiently: "Oh, it's you, is it? Don't stand there like a moonling! What do you want?"

"Nay, I didn't know you'd company!" said the Major sheepishly.

"I have not what you choose to call company! What the devil's the matter with you, sir?"

"Oh, there's naught the *matter!*" Hugo hastened to assure him. "I just wondered whether my cousin was here!"

"And now that you know that I am here, in what way can I serve you?" said Vincent, with smooth mockery.

"Oh, it's nothing of importance!" replied Hugo unconvincingly. He then became aware of Lieutenant Ottershaw, and exclaimed: "Ee, lad, I didn't see it was you! What brings you here this late?"

"Unlike you, sir, I am here on a matter of considerable importance!" replied Ottershaw curtly. "Perhaps *you* can——"

"Eh, I'm sorry!" Hugo said, conscience-stricken. "I shouldn't have come cluntering in on you!" Addressing himself to his grandfather, he added, apologetically: "I didn't know there was anyone with you, sir! I'll take myself off! Vincent lad, if you're not throng, I'd be glad if you'd spare me a minute: got something to tell you! It's just a private matter—nothing of consequence!"

Vincent regarded him with a faint, supercilious smile. "A trifle castaway, coz? I should be interested to know what you can possibly have to say to me of a private nature, but it happens that I am, as you put it, extremely throng. Oh, don't look so discouraged! I'll join you presently—if I must!"

"Nay, it won't do presently: it's what you might call urgent!" said the Major desperately.

"Oh, for God's sake——!" exploded Lord Darracott. "You're disguised, sir! You can take yourself off—and if you'll take this fellow whom you're so devilish pleased to see with you I shall be obliged to you! And as for you, sir," he said, rounding on Ottershaw, "I'll see you damned before I'll let you search my house!"

"Search the house?" repeated the Major, his eyes round with astonishment. "Whatever do you want to do that for, lad?"

"I have no wish to search the house!" said Ottershaw. "As I have already informed Lord Darracott, I am here to see Mr. Richmond Darracott, and that, sir, I am going to do! If his lordship doesn't want his house to be searched, perhaps you can convince him that his only course is to produce Mr. Richmond! He seems strangely reluctant so to do, and I warn you——"

"You impertinent jack-at-warts, how dare you——"

"Nay, don't start fratching!" begged the Major. He looked at Ottershaw, and shook his head. "You know, lad, you should know better than to come up here at this time of night! It's no way to go about things. What's more, you've no need to be in a pelter because our Richmond's been playing tricks on you: I gave him a rare dressing, the night you and I watched him capering about in a sheet, and got the whole of it out of him, the young rascal! There'll be no more of it: take my word for it! Eh, but you shouldn't let yourself be hoaxed so easily, lad!"

The Lieutenant, stiff as a ramrod, held out his warrant. "Perhaps, sir, you would like to read this! I am not here to enquire into any *hoax!*"

Hugo chuckled, but took the warrant, and perused it, apparently deriving considerable enjoyment from it. But he shook his head again, as he handed it back to Ottershaw, and said: "You've made a bad mistake, lad, but if you're set on making a reet cod's head of yourself there's nowt I can do to stop you!"

During this exchange, Lord Darracott, glancing at Vincent, had encountered from Vincent's hard eyes a steady look. It held his own suddenly arrested gaze perhaps for five seconds; and then dropped. Vincent drew out his snuffbox, tapped the lid, and opened it, and delicately helped himself to a pinch, raising it to one sharp-cut nostril. As he inhaled, his eyes lifted again to his grandfather's face, fleetingly this time, but still holding that curiously enigmatic expression. It was on the tip of Lord Darracott's tongue to demand what the devil he meant by staring at him, but he refrained. It was unfamiliar, that hard stare, and it disturbed him; it was almost insolent, but Vincent was never insolent to him. His lordship, grasping that Vincent must be trying to convey a warning to him, but having as yet no clue to what it could be, curbed his tongue, and turned his angry gaze upon his heir.

The Major, as everyone could see, was looking harassed, and rubbing his nose. He cast an eloquent glance at Vincent, who promptly responded to it, saying in a resigned tone: "Well, what is it, cousin? Don't keep me in suspense any longer, I beg of you! It is quite obvious that you have something of great moment to disclose, but why you are making such a mystery of it—dear me, how stupid of me! You appear to be so well-acquainted with Lieutenant—er—Ottershaw, is it not?—that it had not occurred to me that——"

"Nay, I don't mind *him!*" interrupted the Major ingenuously. "The thing is——" He gave a foolish laugh, and again rubbed his nose. "Eh, I've made a reet jumblement of it!" He turned once more to the Lieutenant, who was by this time almost quivering with rampant suspicion, and said confidentially: "Sithee, lad, the fact is, it'll be a deal better if you shab off now, and come back tomorrow!"

"For you, sir, no doubt! But I have no inten——"

"It'll be better for you too, think on!" remarked the Major, with a reflective grin. "You'll get precious little sense out of our Richmond tonight, lad!" He added hastily, and with a wary glance at Mrs. Darracott: "At this hour of the night, I mean! Now, I'm not saying you can't see him, because if you've a warrant to do it——"

"Hugo!" uttered Mrs. Darracott, unable to contain herself another instant. "This—this person is accusing my son of being a—a common *smuggler!*"

His grin broadened. "I'd give a plum to see him at it!" he said. "Nay, then, ma'am, don't be nattered! The Lieutenant's got a bee in his head, but I'm bound to say it was Richmond who put it there, so it's not the Lieutenant you should be giving a scold to, but Richmond, the hey-go-mad young scamp that he is! If ever I met such a whisky-frisky, caper-witted lad! Anything for a bit of fun and gig! that's his motto! You can't but laugh at him, but one of these days he'll find himself in the suds, and all for the sake of some silly hoax! Happen it wouldn't do him any harm if he did get a bit of a fright, but we don't want any more upsets——"

"How dare you say Richmond is a scamp?" broke in Mrs. Darracott, bristling. "He is nothing of the sort! He has never given me a *moment's* anxiety, and as for his being what you call a caper-witted, I have not the least guess what can have put such a notion into your head!"

"No, dear aunt, of course you haven't!" said Vincent. He sighed wearily. "I wondered if that was it. You have all my sympathy, Lieutenant—even though I must own I am devoutly thankful that you, and not I, have been his latest victim."

"Vincent!" she cried indignantly. "Of all the ill-natured, false things to say! You know very well——"

"Be quiet!" interrupted his lordship harshly. "I will not endure any more of this nonsense! The boy doesn't tell you what pranks he gets up to, ma'am, or me either! I've no doubt he plays all manner of tricks—all boys do so!—but let no one dare to tell me he has ever gone one inch beyond the line!" He glared at Ottershaw as he spoke, his breathing a little quickened, his face very grim.

"Eh, I know that, sir!" Hugo assured him, apparently taking this to himself. "Now, there's no need for anyone to go giddy over the lad! And no need for you to think our Richmond's being hidden from you, Ottershaw, just because his lordship don't like getting visits at midnight from Riding-officers, and being told he's to produce his grandson slap! Nor because I told you you'd do better to go away—which doesn't mean that the lad's not here! He's here reet enough, but there are reasons why you've not just nicked the nick in choosing your time! The fact is there's been a bit of an upset——"

"Why the devil couldn't you have said so before?" demanded Vincent. "What sort of an upset?"

"Nay, I can't explain it now! All I want——"

"Major Darracott!" suddenly interrupted the Lieutenant, "you are perhaps not aware that your cuff-band is bloodstained!"

The Major looked quickly at his wrist, and then directed a quelling glance at Ottershaw. "Ay, well—never mind that! It's of no consequence!"

"I must ask you to tell me, sir, how you come to have blood on your cuff, when you appear to have sustained no injury!"

He was somewhat taken aback by the Major's response. Looking at him with a fulminating eye, the Major said, under his breath: "Sneck up, will you, *dafthead?*"

"Hugo, *no!*" Mrs. Darracott cried involuntarily, starting forward. "*Richmond*—? Not Richmond, Hugo, not Richmond! It isn't true—it couldn't be true!"

"No, no, it's got nothing to do with Richmond!" said Hugo, in exasperated accents, adding bitterly to the Lieutenant: "*Now* see what you've done!"

"Whom *has* it to do with?" demanded Vincent. "Come, out with it!"

"If you *must* have it, our Claud's met with an accident!" said Hugo, in a goaded voice. He looked at Lady Aurelia, and said apologetically: "I didn't mean to say it in front of you, ma'am, and, what's more, Claud'll be reet angry with me for doing it! There's no cause for alarm, mind, but happen if you'd go down to the morning-room, Vincent——"

"I will certainly go down. What happened? Did he cut himself?"

"Nay, it's not exactly a *cut*," replied the Major evasively.

Lady Aurelia rose. She had scarcely taken her eyes from the Major from the moment that he entered the room, as he was perfectly well aware, but it was impossible to interpret that steady gaze. She said, with her accustomed calm: "I will accompany you, Vincent."

"Well, I wouldn't do that, if I were you," said Hugo.

279

"He'd as lief you didn't: he doesn't want a fuss made, you see!"

"You would do better to remain where you are, Aurelia!" said his lordship, his voice a little strained. "Depend upon it, he's done something foolish, which he doesn't wish us to know! Elvira, I wish you will go back to bed, instead of standing there like a stock!"

"I will *not* go to bed!" declared Mrs. Darracott, with startling resolution. "If this *insulting* young man is determined to see my son, he *shall* see him! I will take you to him myself, sir, and when you have seen that he is precisely where I told you he was—in bed and asleep!—I shall expect an apology from you! An *abject* apology! Come with me, if you please!"

"Nay, ma'am, I'll take him!" offered Hugo hastily.

"Thank you, I prefer to take him myself!" she said.

Ottershaw, glancing uncertainly from one face to the other, encountered yet another of the Major's fulminating looks. This time it was accompanied by an unmistakeable sign to him not to go with Mrs. Darracott. He began to feel baffled. He had not expected to find that Major Darracott was in any way entangled in Richmond's crimes, but he had very soon realized his mistake. He was a good deal shocked, even sorry, for it was abundantly plain that the Major was desperately trying to fob him off. Then, just as he had decided that the Major was recklessly aiding Richmond to escape from his clutch, it seemed as if it was not from him that this large and somewhat clumsy intriguer was trying to conceal something, but from Lady Aurelia, and Mrs. Darracott. That had puzzled Ottershaw; the signal that had just been made he found quite incomprehensible, for it almost seemed as if what the Major was trying to conceal could scarcely have anything to do with Richmond. Frowning, he stood listening to the Major's efforts to get rid of Mrs. Darracott. It suddenly occurred to him that perhaps he was only anxious to spare her the shock of witnessing her son's inevitable exposure. If that were so, Ottershaw was very willing to further the scheme. He said: "If you will take me to Mr. Darracott's room, sir, there is no need for Mrs. Darracott to come with us."

"That is for me to decide!" said Mrs. Darracott, flushed

and very bright-eyed. "*I*, and no one else, will take you, sir!"

The Major gave it up. "Nay, he's not *in* his room!" he disclosed. "He's downstairs." Looking extremely guilty, he said: "Seemingly, my grandfather ordered him off to bed, but—well, he came downstairs instead! We've been playing piquet."

"Major Darracott, do you tell me that he has been with you all the evening?" demanded Ottershaw. "Take care how you answer me, sir! I have very good reason to suppose that Mr. Richmond Darracott, until less than an hour ago, was not in the house at all!"

"Nay, you can't have," replied the Major. "He's been with me ever since he was sent off to bed—and, what's more, he'd no thought of leaving the house, for he's having such a run of luck as I never saw! Pretty well ruined me, the young devil!"

"Well!" exclaimed Mrs. Darracott. "I must say, Hugo, I think it was very wrong of you to encourage Richmond to sit up late when you *know* how bad it is for him! And as for gambling with him——Well, I shall say nothing *now*, except that I didn't think it of you!" Her voice broke, and tears started to her eyes as she directed a look of wounded reproach at Hugo. He hung his head, looking very like an overgrown schoolboy detected in crime. Mrs. Darracott, tho top of whose head perhaps reached the middle of his chest, said with cold severity: "You will now oblige me by going downstairs again, and desiring Richmond to come to me here immediately!"

The expression of dismay on Hugo's face lured Lieutenant Ottershaw into banishing doubt. Certainly betrayed him into abandoning the dogged deliberation which made him formidable; the light of triumph was in his eye as he said, on a challenging note: "Well, sir?"

"Nay, I can't do that! I mean—I don't think——" Hugo stammered, looking wildly round for succour. "Well,—well, for one thing—happen he won't care to leave our Claud!" His guileless blue eyes, meeting Ottershaw's in seeming horror, took due note of the fact that that dangerously levelheaded young man had at last allowed himself to be coaxed into an unaccustomed state of cocksure excitement. He said, as one driven from his last defensive position: "The fact is—he's just a bit on the go!"

"Do you mean that Richmond is *drunk?*" cried Mrs. Darracott. "Oh, how *could* you? I thought you were so kind, and good, and *trustworthy!*"

"In that case, Major Darracott, *I* will go to *him!*" said Ottershaw. "You are sure, no doubt, that Mr. Richmond Darracot is drunk, and not *wounded?*"

"No, no, *he's* not——" Hugo checked himself suddenly, an arrested look on his face. "Now, wait a minute!" he said. "*Wounded,* did you say?"

"The Lieutenant, coz," interposed Vincent, "was good enough to inform us, before you came upstairs, that Richmond had been shot by one of the men under his command, not an hour since. He appears—perhaps fortunately!—to have been misinformed, but I am strongly of the opinion that an enquire into the incident is called for."

The Sergeant stared woodenly before him. "Upon being commanded to halt, in the name of the King, the pris—gentle—the individual in question, instead of obeying——"

"*Shot?*" interrupted Hugo. He turned his eyes towards Ottershaw. "In the wood, up yonder was it?"

"Yes, sir, in the wood, up yonder! He was challenged——"

"Were there—*two* men posted in the wood?" asked Hugo, in a very odd voice.

The Lieutenant stared at him, suspicious and puzzled. "Yes, sir, two dragoons! They——"

"And was—Mr. Richmond Darracott—wearing a *mask,* by any chance?" enquired Hugo, a look of unholy awe in his eyes.

"His face was *blackened,* sir!"

"Well, happen it may have looked like that," said Hugo, very unsteadily, "but it was only—a sock, with a c-couple of holes c-cut in it!"

At this point his command over himself deserted him, and, to the utter bewilderment both of Ottershaw and of Sergeant Hoole, he went off into a roar of laughter. Feeling much the same sensations as a man might have felt who, believing the ice to be solid, suddenly found it crackling all round his feet, Ottershaw saw the Major helpless in the grip of his mirth: slapping his thigh; trying to speak, and failing to utter more than two unintelligible words before becoming overpowered again; mopping his eyes; and finally collapsing into a large armchair, as though too weak with laughter to remain on his feet.

Watching this masterly performance with every sign of hauteur, Vincent said, as soon as his cousin's paroxysms began to abate: "I think, my dear Mama, that, if Richmond's condition in any way approaches Hugo's, you would perhaps be well advised—and my aunt too!—*not* to come down to the morning-room."

She replied at once: "You need be under no apprehension: I have the greatest dislike of inebriety! Unless you should find your brother in a worse case than I consider probable, I have no intention of coming—or, if I can prevail upon her to listen to me, of allowing your aunt to do so either!"

"Your good sense, Mama, is always to be relied upon!" he said, with his glinting smile, and graceful bow. His glance flickered to his grandfather's face, set like a mask, its harsh lines deeply graven, the fierce eyes fixed in a rather dreadful stare on Hugo. Vincent could only hope that the silence which had fallen upon him would not strike the Lieutenant as strangely unlike him.

The Lieutenant's attention was concentrated on Hugo, who managed to utter, in choked but remorseful accents: "Ee, I'm sorry! Nay, it's no laughing matter, but—oh, Lord, it's better nor like! far, far better nor like!" He gave a final wipe to eyes that so much rubbing had artistically reddened, and looked at Ottershaw. He gave a gasp, and said imploringly: "Don't look at me like that, lad, or you'll start me off again! You come with me, and I'll sh-show you—what you've done!" He got up, now grinning broadly. "Happen you'd better come too, Vincent, but there's no need for anyone else!" He saw Lord Darracott rise stiffly to his feet, and said: "Nay, stay where you are, sir! Richmond will be fit to murder me if he knows I let it out to you that he's had a cup too much!"

"I am coming!" said his lordship gratingly, and, with a repelling gesture, stalked towards the door.

"Yes, and so am I!" declared Mrs. Darracott.

"One moment, Elvira!" interposed Lady Aurelia, firmly grasping her wrist.

"Phew!" breathed Hugo, as he left the drawing-room

in the wake of the Sergeant, and closed the door behind him. "It's to be hoped your mother will be able to hold her, Vincent!"

"My mother is no stupider than the rest of us, I assure you. Is he badly castaway?"

"Well, he was in fairly prime and plummy order when I came away," confessed Hugo. "I wish you will make a push to head his lordship off! I'd as lief not get the boy into trouble."

"I'll try, but it's unlikely I shall succeed," Vincent replied.

As he ran lightly downstairs, after his grandfather, Hugo laid a restraining hand on the Lieutenant's shoulder, saying "Wait! Give him a chance to divert the old gentleman! It'll be the better for you if you do, I can tell you. Eh, lad, I can't but laugh about it, but this is a bad business!"

The Sergeant silently agreed with him. It had seemed at one moment as though Lieutenant Ottershaw's conviction was about to be proved, but the Major's laughter had killed that hope stone-dead. No man, in Sergeant Hoole's opinion, who stood on the brink of exposure as an aider and abettor of criminals could go off into a fit of laughter like that: it stood to reason he couldn't, any more than he could talk to his cousin, like he'd just done, as though it didn't matter a rush who might be listening. Which was a sure sign it didn't, thought the Sergeant, hoping that this jingle-brained Riding-officer he'd been sent to assist wasn't going to make bad worse, and that the haughty young gentleman would succeed in keeping his lordship away.

Lieutenant Ottershaw had not so entirely abandoned hope as the Sergeant, but his state was the more to be pitied, since he did not know what to think, and much less what to do. Until the arrival of Major Darracott upon the scene, everything had gone according to his expectation, with Richmond's family on the defensive; incredulous, belligerent, trying to overawe him, but powerless to divert him from his stern purpose. He had known himself to be master of that situation, for although it might be difficult to handle, it was perfectly straightforward. But within a very few minutes of the Major's entrance it had undergone a bewildering change, always eluding his grasp. He had an uneasy feeling that he had been lured away from the road into a maze; yet he could not, trying to think it over, see at what point he had lost his way; or reasonably blame the Major for that loss. The Major had certainly attempted by every means he could think of to evade the necessity of producing Richmond, but his efforts had been extremely clumsy, causing him to flounder from one position to another, and finally to capitulate. Or so it had seemed, until the moment of his discomfiture, when, instead of being dejected, he had burst into a roar of laughter. Ottershaw, already puzzled by the contradictory nature of his antics, had suffered a shock from which he had not yet recovered. He needed time in which to regain his balance, and to think the whole episode over coolly and carefully; and he felt that he was being rushed. But again it was impossible to blame the Major. Not that leisurely giant but himself had been the one to insist that he should instantly be taken to Richmond. His brain was in a turmoil, with a nagging, unwelcome thought constantly recurring: if Richmond really was drunk, and not wounded, there was nothing in the least contradictory in the Major's behaviour. He had all the time been trying to shield Richmond from his mother and his grandfather, not from the avenging hand of the law. This explanation of conduct which had seemed extraordinary was so simple, and so instantly unravelled every knot in the tangled skein, that the Lieutenant was obliged to cling doggedly to the only certainty remaining: Richmond *had* been wounded, and no matter what the Major did he could not conceal the damning evidence against him.

The Lieutenant said abruptly, as he began to descend the stairs beside Major Darracott: "It will perhaps save time, sir, if I inform you that I have seen with my own eyes the blood on the steps leading to one of the side-doors into this house."

His eyes were fixed on the Major's profile, on the watch for the tiniest sign of dismay. The Major grinned. "I don't know about the steps, but you ought to see the pantry!" he replied. The grin faded, and he shook his head. "Nay, it's all very well; but you've made a rare mess of it, lad! The Lord only knows what the afterclap may be now, for there's more to it than you've any idea of—or I either, think on, at the start of it. I tried my best to tip you the wink, but not a bit of heed would you pay to me!" He turned his head to look down at the Lieutenant, saying, with a quizzical smile: "You know, lad, I'd have something to say to any subaltern of mine who charged tail over top into a quagmire the way you do! Happen we might have hushed it up, between the pair of us, if I could have brought you to your bearing. Eh, I don't know, though, for it's a reet scaddle, and how to button it up is beyond me!" He sighed ruefully. "I could have kept his lordship from finding our Richmond as drunk as a drum, at any hand, if you hadn't insisted on seeing him, you dafthead! You may say it's my blame for letting him get shot in the neck, but the fact is I was dipping rather deep myself. Well, I daresay you know how it is, when you're playing cards! you don't pay any heed to aught else. It's my belief it was as much excitement as brandy that made him top-heavy, too," he added reflectively, "but it's likely to be the devil of a task to persuade his lordship to believe that. And that's what worries me most, because it's taken the lad the Lord knows how long to coax my grandfather to let him have his way, and join the army, and if he flies into one of his passions there's no saying that he won't take back his consent, for it went clean against the pluck with him to give it."

"Going into the army!" exclaimed the Lieutenant, thunder-struck.

"Seventh Hussars," said Hugo. "He's been mad after a cavalry regiment pretty well since he was breeched, seemingly. Well, that's no concern of yours, of course— except that if he gets a nay-say from his lordship now he'll be so crazy with disappointment that happen he really *will* take to smuggling!"

As far as the Sergeant was concerned, that settled it. Descending the stairs behind his superiors, he had absorbed the Major's ruminations with a steadily growing conviction that Mr. Ottershaw had allowed himself to be properly slumguzzled—which, now he came to think of it, was what he'd thought in the first place, because whoever heard of a high-up young gentleman leading a gang of smugglers? There was no sense to it; but these Riding-officers got so that they took to thinking anyone might be a smuggler. The Sergeant wondered uneasily what dire consequences would befall him, if the terrible old lord came the ugly. It wasn't his blame that they'd been hunting an elephant in the moon; on the other hand, no one was going to blame Mr. Ottershaw for what was done by a bottleheaded, addlebrained recruit too raw to be trusted with a pop-gun, let alone a carbine. As far as Sergeant Hoole could see, the only hope of bringing themselves home lay in this lumping great Major, who was the only one of these Darracotts who seemed to be kindly disposed. And ten to one, thought the Sergeant bitterly, Mr. Ottershaw would set up *his* back next.

Reaching the foot of the stairs, after setting a leisurely pace that gave Vincent time to put his grandfather in possession of enough of the truth to prevent his bringing all to ruin by some unwitting blunder, Hugo led the way across the great hall to the corridor that gave access to the morning-room, and to the servants' quarters beyond it. Here Vincent had overtaken his lordship, and rapidly explained the situation to him. As soon as the rest of the party appeared, he said: "Very well, sir: as you wish!" and, turning, grimaced, for the benefit of Lieutenant Ottershaw, and slightly shrugged his shoulders.

Hugo would have much preferred to be rid of Lord Darracott, but since his lordship was obviously determined to take part in the approaching scene he could only make the best of it, and hope Ottershaw was too slightly acquainted with him to think his silence remarkable, or to recognize the stricken look behind the fierceness in his eyes. He said cheerfully, his own eyes twinkling: "We've got him in here, this smuggler of yours. It's a fortunate thing he's too weak from loss of blood to be dangerous, for it would take a battalion to hold him othergates! He's a terrible ruffian!"

With these encouraging words, he walked into the room, and held the door wide for his companions. Over his shoulder, he said, with his deep chuckle: "Pluck up, lad! It was all a mistake, and not Ned Ackleton who shot you. It was Excisemen—and here they are!"

∽∾∽∾∽∾∽∾∽∾∽∾∽∾∽∾∽∾

The scene which met the Lieutenant's suspicious but startled gaze was lurid enough to astonish even Hugo, who
had had no time to do more than sketch for his players
the nature of the rôles allotted to them, before he was
obliged to leave them. The stage had then been by no
means set; but one swift glance round the room now was
enough to satisfy him that his subordinates had more than
obeyed his rapid instructions: they had surpassed themselves.

Not the most uninformed of observers could have failed
to realize that something must have happened to interrupt
two persons in the middle of a game of cards, even if the
obvious cause of the interruption had been hidden from
sight. Richmond was seated at the table in the middle of
the room, with his cards stacked and laid face downwards
before him; but opposite him a hand had been flung down
in such careless haste that two of the cards which composed it had fallen on to the floor. A silver tray, with the
stopper of the decanter lying in it, had been placed on the
table; and beside Richmond a litter of bank-notes and
scraps of paper bore eloquent testimony to the run of luck
he must have been enjoying. The candles in the wall-
sconces behind him had been lit, but since the branched
candelabra, which must presumably have stood on the
table, had been seized, and set down on a chair by the
sofa, to provide Anthea and Polyphant with more light for
their activities, no direct light fell upon his face. Nearly
all the available light was, in fact, concentrated round the
sofa, on which, supported by Polyphant, standing behind
him, reclined Claud, the focal point of the scene.

His aspect was ghastly. From the waist upward he was naked except for the bandages which Anthea, kneeling beside him, had apparently just finished winding round him; as much of his chest as could be seen was smeared with blood; his left arm, which dangled uselessly, its limpy crooked fingers brushing the carpet, was horribly covered with bloodstains; his head lolled on his right shoulder; his countenance, thanks to the thoughtfulness of his valet, who had brandished before his eyes the gruesome dishcloth which had been used by John Joseph to stanch the flow of blood from Richmond's wound, was of a sickly hue; and his breathing was accompanied by a series of faint but alarming moans. The chair which had been dragged up to serve as a stand for the candelabra also accommodated an empty glass, a bottle of smelling-salts, and a bowl containing a revolting reddened water, and the almost empty brandy-decanter stood on the floor within Anthea's reach, together with a heap of lint and torn-up linen; and the final macabre touch was provided by the rent and blood-boltered garments which no one had apparently found time even to bundle out of sight.

Hugo, realizing that his accomplices, not content with such meagre tokens of bloodshed as his neat work on Richmond's wound had afforded them, must have collected from the pantry every cloth and rag which had been used there, surveyed the scene with deep appreciation; but the Lieutenant brought up short on the threshold by the sight of so unexpected a shambles, was badly jolted; and the Sergeant, craning his neck to look over his shoulder, was perfectly appalled.

As soon as Hugo opened the door, Anthea exclaimed, without looking round, or pausing in her task of bandaging the sufferer: "At *last!* What on *earth* can have kept you so long?" but at his frivolously worded announcement, she cast an exasperated glance at him over her shoulder, saying in the voice of one perilously near the limit of her endurance: "For heaven's sake, don't start cutting idiotic jokes! I've had enough to bear from Richmond already! There's nothing *funny* about what's happened, and as for all your fine talk about it's not being serious, either you know nothing whatsoever about it, or you're as odiously drunk as Richmond—which wouldn't surprise me in the least!—Do you think that's tight enough, Polyphant?"

"Nay, I wasn't joking you! Our Claud was shot by a dragoon, lass!"

"To be sure!" she snapped, inserting a pin carefully into the end of her bandage. "Nothing could be more likely! Don't put yourself to the trouble of explaining what a dragoon was doing in our wood, for I've something better to do than to listen to quite unamusing, ill-timed nonsense!" She brought the point of her pin through several thicknesses of the bandage, and said: "I think that should hold it firmly, Polyphant. You can lay him down now. Oh, dear, how dreadfully white he is! Perhaps my aunt *ought* to be sent for—Hugo, did you find Vincent is he com——" She broke off abruptly, for she had turned to ask this question, and now perceived Lieutenant Ottershaw. She stared at him, looked towards Hugo, looked again at the Lieutenant. "But——Good God, what in heaven's name——? Hugo, if this is *your* doing——"

"Now, how could it be my doing?" he expostulated, helping her to rise to her feet.

She pressed a hand to her temple. "Oh, I don't know, but——No, I suppose it couldn't be! But after that Banbury story about dragoons in the Home Wood—I beg your pardon, Mr. Ottershaw, but I am so much distracted—— Oh, Vincent, thank God you've come!"

Vincent, firmly putting the Lieutenant out of the way, had managed to enter the room. "Now, what is all this about Claud having met with an accident?" he began, breaking off abruptly, however, as he allowed his eyes to travel past Anthea to the sofa. "Good God!" he ejaculated. "*Claud——!*"

Polyphant, zealously waving the vinaigrette under his master's nose, said: "He will be better directly, sir, I promise you. He keeps swooning off, but if only we can keep him still and quiet——It's the loss of blood, sir: I thought we should never be able to——*That's* better, sir!——He's coming round, Mr. Vincent! If someone would pour out a little brandy—just a drop or two!—and we could manage to make him swallow it——"

"Ay, that'll pull him together!" agreed Hugo. "Eh, he does look poorly! Where's the brandy?"

For the next few minutes, no one paid the smallest heed either to Ottershaw, or to the Sergeant, except Lord Darracott, who frustrated the Sergeant's instinctive attempt to retreat from this shocking scene, by thrusting him violently into the room, saying as he did so: *"Will you make way for your betters, oaf?"* which terrified him into edging his way along the wall to the corner of the room into which Ottershaw had already been manoeuvred. No one had asked the Lieutenant to move as far from the centre of the room as he could, but Claud's revival spurred his anxious relatives into so much activity that he was obliged to retire into the corner to get out of the way. For all the notice that was bestowed upon him, while the rival merits of brandy and hartshorn were hotly argued, a sling was made to hold up Claud's left arm, his temples were dabbed with lavender-water, his right hand chafed, his brow fanned, and brandy held to his unwilling lips, he might as well have been invisible: and if he had not been a very dogged young man he would have yielded to the Sergeant's whispered suggestion that they should both of them slip away quiet-like without any loss of time.

To the surprise and the relief of his fellow-conspirators, who had feared he might prove the weak link in their chain, Claud, perhaps because he found himself for the first time in his life the star round which the other members of the family revolved, came artistically to his senses, and, seizing the cue afforded by Lord Darracott's demanding to be told how the devil he had come to be shot, at once took command of the scene, in a manner that won even his brother's admiration. Punctuating his utterances with winces, stifled groans, and dramatic pauses during which he stiffened into rigidity, with his eyes closed, and his lower lip clenched between his teeth, he disclosed that he had been set upon by two Bedlamites, both of whom had jumped out from behind a bush, roaring at him like a couple of ferocious wild beasts, and one of whom had fired at him. "Knew at once!" he said, shuddering at the memory. "Ackletons!"

The Sergeant cast a doubtful glance at Lieutenant Ottershaw, for, in his opinion, this had a false ring. His men, as he frequently informed them, put him forcibly in mind of many things, ranging from grapeseeds, hedge-birds, slush-buckets, and sheep-biters, to beetles, tailless dogs, and dead herrings, but none of them, least of all the two raw dragoons in question, had ever reminded him of a ferocious wild beast. Field-mice, yes, he thought, remembering the sad loss of steel in those posted to watch the Dower House; but if the young gentleman had detected any resemblance to ferocious wild beasts in his assailants, the Sergeant was prepared to take his Bible oath they had not been the baconbrained knock-in-the-cradles he had posted (much against his will) within the grounds of Darracott Place.

But Sergeant Hoole had never, until this disastrous evening, set eyes on Mr. Claud Darracott. Lieutenant Ottershaw had beheld that Pink of the Ton picking his delicate way across the cobbles in Rye, clad in astonishing but unquestionably modish raiment, and holding a quizzing-glass up to his eye with one fragile white hand, and it did not strike him as remarkable that this Bartholomew baby should liken two overzealous dragoons to wild beasts.

"Did you recognize them, Claud?" Vincent asked.

Claud feebly shook his head, as it rested on one of the sofa-cushions, and instantly contracted his features in an expression of acute anguish, drawing a hissing breath, and ejaculating: "O God!—No, how could I? Too dark to recognize anyone at that distance. Besides,—only saw them for a minute. Dash it!—you don't suppose I stopped to ask 'em for their visiting-cards, do you? Knew it was the Ackletons. Couldn't have been anyone else!"

"As I apprehend the matter, it might well have been somebody else," said Vincent.

Claud opened his eyes, and regarded him with disfavour. "Well, it mightn't!" he said. "I daresay half the county may want to murder *you*, but——" He broke off, recalling his injury, and groped with his right hand. "Vinaigrette!" he uttered, in failing accents. "Polyphant!"

"Don't *agitate* him, Vincent!" begged Anthea, as Polyphant hastened to his master's side. "It must have been a terrible experience for him, poor Claud! And how he contrived to escape from those murderous bullies, and to struggle to the house, bleeding as dreadfully as he must have been, I can't imagine! I think it shows the greatest determination!"

"Yes, indeed, cousin: most creditable! But I think you have not exactly understood how the case stands. We have every reason to suppose that Claud was not attacked by the Ackletons, but by a couple of dragoons, precisely as Hugo told you."

"But that's nonsensical!" she exclaimed.

Lord Darracott, who, after one glance at Richmond, had stalked over to the fireplace behind him, and taken up a position there, with his hands gripped behind his back, said in a voice of suppressed passion: "Is that what you call it, girl? Preventives posted in my grounds without my knowledge or consent, one of my grandsons accused of being a common felon, another fired upon—*fired upon!*—because he don't choose to account for himself to a couple of loutish dragoons—"

"*What?*" interrupted Claud, once more opening his eyes. "Dragoons? *Dragoons?*"

His lordship swept on remorselessly. "My house broken into at midnight, warrants thrust at me by a damned jack-at-warts with no more conduct than wit——"

"What's a common felon?" suddenly demanded Richmond. He had been lounging in his chair, with his left arm on the table, an empty glass loosely held in his hand, his right hand dug into his pocket, and his gaze fixed on nothing in particular, but he now judged it to be time to demonstrate to Lieutenant Ottershaw that he was in no way incapacitated. His left arm was not entirely powerless: if the elbow was supported, he could make slight movements with his forearm, and he knew that he still had the use of that hand. He was in considerable discomfort, any strain on his hurt shoulder was exquisitely painful, and he had lost enough blood to weaken him to the point of hovering on the brink of collapse; but none of these ills had the power to daunt him, or to subdue the fearless spirit that responded with alacrity to the spur of danger, and found a strange enjoyment in flirting with disaster. It had flickered and sunk for an instant when a single, fleeting glance at his grandfather's face has brought home to him the enormity of what he had done, but only for an instant. Somewhere, at the back of his mind, lurked shame, repentance, grief for an old man's agony, but there would be time enough later to think of such things: no time now, when disaster, so often defeated, was grinning at him in triumph. Richmond Darracott, pluck to the backbone, grinned back at disaster, gaily accepting a grim challenge.

He sat up. "'Nother thing!" he pronounced, staring frowningly at the Lieutenant. "That's Ottershaw! What's he doing here?"

The Lieutenant, watching him with narrowed eyes, took a few steps into the room, and replied: "I am here to see *you*, sir!"

"See me," repeated Richmond, slurring his sibilants. His gaze remained fixed on the Lieutenant's face, frowning in an effort of concentration. Suddenly, to that serious-minded officer's discomfited surprise, his eyes began to dance, and a mischievous smile curled his lips. He giggled.

"Be silent, Richmond!" commanded Lord Darracott. "You're drunk!"

"But I don't understand!" complained Anthea, looking helplessly round. "*Why* should you want to see my brother, sir? At this hour, too? *Why* did dragoons shoot Claud? Why——Oh, for goodness sake, *tell* me, somebody, before I go into strong hysterics, which, I warn you, I shall, at any moment!"

"Nay, lass, it's naught but a storm in a teacup!" said Hugo soothingly. "There's no need to be in a worry!"

She rounded on him. "No need to be in a worry, when I find Richmond in this *odious* condition, and Claud bleeding to death?"

"None regrets the accident to Mr. Claud Darracott more than I, ma'am," said the Lieutenant. "It is a mistake which——"

"It is a mistake which is going to cost you dear!" interrupted Lord Darracott. As Richmond Darracott responded to the challenge of danger, so did Lieutenant Ottershaw to that of threats. Where the injury to Claud was concerned (if such an injury existed), he knew himself to be standing on thin ice, but he answered at once: "I would remind you, my lord, that it is the absolute duty of any person, when commanded to halt in the King's name——"

"Help me up!" commanded Claud, making ineffectual efforts to heave himself on to his sound elbow.

"Take care!" cried Anthea, hurrying back to the sofa. "No, no, Claud, pray be still! Vincent—Polyphant!"

"Help me up!" repeated Claud. "Dash it—can't—talk to that fellow—like this! Going to sit up! Going to—sit up—if it kills me!"

"Keep still, brother!" Vincent said, pressing him down again. "*I* will talk to the fellow—have no fear of *that!*"

"There are some questions I wish to put to Mr. Claud Darracott," said Ottershaw, "but—*if* he has sustained serious injury, will refrain until his condition is less precarious. Perhaps Mr. *Richmond* Darracott will be so good as to answer a question I wish to put to *him?*"

"*If* I've sustained——*If?*" gasped Claud. "Let me up, Vincent! By God, if you don't——"

"Gently, lad! You shall sit up!" intervened Hugo. "Better let him have his way!" he added, to Vincent. "And as for you, Ottershaw, just keep quiet for a few moments, will you?"

"Hugo, if that bandage were to slip——!" Anthea said, in an urgent undervoice.

Sergeant Hoole, surreptitiously wiping the sweat from his brow, tried in vain to catch the Lieutenant's eye. Dicked in the nob, that's what he was! As though anyone couldn't see that the young chap wasn't bandaged, let alone he was as drunk as an artillery-man, sitting there, giggling to himself. As for the other young gentleman, a nice set-out it would be if he was to start bleeding again, all through Mr. Ottershaw not believing his own eyes! Why, there was blood all over everywhere! The gentleman was as green as a leek too: if they didn't take care he'd go off again.

"Quick, Polyphant! Brandy!" said Vincent, as Claud, tenderly raised against a bank of cushions, allowed his head to loll on to his shoulder again.

Richmond, when he saw both Ottershaw's and the Sergeant's eyes fixed on the fainting Claud, got both his elbows on the table, and, lifting his left hand with his right, dropped his chin on both. In this position, and keeping his weight on his right elbow, he watched Ottershaw, mockery in his eyes, an impish grin on his lips; and when the Lieutenant, as though feeling himself to be under scrutiny, turned his head to look at him, he said: "*I* know why you shot Claud!"

"Oh, I wish you'd go to bed, Richmond!" exclaimed his sister exasperatedly. "Things are bad enough without you to make them worse! Mr. Ottershaw did *not* shoot Claud!"

"Yes, he did," insisted Richmond. "You think I'm castaway, but I'm not. *I* can carry my wine! *All* the Darracotts can carry their wine. He shot Claud because Hugo wouldn't let him shoot me!" He chuckled. "Silly clunch!"

"The Darracotts do not appear to be able to carry their brandy with any very notable success," remarked Vincent dryly.

"Tell me, sir!" said Ottershaw, looking at Richmond very hard. "*Why* should I have wanted to shoot you?"

If he thought to disconcert Richmond by his searching stare, he was disappointed: those dark, gleaming eyes were brimful of wicked laughter. "Because I made the dragoons run away!" Richmond let his clasped hands drop to the table, and bowed his head over them, idiotically giggling.

Vincent regarded him with raised brows, and then said to Hugo: "I wonder what gave rise to that—admittedly enchanting!—delusion? I fear we shall never know."

"Nay, it's simple enough! The dragoons were set to keep watch on the Dower House, and they weren't very well suited with that duty—eh, Sergeant?"

"Well, sir..."

Hugo's eyes twinkled. "Eh, Sergeant, *you* know, and *I* know—the things we both know!"

The Sergeant smiled gratefully at him. "Yes, sir!" he said, feeling that all might not be lost if this Major would take command. He'd thought him a queer sort of a gentleman at first, but he was what the Sergeant called a right officer: any soldier could tell that, he thought.

Richmond lifted his head. "Ran all the way to the Blue Lion!" he disclosed. "Only me! Not a ghost." He stopped giggling, and frowned. "*Not* a silly clunch. Forgetting!" He looked vaguely round, his eyes coming finally to rest on the Lieutenant. He smiled in a friendly way. "*You* weren't frightened. My cousin said you weren't. Mustn't hoax you any more. Might get shot, like Claud. That's what Hugo says. *I* dunno!"

Vincent cast up his eyes. "So far as I understand these cryptic utterances, I collect that my extremely tiresome young cousin has been playing at being a hobgoblin—with, apparently, disintegrating results. Very improper! But it in no way explains why my brother became a target, Mr. Ottershaw. Perhaps you would care to enlighten me?"

"If your brother was shot, sir, the reason was that he was mistaken for Mr. Richmond Darracott!"

Claud, listening to this with dropped jaw, said, in a

dazed voice: "*I* was shot, because I was——Dash it, I don't look like Richmond!"

"You are of much the same height and build, sir, and I had good reason to believe that he was abroad tonight."

"But you can't shoot at everyone who's the same height and build as my cousin! Besides, what's it got to do with you if he was abroad? Never heard anything to equal it in my life! You must be mad!" said Claud, stunned.

"He's got it firmly fixed in his head that our Richmond is mixed up with the free-traders," explained Hugo.

"Well, that proves he's mad. If my head weren't swimming so——What I mean is—nothing to do with *me*, if he was mixed up with them! Silly notion, anyway. And when I think——" He put up a hand to his shoulder, cautiously feeling it, and wincing. "I don't know what you've done to me," he said fretfully, to his valet. "It's too tight. Devilish uncomfortable!"

"Pray do not touch it, sir! I implore you, sir, do not try to shift those bandages!"

"Something sticking into me," muttered Claud, closing his eyes again.

"Yes, sir, but it was necessary to bind a thick pad over the wound," said Polyphant soothingly. "We fear that the bullet may be deeply lodged, so you must not——"

"What!" Claud's eyes flew open. "You mean to tell me I've got a bullet in me?"

"It'll be dug out, never fear!" Hugo consoled him.

"Oh, *no!*" moaned Claud.

"Mr. Darracott, I have two questions which I shall be obliged if you will answer! That will not, I trust, exhaust you! Why were you wearing a mask, and why did you run away when commanded to halt in the King's name?"

"Take this fellow away!" begged Claud feebly. "A bullet lodged in me! It may be *fatal!* And all the fellow can do is to stand there, asking me questions! How was I to know what they were shouting? Next you'll say I should have begged pardon and asked them to speak more clear—Polyphant, *where* is the bullet lodged? I am feeling very low."

"And the mask, sir?" demanded Ottershaw inexorably.

"Very low *indeed!* Shouldn't wonder if I fainted away again. Dashed if I'll answer you! No concern of yours!"

"Were you wearing a mask, Claud?" said Vincent, looking amused. "Now, I wonder if I could hazard a guess? Rather a late hour for a ramble in the wood, was it not? Unless you wished for some reason to go by the shortest way to the village—or to meet someone, not far from—perhaps—the smithy?"

"You go to the devil!" said Claud sulkily. "And you can take that nosy tidewatcher with you!"

"I wonder if any of my cattle want shoeing? I feel sure they do. I have a positively burning curiosity to see that game-pullet of yours, Claud. But I shan't wear a mask, however savage her brother may be. What Hugo can do, I can!"

"Leave the poor lad alone!" said Hugo reprovingly, but with a grin. He laid his fingers on Claud's limp wrist for a minute. "Yes, I think the sooner we get him to bed the better it will be."

"If I may say so, I am entirely of your mind, sir!" said Polyphant. "Knowing Mr. Claud's constitution as I do, I shall make bold to say that he will be in a high fever if we do not procure for him a little *quiet!*"

Hugo nodded, and looked at Ottershaw. "Well, lad, you've had your wish, and kicked up a rare scrow-row into the bargain, but happen it's time you took your leave now," he said, not unkindly, but with a certain authority in his deep voice.

The Lieutenant stared up into his face, his eyes hard and searching, his lips tightly compressed. For several moments he did not speak: to the Darracotts the moments seemed hours. The Sergeant cleared his throat, and moved towards the door, but Ottershaw paid no heed. He could read nothing in Hugo's calm face but slight amusement, nor did those very blue eyes waver. Could any man appear so totally unconcerned unless he was as innocent as the Major looked? Some, perhaps, but this enormous, simple creature——? Nothing could have been clumsier than his efforts to keep Richmond's mother and grandfather in ignorance of his condition; his naïve attempts at deception had been the big, good-natured, stupid man he appeared to be. But was he? There was no subtlety in his face, as there was in Vincent Darracott's; his eyes were sometimes grave, and sometimes twinkling, but they were the eyes of a child: they gazed innocently upon the world, there was no thought behind them.

The Lieutenant glanced at Richmond. It struck him that Richmond was too pale; paler, surely, then he had been a few minutes earlier? His eyes narrowed, intently watching the boy. It was useless to question him: if he was drunk his answers would be valueless; if he was pretending to be drunk he could make them so. He was leaning forward, both his arms on the table, foolishly trying to stand the stopper of the decanter on end, using both hands impartially. It was incredible that he could sit like that, vacantly smiling, if he had a bullet lodged in him; it was incredible that he should be sitting in that chair at all under such circumstances: surely he must have swooned from sheer weakness? But he was certainly growing paler.

"Vincent!"

The Major's voice was lowered. Ottershaw's suspicious eyes went instantly to his face, but Hugo was no longer looking at him, he was looking at Richmond, a rather rueful smile on his lips. He glanced towards Vincent, and significantly directed his attention to Richmond, saying, in an under-voice: "From the looks of it, he'll be casting up his accounts before he's much older. Better get him to bed."

"Damn the brat!" said Vincent. "Inevitable, of course! He will in all probability cast 'em up as soon as he gets to his feet. What a singularly disagreeable evening this has been, to be sure!"

He went up to the table as he spoke, and grasped Richmond's left arm, just above the elbow, as though to pull him to his feet. "Come along, bantam!" he said. "Bedtime!"

Richmond hiccuped. "I don't want to go to bed."

"One moment!" Ottershaw said suddenly, obedient to an insistent, inner prompting. "Before you retire, Mr. Richmond, oblige me, please, by removing your coat!"

⟨⟩⟨⟩⟨⟩⟨⟩⟨⟩⟨⟩⟨⟩⟨⟩⟨⟩⟨⟩⟨⟩⟨⟩⟨⟩

"Well, upon my word!" cried Anthea, as though she could no longer restrain herself. "Mr. Ottershaw, are you indeed mad, or merely determined to insult us! I never heard of anything so outrageous in my life! Who are you to throw orders about in this house? Pray how *many* people have been fired on tonight?"

Uncertainty, chagrin, the intangible feeling that he was being fooled to the top of his bent, were making the Lieutenant lose his temper. He snapped back accusingly: "Only *one*, Miss Darracott!"

She stared at him, her eyes blazing. "Only——Why, you—you *impertinent* idiot! Do you know what you are saying? Do you seriously imagine that *I*—my grandfather—my sousins—all of us, in fact: every member of the household!—are engaged in the smuggling trade?"

"No! But that you are engaged in protecting Mr. Richmond Darracott, *yes!*" he said recklessly.

"Don't be so daft, Ottershaw!" said Hugo quietly.

Anthea paid no heed, but gave a scornful, angry laugh, and said: "Well, I hope *you* know how my brother has contrived to become a smuggler without anyone's being the wiser, for I can assure you I don't! When I think of the way every single soul at Darracott Place fusses and cossets him——Oh, what is the use of talking to you? You are out of your senses!" She swung round towards Lord Darracott, demanding impetuously: "Grandpapa, how much more of this do you mean to endure?"

"Let him go his length, my girl!" he replied. "The farther the better! Do you think *I* mean to stop him tieing the noose round his own neck? I don't pea-goose!"

300

Sergeant Hoole stepped forward, laying a hand on the Lieutenant's arm. "Sir!" he uttered imploringly. "Begging your pardon, but——"

Ottershaw shook him off. He had gone too far to draw back, and the voice within his brain that urged him not to let these Darracotts outjockey him was growing every second more insistent. Rather pale, but with his jaw outthrust, he said: "If Mr. Richmond Darracott is unhurt, why should he hesitate to remove his coat, so that I may be convinced by the evidence of my own eyes that it is so?"

Hugo, who had bent over Claud, adjusting the sling that supported his left arm, straightened himself, saying: "Oh, for God's sake, take your coat off, Richmond, and your waistcoat too! Let's be done with this business!"

Richmond might be pale, but his eyes, tremendously alive, gave the lie to the drawn look on his face, not a trace of fear in them. He gave a gleeful chuckle, and pointed a derisive finger at the Major. "*Who* said I couldn't bamboozle the Exciseman? *Who* said he was too fly to the time of day to be hoaxed by a *silly schoolboy*? I've *done* it! Vincent, do you know what Hugo——"

"I'm going to say something more, when you're sober enough to attend to me," said Hugo, somewhat grimly. "Happen you won't find that so amusing! In the meantime, we've had more than enough of your hoax, so take your coat off, and let me have no argument about it!"

Richmond's laughter was quenched. He looked resentfully at his large cousin, saying sulkily: "I don't know why I need do as *you* say. I don't care for what *you* think. Nothing to do with you!"

"Help him off with it, Vincent!" said Hugo curtly.

At this point Claud, who had opened his eyes some few minutes previously, demanded, in bewildered accents: "What the devil does that fellow want with Richmond's coat? Dash it, he *is* mad!"

"Don't fatch!" said Hugo. "He thinks it's Richmond that was shot, and not you at all, so the easiest way to prove him wrong——"

"Thinks—thinks *I* wasn't shot?" gasped Claud, galvanized into struggling up on to his right elbow. "Oh, so that's what you think, is it, you murderous lunatic? Then let me tell you——"

"You young fool, keep still! *Claud——!*" exclaimed

301

Hugo, taking two hasty strides to the head of the sofa, as Claud, with every sign of one exerting a superhuman effort, dragged himself up from the cushions, panting, and making unavailing attempts to speak. "Nay then, lad! Gently now!" he begged, his arms round Claud. "You'll do yourself an injury, you silly lad! You mustn't——"

"Don't you talk to me!" raged Claud, between laboured breaths. "If you think——*Ow*——!"

The anguish throbbing in this sharp cry was so real that even Vincent was startled, while Anthea could almost have exclaimed Bravo! Ottershaw, who had been paying no heed to him, but keeping his eyes fixed on Richmond, just about to let Vincent pull off his coat, turned involuntarily.

"Hugo, you—you—!"

"Nay, lad, it's your own fault!" protested Hugo. "Stop wriggling about like——"

"You put your great, clumsy hand right on——Oh–ah—ugh——!" moaned Claud, reduced again to *extremis*.

"Brandy, Polyphant!" Hugo said, his anxious gaze on Claud's face. He shifted him slightly, and stretched out an imperative hand. "Or the salts! Anything, only give it to me quickly!"

A tiny, perfectly spontaneous shriek escaped Anthea. "Hugo——! Your *hand!*" she stammered, her dilating eyes riveted to it.

"Good God!" ejaculated Vincent involuntarily.

Hugo looked round, surprised at Anthea, and then at his own bloodstained palm. "Oh, my God!" he uttered, swiftly glancing down at Claud's back, which only he was in a position to see.

"*Sir*——!" exclaimed Polyphant reproachfully, and darting forward to snatch up some lint from the pile on the floor. "No, no, let me, sir! I beg pardon, but *pray* don't——Just hold him, if you please! Oh, dear, oh, dear! Miss Anthea, the longest strip of linen you can find—or knot two together—anything! Don't move, Mr. Claud! I implore you, sir, *don't move!*"

Since no one in the room had seen the Major pick up several of the blood-soaked swabs from the bowl still standing on the chair beside the sofa, and close his hand on them, it was hardly surprising that the sight of his horridly reddened palm should have come as a shock to the rest of his family. Had Lieutenant Ottershaw not been far too much shocked himself to think of studying the expressions on the faces of his companions, one glance must have satisfied him that the Darracotts were honestly horrified.

Anthea was the first to recover her wits, and to rush to the sofa, scolding distractedly; Vincent was swift to follow suit. Both blamed Hugo for having handled the drooping Claud with abominable clumsiness; my lord joined in, directing his menaces, however, towards Lieutenant Ottershaw, for being the real cause of this fresh disaster; and the Sergeant, prompted by real dismay, and a very lively dread of the consequences, seized the opportunity provided by all this commotion to represent to Ottershaw, with all the eloquence at his command, that any more attempts to exacerbate the Darracotts would only bring them both to ruin.

It was at this moment that Lady Aurelia entered the room, and, halting on the threshold, demanded, in a voice which, without being raised to any vulgar pitch, easily penetrated the hubbub: "*What*, may I ask, is the meaning of this *extraordinary* scene?"

Such was the effect of her commanding eye, and air of supreme assurance, that Lieutenant Ottershaw found himself to his subsequent fury, adding his voice to those of Anthea and Vincent, in an attempt to present her ladyship with the explanation she desired.

She seemed to grasp the gist of what was told her with all the rapidity of a powerful intelligence; and, considerably before the various accounts had been brought to their conclusions, paralysed the company by uttering, in icy yet ominous accents: "Be silent, if you please! I have heard enough!"

She then swept forward to the sofa, Anthea, Vincent, and the Major giving way instinctively before her, and bent over Claud, feeling his brow, and his wrist. Magnificently ignoring everyone else, she exchanged a few words with Polyphant, who had remained devoutly at the head of the sofa; and, upon Claud's venturing to open his eyes sufficiently to cast a doubtful, slightly nervous glance up at her, said with calm kindness: "You will keep perfectly still, my son: do you understand me? You have no need to trouble yourself about anything, for Mama is here,

303

and will make you better directly."

She then turned, and looked round the room, with all the lofty contempt natural to the descendant of eleven Earls, all of whom, if not otherwise distinguished, had been remarkable for the high-handed and very successful way with which they had dealt with inferior persons, and overridden all opposition to their domestic decrees. No one saw these august personages range themselves at Lady Aurelia's back, but (as her appreciative elder son afterwards asserted) no one could doubt that they had all of them hurried to the support of so worthy a daughter.

"I do not know," she stated, in a tone of dispassionate censure, "why I have been obliged to come downstairs to discover for myself the precise nature of Claud's injury, but I do not attempt to conceal from you that I am excessively displeased. *Your* conduct, Vincent, I consider particularly reprehensible, for it was on the understanding that you would instantly apprise me of it, if you found your brother's injury to be of a serious character, that I allowed myself to be persuaded to remain upstairs. Neither you nor Anthea, whom I must deem to have been gravely at fault, are so stupid as to have supposed that the *accident* was of a *trifling* nature. I shall say no more to *you*, Hugo, than that I trust you will in future refrain from making well-meaning but foolish attempts to conceal from some other female in my position the very dangerous state in which one of her children may be lying. Pray do not answer me! I have neither the time nor the desire to listen to excuses or apologies. You will all of you, with the exception of Polyphant, be so good as to leave this room immediately. Vincent, since I apprehend that Richmond is disgracefully inebriated, you will please assist him to his bed-chamber. I do not presume to dictate to *you*, my lord, but since there is nothing for you to do here I am persuaded you will be very much more comfortable in your library." Her eyes next fell on Lieutenant Ottershaw, and after considering him for a moment or two in a way that made the Sergeant feel profoundly thankful that her gaze had swept past him, said, without the slightest change of intonation: "You, I believe, are the author of this outrage. I collect that you are in the service of the Board of Customs. I shall be obliged to you if you will furnish me with your name, and style."

304

The Lieutenant's colour was considerably heightened, but he replied with commendable readiness: "My name is Ottershaw, ma'am—Thomas Ottershaw, and I am a Riding-officer of the Customs' Land-Guard. Allow me to assure your ladyship that, while I do not seek to disclaim responsibility for whatever injury Mr. Darracott has suffered, my explicit order was that no shot was to be fired, other than a warning shot over the head of any person failing to obey a summons to halt in the King's name. I regret very much that an accident should have occurred, but I must take leave to inform your ladyship of the circumstance which led——"

"Pray say no more!" she interrupted. "I am neither deaf nor slow of understanding, and since I was present when you made known to his lordship the precise nature of your errand any further explanation would be superfluous. Let me make it plain to you that whatever may be my opinion of the accusation you than made, I am not concerned with my nephew's affairs, but with the attack upon my son. I have nothing further to add, except that I shall immediately lay the matter before my husband. No doubt he will know what action to take. As a mere female, I cannot consider myself competent to deal with such an affair. I will not detain you any longer. If you have anything further to do in this house, pray desire Major Darracott to conduct you to some other room!"

With these measured words, she turned to Polyphant, and began to question him on the exact nature of Claud's injury, wholly ignoring her stunned audience.

The Major, a phlegmatic man, was the first to recover from the shattering effect of this encounter with a mere female, and he acted with great promptitude and good sense, saying meekly: "Yes, ma'am! I will do so immediately," and thrusting the Lieutenant out of the room. Sergeant Hoole, holding the door for them, needed no urging to follow, the manner of his exit suggesting that only a rigid adherence to discipline restrained him from preceding his superiors.

No one moved or spoke for several moments, the actors in the conspiracy remaining as though frozen, nearly all of them looking towards the door, intently listening. Then Lord Darracott sank into a chair beside the fire, and with shaking hands grasped its arms, his countenance grey, and his eyes staring straight before him, fixed and sight-less. Lady Aurelia glanced at him, and then away from him, as though averting her gaze from some indecent spectacle. As Claud sat up, saying: "Well, thank the lord that's over!" she lifted a warning finger, and said: "Do not abandon your position until we are assured that those men have departed! Since you have all of you chosen to pursue a line of conduct as criminal as it is grossly improper, I must beg you to maintain the imposture!"

Claud sank back obediently, but said: "Dash it, Mama, if you think we *chose*——Besides, I should like to know what *you* were doing! Well, what I mean is——"

"I know exactly what you mean, Claud. Pray do not imagine that my participation in this disgraceful affair in any way alters my sentiments!" said her ladyship severely.

"You are quite superb, Mama," said Vincent. "May I make you my heartfelt compliments on a performance that will ever command my admiration? Your entrance I can only describe as a clincher."

"I have the greatest objection to cant terms," responded her ladyship. "I trust I may have *expedited* the departure of the Preventive officer, but I must suppose, from what I have seen of your powers of what I can only call decep-tion, that you would have done very well without my intervention."

"Hugo did it," Anthea said, with a wavering smile. "It was all Hugo. We didn't know what to do. Even Vincent didn't. We just—did what Hugo told us." She dashed a hand across her eyes, adding: "It was the *pageant of Ajax!* Not that I mean the others weren't wonderful too, *par-ticularly* Claud! Claud, that shriek you gave almost per-suaded me to believe you *had* suffered a spasm of an-guish!"

"Oh, it did, did it?" said Claud bitterly. "I should rather think it might! Hugo jabbed a pin into me!" He eyed his relatives with disfavour. "Yes, I daresay you think it's devilish funny, but when *I* see Hugo next——Well, dash it, I knew what he wanted me to do, because he told me, when he pretended to be arranging this damned sling, and there was no need to stick pins into me! When I think of the things I've had to do this night, let alone being smeared all over with young Richmond's blood——Yes, and how much longer have I got to lie here, swaddled up in bandages which are dashed uncomfortable, besides——"

"You have my sympathy, brother, but Mama is, as usual, right. It will not do for any of us to be caught off our guard. I have no real apprehension—the hideous experiences of the past hour have taught me that our cousin's bovine countenance is, to say the least of it, misleading—but we will take no eleventh-hour risks. I wonder what glib lies he is telling that unfortunate Exciseman now?"

"It is a very distressing reflection that any gentleman of birth—and particularly one whose military rank is distinguished—should have been obliged to lend himself to so disreputable a business," pronounced her ladyship, with undiminished severity. "It is, however, to his credit that he appears at least to know what is his duty to his *Family*, and although I am far from approving of his conduct I cannot deny that I regard his arrival at Darracott Place as the greatest piece of good fortune that has befallen the Family for very many years. As to whether the Family is deserving of its good fortune—*that* is a subject upon which I prefer to remain silent!"

This measured speech not unnaturally reduced its auditors to speechless discomfort; and when Hugo presently came back into the room, he found his actors so apparently petrified into the positions in which he had left them that he grinned, and said: "Eh, you look just like a set of waxworks!"

"Not waxworks, coz: puppets!" retorted Vincent. "What unnatural antics must we next perform?"

"Hugo, have they gone?" Anthea asked anxiously.

"Oh, yes, they've gone, lass!" He smiled cordially upon Lady Aurelia. "Thanks to you, ma'am! I'm reet grateful to you. Nay, till you came in there was no deciding which was the best actor amongst the lot of you! Myself, I couldn't make up my mind between Claud and Richmond, but, eh, when you took command, there was——"

"Yes, dear cousin," interrupted Anthea firmly, "we are well aware that everyone, except you, acted to admiration, but what we are desirous of knowing is how you contrived to rid us of Ottershaw."

"Oh, there was no difficulty about that, lass, once her
307

ladyship's guns had broken the square!" he assured her. "You might say that I'd nothing to do but to harass the retreat."

"I might, but it is very unlikely that I shall," she retorted. "Hugo, are we *safe?*"

"Nay, love, don't look so fatched! We shall be safe enough, once we've tied up a few knots, which we'll do easily, never fear!" he assured her.

"Did you succeed in convincing that damned, obstinate tide-watcher!" demanded Vincent.

"Nay, I'm not one to level at the moon. Happen he'll suspect to the end of his days that he was made a Maygame of, poor lad! But what with her ladyship setting him in a quake, and me telling him that you'd so much influence, ma'am, that if he'd caught our Richmond redhanded you'd have seen to it the whole business was hushed-up, he didn't know which way to turn. He's no turn-tail, but he knew well he'd exceeded his commission, and when he saw I knew it too, there was naught he could do but retire—the position being untenable, as you might say! I don't know much about Preventive work, but I do know that unless they find a smuggler in actual possession of run goods the Preventives are pretty well hamstrung—even when they've been nose-led after a decoy-train of rascals rigged out in smocks to deceive them, and leading a string of ponies carrying nothing more than loads of faggots. They know full well they've been bamboozled, but it's no crime to carry faggots across the country in the middle of the night, so the poor devils have naught to do but own themselves gapped. Well, it was plain enough that, whatever Ottershaw *had* seen, he hadn't seen our Richmond in possession of anything other than a load of devilry. All he was doing tonight was trying to catch the lad, or at any road to discover how he was contriving to flit in and out of the Dower House, no matter how strong a guard was set on it. He'd no more intention of executing that warrant than he had of getting the lad shot. Once that had happened, he may have felt there was naught to do but go through stitch with the business, or he may have gambled on the chance that if he found the lad here, wounded, he could scare him into making a confession. If he couldn't do that, he knew he'd be taken at fault, so you can't but allow he's got plenty of courage. I must say, it went to my heart to cheat him, poor lad! However, a back-cast won't harm him, for he didn't handle the business well, and happen he'll do better in future." His rueful grin dawned. "It was a reet shame," he confessed. "I gave him a dressing, just as I would any skelterbrained subaltern that had plunged stickle-butt into trouble all because he was too pot-sure, and that took the last bit of fight out of him. So I told him when he was fairly down that I knew it was our Richmond's mischief that had led him into the hobble, and I'd do my best to bring him safely home, and no one the wiser as long as he kept his tongue between his teeth. So we'll hope that's buttoned the thing up, which there's no reason to think it won't— once he knows *that* young scamp's not here any longer to plague the life out of him."

There was a tiny pause, several pairs of eyes instinctively turning towards Lord Darracott. He gave no sign of having heard what Hugo had said, still sitting immobile, and staring straight ahead. Anthea glanced from him to Richmond, no longer tense, but sitting rather limply, his right elbow on the table, and his brow dropped on to his hand; her eyes travelled to Vincent, reading the look of strain on his face; and suddenly she began to laugh rather tremulously, realizing that the only one whose nerves were not in some way or other disordered from the ordeal they had passed through was the one on whom the success of an enterprise fraught with peril had depended, and thinking how ridiculous it was that he should rejoin his shattered accomplices as placidly as though he had done nothing more than escort two harmless morning-callers to the door. She saw that he was looking at her in mild surprise, and said: "Oh, Hugo, Hugo! I don't know what to say to you!"

"Well, we've no time to waste on any more talk now, love, so happen that's just as well," he replied matter-of-factly. "We must dispose of Richmond's clothes, and clear up all this mess. Nay, then, Polyphant! don't stand gauping! There's work to be done!"

Polyphant, who had indeed been standing staring at him, gave a start, and recalled his scattered wits. "Yes, sir—to be sure! I fear I was indulging in reflection—I will remove the bowls first, and then Mr. Claud will be comfortable again!"

"You'll find the swabs I squeezed in my hand behind the sofa cushions," Hugo warned him. "Vincent, will you see all these clothes disposed of? I've been trying to decide what had best be done with Richmond, and it seems to me that we'll have to put him to bed in Claud's room, for that wound of his must be attended to, and since it's Claud who's supposed to be the wounded one we mustn't have any bloodstains anywhere but on his sheets. Now, there's no need to start shuddering, lad! I'm not asking you to sleep on them!"

"No, and it wouldn't be any use if you did ask me to!" Claud informed him, pausing in his struggles to unwind the bandages from round his slim person. "Dashed if I ever met such a fellow as you are!"

"How seldom it is that I find myself in accord with you, brother!" remarked Vincent. He looked at Hugo, and said, with a wry smile: "You irritate me intensely, you know. I have little doubt that you always will, but if ever I should get into a tight corner I do hope to God you will be at hand to pull me out of it, coz!"

"Never mind throwing the hammer at me!" replied Hugo, unmoved by this tribute. "If you want to throw it at anyone, throw it at Claud, because he's the one who saved our groats!" His eyes were on Richmond, and he went to him, saying: "I think I'll carry you up to bed, lad, before I do aught else."

Richmond lifted his head with an effort. The fire had gone out of his eyes, and with the passing of danger the spirit that had upheld him so indomitably had sunk, allowing his physical weakness at last to overcome him. He managed to smile, and to say, in the thread of a voice: "A close-run thing...! Thank you—so very grateful—so *sorry*, Hugo——Grandpapa..."

Hugo caught him, as he collapsed, and lifted him up in his arms. "Eh, poor lad, I ought to have got him to bed sooner, instead of standing there chattering!" he said remorsefully. "Anthea, run upstairs to see if the coast is clear, will you, love?" He looked at Lady Aurelia. "I take it you warned his mother, ma'am?"

"Certainly," she replied. "She was cast into very natural affliction, and dared not come down to this room for fear that her agitation might overcome her, and so betray you all, but I left her in Mrs. Flitwick's care, and have no

310

doubt that she will be more composed by now."

"I'm very much obliged to you, ma'am," he said.
"Breaking it to her was the thing I dreaded most."

"An unpleasant task," she agreed. "I am happy to have
been able to relieve you of it, for, however little I may
approve of your conduct this evening I must own myself
to be deeply grateful to you for all that you have done,
and, I may add, very conscious of the magnanimity you
have shown."

"Nay——!" begged the Major, reddening.

She said graciously: "You have no need to blush, my
dear Hugo. I do not mean to flatter you, and will only say
that I have from the beginning of our acquaintance believed you to be a most estimable young man. I have little
doubt that when you have overcome your tendency to
levity you will do very well at Darracott Place."

Fortunately, since Hugo was showing signs of acute
embarrassment, Anthea had by this time come back into
the room, to report that it was safe to carry Richmond
upstairs. Lord Darracott rose stiffly from the chair into
which he had sunk, and looked at Hugo, saying, as though
the words were forced from him: "I am obliged to you,
Hugo."

"There's no need for that, sir," Hugo replied cheerfully. "The young scamp's as near to being my brother-
in-law as makes no odds—though happen I'd have better
not to have said that, because, now I come to think of it,
you've not accepted my offer yet, have you, love?"

"*More* levity?" she murmured.

He grinned. "You're reet: I'm past praying for! Come,
now, lead the way, lass!" He saw that Lord Darracott was
looking at Richmond's white, unconscious face, and
paused for a moment, and said gently: "He's got spunk,
you know, sir."

His lordship's grim mouth twisted. "Yes," he said, turning away. "He was always—full of pluck. Take him up to
his mother!"

It was some considerable time later that Hugo came
downstairs again. Claud had retired to bed, but Lord Darracott and Vincent were still up, seated in the library.
As Hugo came into the room, Vincent looked up with a
flickering smile. "Well? How is that abominable brat?"

"Oh, he's nicely!" Hugo replied. "He won't be very

311

comfortable till he's had the bullet dug out of him—and that's something he won't enjoy, think on—but it would take more than one bullet to daunt *him!* I won't deny that he's caused a deal of trouble—eh, if ever a lad wanted a good skelping——! But I can't but like young devils as full of gaiety as he is."

"Yes, excellent bottom," Vincent agreed, getting up, and walking across the room to a side-table. "I owe you an apology, Ajax: you warned me, and I paid no heed. I'm sorry. Had I attended to you, I might have averted the singularly nerve-racking events we have survived this night, thanks, I admit,—and you have no notion how much it costs me to do so!—to your unsuspected genius for—er—diddling the dupes! Accept my compliments, and allow me to offer you some brandy! Unless the very word has, for reasons which I need not, I feel, explain to you, become repulsive to you, I am persuaded you must stand in urgent need of it."

Hugo grinned, as he took the glass Vincent was holding out to him, but said quite seriously: "Well, it nattered me at the time that you wouldn't heed me, but I'm not so sure now that it would have made any difference if you had. The best thing about this business is that, while that cargo was hidden in this passage of ours, it didn't matter to Richmond how close the hounds were: it was his doing that they were stored there, and nothing anyone could have said would have turned him from what he saw to be his duty. You heard him, Vincent: he said he couldn't leave his men in the lurch, because it was his scheme, and he was in command. Never mind the rest!—that's the stuff out of which a damned good officer is made!" He looked down at his grandfather. "You don't like round-aboutation, sir, and nor do I. I told Ottershaw that Richmond had won your consent to his joining, and I'm looking to you to make my word good. Will you let me purchase a cornetcy for him?"

There was a long silence. Vincent broke it. "You have no choice, sir."

"Do as you will!" his lordship said harshly. "That any grandson of mine could—and, of you all, *Richmond!*——

"It's no wish to mine to fratch with you over what's done, and can't be mended," interrupted Hugo, "but ask yourself, sir, whose fault it was that a lad of his cut, crazy with disappointment, and hearing nothing but praise of smuggling all his life, was brought to this pass?"

"I have said you may do as you will! I am not answerable to you for Richmond's upbringing!"

"Not to me, but to him, sir."

Lord Darracott threw him a strange glance, and lowered his eyes again. After a slight pause, Vincent said: "And so, coz?"

"If it's left to me, I'd like to see the boy in the Seventh Hussars. I've several good friends in the regiment, who'll need no urging to keep an eye on a lad who bears my name."

"That, cousin," murmured Vincent, "*is the most unkindest cut of all! Proceed!*"

"Nay, I didn't mean it so! For the rest, we've settled it between us—my aunts and I—that it will be best to get the lad away from here, and Claud too, at first light, before the servants are up and about. It will be easily done, and accounted for: your mother wants her own doctor to deal with Claud, and Richmond goes to help her with him on the journey. John Joseph will drive them to Tonbridge in her ladyship's own carriage, and see to the hiring of a post-chaise there to carry them on to London. I've promised my Aunt Elvira I'll take her to London myself as soon as I get back from the north, but it won't do for her to join Richmond too soon, for we don't want to set tongues wagging."

"Have you induced her to let him go without her? Good God!"

"She'll do nothing to hinder us from doing what's best for him, little though she may like it. She knows your mother will take good care of him, too."

"Your staff work is admirable, coz. Why, by the way, does Richmond go to succour Claud while I remain here?"

"No one will wonder at that, lad! Claud's in no state for fratching!"

"*Touché!*" Vincent acknowledged, throwing up a hand. "You don't feel that I ought to drive myself to town in the wake of the chaise, as—er—rearguard?"

"I don't," replied Hugo. "You and I, lad, have got work to do here! Something must be done about that secret

313

passage. If we can do no more, between the pair of us, than block it, as it was when Richmond first saw it, we'll do that."

"What an enchanting prospect!" said Vincent faintly. "How right you are—*damn* you!"

Hugo chuckled, but addressed his grandfather. "There's one thing more, sir. That young good-like naught of yours won't rest until he's seen you. He knows well the blow he's dealt you. He bade me tell you so."

Lord Darracott rose from his chair. "I'll go to him," he said curtly.

Hugo moved to the door, to open it for him. His lordship paused for a moment before he went out, passing a hand across his brow. "I suppose you will do what's necessary. There will be many things—his boat, his horses—I'm too tired tonight, but I'll discuss it with you tomorrow. Goodnight!"

"Goodnight, sir," Hugo replied. He shut the door, and came back into the room. "Happen I'd best do something to put him in a passion tomorrow," he said thoughtfully. "It won't do to let him fall into a lethargy."

"You will, cousin, you will!" Vincent said, with his mocking smile. "I own, however, that I shall greet the familiar storm-signs with positive relief."

Ten minutes later, Anthea was saying much the same thing. "I never thought I *could* be sorry for Grandpapa," she told her cousins, "but I am, and, what's more, I had rather by far have him cross than stunned!"

"Have no fear!" said Vincent. "Ajax is already considering how best to enrage him."

She smiled, but said: "Well, anything would be preferable to having him so quiet and crushed. He didn't utter one word of reproach to Richmond. But what almost sank me to the floor was his saying to Mama that she had much to forgive him! It was precisely what she had been saying to me, except that she said she never *would* forgive him, so you may imagine my astonishment when she burst into tears on his chest! As a matter of fact I nearly burst into tears myself."

"Dear me, what a lachrymose scene!" remarked Vincent. "I shall go to bed to fortify myself for the inevitable reaction—not to mention the exhausting labours I shall no doubt be expected to undertake in that accursed passage. To think how much I once wanted to discover it, and how much I wish now that it never had been discovered!" He went to the door, and opened it, looking back to say: "My dislike of you is rapidly growing, Ajax: I shouldn't make the smallest attempt to drag you back from that cliff-edge!"

"What cliff-edge?" enquired Anthea, as Vincent left the room.

"Just a joke, lass. Eh, you look tired out!"

"I am tired out, but I couldn't go to bed without coming to thank you, Hugo. I—oh, Hugo, I can't believe yet that it wasn't a nightmare!" she said, walking straight into his arms, and hugging as much of him as she could.

He received her with great willingness, enfolding her in a large and comforting embrace. "Well, that's all it was, think on," he said. "Now, don't *you* start on cry, lass!"

"I won't," she promised. She took his face between her hands, smiling up at him, and saying: *"Noble Ajax, you are as strong, as valiant, as wise, no less noble, much more gentle, and altogether more tractable!"*

"Nay then, love!" expostulated the Major. "Don't be so daft!"